The Chronicles of Anaedor

The Prophecies

KRISTINA SCHRAM

To read is to be free...

Kristina Sch

BLiP

An imprint of Variance

Variance Publishing
1610 South Pine St.,
Cabot, AR 72023
(501) 843-BOOK
www.variancepublishing.com
Printed in the United States of America.

Library of Congress Catalog Number—

ISBN: 1-935142-10-0
ISBN-13: 978-1-935142-10-2

Cover Design: Erik Hollander,
        www.hollanderdesignlabs.com
Cover Layout: Stanley Tremblay
Interior Design: Stanley Tremblay
Interior Illustrations: Jeremy Robinson,
        www.jeremyrobinsononline.com

Visit Kristina Schram on the World Wide Web at:
www.kristinaschram.com

        10   9   8   7   6   5   4   3   2   1

For my Loves,
Daniel, Gordon, Keegan and Jaren

ACKNOWLEDGEMENTS

I would like to take this opportunity to thank all the people who helped me with this book, either by offering encouragement, by reading and re-reading every single word and page, or by not killing me for talking endlessly about the world of Anaedor.

To my husband, Dan ~ You have been the greatest cheerleader a person could ever ask for. You never give up on me. Thanks for being there, through thick and thin, especially when I grow needy and self-pitying. You're a saint.

To my children, Gordon, Keegan and Jaren ~ You are an endless source of inspiration to me, even when you're constantly interrupting me to ask for food, to help you catch a grotesque bug, or to show me your latest creation. I'm glad you trust me enough to keep coming back.

To my family ~ To Mom, thanks for reading my books, for offering suggestions and for feeding me when I was a kid. You rock!

To Heather, thanks for all the endless editing . . . and the cool drawing you did of the *Gule*!

To Shawn and Danielle, thanks for being my guinea pig readers and going easy on me when you had me at your mercy.

To Terry ~ Wherever you may be, thanks for your editing and encouragement!

To Breakneck Books ~ Thanks for giving me my first publishing deal!

To Variance ~ Thanks for making this a better book, for putting up with my demands, for being patient with me (that would mean you, Tim)!

To Shane ~ You forced me to make changes and you were right. Bless your heart. And I mean that.

To Anastasia ~ Thanks for your editing input!

The Chronicles of Anaedor

The Prophecies

I awoke with a start and shot up straight in my small, rumpled bed. My heart pounded like a jackhammer as my eyes darted rapidly about the shadowy room. It was only when I realized I was still safe in my bed, still living in the cramped apartment I shared with my dad, that the wild thumping went away.

I pushed strands of dark brown hair off my sweaty forehead and flopped back onto my flattened pillow. I'd just had that awful dream . . . again. In the fifteen years I'd spent on this planet, I'd had that dream more times than could be considered normal. Or healthy. Or sane.

I can't ever remember the details of what happens, thank goodness. But the feeling of horror I experienced every time I woke up from that dream, which haunted my nights more and more often, was starting to wear me down. I couldn't stand it—this sense of impending doom. But what I hated even more was that I was absolutely convinced my dream was going to come true some day.

That's what I dreaded most of all.

~PART ONE~

PORTAL MANOR

CHAPTER ONE

THE GATE

Todd Crow raced his dusty Toyota along the curvy road. He wanted to drop his beastly passenger off as soon as humanly possible and get out of this godforsaken backwoods maze. This place gave him the creeps.

As he drove, he savored the thought of getting rid of Viddie Mors. He'd had to put up with her antics for four long years, far too long for any decent person to handle. During that time, she'd done a lot of weird things, though her annoying habit of staring at him and then telling him exactly what he was thinking was the worst. The tiresome girl's seeming ability to read his mind was unnatural, and he was thoroughly sick of it.

Even more unsettling was the notion that one day she might share some of his less-than-loyal thoughts with her dad. If his professor and mentor, the illustrious Dr. Andrew

Mors, found out what his teaching assistant really thought of him, all his tedious brown-nosing and schmoozing would go down the toilet. Then where would he be? It was too disturbing to think about.

He braked around a sharp curve, then sped up again. He was shifting into fourth gear when something large loomed up out of the thick fog directly in front of him. He slammed on the brakes, and the old car skidded sideways on the loose gravel. It rattled to a stop in time to avoid crashing into a massive wrought-iron gate rising out of the heavy mists like black, skeletal fingers. Mumbling curses, he backed up the battered car, spitting small rocks into the air.

"Watch out!" a high-pitched voice hollered from the back seat.

Todd glanced in the rearview mirror to see the girl's screwed-up mouth and tightly crossed arms—her typical pose whenever she looked at him—and rolled his protuberant, yellow-brown eyes as he gave a martyred sigh.

"How was I supposed to know they'd put a gate in the middle of the road? You should be grateful I was willing to take time out of my busy schedule to drive you here, you little brat! Your dad should've made you take the bus." He shifted the car into park, grinding the gears. "I've never known anyone so ungrateful."

"So you've been saying for the last three hours," the girl replied.

Todd heaved another sigh and glared at her in the mirror. It had been a long trip.

It *had* been a long trip, I thought to myself, but only because the Toad had made it that way. For most of the drive we fought about stupid stuff, like bathroom breaks. I wanted to take them; he didn't. After the two-hour mark, I nearly lost my battle with the call of nature before he finally caved in and pulled into the grungiest gas station he could find.

The Toad doesn't like me. In fact, he loathes me, a sentiment which comes through loud and clear every time he glares at me, tells me to shut my trap, snaps my bare arm with the red comb he always carries in his back pocket, or tattles on me to my dad, to name just a few of the despicable things he does when no one's looking.

It wasn't his toady behavior, however, that earned him his nickname. The first day Dad introduced his new teaching assistant to me, I renamed him "the Toad" and refused to call him anything else after that. He has these big, bulgy eyes hooded by heavy lids that open and close very slowly, exactly like a toad's. His cold, clammy skin is dull gray and covered with warts, and his broad face is mostly nose, with no chin to speak of. Rumor has it that when he was born, his own mother took one look at him and fainted.

Obviously we can't stand each other, which is why this seemingly endless trip has been so awful. To make matters worse, we were now stuck in the middle of a dark, foggy road, both of us staring miserably up at the massive gate blocking our way and wondering how much longer this nightmare was going to last.

After several minutes of uncomfortable silence, waiting nervously for someone to open the gate, the Toad honked the horn with as much force as his puny forearm could muster. When no one appeared, he lowered his window to peer out. Watching his head swivel back and forth, as though searching for flies to eat, I realized something . . . the Toad didn't like this place; in fact, he was scared of it. He was actually sweating as he looked around, beads of perspiration popping out on his big forehead like dewdrops gathering on a mushroom. His increasing uneasiness made me feel less wretched about our situation, though only a little. He was the one who got to go home again.

"Why couldn't my dad drive me himself?" I mumbled as I stared out the window. My dad's decision to have the Toad drive me to my destination really bothered me. It was bad enough to be sent away from home like some kind of juvenile delinquent—which I wasn't—but to have my dad refuse to take me himself, condemning me to ride with the Toad? That was cruel and unusual punishment.

"Listen, kid,"—the Toad's croaky voice dripped with impatience as he raised the window, then turned on the wipers to clear away the mist that had settled on the wind- shield—"I've told you a hundred times already: Dr. Mors has to finish his presentation for the annual Scientific America Chemistry Convention coming up. He's a busy man."

I sniffed moodily. My dad was always busy with some paper he was writing or experiment he was working on or class lecture he was preparing for. He didn't have enough time for me—had *never* had enough time for me. I accepted that he had a lot to do, really I did. What I didn't like was that he never made any effort to spend time with his only child. Driving me to my new home would have been a nice place to start.

I wondered whether he wanted to be around me at all. From the time I was a little kid, I'd picked up on the strange way he would sometimes look at me, as though he was afraid of me. I didn't mind that the Toad was scared of me, but my own dad? Parents shouldn't be afraid of their kids, no matter what strange things they might do, and especially after they'd worked so very hard to stop doing them.

I felt a familiar stinging sensation in my eyes and pinched my arm hard enough to hurt. I'm not going to cry, I threatened myself. I'm *not* going to cry. Unfortunately, it seemed that all I had to do lately was think about my miserable life and the waterworks turned on like a faucet. But darned if I was going to let myself cry in front of the Toad! That would make his day.

"Is this the place?" I asked, although I was afraid to hear the Toad's answer. There was something familiar about the gate, in an unsettling kind of way. I shuddered and looked away.

"It better be," the Toad retorted. "It took long enough to get here, and it's a long drive back."

I sighed. *A long drive back.* How many chocolate bars would it take to bribe the Toad into turning around and taking me with him? I wondered. The ride would be horrid, but it'd be better than being left behind, especially since I hadn't wanted to leave home in the first place. From the start, I'd had a bad feeling about this whole scheme. But the Toad would never take me back with him. To say he was thrilled I was leaving would be an understatement. He was ecstatic.

My eyes drifted toward the window again. Chin propped on my fist, I stared at the huge gate, which connected two high stone walls, then stretched endlessly off into the distance on either side. Thick, brown vines covered with spiky thorns and dark green leaves climbed the rough surface of the walls like snakes racing each other to the top. Through the heavy fog, I could barely make out the black iron spikes standing alertly on top, daring anyone to try to enter the

premises without permission. Or . . . maybe the sharp
sentinels were there to keep people in. People like me. I
shuddered at the thought.

To distract myself from the depressing image this
created, I focused harder on studying the gate. As I stared
at it, the letters *P* and *M* popped out from amongst a thick
tapestry of iron curlicues and spikes. I wondered what the
letters stood for, then wondered why I cared. I wasn't staying here. First chance I got, I was heading back home to
prove to my dad that I was a normal kid, even if I had to
lock him in a room to do it. I'd throw the Toad in there, too,
and leave him there to rot, I thought defiantly as my eyes
continued to follow the patterns in the ironwork.

A light breeze picked up and cleared away the fog,
revealing the entire gate in all its glory. At that same
moment something clicked in my mind, like a key turning
in a lock, and I knew at once why the gate looked so
familiar to me and why I'd had a bad feeling about this trip.
My heart thudded in my chest as I shook my head in denial.
It couldn't be! I pulled back and looked up at the imposing
structure again. It *could* be. Goosebumps prickled my
skin. It seemed impossible, but my dream, my lifelong
nightmare, was coming true. My hands rubbed together
nervously. I had to get out of this car. I *couldn't* go through
that gate—it was the one in my dream!

I grabbed the door handle and pulled as hard as I could,
but the door wouldn't open. I jiggled the handle again and
then realized the door was locked. I hit the automatic lock
button and the knob popped up. When I tried the handle
again, the door remained shut fast. I pulled and tugged at
the handle, my heart thudding in warning, until I heard a
snicker coming from the front seat. I met bulging eyes in
the rearview mirror. The Toad was smirking at me.

"Child-proof lock." He grinned. "I flipped the switch

when you got out to use the bathroom at that last gas station. Now you can't get out of the car until I want you out. We wouldn't want anyone getting lost, would we?"

"Let me out of here, Toad!" Panicking and angry, I whacked him on the back of the head with the paperback book I'd been reading. I wished I could have afforded the hardcover version; it would've made a better club.

The Toad whipped around in his seat, his usually gray face red with fury. I shrank away from him, driving my legs against the vinyl seat. "If you don't shut your trap, Viddie Mors, I'll tell your dad about your little *incident* at school."

My mind spun like a top, and I felt myself grow cold with dread. My dad had never heard that particular story. I'd never intended that he would. So how had the Toad found out? This was bad.

"Who told you about that?" I managed to choke out through a suddenly dry mouth.

The Toad grinned malevolently. "Your teacher called about it one day when I was at your apartment picking up papers to grade. The professor was busy, so I answered the phone. She thought I was your dad—a mistake I didn't bother correcting." He chuckled. "She told me the whole story. I never said anything to your dad because I didn't want to bother him with his crazy daughter's problems. I also knew that one day this information might come in handy." He grinned as he turned back around, knowing he'd won this battle. "And now it has."

That *jerk*! He knew I didn't want my dad to find out what had happened that day at school, or at least not the version the Toad had probably heard. If my dad learned the truth, he'd have tangible proof that something really was wrong with me and would never let me come back.

With a defeated sigh, I dropped my cold hand from the door handle and nibbled on my pinkie fingernail. I needed to get out of this car. But to do that I had to calm down or figure out what to do next in a rational, logical manner. Unfortunately, I'm not too good at doing things calmly, or in a rational and logical manner. I unwrapped a candy bar and munched on it in silence, wondering with each bite how long it would take the caffeine to kick my thought processes into gear.

"They better not expect me to open those gates myself," the Toad muttered. "I can't afford to pull something. My teammates would kill me." He was the coxswain for the rowing team at college, which meant he steered and yelled.

"*That* would be a tragedy," I replied, as I peeled back more wrapper.

He gave me an evil look in the mirror and honked the horn again, putting all his weight into it. After the seventh or eighth honk, the sound reverberating like a foghorn in the misty silence, a part of the wall began to move, startling the Toad and me. A teenage boy about my age pushed his way through a small opening next to the gate, battling against the tangled mess of leaves and vines that hid a door.

Free of the grasping vines, he loped toward the car, covering the ground between us quickly. With each step, his features solidified. He was almost as tall as my dad, who was six feet tall, and beanpole skinny, as if he couldn't eat fast enough to keep up with a recent growth spurt. He wore a navy blue turtleneck sweater, faded blue jeans, and a scowl. I thought about asking him to open my car door for me, but changed my mind when I saw the look on his face.

The boy walked around the front of the car and came to my side. Leaning over, he motioned to me to lower my window. When I did—it was one of those windows that only went halfway down, barring *that* escape route—he leaned forward to study me suspiciously, as though I were some kind of criminal intent on robbing the place.

He had bright, blue eyes and dark brown, unruly hair that covered his forehead and tickled the tops of his bushy, black eyebrows. All that extra hair was probably meant to hide the red spots spattered on his tanned forehead. Freckles, along with a few more pimples, covered the crooked bridge of his nose, and a thick, white scar cut through his left eyebrow, giving him a satirical look. He seemed strangely familiar to me, although I was certain we'd never met.

Without saying so much as a "how's it going," he pushed himself away from my window and took his time walking around the car before stepping up to the driver's window. I squirmed nervously. This guy was trouble.

The Toad lowered his window. "Is this going to take long?" He had deepened his voice to sound manlier. "It's getting late, and I've really got to get back and study for my Bio-chem test tomorrow."

"I need to see some identification," the boy told him, holding out his hand.

The Toad dug out his wallet and showed his driver's license to the teen. "I'm Todd Crow. Dr. Mors sent me." He jerked his thumb back at me. "This is the prisoner."

I kicked his seat; he sniggered at me in the mirror. He loved torturing me. Why couldn't my dad ever see this side of the Toad?

"Knock it off, will you? You're acting like a three-year-old. Anyway,"—he turned back to the teen—"this is Dr. Mors' kid. I'm his teaching assistant." He added the last part importantly.

When the boy said nothing, the Toad frowned. "He asked me to take time out of my busy schedule to bring her here. I hope this is the right place. I've really got to get back. It's getting dark and I don't have good night vision and there's my test . . ." He looked out the window nervously.

"This is Portal Manor, all right," the boy replied. *Portal Manor*. That explained the letters *P* and *M* in the ironwork. He looked down at the Toad's driver's license and carefully studied the piece of plastic. "Go on ahead," he directed as he handed back the card, giving me a sharp look. He pointed a black object toward the gate, and the metal structure began to open.

The Toad gave a dramatic sigh of relief as he shifted the car into drive. "Thanks, kid. I appreciate it." The "kid" frowned, and I smiled to myself. Apparently he didn't like being called kid either.

The car lurched forward and my amusement quickly died. We were going in. I unbuckled my seatbelt and stuck my head out of the car window. Seeing the ground pass by below me, I didn't hesitate. I shoved my body through the narrow opening and got my arms out the electric window before the Toad could shut it. It whirred as it slid upward, catching me mid-torso. I pushed down on the glass and leaned farther out. "You've got to help me!" I pleaded to the boy, who stood watching us go, an unreadable expression on his face. "Don't make me go in there!"

He stared at me, his countenance stony.

The Toad stomped on the gas and the car sped through the gates.

"Please!" I begged as the window threatened to crack a rib.

"Sorry," he shrugged. "It's not up to me." He aimed the object at the gate to close it.

With a resounding clang, the gate swung shut behind us. We were inside now, the boy nowhere to be seen in the thick fog.

There was no going back.

CHAPTER TWO ☉

A GHOST TO GREET ME

The car rolled forward into the fog and . . . nothing happened.

I tried to recall what my dream had prophesied about this day, but I couldn't retrieve anything solid. I could only remember the gate and feeling like something bad was going to happen to me once I went through it, though I had no idea what that bad thing was or when it would occur.

Maybe it wasn't meant to happen right away.

I fell back against the seat of the car and thought about the boy back at the gate, the one who'd left me to my fate. Why wouldn't he help me? *Sorry*, he'd said. *It's not up to me.* Well, who *was* it up to? And who was he, anyway? Being only a teenager, he surely couldn't work for my dad, who owned the place. My dad's mother, Grandma Mors, had left it to him years ago, although I had found out about its existence only the week before when my dad informed me I'd be moving. Alone. He'd also mentioned that my "guardian" would be a Mrs. Keeper, but said nothing about doofus back there. Not for the first time, I wondered how much my dad knew about the people living at this place, this prison I was being sent to against my will.

My imagination was running amok about my future and what my guardian might do once she got ahold of me, when I saw something strange up ahead. A group of people rose up out of the mists and moved rapidly toward the car.

Still wedged half out the back window, I strained to get a better look, the misty air cool on my face as I stared at the approaching figures. I soon realized they weren't people at all, but life-sized stone statues. We were the ones moving, not them. The grayish-white figures peered down into a small, dark pool of water as though searching for answers— all of them, that is, except one. This particular statue gazed directly at me, his hands reaching out, imploring me to help him.

Time froze as I stared into those large, round eyes. The statue looked so real, I would almost swear he was alive. And I would almost swear that I'd seen him somewhere before. We gazed into each other's eyes for what seemed an eternity—I couldn't look away—and then time snapped. The car left him behind, the fog enveloping the statues around the pool as we drove onward.

Up ahead, the fog cleared a bit and a large shadow loomed into view—a pirate ship sailing on a sea of green grass. My eyes widened in amazement, and I promptly forgot about the stone statue. Portal Manor wasn't a house; it was a mansion.

The Toad let out a low whistle. "I thought you guys didn't have any money," he said, staring up at the massive building. He was obviously thinking about all the time he had put into writing grants, begging for money for my dad's latest experiment, time he could've spent getting better grades (like more time could have helped him).

"That's what I thought," I replied.

I studied the mansion we owned. A tangle of dark, leafy vines crawled up the smooth stone walls, covering most of the facade. The tendrils seemed to know not to grow on the many windows of varying shapes and sizes that stared blankly out at the front yard. I wondered why there weren't any lights shining through them on such a dreary day. Could it be that a house in this day and age didn't have electricity? The thought was distressing.

The Toad lowered the window a little and I knocked my head against the window frame as I drew myself back inside the car. Rubbing at the sore spot, and still searching for any sign of light, I suddenly realized I was staring directly at a figure standing in one of the upper windows. But before I could be sure of what I was seeing, it disappeared.

Feeling apprehensive, I forced myself to look over the rest of the building. I'd learned from my experiences at my old school that you should know where all your escape routes are—a sad lesson to learn, but a necessary one after the Incident.

On each side of the house, immense, vine-covered towers pressed up against the main walls, supporting the giant building between them. The two towers rose high above the mansion's roof, their tops disappearing into the fog. A large glass structure leaned against one of the towers and the south part of the main building. Yellow leaves from a nearby tree spotted the top of the glass roof with bright bits of color. Inside, large, shiny green leaves pressed against the glass, straining toward the sky. I wondered what grew within those fragile walls. From my vantage point, the

scene resembled a jungle. At any moment, I expected to see
Tarzan swinging past, searching for Jane.

In front, wide stone steps led up to two doors made of
rich, dark wood large enough for two elephants to pass
through side by side. On the face of both doors, surly gar-
goyles gripped large iron rings bigger than my head in their
petulant mouths and challenged any normal-sized person
to lift them. Maybe I could convince the Toad to make an
attempt. With any luck, he'd hurt himself trying and leave
here with a little injury to remember me by.

On either side of the stairway leading up to the doors,
two lion statues crouched arrogantly on broad pedestals.
Their hungry mouths, opened in a threatening roar, did
nothing to make a person feel warmly welcomed. In fact,
the entire house looked ready to eat whatever victim was
dumb enough to enter.

If I had any say in the matter, that dumb victim wouldn't
be me.

Behind the building a mighty hill rose up like the back of
the Loch Ness monster, adding to the dark, Gothic atmos-
phere of the mansion. Trees covered the hillside like a
heavy fur coat, and I wondered what monsters might be
hiding amongst them.

I bit my lip. Portal Manor was supposed to be my home
until I finished my schooling. Four long years. I shook my
head in disbelief. No way was I staying here for that long,
not if the mansion was the same place as the one in my
dream. Then again, maybe I was being an idiot about all
this. Most kids would jump at the chance to stay in a big
mansion and attend private school. Especially if the apartment you'd been living in was a tiny hovel and your old
school was crammed full of Neanderthal creeps who
thought you were a witch because of something you might
have done once.

Going to a private school, however, did not sound at all appealing to me. The afterschool specials I'd watched over the years depicted private schools as torturous institutions filled to capacity with snobby rich kids picking on a few nerdy poor ones. *Not* my idea of a good time, especially since I happened to be one of those nerdy poor kids. On the other hand, living in a mansion might be pretty cool. Under normal circumstances, I would probably be psyched about staying here. But these were not normal circumstances; everything I'd felt and experienced up to this point warned me to stay away from Portal Manor.

More worried than ever now, I reached up to stroke the large medallion I wore on a thick, tarnished silver chain around my neck. My dad had told me once that it had been a gift to me from my grandmother, his mother, to be given to me at my birth. When I asked him what had happened to her, he replied that not long before I was born his mother had left on a trip to Alaska—from time to time she took these sojourns about the country—and had never returned. Apparently, while driving to a small town outside Anchorage, a blizzard blew up and she was never seen or heard from again. After telling me this much, Dad refused to say any more on the subject.

Up until now, I'd always thought Grandma Mors' disappearance was a fascinating mystery, but after seeing this place, I no longer found the idea of someone disappearing so intriguing. More like terrifying.

Still, I wore the necklace everywhere I went, even in the shower. It wasn't clear to me why, since I hadn't even known my grandma, but it seemed like the right thing to do. Now I was glad I had it on. Simply knowing the necklace was there made me feel a little better, like I was taking a small bit of home with me.

The Toad pulled the car up to the front steps, tires

screeching. He didn't bother to turn off the engine before leaping out of the car and running to the trunk to unload my luggage. I wondered whether he shared the same uneasy feeling I did, that someone or something was watching him. He probably regretted convincing my dad it would be best if he drove me to my new school. He'd volunteered because it was the only way he could be sure I wouldn't talk my dad out of going through with the plan. My dad was a genius in the science field, with several journal articles, books, and inventions to his name—that's why the Toad sucked up to him—but the Toad also knew that when it came to dealing with his own kid, my dad was hopeless.

Untying the rope holding the trunk lid down, he pulled out the first of three steamer trunks and heaved it to the steps, where he dropped it with a thud. He then moved to the one strapped onto the roof of the car. I sighed and unwrapped the last bit of my third candy bar of the trip. It looked like bribing the Toad wasn't going to happen. His behavior confirmed what I'd already suspected . . . he was overjoyed at the prospect of dumping me here to live with the Addams family.

I popped a piece of chocolate into my mouth, savoring the buttery richness for perhaps the last time, then leaned over Ms. Penny Dolittle and carefully gave her a vigorous shake. Having learned from hard-earned experience, I quickly pulled my hand back, as waking Ms. Penny was like trying to wake a hibernating bear . . . nearly impossible and almost as dangerous. That little coon had sharp teeth.

Ms. Penny is the result of my dad's nearly forgetting my tenth birthday. That morning I'd reminded him, as usual, that I was now a year older. The look of bewilderment on his face told me that, true to form, he'd once again forgotten. But luck was on Dad's side that year, or on mine, really, because one of his colleagues had discovered, upon bringing home an abandoned baby raccoon he'd found in one of the university dumpsters, that it didn't like the competition of his nine-month-old baby daughter. Obviously, Ms. Penny had to go. My dad, who'd just happened to be looking for a gift for his own daughter before going home to her that night, told his colleague he'd take the animal.

She's the best present I've ever gotten.

Ms. Penny's about the size of a large cat and has a poofy black-and-gray-ringed tail. A dark mask frames her beady little eyes, and she has a cute, tiny, black nose. Despite the mask, she looks very sweet and innocent. Don't be fooled, though; she's a terror, and an incurable thief, stealing anything that isn't nailed down, especially if it's shiny. She also likes to make messes. Even though she's a pain in the butt, she's a loyal friend. She's always been there for me, and *she* doesn't think I'm scary or weird . . . unlike everyone else who knows me. She loves me for who I am, and I love her, too.

Fondly, I pushed the little imp again. Ms. Penny groaned and scooted away from the annoying finger rudely disturbing her blissful dreams of termite shakes and giant mango pies.

"Wake up, sleepyhead. We're here."

Ms. Penny whimpered and tried to move away, but I poked her again. Finally, after a few more well-placed prods, she opened one brown eye and gave me a dirty look before sitting up on her haunches to peer out the window. Apparently satisfied with what she saw, which wasn't much with all the fog, she leaped to my shoulder. I gave a sigh of relief. When Ms. Penny didn't like something, she'd sulk about it for days. It could be very trying.

The Toad flung the door open for me, and I climbed out

of the car with Ms. Penny precariously balanced on my shoulder. She was small for a coon, but big enough to do damage if she felt the need to dig her sharp claws into my skin to keep from falling. She looked around, then gave a screech of approval, ready to explore. I wasn't sure I felt the same way. I was all for adventure (I liked it in my books, anyway), but my dream made me afraid of what I might find while poking about. With my luck, I'd end up finding a severed head.

Taking a deep breath for courage, I climbed the broad steps leading up to the door and, as the Toad was nowhere to be seen, struggled to lift the heavy knocker. I was about to give up my fight to raise the iron ring when the doors swung wide open, as though a giant, powerful hand had punched through them.

"Hello?"

After a few seconds, when no one appeared, I took a cautious step forward and peered into the darkness. Ms. Penny followed my example, peeking around my head for a closer look. I saw no one through the crack, nor did I hear anything. I was about to take another step forward when a ghostly figure appeared in the doorway, quick as a flash of lightning. I stumbled backward, catching myself with the railing in time to keep the two of us from tumbling down the stairs.

CHAPTER THREE
LIFE AS I KNEW IT

I sucked in several deep breaths and tried to calm myself. Shades of my dream clawed at my memory and my mind swirled. Before I knew what was happening, I was floating above my body like a cloud, dispassionately observing myself below as I clutched the stone railing and stared straight ahead, wide-eyed and panting. Ms. Penny clung to my neck and screeched, then jumped down and hid behind my legs. Whatever was waiting for me in that house meant the end of my life as I knew it. I also knew that I should turn and run back to the car, but I couldn't seem to make my cowardly legs move.

The ghostly figure chose that moment to step forward. I gasped.

Then heaved a sigh of relief.

The person standing before me was not a ghost, but a

little woman with a nice, if rather vague, smile. She was short, a bit on the plump side, and appeared quite harmless. Small, round glasses perched delicately on the tip of a tiny nose, ready to fall off at any moment, but were fortunately attached to a rainbow-colored cord around her neck. She had light brown hair, hastily pulled back into an untidy bun, with wings of gray spreading back behind her ears. Despite the gray in her hair, however, her round face looked youthful. She could have been anywhere from forty to sixty.

She wore a threadbare, flower-print dress, dull and faded to a rose color, along with a badly matched green and blue argyle cardigan over it. A brown crocheted shawl, nearly as large as a blanket, topped off the ensemble. From beneath the hem of her long, full dress, sturdy black shoes peeked out, each coated with a fine layer of dust. The strange little woman clasped a large book to her chest, some of the pages loose and the leather binding frayed. It looked *very* old.

A bit of my fear faded. This woman certainly didn't *look* like someone to be scared of—unless you ran a fashion magazine. But then again, appearances could be deceiving. Sweet-looking Ms. Penny had taught me that.

The woman studied me, small, dark brown eyes squinting as she peered over the tops of her glasses, giving me a rapid once-over. I squirmed under her cursory scrutiny. "You look as though you've just seen a ghost, dear," she said at last, startling me.

I was surprised to hear an English accent. Dad hadn't said anything about my new guardian being English. Had he even met the woman? Yikes. He had sent his own flesh and blood to live with someone he'd never met! I shook my head at his ignorance. Did the man not watch *any* TV? As far as he knew, Mrs. Keeper could be some crazy woman who chopped people up and made stew out of them. "Saw a ghost?" I laughed as my cheeks flushed a hot red. "That's a good one. It's just I wasn't expecting the door to open like that. I hadn't even knocked yet and—"

"I was anticipating your arrival at any moment, dear," the little woman interrupted, her eyes dark with mystery as she watched me. "It's been a long time."

Uncertain how to reply, I peered down at the tips of my scuffed brown boots, which stuck out from beneath the frayed hems of my faded blue jeans. I'd bought the boots at a thrift shop for the bargain-basement price of five bucks. They were a little big, but I was used to that. "Oh, well," I began, "I'm sure my dad called ahead to let you know I was coming." I smiled nervously. "Right?"

She smiled back at me, the darkness gone. "Ah, yes. Pity he couldn't drive you himself." She sighed. "I'm not surprised, though. Considering the circumstances, I don't expect he'll ever return to Portal Manor. I believe it's been over twenty years since he left here and he hasn't been back since." She shook her head sadly. "Poor man. He never could handle it."

I frowned. "That can't be right. I mean, he grew up here. Why wouldn't he come back?" It seemed a strange thing to do, even for my dad. When the woman didn't answer my question, I looked up to see her once again watching me closely with an expression that looked an awful lot like pity. I felt an overwhelming desire to elaborate. "Well, I'm sure he would've come with me this time, but he had a paper to prepare for an important convention. That's why he couldn't come." I regretted the words as soon as they left my mouth. How could I defend him after what he'd just done to me? If he hadn't returned to this place for over twenty years, he wouldn't have made an exception for a daughter he didn't even like. He would've hated spending three hours alone with me in the car.

"Either way, dear," the woman said kindly, interrupting my straying thoughts, "you made it here safely, and for that we're grateful."

"Barely," I replied, looking back at the Toad in time to see him hopping into his ratty, old car and peeling away, his headlights cutting through the fog. He tossed me a triumphant wave out the window, and I sighed. He was a horrid humanoid anomaly, but I'd have given anything just then to have been in that car with him. As the saying goes, better the evil toad you know . . .

"So, Viddie . . ." she began. Viddie was the name my dad called me. I couldn't remember his ever calling me by my full name, Lavida. I always gave my nickname when introducing myself to new people, even though I thought of myself as Lavida. It was one of the few things I did that seemed to please him.

Fat lot of good *that* had done me.

"Um, yeah?"

"Welcome to Portal Manor." She smiled, and this time the expression lit up her face, making her look quite young. "I'd shake your hand, only mine"—she glanced down at her burdened arms, and her glasses fell off her nose—"oops!" She struggled to put the glasses back on without dropping the heavy book. "Glad to have this bit of rope. I'd lost plenty a pair of specs underfoot before it was given me as a present." She laughed heartily.

"Anyway, as I was about to say, my hands are a bit occupied at the moment. So nice to finally meet you." She examined me for a third time, peering over the rims of her glasses. "I believe you are the spitting image of your dear mother, may she rest in peace. Though I don't know that she does, poor lass, after . . ."

"After . . . ?"

She paused, then smiled brightly. "I knew your grandmother, too, you know. Difficult woman, your gran, but she always made life interesting . . ." Her voice trailed away as she looked into the distance. The misty, gray sky reflected off her glasses, and her brow furrowed as though deep in thought.

I shuffled my feet uncomfortably, waiting for her to continue. Should I say something? I wondered. A crow flying low across the sky cawed loudly, making the choice for me. The little woman shook her head before returning her attention to me. Laughing, she asked, "Where was I? Oh, yes. To answer your question . . . yes, Mrs. Keeper is here. Standing right in front of you, in fact."

Question? I hadn't asked any questions—not out loud, anyway—but she told me what I'd wanted to know. This strange little English woman was supposed to be my guardian for the next four years.

Not if I could help it.

Mrs. Keeper scanned the front yard. "Count ninety days from a foggy day and you'll be having yourself a storm," she informed me. "You'd better come inside now. Won't do to linger outdoors on a damp day like this." She motioned for me to come into the house, a mischievous gleam in her eye as she added, "Besides, you never know what's out there lurking in the fog."

Suddenly she spotted Ms. Penny hiding behind my legs. "Well, now. Who might this be?" She leaned forward for a closer look and her glasses fell off again. But this time, when she straightened up, she let them rest on her stout bosom.

I squared my shoulders. It was time Mrs. Keeper found out that her job as my guardian wasn't going to be an easy one. "This is Ms. Penny Dolittle," I announced. "She's my pet, and where I go," I boldly proclaimed, "she goes."

"You don't say? A pet raccoon, hm? How exciting," Mrs. Keeper murmured, a touch of mirth turning up the corners of her mouth. "Oh, dear," she began again, "this *is* a pickle. I'm not sure if she'll—"

"She *has* to stay," I said. To my disgust, the tone of my voice came out sounding more pleading than commanding. "I couldn't leave her at home 'cause there's no one to take care of her but me. The Toad would try to eat her and Dad would forget about her—"

Mrs. Keeper held up a tiny hand and I bit down on what I was about to say next. "I was going to say that I'm not sure if she will get along with the cats. We have twelve of them, so they're a bit hard to avoid." She shook her head and smiled. "But this is a big house. There should be enough room for everybody. At any rate, your pet should make life more interesting, and those cats could use some exercise."

I raised my eyebrows. Hmmm. What a great excuse to get myself sent back home. I leaned down for Ms. Penny to jump onto my shoulder, and when the coon was safely in place I said, "You know, Mrs. Keeper, I wouldn't want any of your cats getting hurt because of Ms. Penny." I covertly gave her a little pinch to make her squeak menacingly. "As you can see, she's not the nicest pet. She doesn't get along well with other animals, or most people, for that matter. Maybe you should call my dad and tell him this isn't going to work out. I could easily take the bus back," I added, fluttering my lashes.

Mrs. Keeper smiled brightly. "Oh, but my dear girl, that won't do. That won't do at all." Without another word, she turned on her heel and disappeared into the house. I scrunched up my fists in frustration. My new guardian was smarter than she looked.

I grabbed Ms. Penny's tiny paw for moral support and

tentatively walked through the doorway into the house, feeling as though I was stepping directly into the monster's mouth. Again the sensation that I should turn and run away gripped me, but I couldn't move. My feet were frozen to the floor.

Long seconds passed as my eyes adjusted to the dim light in the room and I began to make out shapes, then details. My mouth dropped open as I looked about in amazement. The inside of this house—this mansion—had been built to resemble a castle straight out of the Middle Ages. It seemed, if possible, to be even larger on the inside than it appeared from the outside—deceptively so.

Massive, colorful tapestries depicting medieval hunting scenes, family crests, and strange creatures, all faded now from time, covered broad sections of the rough stone walls. Throughout the room, torches were tucked safely into sconces flickered in the draft slipping around the open doors behind me. A huge fireplace to my left, which took up nearly half of one entire wall, barely contained the flames of a roaring fire. Large, elaborately carved chairs took their places around the room, and a battered, old leather couch sat in front of the fireplace. Two furry black cats stretched out on an old Persian rug in front of the fire, enjoying its warmth. To my disappointment, Ms. Penny ignored them altogether.

Opposite the fireplace, an assortment of candles decorated a long table that ran along the wall. A hat rack, concealed by dozens of brightly colored hats, stood guard by the door. Next to the rack sat a bench, underneath which stood three pairs of Wellington boots. Wooden doors of all shapes, sizes and colors took up the remaining wall space.

"This is the Great Hall," Mrs. Keeper explained, noticing my wide eyes. "In the past, all the folks who lived in the castle—er, house—used this room for dining and socializing. Heating one big room was much more efficient than many little ones. Not until the invention of modern heating contraptions did people begin to spend more time in their private rooms. Nowadays people actually seem to *want* to be alone. Not me. I prefer the old ways, with all sorts of people around." She sighed wistfully and stroked the back of a worn settee. "You may explore the rest of the house some other time," she went on, her round face brightening. "Right now I'm going to show you to your room. I think you're going to like it." She rubbed her hands together excitedly. "Ian and I spent hours preparing it for you."

I looked back at the oversized entry doors, wondering whether I should fetch my luggage before we went any farther.

Mrs. Keeper caught me looking at the doors. "Ian will bring your things up to your room for you," she said, answering my unspoken question. "Now, shall we go?" Without waiting to hear my reply, the squat woman pivoted on one square heel and marched toward the first door on the left. Using a large skeleton key hanging from a ring crammed with an assortment of others like it, she unlocked the arched door, but before dropping the key ring back into a large pocket in her cardigan, she pulled off the key she had used to open the door. She lifted a crude torch from its sconce and held it up high. With her free hand, she grandly swung the door open, and gathering up her worn, flowered skirt, she scurried up the stairway.

Behind me, the monstrous outside doors slammed shut, jolting my nerves. I glanced back and saw no one. Had it been the wind? Not likely. Only a hurricane could blow those doors shut.

I stared up after Mrs. Keeper, took a deep breath, then obediently followed the bustling figure up the narrow, spiraling staircase. It looked like I'd be staying overnight; I might as well make the best of it—it wouldn't hurt to get a good night's rest before I flew the coop. I was going to need all my energy to get back to the city and, once there, convince my dad that leaving me at Portal Manor would be a huge mistake.

Glancing around, I soon determined that making it through the night wasn't going to be easy. As we climbed the stairs, the flames from Mrs. Keeper's torch conjured up monsters peeking out from every nook and cranny. Out of the corner of my eye, I spotted something odd creeping along the wall, and when I turned to get a better look, I swear the thing disappeared into a crack between two stone blocks. I gulped. I'd only been here for twenty minutes and was already losing it. It was going to be a long night.

Ms. Penny Dolittle wasn't the least bit nervous. Once we reached the stairway, she hopped down from my shoulder and trailed after us, giving small chirrups of pleasure. She liked climbing anything, stairs included. Every few steps Ms. Penny stood on her hind legs and pushed against my butt, trying to make me go faster. After she nearly knocked me into Mrs. Keeper's broad backside, I hissed, "Stop it!" She replied, as she usually did to reprimands, by sticking her tongue out at me and screeching like a spoiled toddler.

Unfazed, Mrs. Keeper glanced back to see what was going on. "Are you all right, Viddie dear?"

"Uh, yeah," I responded as an idea formed in my mind. "Sorry about that. Ms. Penny is already causing trouble. She almost pushed me right into your . . . um, you know . . ."

"My derriere?" the older woman replied calmly. "Don't fret yourself. I've quite a bit of padding back there, as you can see." She turned and continued waddling up the steep stairs as quickly as a mountain goat up a mountainside.

Rats.

A few more twists of the staircase brought us face to face with a small, dark door. A tarnished brass knob shaped like a lion's head presented itself to us. Mrs. Keeper approached the door and slid the same key she'd used for the downstairs door into the keyhole. She turned the key and then pulled it back out.

"Well, Viddie," she said, handing me the key, which was as long as my hand, "this is where you'll be staying."

I hesitated, fingering the cool metal, not sure I really wanted to see what was behind the door. Maybe it wasn't a bedroom; maybe it was a torture chamber.

"Open the door, dear," Mrs. Keeper encouraged me. "There aren't any surprises behind this one. Well, there *shouldn't* be . . ." My new guardian frowned as she thought about it, then laughed with gusto. "Go ahead."

I pocketed the hefty key and stepped toward the door. Weakly, I pushed it open and peered into the darkness. In front of me I saw yet another set of steps, but no monsters.

"It may not look like it, but we do have electricity here," Mrs. Keeper cheerily informed me. I breathed a sigh of relief. "I prefer candles or firelight, though," she went on. "So much more flattering for the complexion, don't you think?" She winked at me. "At my age, a gal needs all the help she can get."

I nodded absently, then realized what I was nodding to. With an effort, I stopped the movement of my head.

Mrs. Keeper continued, unperturbed. "The power goes out all the time so far out in the country, so it helps to have back-up. But go ahead and flip the switch to your right, just inside the door."

Like a robot, I did as I was told, and a feeble light flickered on. Another door stood open at the top of the staircase. To my right was a small nook, just large enough for a cot.

"On the left is your bathroom. It's small, but should serve your purposes."

I sincerely hoped it was large enough to hold a working toilet. I'd read about people using chamber pots in the good old days and had no desire to use one myself. I looked back at Mrs. Keeper. "Should I go up?"

She nodded excitedly. "Yes, do. I'll be right behind you, dear. I can't wait to see the look on your face. Be careful of the steps, now. They're a bit steep."

After an enthusiastic shove from my new guardian, I put my foot on the first step, looked up at the doorway one last time, then began to make my way up the sharply sloping staircase. Ms. Penny, impatient as always, zipped past me and darted through the open door.

"Ms. Penny!" I cried and rushed up the remaining steps. When I reached the landing, I let out a gasp.

I was standing in a tower.

CHAPTER FOUR

MY VERY OWN TOWER

I don't know what I'd been expecting (other than the torture chamber scenario), but it wasn't anything like this. The room, with its rounded walls and high ceilings, couldn't be more different than my tiny, dark bedroom back home. Here, everything smelled fresh and clean. The polished wood floors glowed. The dark beams overhead gave the room a cozy feeling, yet even on such a foggy evening, enough light flowed in from three large, arched windows to brighten the tower. Underneath one of the windows opposite the stairwell rested an ornately carved canopy bed, complete with red velvet curtains hung round it like a sultan's tent. Close by, a cheery fire burned in a small fireplace. An old wooden trunk with worn leather straps and handles was parked at the foot of the bed. It looked well traveled. I wanted to peek inside, then thought

I might not want to know what it held. It might be where they kept the severed head.

Against the wall and to the right of the stairwell, stood a tall mahogany dresser and wardrobe. Under the window facing the front yard, a roll-top desk awaited my scholarly activities. A window seat adorned the third window, which looked out over the hill and its blanket of yellow-leaved trees. I strolled over to the seat and peered out into the woods below. It was a perfect spot to read or to just look out at the trees and daydream.

I felt myself growing excited at the prospect of staying here. Then I frowned, angry with myself. I had to stop thinking that way. I couldn't start imagining living here, not if I wanted to get back home.

"Well?" Mrs. Keeper said, startling me. I turned to see her standing behind me, tiny hands clasped together. She was practically dancing with excitement. "What do you think?"

"It's not bad," I replied. There was no way I was going to let on that I loved everything about my new room. I couldn't afford to give Mrs. Keeper, or my dad, the leverage they'd need to convince me to stay. "Is this my dad's old room?"

"Your father preferred a regular room with four walls and a flat ceiling. He was never one to like anything out of the ordinary. He wanted life to be normal and predictable." She cast her eyes about and sighed.

"Is that why he's never come back?"

"Oh, I'm sure that's one reason. But there are others— which reminds me . . . there is something you need to know about this room."

I brightened. I knew this place was too good to be true. I already had a good idea what my guardian was going to tell me . . . *It's a nice room, dear, if you don't mind bats. Or rats. Or that mysterious, toe-curling smell we can't seem to get rid of.*

"Go stand by the bed and face the wall," Mrs. Keeper directed, putting a stop to my imaginings. I went over to face the wall, the only part of the room paneled in wood instead of the stone blocks that composed the rest of the tower. The dark wood paneling stretched from about four feet on one side of the bed to four feet on the other. "Put your hands on the wall right next to the bed and give it a shove, will you, dear."

I shrugged at the mysterious request, but pushed anyway. To my surprise, part of the wood panel moved. What appeared to be a solid wall was actually a spring-hinged door. *This is exactly like a book,* I thought, feeling dangerously exhilarated. Preparing myself for a massive surge of bats, I leaned forward to look around, but could see nothing, not even bats.

"It's a door."

"Of course it's a door, dear," Mrs. Keeper chuckled. "It leads to a stairwell which will take you directly to the conservatory. This back way is a much faster way to get downstairs. It was installed in case of . . . well, just in case."

I swung to face Mrs. Keeper. "There *are* bats, aren't there?" *There had better be,* I thought. I was already feeling way too attached to this room.

"Oh, no, no . . . at least not that I know of. But you never know what could happen in this house, dear—in any old house," she quickly amended. "It's best to always be prepared."

Before I could respond, Mrs. Keeper pointed toward the window with the window seat. "See that hill?"

I returned to the window to look out at the hillside and nodded when I saw the dark incline. It was hard to miss, even with the sun already set.

". . . and Killiecrankie Wood?" The wood was deep and shadowed and filled with slender beech trees, their silver-gray trunks ethereal as ghost limbs.

I nodded.

"Good. Best to stay clear of it. Just to be on the safe side. Wild animals and such. No sense waking the dragon, so to speak."

I nodded again, more slowly this time.

"Have you eaten?" she asked.

"Yes." I'd packed a sandwich and an apple. And then there'd been all those candy bars.

"That's fine. When you come down for breakfast in the morning, take the back stairs to the conservatory. It'll let you out right next to the kitchen, which leads to the dining room, where we eat." She clapped her hands together. "Now then, Ian is on his way up with your trunks. Is everything to your liking?"

She didn't bother waiting for my answer. Judging by her happy tone, I had a funny feeling she already knew what it would be.

"I imagine you're tired, dear, and you have your first day of school tomorrow, to boot. We leave here at half past seven. If you have trouble settling, come down for a cup of tea; we always keep a kettle on the stove."

"Okay, Mrs. Keeper." The sea of yellow leaves down below was mesmerizing, enticing me to explore the woods despite Mrs. Keeper's warning. I felt unable to look away. Caught up in my daydreaming, it took a moment to realize that my guardian hadn't answered me. When I turned around, I saw that she had disappeared. Seconds later, I heard a loud thumping noise on the stairs. Either Mrs. Keeper was charging down them like a bull on the loose or someone was coming up in a major huff.

A tall figure emerged from the dark stairwell. His dark

hair was damp from the misty fog swirling about outside. I stared at him and shook my head at the irony of it all. This was the mysterious Ian, and either he had a twin, or this guy was none other than the very unhelpful boy at the gate.

"Look out!" He lunged past me and dropped the red steamer trunk with a bang. Without looking at me, he pounded back down the stairs to fetch the rest of my things. According to my dad, the trunks had once been my Grandma Mors'. Sensing my interest in them, he had told me that I could have them for the trip if I wanted. While packing, I'd filled all three trunks to the brim. I didn't dare leave anything behind for the Toad to sell to the highest bidder while I was gone.

"Do you need help?" I asked after he dropped the second trunk on the floor.

"I've got it," he replied and thudded back down the stairs. I smiled wickedly as I thought about his dragging the last trunk up that endless flight of stairs, especially as he hadn't yet fetched the one filled with my books.

By the time he reached the top of the stairs with the last trunk, he was breathing hard and sweating profusely. He pushed the heavy box over by the bed, then collapsed on top of the mattress. "What'd you do, pack everything you own?"

"I did leave my brick collection at home."

Ian closed his eyes and shook his head, snorting in disgust.

"It wasn't *that* bad of a joke," I said.

"Yes, it was." He sat up and ran his fingers through his damp, scruffy hair.

My teeth clenched. First he refuses to help me, then he acts like a jerk. "My dad owns this place, you know." The words spilled out before I could stop them. Ugh. That was a new, all-time low for me.

"Big hairy deal. So you're rich." He fixed me with a tough stare and cracked his knuckles one by one. The popping sound made me cringe. "You think that makes you better than me?"

"We're *not* rich." I didn't want him thinking that I was one of *those* people. Besides, despite my dad's well-known reputation, we lived in a cramped, dark apartment on campus, and Dad bought most of his clothes at consignment shops. Mine, too. It wasn't *my* fault I looked so weird. Growing up, whenever I needed something new, I'd use the old door-in-the-face technique—ask for something absurdly big so you'll have a better chance of getting the smaller thing that you actually want. "Dad, can I have a big-screen TV?" I'd ask. "No," he'd reply automatically, "you know we don't have the money for that." "How about some new underwear?" I'd beg, getting to the real heart of the matter. "We'll see," he'd murmur absently. Sometimes I had to abandon all pride and resort to showing him the remains of my tattered drawers, though not when I was actually wearing them, of course. Usually, my unmentionables had to be holier than the Shroud of Turin before he'd give in and fork over the dough for new ones.

So anyway, I'd always thought we were poor, which is why I had to ask, How are we going to pay for it? when he told me he was sending me away to a private school. I was looking for a reason—any reason would do—to get out of going. His excuse for sending me away was that my grades had been slipping over the past three years and a private school might do me some good. Well, they hadn't been slipping, as he so delicately put it; they had plummeted—after the Incident—so why start caring about them now?

"I'm working on an idea that should bring in some money in the near future," he replied quickly to my question. A little too quickly. I knew all about his recent work creating an anti-pollution chemical, but I didn't think my dad was close enough to completing it to pay my tuition. If we'd owned this mansion all along, why did my dad need to make more money? Why not just sell this place? It didn't add up.

"We're not rich," I repeated to Ian, though rather feebly this time.

"Whatever you say," he replied in a bored voice, running a hand through the dark mop on his head, again. He must really like the feel of his own hair.

Ms. Penny, curious as always, decided at that moment to find out who this new creature sharing her bed was. She dropped down from the bedpost, right next to him.

"What the—" His voice cracked. "Oh, it's you. Saw you in the car."

Too bad. I had hoped he'd start screaming.

"Ms. Penny!" I hurried over to grab the squirmy coon, but before I could get a grip on her she wiggled away and jumped onto Ian's shoulder. He reached over and scratched her under the chin.

"You can stay, girl," he said.

Ms. Penny grinned at me and made herself at home. Once she settled herself, she started to groom him.

"I'll get her off you," I blurted out. "She's been known to pee on people she doesn't like." I wasn't making that up. One time, Ms. Penny had peed on the Toad's head when he'd tried to befriend her. He knew it would make me mad, and she'd let him know in no uncertain terms that she didn't need friends like him.

"She's all right." He grinned at the cheeky beast. "Animals like me." The grin disappeared when he looked over at me. "So, I hear you're going to Smellmont Academy."

"It's Bellemont Academy, not—" I saw the laughter in his eyes and mentally kicked myself. "That's very clever. Did you come up with that name all by yourself?"

He shrugged. "Someone made it up way before my time. The name fits, though. All those rich girls thinking they're better than everybody. Them and their attitudes stink."

I felt myself go cold. "Are they that bad?"

"That snob factory? Better believe it."

I flushed. I was *not* a snob. If anything, I was anti-snob. I knew very well what it was like to be treated badly just for being different. "For your information, my dad is making me go. He thinks . . ." I couldn't tell Ian the real reasons— my poor grades, my dad not wanting me around. "He thinks it would be good for me. But I don't plan on sticking around long enough to find out. As soon as I can find a way, I'm going back home."

He eyed me speculatively. "You think so, huh? Well, good luck with that." He scratched Ms. Penny under the chin again after she batted him on the head when he stopped. "You can't drive, and there isn't anybody in town who would come and get you here. And trust me, you don't really wanna be alone out there." He jerked his head toward the dark window. "Some strange things hang out in those woods."

He stood suddenly. Ms. Penny swayed, but hung on. "I have to finish my chores." He stopped at the door, his hand on the knob, and looked back at me. His blue eyes scanned my face. "How old are you, anyway? Twelve?"

I frowned and thought about throwing one of my trunks at his head. I replied with as much dignity as my four-eleven frame would allow, "I'm fifteen, if you need to know."

"Really? So am I," he told me, squaring his shoulders. "But everyone says I look at *least* sixteen." He grinned, looking just like a fifteen-year-old would. "I think it's the beard," he confided, stroking a strange little tuft sprouting from his chin. He glanced over at Ms. Penny. "All right, raccoon. You can get down now," he said, and Ms. Penny stuck out her bottom lip, jumped to the floor and galloped over to the bed. "See you later, kid," he added, and disappeared down the stairs.

I watched him go, muttering curses at his back, then hurried over to study my reflection in the cheval mirror standing next to the dresser. In the dark glass, and much to my annoyance, I had to admit that I did look like I was only twelve. My short stature and scrawny frame didn't help matters. The face looking back at me was pixie-like, with large, round eyes as gray as the fog outside and a pert, up-tilted nose. When it wasn't getting in my face, my straight, dark hair fell just below my jaw line. Surprisingly straight, bluntly cut bangs bisected my high forehead. I say surprisingly because I cut my own hair.

On the whole, I looked like an Elf, something I'd always secretly liked, especially since my mother had looked the same way. I only knew this because one boring, rainy afternoon while snooping around the apartment, I'd found a cardboard box filled with pictures in my dad's closet. One silver-framed photograph of my mother showed an almost eerie resemblance to me. In the picture, she was laughing, her head thrown back and her white teeth flashing. She looked so happy and alive. My dad stood with his arm draped over her shoulder. He, too, looked uncharacteristically cheerful and not too shabby in his typical professor's uniform of a turtleneck and tweed jacket.

I filched the picture from the box before restoring it to the shelf, leaving the rest so my dad wouldn't know I'd borrowed one. Once in a while, I'd take the photo from the drawer in my bedside table and stare at it, willing the person my mother had been to show herself. But nothing ever happened, no connection, no spark, as though Kelly

Mors had never existed. Sometimes I got mad at her for leaving me, even though I knew it wasn't her fault. She'd died when I was only a baby. Mostly, though, I felt sad. I missed what our family could have been.

I shook my head and refocused on my image in the mirror. Thinking about my mother for too long wasn't good for me. It was easier to stuff that emotion away in a place deep down inside. Someday my feelings would likely all come out in one big explosion, and someone, somewhere, was going to get hurt.

I tilted my head to one side, then to the other. I pulled my hair back and tried to pile it on top of my head. Silky and fine, strands kept slipping between my fingers. Not a bad look, I thought. Maybe if I got glasses too, I'd look older. Then I frowned. Why did I care? I wasn't like the other girls at school, so caught up in their looks that they'd forgotten to develop a personality. The fact that I was giving my appearance some thought irritated me.

I dropped my arms and scowled at myself. My eyes strayed to my flushed cheeks, stopping in horror at a rather large streak of chocolate close by my right ear. "Oh, man." I wet my finger on my tongue and rubbed at the brown smudge. Having chocolate smeared on my face certainly didn't help me look any older.

Noting the time on my pocket watch—yet another thrift-shop gem—I began unpacking my trunks only to stop myself. What was I doing? Why bother to unpack when I only planned to be here a day or two—a week at the most?

I flopped down on my bed. Maybe I should just give up and stay. It was obviously what my dad wanted me to do. Then I remembered why I couldn't: Portal Manor was the place in my dreams. The wrought-iron gate, the feelings of familiarity, the sense of danger. All these signs told me that this portion of my dream was coming true, which meant the rest of it could, too. And the part that I couldn't remember, but *knew* was real, frightened me more than anything.

Rolling off my bed, I decided to unpack only the bare necessities: a book to read, a ready supply of chocolate bars, and mine and Ms. Penny's pajamas. I finished my tasks, then hurried downstairs with Ms. Penny to use the toilet (it hadn't been easy training her to do that) and to brush my teeth. Inside the bathroom, a claw-foot bathtub, a basin sink, and a shelf stuffed with towels and various other bathroom necessities filled the small space. There was a real toilet, I noted happily. Back upstairs, I changed into my PJs, dressed Ms. Penny in her nightgown, and grabbed my book. Once in bed, I snuggled beneath the covers.

It's not that I wanted to stay overnight, it's just that I had no intention of sneaking off under the cover of darkness, not after hearing Ian's and Mrs. Keeper's warnings about strange things lurking in the woods.

Tomorrow, I murmured to myself. I'll leave tomorrow.

CHAPTER FIVE
SMELLMONT ACADEMY

When I awoke the next morning, I glanced at the clock and saw that it was already seven o'clock. Crud. I was supposed to leave for school in half an hour. I leaped out of bed, hustled over to a trunk and pulled out the wrinkled school uniform my dad had ordered from the academy. It looked awful. I shrugged. I didn't really care what I wore as long as it was comfortable. This outfit—a white oxford shirt, a blue-and-green plaid skirt, navy blue tights and a navy blue cardigan—didn't look too bad in that department.

By the time I finally managed to get the tights on, I was singing a different tune. Who invented these leg girdles? They were like little torture machines. And were they itchy! I couldn't wait to return to my old school and get back to wearing my regular outfit of jeans and a t-shirt. My clothes might have been way too big on me, but at least they were comfortable. Every minute I had to wear a uniform would only further motivate me to leave this place far behind.

After Ms. Penny and I used the facilities, I hurried down the front stairs chewing on a handful of dried peaches, leaving Ms. Penny in my room with the rest of the bag. One of the large doors in the Great Hall stood ajar, and I slipped through the crack into the cool air of the early October morning. Seeing my breath floating in puffy clouds in front of me, I snugged my cardigan about me.

Parked in front of the main doors, looking like a cross between a tank and a hearse, a big black car cut the strangest figure I'd ever seen, especially in the fog that still lingered in the morning air. I liked it. No one sat in the driver's seat, but since it was rather chilly, I decided to wait inside. Climbing into the back seat, I fastened my belt and waited for the others to arrive. Ian soon came racing out of a vine-covered door directly below the tower on the north side of the house. Was that where he lived? The other tower? I couldn't imagine he'd pick any other room when there was a tower to choose from.

He sprinted toward the car, pulling on a jean jacket as he ran. A pastry shoved firmly in his mouth oozed raspberry jam from its center. My stomach rumbled at the sight of it. Instead of climbing into the passenger seat next to me, he slipped behind the steering wheel.

"Hey," he greeted as he chewed on a mouthful of Bismarck, "looking forward to your first day at Smellmont Academy?"

"No." I stared at the back of his head. His dark hair was still wet. "You're not driving, are you?"

His answer was to turn the key in the ignition. The car rumbled and groaned, then turned over. Once started, the engine purred like a kitten. Ian leaned back in his seat and devoured the rest of the Bismarck. He had just swallowed his last bite when Mrs. Keeper scurried out the main doors like a tiny tornado, the large doors banging shut behind her. I wondered how the tiny woman did that. She must work out with some massive weights to get that kind of power.

She yanked open the driver's door. "Shove over, Ian. You've still got loads of time before you get your learner's permit. Until then, I don't want to see you anywhere near this steering wheel."

He gave her a sheepish grin and slid over. Mrs. Keeper shook her head with exasperation, but didn't seem to really be mad. Shifting the car into drive, she tore down the driveway and through the open gates. Once on the other side, she pressed the button on the remote clipped to her window visor and the gates closed behind us like automatic garage doors.

"You're ready for school, then, Lavida dear?" Mrs. Keeper asked, looking at me in the rearview mirror.

Mentally urging her to keep those brown eyes of hers on the winding, foggy road, I clutched the seat for dear life and stammered, "I—I think so."

Mrs. Keeper glanced at the road, then back in the mirror. "Do me a favor, dear, and try not to run away on your first day."

I blushed. How had she known I was even thinking of running away? Then it occurred to me how she knew, and I glared at the back of Ian's head. He swung around in his seat. "Don't look at me like that!" he exclaimed, pushing a lock of hair off his forehead. "I never said anything."

"Of course he didn't," Mrs. Keeper assured me. Ian gave me an I-told-you-so smirk. "It was your father who told me. He warned me you might not be too happy living at Portal Manor or going to school at the academy." She caught my eye in the mirror. "Give it a chance, dear. You might learn to like both."

I folded my arms and stared out the window, tuning out Ian's complaints about not being able to drive yet. I hadn't counted on Mrs. Keeper finding out about my plans to escape. Great. She was already keeping a close eye on everything I did, making it that much harder for me to make my getaway. It really was like living in a prison.

I focused on the road that led into town, hoping to memorize the route. It wasn't hard to remember the way. The road had a lot of hills and curves, but basically, after one turn, it was a straight shot to the town of Bellemont. A white sign, planted in the ground just past a narrow bridge that spanned a frothing stream, welcomed visitors to the small, typical New England town. Lined with immaculate white buildings, Main Street was a Mecca for tourists: signs for expensive shops and restaurants, a grocery store, a little red brick library, and a small theater were neatly lettered in Gothic script.

Halfway along the row of buildings, the street split. A town green filled the divide, complete with thick, healthy grass and the customary statue of a man astride a rearing horse, most likely capturing the moment just before he fell off. A white church with a tall steeple stood at the end of the street, seemingly cut off from the hustle and bustle of the town. A graveyard hid in its shadow, with a knot of old gravestones crammed into the small space.

"Welcome to Bellemont," Mrs. Keeper said gaily. "It was named after your mother's family, you know."

I sat up. I hadn't known that. My dad had only just told me a couple days ago that my mom had grown up in Bellemont and attended Bellemont Academy. He hadn't suddenly decided to become open about my mom; he'd only brought it up to make me want to go. A sure sign of desperation, his giving out information like that, but his ruse had worked. After he'd told me, I stopped fighting him about coming here. I was curious about my mom.

It made sense she'd lived in Bellemont, since she and my dad had met here. They must have gone on dates in this very town, maybe getting ice cream at the Soda Shoppe on the corner. But as I looked around the picturesque village, I simply couldn't imagine her being here. I slumped back down in my seat. I had hoped that coming to this place would make me feel more connected to her, but it didn't. I felt as cut off from her as ever.

"Here we are," Mrs. Keeper announced, startling me out of my depressing reverie. The car screeched to a stop in front of an impressive building boasting the name Gates Hall. "Have a good first day, dear." Her eyes were sympathetic.

I clambered out the side door, dragging my backpack after me, reluctant to leave the car. I didn't want to do this. I didn't want to a meet a bunch of snobby girls, and I didn't want to go to this school. I didn't have much of a choice, though. Prisoners usually don't.

"Seeya, kid," Ian called out the window as they drove off.

"Stop calling me kid!" I shouted at him, sounding very much like one, even to my own ears. Standing there, all alone, I wrapped my arms around myself as a shiver of foreboding shook my frame. Slowly I turned around. Bellemont Academy looked exactly the way I had thought it would: old and intimidating, with ivy-covered buildings rising out of the fog like malevolent giants. The grass was perfectly cut, the grounds immaculate. Girls in uniform hurried to their classes, chattering and laughing. It took all my willpower to keep from thinking they were laughing at me.

New students were required to register at Gates Hall, at which time they'd get their class schedules. I glanced at my pocket watch. Classes started in fifteen minutes. I broke into a run, nearly knocking over another girl as I scrambled up the steps. Inside, Mrs. Petticoat, the admissions dean, had her secretary print out my schedule. My dad had registered me a few weeks ago, choosing the classes he thought I should be taking. I noticed Chemistry was on the list and sighed. Why did he think I'd have any interest in that? With my track record, I'd probably blow up the building and everyone in it.

After I'd finished perusing my schedule, Dean Petticoat gave me a folder that contained a map of the campus printed on the back. She then showed me where my classes were, marking each building with an X and, wishing me good luck, she escorted me to the door. She'd been pro-fessional, yet kind.

So far, so good, I thought, as I sprinted toward my first class. I found the right building on the first try and made it to my class before the final bell rang. I settled into a desk at the back of the room and tried hard to lie low. I can do this, I told myself.

As it turned out, all my morning classes—Civics, English, Mathematics (in my old school it was plain old math), and French—weren't as hard as I had expected. But they also weren't easy. I didn't talk to anyone, and no one talked to me. It didn't take long for me to see that Ian was right. No one here would want to hang out with someone like me. These girls came from money. Still, it wasn't long before I started to relax a little. As long as I remained unnoticed, I might do all right. Even if I had to stay in Bellemont, God forbid, I thought I could survive this school better than the one back home. At least here I didn't have to worry about the other kids being afraid of me.

The lunch bell rang and I followed a group of girls heading toward the cafeteria. I stood in line for my lunch along with the rest of them, my stomach rumbling fiercely. They chatted around me as the lunch lady plopped my selections onto my tray. Once I had my meal, I found an empty table and headed for it.

My stomach had been growling since the beginning of second period, and I was really looking forward to eating my lunch. I gazed down at my red tray bearing a plateful of steaming spaghetti and meatballs, two pieces of fragrant garlic bread, a small garden salad, and a cannoli. The food smelled delicious. I shivered in anticipation.

That's when it happened.

Not looking where I was going, I ran right into another girl. Horrified, I watched as my veggies, garlic bread, and milk carton flew up into the air, while my spaghetti splashed up against my front before it slid off the tray and onto the floor, the plate shattering next to it.

"Watch where you're going!" the girl spat, her blue eyes raging. She had a perfect figure—tall and slender—to go along with the perfect blonde hair that fell in a cascade of curls around her head. As thin as she was, she was obviously one of those girls who'd never have to worry about seeing womanly curves. She had them in spades.

"My lunch!" I stared down at the mess on the floor. Spaghetti and lettuce and milk were everywhere.

"I'd be more concerned about my shirt if I were you," the blonde smirked, and the whole cafeteria burst into laughter around me.

"Good one, Fiona," someone called out.

I looked down to see saucy noodles clinging to my once-white blouse. I swiped them off. "Next time stay out of my way." She flipped her hair. "Come on," she barked to the gaggle of girls following her, "let's go."

I watched them leave before staring down at the mess that had once been my lunch. My empty stomach gave a disappointed lurch as I kneeled down to clean it up.

The day went downhill after that. The girls that had been with the blonde in the cafeteria were in my afternoon classes. They pointed and laughed at me whenever they could. Notes found their way into my lap, scrawled with words like *dork* and *klutz* and *freak*. The insults were lame and uncreative, but hurtful all the same.

After reading the last note, which questioned my sanity along with my hairstyle, I sank low in my chair and chewed on my pinkie nail, what was left of it. I had thought things might be different here at Bellemont Academy.

I had thought wrong.

CHAPTER SIX

MRS. DOOLEY'S KITCHEN

Mrs. Keeper and Ian picked me up outside Gates Hall a little after three.

"How was your day, dear?" Mrs. Keeper asked when I climbed inside the car.

"Great," I mumbled. During my wait, I'd had to endure stares, snickers, and a balled-up piece of paper upside the head.

"Make any friends?"

"I'm the most popular girl at school," I felt tempted to say. Instead I replied shortly, "No."

Ian snorted, then took over the conversation, complaining about some kid at school who'd seemed determined to pick a fight with him. Again, I tuned him out, preferring to brood and plan my escape from this awful place.

Once home, I leaped out of the car and flew up to my room, changed clothes, repacked my stuff, then found Ms. Penny curled up in a ball on the bed. I shook her. "Wake up! We'll get something to eat and get out of here."

She perked up immediately. *Eat* is one of her favorite words. She jumped off the bed and galloped toward the door, chirruping with excitement the whole way.

I called her back. "Not that way, Ms. Penny. This way." I pointed to the hidden door. Just because I didn't plan on staying here was no reason why I couldn't satisfy my curiosity about the strange door and the conservatory that waited for us down below.

The furry little creature cocked her head to one side, then scampered back to me and jumped up on my shoulder. With Ms. Penny clinging tightly to my shirt, I approached the door and was about to push on it when it occurred to me: Why was there a hidden door in my bedroom? Why did someone living at Portal Manor need an escape route? Who, or what, would they need to escape from?

Probably just a fancy fire escape, I told myself. Thoughts of the bogeyman made me shiver; still, I went ahead and pushed open the door. Blackness rushed out to greet me like a frightened bird, and my hand shot out to find the light switch. When I stumbled upon a protrusion on the wall, I flipped it up. A dim glow appeared from a single bulb over my head, allowing enough light to see a flight of steps descending directly before me.

Even with the glowing bulb, the stairway was still quite dark, though I could make out a thin crack of light at the bottom. I felt a thrill of excitement slip through me as I crept down the rough stone stairs, my boots thudding against the hard surface. Halfway down, my foot caught on one of the steps and I stumbled. Leaning quickly to my right, I fell against the wall and grabbed hold. Steadied now, I quickly pushed away from the wall, which was as cold as a tombstone in November, then wiped my damp hands on my jeans.

At the bottom of the steps, I slowly pushed open the heavy wooden door. The hinges squeaked loudly in protest, as though the door hadn't been used in years. I cautiously stepped through the doorway and was met with a curtain of leafy vines. When I finally emerged from the tangled web and looked around me, I was amazed to find myself in a lush rain forest. Everywhere hundreds of exotic plants grew wildly and luxuriantly; the fragrant scent of blooming flowers tickled my nose. A bird hooted loudly overhead, startling me, then something wet hit me on the cheek. It wasn't bird poop, I discovered to my relief after wiping it away, only a water drop from one of the sprinklers hanging from a network of metal pipes close to the glass ceiling.

Ms. Penny let out a whinny of delight and jumped down from my shoulder. She raced over to one of the larger trees, and I watched nervously as she shot up its broad trunk. To my knowledge, Ms. Penny had never climbed a tree before, yet she easily made it to the top without so much as a slip of the paw. Unfortunately, she then began to jump from branch to branch, using her front legs as arms, like a fat, furry trapeze artist. Dashing around like a maniac, I tried to stay under her to catch her in case she lost her grip. But after a few minutes, I relaxed; Ms. Penny was handling the tree just fine.

Leaving her to her fun, I looked around the conservatory. The glass-paned wall facing the front yard framed a door leading outside. Next to the door grew an immense tree, and from one of its thick branches hung a swing. When I had assured myself no one else was in the room to see me, I ran toward it like a kindergartner let out for recess and climbed up. After three strong pumps, I was flying high into the air, where I could see all over the enormous room.

The two walls not made of glass were built from a patchwork of rough stones. The other, punctuated like gems in a crown by windows, both clear and stained-glass, faced the hill behind the house. I could only imagine how beautiful the conservatory must look on a sunny day, with a rainbow of colors flashing about. A large rectangular pool filled with clear water jutted out from the center of the wall, a blue-and-aqua mosaic coloring the floor, giving the water a bright glow. The floor pattern appeared to form a picture, but I couldn't make it out.

A balcony ran the length of the pool and could be reached by climbing a stone stairway flanking either side. Beneath the balcony, water spewed from the mouth of a large, grotesque head—eyes fierce and leering, nose bulbous and flaring. Carved lion heads protruding from a low, crenellated wall surrounded the rest of the pool, spurting streams of water from perpetually roaring mouths, an assortment of plants in large pots filling the spaces in between. Several feet from the pool, a wide tree branch dipped down so you could sit on it as though it were a chair. In one corner of the enclosure, a large hammock, perfect for napping, hung between two smaller trees. All around, lush flowers grew in colorful masses, butterflies flitted from blossom to blossom, and little fat birds pecked at specks on the ground.

A squawk drew my attention up to see more birds flying overhead. They reminded me of buzzards circling a dying man, which reminded me of school and those stupid girls. I couldn't believe I'd screwed up already. One mistake and I was already being ostracized—just like at my old school. The carrion birds also reminded me that I'd missed lunch.

My eyes followed the wall until I spotted a dark wooden door tucked away in a corner to the right of the pool. I made my way toward it along a narrow stone path flanked by bunches of fragrant herbs. When I reached the door, I turned the cool glass knob and entered a large room. The first thing I noticed in the warm, delicious-smelling space was a woman of immense proportions peeling potatoes over a two-basin, white ceramic sink. She wore a blue apron over an orange muumuu, and her sizeable hips swung from side to side as she belted out the words to a pop song. The color of her full cheeks blended into her frizzy, dark red hair, the majority of which sprung outward from her head like broken bed-springs.

Opposite from where the woman worked, a cavernous fireplace, twin to the one in the Great Hall, spread itself along one of the walls. A bright fire crackled cheerily, warming the room. All kinds of glass jars, filled to the brim with apples and beans and peaches and various indiscernibles, crammed wooden shelves lining the walls. A long wooden table dominated the middle of the room. Deep-dish pies, every kind of vegetable you could imagine, yellow apples in a blue ceramic bowl, an assortment of cutlery, and empty jam jars covered the dark golden surface, mottled and scarred from centuries of contact with greasy food, wine spills, and knife nicks. A pair of long benches flanked the table, and a wrought-iron rack hung from the ceiling overhead, from which fire-blackened pots and bunches of dried herbs dangled on hooks. Despite its old-fashioned look, the kitchen boasted a few modern appliances—a refrigerator, a double-stacked oven and a black gas stove.

"Find what you're looking for, lassie?" the woman asked in a rich Irish brogue. I jumped. She hadn't turned around, but somehow sensed that I was in the room.

"I was hungry," I said, feeling the need to give an excuse as to why I was here in this woman's kitchen.

She stopped what she was doing and reached up to snap the radio off before swinging around to face me. I braced myself. "You had a hard day of it, didn't you?" Her voice was soft and kind.

My breath rushed out. How had she known? I slowly nodded.

"Come on, then. Sit," she said, motioning to the table. "Let Mrs. Dooley take care of you."

Letting go of the doorknob, I took a few cautious steps forward, then quickly sat down at the long table. Mrs. Dooley plunked down a large glass of milk and a plate of freshly baked oatmeal raisin cookies in front of me. As I chugged down the milk, she waddled over to the sink and turned on the faucet. When the water was running, she picked up a stoneware mug, leaned back against the sink and took a long swallow. I read her apron—*You can help me by getting out of my kitchen*—and wondered if I should take the warning seriously. As I took a giant bite from a warm, gooey cookie, she set the cup down next to the sink and added a large dose of dish soap to the water.

I watched her every move.

"So you're Andrew Mors' little girl," she said at last.

"I'm Viddie," I told her around a mouthful of cookie. "My dad sent me here to attend Bellemont Academy."

"Ah, yes. Bellemont Academy. I don't believe in private schools myself; they breed snobbery, in my opinion. Mind you, some good girls go there."

"They must all be in hiding," I mumbled.

She chuckled. "You'll just have to look harder, then."

"These are good cookies," I told her, hoping to change the subject.

"Well, finish them up. You're too skinny." She shook her

head ruefully as she eyed my slender frame. "The grass wouldn't even know you're walking on it, to be sure. I'll be making your lunch from here on out. Less trouble that way."

I nearly blurted out that there wouldn't be any "here on out," but thought better of it.

"Moving to a new place can be hard," she went on, "especially to a place like Portal Manor. It's different here. But then, different can be a good thing."

"Different gets you in trouble," I said quietly, then rushed on. "So I was wondering if I could get some food for my raccoon, Ms. Penny—"

"Raccoon!" she echoed, as though I'd just told her I had a pet rhinoceros, then she cautiously peeked behind me.

"She's in the conservatory."

"Ah, well." She relaxed. "That's all right then. I'm not sure I'll be wanting wild animals and such running loose in my kitchen. All those birds and reptiles Ian adopts are bad enough." She frowned. "So what do raccoons eat?"

"Well, they eat—"

"Pretty much anything," she interrupted, "judging by the mess they make out of my garbage cans. Go ahead and look there." She indicated the refrigerator behind me. "There should be plenty of food to choose from. I keep my kitchen well-stocked, which isn't always easy, if you know what I mean." She winked at me and patted her rounded belly before turning off the water.

"Supper's in the dining room." She nodded at the opposite side of the room. "Hurry along and feed your pet. We'll eat in an hour." Leaning over the sink, she switched the radio back on and began singing along as she kneaded a lump of bread dough the size of a watermelon.

Scanning the contents of the gaping refrigerator, I was stunned by the array of choices. I'd never seen so much food, or such variety, in a fridge before. Ours at home was often empty. I placed two apples and a stalk of celery into the pouch I'd made with my oversized Jim Morrison t-shirt and grabbed two bananas and a bag of sunflower seeds from the counter. Afraid Mrs. Dooley would call me back and scold me for taking so much, I hurried over to the little door. She *seemed* nice.

But nice, I'd learned, could turn on you.

I found Ms. Penny by following the sound of her chatter, which she was aiming at the birds. When I called to her, she refused to come down. The pain-in-the-behind wanted me to climb up and bring the food to her. Not going to happen. I had to pretend that I was eating her dinner before she practically took off my head in her race to get at it. She climbed back up the tree with a banana and an apple, and I sat in the hammock to plan my escape. Nothing came to me. All I could think about was Mrs. Dooley's kindness and that I was going to have a hard time getting Ms. Penny away from here. Plus, it was already getting late and I was still really hungry. I'd stay for dinner, I decided. And one more night. But tomorrow afternoon, I was out of here.

Stomach growling, I returned to the kitchen, where Mrs. Dooley was washing the dishes. Not wanting to disturb her singing, I tiptoed past her toward the large archway on the other side of the kitchen and entered the long, narrow room that was the butler's pantry. Wide, polished wooden shelves stood at attention against the walls, displaying row upon row of beautiful china. Below the shelves, open-faced cabinets housed stacks of thicker, sturdier plates, enough of them to feed an army. Who needed that many plates? Who were they all for?

At the other end of the pantry, I spied a set of pocket doors and moved toward them. After sliding them into their respective spaces in the wall, I peered into the grandly decorated dining area. I quietly stepped inside and looked around. It was a dark room, lit only by torches, though a large chandelier hung over the table if needed. Against one wall, a long serving table supported a mismatched, dented sterling silver service, which had obviously seen better days. On the opposite wall, the now-standard, giant stone fireplace gave off waves of heat. A large, oval mahogany table set with three place settings, a pitcher of creamy white milk, a dish of butter, and a loaf of freshly baked bread occupied the middle of the room. The table legs had been carved to look like those of an animal, each ending with a large paw that rested on the flagstone floor. As in the Great Hall, tapestries graced the otherwise bare spaces on the walls.

Drawn to one of the tapestries, I walked over to get a better look. A massive scene depicting a medieval hunt had been painstakingly woven into the fabric. A party of riders dominated the picture, each mounted on a solid horse and wearing the tunics and long hosen of the time. They clutched swords and raised pitchforks high into the air, a zealous fire burning in their eyes. Hounds sniffed the ground and howled forever into the dark mists of the densely wooded forest.

At the edge of the hunt, just out of sight of the hunters, crouched a strange creature. I could not think of any other word to describe it, as the artist had slightly blurred the face and body, depicting only the eyes clearly. Head turned, the odd being looked out of the picture, directly at the viewer.

At *me*.

Enticed by its dark, haunting eyes, I moved closer. Like the strange statue out in the front yard, the creature's beseeching gaze pulled me in like a magnet. I couldn't stop looking at those eyes. Suddenly, fear—a hopeless, mindless terror—dried my mouth and churned my stomach.

The creature was alive.

CHAPTER SEVEN
MS. PENNY'S DISCOVERY

A floorboard creaked ominously, startling me out of my reverie. I swung around to see Ian standing in the doorway to the butler's pantry, eating a thick slice of bread. "What are you staring at?" he asked.

"I'm not staring at anything," I blurted, and then, assuring myself that the creature wasn't alive—only an image composed from old, worn thread, and certainly nothing threatening—I stepped away from the tapestry.

"You're kind of weird, aren't you?" Ian said around a mouthful.

"Shouldn't you be working somewhere?"

"I'm done with my chores." He took another bite of bread.

"Then go torment somebody else."

He frowned. "What's your problem?"

"*My* problem?" I couldn't believe what I was hearing. "I asked you to help me at the gate and you wouldn't. For all you knew, the Toad could have been kidnapping me."

Ian's thick, dark eyebrows drew together, nearly forming an upside-down V. "Yeah, sure. He kidnapped you and brought you *here*. Besides, I was told to . . . Oh, forget it," he growled. "Just sit down, will you? I hate it when people pace."

"I'm not pacing," I replied, suddenly realizing that I was. "I'm just getting a little exercise."

"Well, it's almost time to eat. Would you sit down for that? Besides," he said reluctantly, "Mrs. K. said I was to make you feel at home."

"Well, you've been doing a bang-up job so far." Despite a childish desire to remain standing just to annoy him, I pulled out a chair and sat down before my knees buckled beneath me. "I feel about as welcome here as an alligator in a swimming pool full of baby ducks."

He glared at me, opened his mouth to say something, then snapped it shut. The room settled into silence. He played with his fork, cracking an occasional knuckle as he stared into the fire while I summoned up the nerve to look at the tapestry again. The scene looked normal enough, yet what I'd imagined moments before had felt so real.

A door opened behind me and Mrs. Keeper bustled in. "Hello, Viddie. Hello, Ian." She actually looked happy to see us, both of us. It was a strange sensation. No one in my life had ever even *acted* happy to see me. "I just love foggy days, don't you? They make it easier to get important things done without being seen doing them." Her dark eyes sparkled.

Odd.

She sat down at the head of the table, her chin not rising much higher than the surface itself. "Are you two getting along?" She unfolded a white linen napkin and laid it across her lap. I followed her example. "Of course, you are," she continued. "You're the same age, after all. You must have something in common, like a favorite music band or a show on the telly, hm?"

Ian started to point out that we didn't even look the same age, but Mrs. Dooley shuffled through the doorway, balancing two large platters of food, one in each meaty hand. She plunked one down in front of Mrs. Keeper and the other next to Ian. She rubbed his head good-naturedly and gave me a warm smile before leaving again, humming a popular game-show tune.

"Oh, this looks lovely," Mrs. Keeper remarked, pulling her brown shawl more tightly around her shoulders. "I love to eat. How about you, Viddie?" She looked me over, her small, brown eyes narrowing thoughtfully. "Not nearly enough, I can see." She turned her attention to serving the food, heaping a large slice of Shepherd's pie onto my plate. I stared at the huge helping in awe; I was used to surviving on tomato soup, peanut butter and jelly sandwiches, and applesauce. Dad rarely made it home for suppertime, so it was left to me to make do. Unfortunately, I couldn't cook worth beans. Heck, I couldn't even cook beans.

When our plates were full, Mrs. Keeper held out her tiny hands, one to Ian and one to me. Ian took her hand, so I did the same, unsure what was expected of me. Mrs. Keeper spoke in a low, reverent voice as she gazed up at the ceiling. "Help us to care for those poor souls who need us the most—the ones who have nowhere to go, the ones who do not fit in, the ones who are unhappy, the ones who suffer. Guide them to our door that we may protect them. Blessed be." She gently pulled her hands away from ours and started to eat with enthusiasm. I lowered my own hand, grabbed a fork, and followed her lead. I was too hungry to think about the strange blessing I'd just heard, but stored it away for future ponderings.

Her hunger finally satisfied, my guardian turned her attention to me. "Viddie . . ." she said thoughtfully. "Viddie, Viddie, Viddie. That just doesn't sound right. Sounds more like a name for dog food." Ian snorted, but looked down at his plate when Mrs. Keeper glanced over at him. She patted my hand. "I wasn't being rude, dear. It just does. Viddie must be short for something."

"Actually it is," I replied, lowering the fork that hovered halfway between my plate and my waiting mouth. "My real name is Lavida, but my dad never calls me by that name. I think my Grandma Mors picked it out."

Mrs. Keeper's merry eyes sharpened. "Are you sure about that?"

Ian stopped shoveling food into his mouth and looked at her. He seemed as intrigued as I was by the sudden change in her demeanor.

I looked back and forth between the two. "Sure that it's short for Lavida, or sure that my grandma suggested the name?"

"Just the grandma part, dear," Mrs. Keeper replied, leaning forward.

"Pretty sure. At least that's what my dad told me once." It had been one of the rare times when he'd actually answered questions about my life, and he only did it because I said I needed to know about my past for a school project. I didn't, but after the Incident I was desperate to learn what it was about me that made me so different.

Mrs. Keeper leaned back, the look on her face far away. "So she thought that you might be . . . hmmm . . ." She tapped her rounded chin. "Even though . . . hmmm." She tapped her chin again, then looked at me, her eyes filled with excitement. "Did your father ever tell you what your name means, Lavida?" She was practically humming with anticipation.

I shook my head, starting to feel a little strange.

"All names have a meaning, dear. But *your* name has a particularly special one."

Ian burst out laughing. "Yeah, it means discount dog food."

I couldn't believe he just said that.

"Hush," Mrs. Keeper gently admonished him. "It's nothing to worry about, dear," she continued, turning back to me, "at least for the moment. Later, perhaps, it might become something of an issue. But for now . . ." She looked toward the tapestry on the wall, her forehead creased, her lips curled fretfully inward until they disappeared. "I have to get back to work," she said suddenly. "So much to do. You'll be all right, then? Do your homework on your own?"

"Sure thing," Ian replied.

I nodded absently, wondering what my name meant, then switching to considering all the ways I might ruin Ian's life as he sat there grinning at me.

Mrs. Keeper rubbed her dimpled, little hands together. "Such exciting news!" She scooted her chair back from the table and hastened away.

"What exciting news?" I asked after she had left the room.

"What's that, Viddie Chow?" The expression on Ian's face was mostly innocent, though his blue eyes gleamed wickedly.

The ticked-off look I aimed at him sent him into paroxysms of laughter. He continued laughing hysterically as he shoved away from the table and stumbled out of the room, holding his gut. I could hear him laughing all the way into the next room. I could only hope he laughed so hard he heaved all over himself.

Pushing back my chair, I decided to track down Ms. Penny. I entered the conservatory and called for her. After some pathetic begging, I resorted to bribing the ornery beast with promises of a special treat if she came down, which she finally did. But she wasn't happy about it.

I searched for the hidden door amongst all the vines, but only succeeded in getting tangled up in them. Giving up, I made my way to the Great Hall through a small door at the other end of the solarium. Passing through the Great Hall, I spotted an old-fashioned phone lurking in one of the dark corners and thought about using it to call my dad. Maybe, just maybe, he'd come and get me. Then I remembered that he had already flown out to attend his science conference. Disappointed, and a little bit scared, I headed toward the door leading up to my room. Cut off from anyone who might be able to help me, I was on my own in this strange place. This dismal thought haunted me like a spook as I climbed the long and dreaded spiral staircase to my tower room. I kept an eye out for strange apparitions, but nothing showed itself.

Once in our room, Ms. Penny ran around the place looking for the promised treat. Unsure which trunk held her stash, I had to go through each one. Of course it was the last one, closest to the wall and at the bottom of the stack. I pulled it away from the wall, opened it and gave Ms. Penny a box of raisins, her favorite. Once Ms. Penny had devoured her treat, she screeched and motioned toward the wall.

I shook my head. "Not tonight," I said. "You're not going back to the conservatory."

Ms. Penny had other ideas. She gave me a raspberry—I sincerely regret teaching her how to do that—and jumped up and down as she pointed at the wall again.

"It's time to get ready for bed. We're going to need our sleep for tomorrow when we run away. The last thing I need is a cranky raccoon giving me a hard time."

She reared up on her hind legs and had the nerve to give me another raspberry. Despite her defiance I was determined to win this fight. I did not want to be alone tonight.

"Come and use the bathroom," I told her. She joined me, and when we reached the bottom of the stairs, I saw a light coming from under the door. The doorknob started to turn.

"Who's there?" I called in a quivering voice. Silence answered me. "Hello?"

"It's just me," a voice answered.

I opened the door. "What do you want?" Ian held out a pile of towels. I peered at him suspiciously. "You could've just left them there outside the door."

"I will next time, Viddie and Bits." He dropped the stack on the floor and turned away, mumbling to himself about certain people's lack of gratitude.

I grabbed the pile of towels and shut the door behind me. Then I took out my key and locked the door; I didn't want any more unexpected visits. The main door locked, I opened the small door by the staircase and entered the bathroom. Ms. Penny followed me, used the toilet, then took off. As I brushed my teeth, I stared at the abundance of neatly stacked towels on the shelf. It was obvious I hadn't really needed the towels Ian had brought. So why did he bring more of them? Was he spying on me, or had he come just to harass me about my name?

Finished brushing, I shoved the worn green towels onto the shelf and gazed longingly at the tub. I decided I'd better get back to Ms. Penny before she decided to take matters into her own paws. I quickly readied myself for bed, then hurried back up the stairs. "I'm baaaack," I called out as I entered the room. Usually when I say this, Ms. Penny leaped into my arms. Not this time. "Oh, for Pete's sake, Ms. Penny! You can stop pouting, you big baby. You're not going down to the conservatory and that's that, so you might as well come out from wherever it is you're hiding."

Nothing.

"Ms. Penny?"

Nada.

I searched under the bed, up in the beams, and behind the curtains on the bed. The raccoon was nowhere to be seen. Scanning the room again, I noticed a slight gap in the wall behind my trunks. A bad feeling sprouted in the pit of my stomach as I hurried over to the spot, shoved the trunk aside, and pulled on the protruding bit of wood. A section of the paneling moved—it was another door! My room had *two* secret doors. But why hadn't Mrs. Keeper told me about this one?

So where did it lead to? A torture chamber? An oubliette? Certain doom? A distant, and frightful, screeching told me I might be right on all three counts. Hands shaking, I stepped through the doorway and groped about for a light switch. Unable to find anything, I chewed on a last bit of fingernail. It looked like I was going to have to go after Ms. Penny in the dark—it was the only right thing to do, what any good pet owner would do—but I couldn't help feeling like something bad was going to happen if I went down those stairs. Bad, as in Stephen King bad. I really shouldn't go by myself, not after all the paranoid feelings I'd gotten about this place, not with this tingling zipping up and down my spine. But I had no choice. My pet needed me.

Trembling from head to toe, I inched forward until my foot dropped over the edge of the first step. As carefully as I tried to make my way down the stairs, my foot slipped anyway, and before I could catch myself I fell, landing hard on my back. But instead of tumbling down a flight of stairs, I started sliding. Down I went . . . through absolute darkness. The slide curved to the left, then to the right, and then back again. I flew downward in a blinding rush of speed until, without warning, I shot off the slide and sailed through the air, screaming myself breathless. Then with a thump, I hit the rough floor and bounced forward like a basketball.

When the throbbing in my backside had subsided, I looked around to see where I was, but couldn't make out a thing in the darkness. "Ms. Penny?" I whispered. Something furry leaped onto my head and I squealed like a cheerleader before realizing what it was. "Don't ever do that again, you naughty beast!" I scolded, thrilled to see her. She hugged my head and hooted softly.

As we sat there in the dark I felt a chill seeping into my legs. Running my hand over the cool stone floor, I wondered how to get out of here before we both succumbed to hypothermia. Maybe we could climb back up the slide. I was about to stand up and look for it when I heard a noise.

Footsteps, quick and light.

Ms. Penny chattered nervously.

"Shhh!" I clapped a hand over her tiny mouth. "I think I hear someone coming." Ms. Penny responded by grasping me tighter, nearly pulling my hair out with her death grip. I listened more closely, then felt my stomach turn inside out. "Oh, Ms. Penny, I don't think it's coming anymore. Whatever it is . . .

. . . it's already here."

CHAPTER EIGHT
UNINVITED GUESTS

Suddenly it was quiet. Too quiet. Silence surrounded us, gripping us like a giant fist. I was desperate to run, but my frozen nerve-endings kept me rooted to the floor. I *knew* something was with us.

"Do you remember what we are supposed to do, Darian?" a voice whispered loudly in the darkness. "I always forget."

I turned swiftly toward the strangely accented voice, nearly dislodging Ms. Penny from her perch on my head, and jumped to my feet. The tone was soft and melodic, like a flute. The speaker didn't sound scary, but I wasn't about to trust a disembodied voice in the dark.

Another voice hissed back, "You cannot forget what you never heard in the first place, Loria. If you would only pay attention during training, instead of talking to your friends all the time—"

"I know, I know!" the first whisperer responded at full volume, forgetting to be quiet. It was a girl's voice. "But those meetings are *so* boring, Darian. I try hard, but I simply cannot concentrate. I never remember anyway. *You* are the one who remembers everything, you know."

"That is true." The second whisperer sounded matter of fact.

"So what are we to do?"

"It is obvious. In a situation like this, where unauthorized infiltration has occurred, we are to determine if the invading creature, or creatures as in this case, constitutes an immediate threat."

"I cannot imagine either one is a threat," the female laughed. "The bigger creature is a Human, I believe."

"She does appear to be Human," the other agreed, speaking now in a masculine voice, no longer taking care to whisper.

What else would I be? I wondered.

"I hope she is! She is so very little, though. She could not harm us if she wanted to. And the furry one—I have never seen a creature like that. It is so cute! Perhaps we could keep it? It would make a nice hat. I would be the envy of all my friends wearing such a daring accessory."

Finally finding my voice, I gasped, "A hat! You'd use Ms. Penny's fur for a hat?"

"So you *can* speak!" the girl trilled. "Good! I have lots of questions I want to ask you. Let us turn on the light, Darian. I want to better see the Human. She looks just like the drawings." She giggled. "I guess I do pay attention to some things."

"You can't use my raccoon as a hat," I cried. "That's sick!" Besides, if anyone were going to wear Ms. Penny as a hat, it would be her long-suffering owner.

"But you are using her for a hat."

Belatedly I remembered Ms. Penny's position and wondered how the girl could see us in this dark. "I'm not wearing her as a hat. She's sitting on my head because she's scared."

"Scared?"—she laughed lightly—"of what? We are harmless. Darian, turn on the light."

"That is not proper protocol, Loria," the other replied stiffly. "We would not want her to see us as we are."

As we are? What was wrong with them?

"We shall blend, of course," she replied. "I remember that part of class, too. *Appear to others as they are*," she quoted. "I want to look like the furry one." She clapped her hands together excitedly.

"Shhh, Loria!" His tone of voice was irked. "You are giving away too much."

"Sorry, Darian. I forget myself." The girl laughed once more. The sound, like wind chimes, echoed in the darkness. "We shall both take our usual Human forms." She said this confidently, as though she were quite sure Darian would agree with her.

"I suppose we could do that." A tapping sound filled the room. "Awake," he commanded, and a dim glow slowly pushed away the black ink. The light grew brighter, and the outline of an old-fashioned kerosene lamp emerged from the darkness. Inside the glass cylinder a handful of abnormally large fireflies flitted about.

My eyes moved from the lantern to the two strangers. They stood about five feet away from me, in the middle of a small, empty room. Both were tall, dark-haired and paleskinned, and looked very much like one another. The taller one peered searchingly at me from around the lamp he held. He wore a long-sleeved, dark-brown jacket, belted at the waist, over close-fitting tan pants. Pointy leather boots, polished to a high sheen, completed the strange outfit, and his hair was curly, but neatly cut. Everything about him looked tidy and put together. This one must be Darian.

The other one, Loria, was shorter. Her hair, too, hung in curls, but she wore it longer and wilder. A soft, velvety green hat, perched rakishly on her head, attempted to hold her riotous curls in place. Her dress came to her knees and resembled a patchwork crazy quilt. Green leather boots that matched her cap reached up to meet the flowing skirt.

The strangers were dressed a bit oddly, but other than that, they looked normal, which meant they looked as human as I did. I paused. No, that wasn't right. What I normally would have dismissed as floaters in my eyes or an illusion caused by the light turned into something else when I focused hard on the girl. Her face and body shimmered, and her skin rippled and wavered like skipping stones disrupting the smooth surface of a pond. Her ears grew and turned pointy, then shrank and disappeared just as quickly. Her nose stretched, then flattened, and her eyes glowed and sparkled. These tiny transformations occurred all in a flash. When I blinked or lost my concentration, the crazy shifting about stopped. I could only see the effect if I focused hard, and even then, with Darian, it was hardly noticeable. I must have hit my head on the floor when I landed and given myself a concussion.

"What is she staring at, Darian?" Loria's long, curly hair swung in an arc as she peered behind her. She peeked behind Darian, then shrugged, seeing nothing.

Darian looked at me shrewdly. "I do not know." He took a step closer to me. "Human, what is it that you see?"

I stepped back. I wasn't sure what he was, or what he was capable of doing. The strange business with the changing features, and the fact that he kept calling me Human, made me think my two new acquaintances didn't think of themselves as such.

When several seconds had passed in silence, Loria pursed her heart-shaped lips. "She will not say, Darian. I wish we could read minds as well as the Amorals do."

"Shhh," Darian hissed, more urgently this time. "Do not speak of them. They might hear you and then want to come see for themselves what is going on."

"That would be so exciting!" Loria breathed, her large, dark eyes shining. "A real challenge!"

"That would be a disaster," Darian retorted. "We do not want the Amorals around making trouble when we are guiding the, um, others. You know how they are."

I decided to interrupt. I was cold and I'd had enough of this weird dream, or joke, or whatever it was. "I don't know who you guys are, but that's okay. I don't want to know. Just show me the way out of here and you'll never see me or my raccoon again. Deal?"

"We cannot simply let you go," Darian replied coolly, gazing down at me disdainfully. "We have rules. The Magistrate needs to know about your infiltration and will decide what to do with you."

That didn't sound good.

"Listen, I don't want to cause any trouble," I said. "Help me get back to my room, and I will never *infiltrate* you again."

The two looked at each other. Loria whispered something in Darian's ear. He shook his head and whispered something back. The stubborn expression on both their faces told me they were in disagreement.

"*Please* let me go," I tried again.

Loria glanced at Darian. "She is saying the magic word, Darian. You know I cannot say no when someone says please."

Darian looked at her fondly. "Everyone knows that,

Loria, which is why you get stuck watching the Piggerel brats all the time."

Loria smiled and winked at me, like we were co-conspirators. "She is not a threat to us, Darian. Look at her. She will tell no one about us being here, right, Human?"

"Of course, I wouldn't tell anyone about you," I promptly agreed. "They wouldn't believe me anyway."

"Perhaps she is one of the Helpers," Darian mused, "a new one I have not yet met." He regarded me closely. "And I would not want to cause trouble with them."

Loria grinned, knowing she'd won. "We will let you go, Human," she said, turning to me.

"First, tell us your name," Darian added. "I will need it for my report."

I hesitated before figuring there was no harm in telling them. "My name is Viddie . . . Well, actually," I went on, any lingering desire to pacify my dad gone, "you can call me Lavida. Lavida Mors." When they didn't respond, only stared wide-eyed at me, I laughed nervously. "I know it's a weird name, but it's not *that* bad. Is it?"

Loria grabbed her companion's arm. "Did you hear, Darian? She said her name was—"

"I heard, Loria," Darian said calmly, patting her hand, and laughed as though some utterly ridiculous idea had just occurred to him. "But she is much too small, and she is a *Human*." He spoke the word snidely, as though to imply that humans were lower than maggots. "A Human could never be the *One*."

Loria stared at me, shaking her head in wonder. Then she shrugged. "You are probably right. She is obviously not one of us." She sighed, then brightened. "I nearly forgot. Why were you staring at us?"

I pushed back an errant strand of hair that tickled my cheek every time Ms. Penny squirmed. Did I want to tell them what I'd seen? The effects could simply have been a result of overtired eyes, or my imagination. Then again, Loria wasn't about to give this up. The sooner I satisfied her curiosity, the sooner I could go.

"I'll tell you what I saw, but then I have to get back to my room."

Darian frowned, but both he and Loria nodded their agreement.

"When I was watching you, I saw something strange happening, especially with Loria. One moment you had long, pointy ears,"—I demonstrated—"and the next moment they were gone. Then you were dark and small, then tall and fair. Your parts kept shifting about like puzzle pieces. It was only my imagination, of course, and I am awfully tired . . ." My voice trailed away when I saw the look on their faces.

"She sees, Darian!" Loria shouted, practically jumping up and down. "She can see what we are! How is that possible? She should not be able to see our blends."

"I do not like this. Not only is she somewhere she is not supposed to be, she has exhibited behavior not befitting her kind. It is most suspicious." Darian glared at me distrustfully. "It is our duty to bring her in, Loria."

"But you said you'd let me go!" I cried, my cheeks suddenly hot.

"We are sorry," Darian replied, sounding not at all sorry as he reached out to take my arm. Before he could grab hold of me, I pried Ms. Penny off my head and tossed her toward the slide. She didn't hesitate to bound up the slide quicker than a rabbit and, giving Darian a hard shove, I dashed after her.

The sound of footsteps chased after me as I struggled up the steep slide. My foot caught the raised edge of the slide and my palms registered the slide's smooth wood before I pushed myself back up again. Just as I was about to start running again, a hand grabbed my shoulder. I gasped in fright and tore away from the vise-like grip. My breath roared in my ears as I scrambled up the slippery surface as fast as I could go. I saw a light flickering up ahead and knew I was near my room. My feet found the short set of stairs and I frantically stumbled up them. I didn't think I was going to make it; Darian was too close behind. But then, with a burst of energy spurred by panic, I crashed against the door and, tumbling through it, kicked it shut and held it with both feet.

I stopped and listened.

Other than the sounds of my own labored breathing, I heard nothing. If Darian had given up chasing me, I wasted no time finding out. I leaped to my feet and shoved all my trunks in front of the door.

Ms. Penny huddled nervously beneath the bed covers, and I ran and jumped under them with her, pulling her close. We were safe.

Funny, though, I didn't feel that way.

CHAPTER NINE

THE INCIDENT

I awoke with a start and sat up, my heart pounding fiercely. My eyes darted around the room, searching for the source of the sound that had awakened me. I soon found the culprit. Ms. Penny was playing her favorite game: attack the weird-looking creature in the mirror. She has yet to figure out that the creature is *her*.

I stood up and stretched, then joined Ms. Penny in front of the spotted glass. I studied my reflection. I hadn't slept well, and it showed in the dark circles under my eyes. I looked like Wednesday Addams . . . on a good day.

Even with all those trunks shoved in front of the secret door, I hadn't fallen asleep right away. For at least an hour I'd lain in bed and wondered whether or not to tell Mrs. Keeper what had happened. In the end, I decided not to say anything to her; not only was I not sure I could trust her, but also because I'd finally figured out what was going on. I hadn't been dreaming, and I hadn't met aliens from another planet. That loathsome Ian had played his idea of a joke on me. He must have invited some friends over to play Loria and Darian, their strange, shape-shifting behavior brought about using some kind of holographic projection technique. It was an elaborate prank to play on someone he'd only just met and had to have taken some time to plan out. He must have decided to trick me before we'd even met, suggesting that he didn't like the idea of me coming here. But why? What was he afraid of? Certainly not me. He couldn't possibly have known what I was hiding.

Leaving Ms. Penny to her strange little game, I crept over to the wall. After moving the trunks out of the way, I pressed on the place where I thought the secret door had been. The wall didn't budge an inch. I pushed on other parts of the wood paneling, but nothing gave way. Ian had probably locked the door from the other side after I'd fallen asleep. He had to have known it would be hard for me to stay in a strange place for the first time, that I'd be imagining all sorts of weird things going on in a house like this, and he had taken advantage of that fear.

That jerk!

Seething, I shoved the trunks back against the wall, ensuring no one could go in or out. I chewed furiously on a nail. I must avenge myself. And soon.

After digging out a fresh shirt and sticking the stained one in the tub to soak, I pocketed a stash of fruity chews in my cardigan pocket in case Ms. Penny acted up and went downstairs. Stepping into the conservatory, I tied several vines into a knot, then took a step backward. The knot was reasonably easy to spot, so I felt satisfied that I could find the door again. To my relief it was locked on the outside, but opened easily when I tried my key. Good. If Ian knew about this door, he wouldn't be able to use it unless he had the right key. Hopefully he didn't.

Mrs. Dooley was washing a large pot in the sink when I entered the kitchen. "Did you have a good night, Lavida?" she asked without turning around. I jumped, startling Ms. Penny, who squeaked at me in annoyance. That woman should have her own psychic hot line.

"It was all right," I told her as I calmed Ms. Penny with a pat and a fruit chew.

"Just all right?" she questioned over her shoulder as she wiped her large hands on a worn, white dishtowel. "You seem a bit peaky to me."

I wondered how she could tell what I "seemed" without turning around to look at me. "I did have a little trouble sleeping," I admitted, wondering what Mrs. Dooley would think if I told her what my night had really been like. Would she be mad at Ian for scaring me, or would she take his side, saying boys will be boys? Or maybe she had already heard all about it, and that's why she knew I looked peaky. My stomach soured at the thought.

The heavyset woman set the pot upside down to dry, then turned around. "Lord, have mercy!" she squawked like a chicken and ran straight at me, swinging the dishtowel like a weapon. "I'll save you, dearie!"

Ms. Penny yelped and clung to my head as I darted around the table. "Mrs. Dooley!" I shouted over the bellowing and screeching. "It's my raccoon! She won't hurt you!" Well, she might bite, but now was definitely not the time to impart that tidbit.

Mrs. Dooley stopped swinging the towel and patted her heaving chest. "Oh, my! I really do need to get myself some spectacles. I thought you had a feral cat on your shoulder."

I pretended to cover Ms. Penny's ears. "Don't let her hear you say that," I laughed. "She's actually pretty nice.

Would you like to hold her?"

Mrs. Dooley chuckled and pushed several curly strands of dark red hair off her sweaty forehead. "Maybe later, dear, when my heart's had a chance to settle down."

"Ms. Penny's hard to resist once you get to know her," I said proudly.

Mrs. Dooley smiled weakly. "You're probably right." She shuffled over to the oven and checked on something baking inside. A heavenly aroma drifted toward me. Satisfied with what she saw, she shut the door and straightened up with a groan, rubbing her hip. "Now, run along and get yourself some breakfast. It's in the dining room. Self-service. Take as much as you want. You could gain a stone and still be thin as a pole. I could stand to lose a couple myself, though it's probably best that I don't." She pointed to her apron. Today it read *Never trust a skinny cook*.

I grinned and headed for the dining room. I liked Mrs. Dooley. She had been so protective of me—both after school yesterday and then again today, trying to save me from Ms. Penny—I couldn't envision her conspiring with Ian. I liked Mrs. Keeper, too (odd as she was), which was troublesome. I should know better than to let my guard down around other people, to get involved with them, to care about them.

No one else was in the dining room when I entered with Ms. Penny in tow, which was disappointing; I'd been hoping Ian would be there. I wanted to be absolutely sure he'd set me up before I put my plan for revenge into action. Compared to his scheme, mine was almost primitive. A bagful of snakes, a jar of spiders, a bucket of slime and his bed were all I needed.

Following my nose, I headed straight to the walnut-colored sideboard covered with silver serving dishes. Lifting lids, I discovered a surprising variety of foods, from bacon and sausages to pancakes and homefries. It was a lot of food for so few people. Who ate the rest of it? I wondered. Surely not Mrs. Dooley . . . I giggled as I helped myself to a stack of blueberry pancakes, a generous dose of maple syrup and a glass of orange juice. For Ms. Penny, I put together a plate of melons, bananas and kippers. When we were done eating, I carried our dirty dishes into the kitchen, noting as we passed through the butler's pantry, that several of the plates from the lower shelves had disappeared.

"Great breakfast," I complimented the cook as I entered the kitchen. Mrs. Dooley was tidying up the trestle table.

"It was my pleasure," she replied gruffly as she cautiously sniffed at one of the jars she'd just opened. "Just put the dishes by the others," she said over her shoulder. "I'll do them in a bit."

"Do you want some help?" There were an awful lot of dirty dishes piled on the counter by the sink, leading me to believe I'd found the missing dinnerware. But who'd used them?

Mrs. Dooley shook her head. "Thanks, luv, but you've got school today. Grab your lunch," she reminded me. "I'll see you when you get home, and you can tell me all about your day."

I set my dishes next to the others, grabbed my lunchbox, and after saying goodbye headed into the conservatory. Ms. Penny immediately ditched me for the hammock, where a large tomcat lay sleeping. The cat hissed in annoyance, then shifted over. Ms. Penny had found herself a friend, whether he knew it or not.

The ride to school passed way too quickly. I had wanted to subtly grill Ian about his little joke, but every time I tried, Mrs. Keeper asked me a question about my classes. As soon as I finished answering, she came out with a new one. Why she cared about how many people sat in my row in French class, I haven't the foggiest.

Outside Gates Hall, I crawled out of the car and then, spotting Fiona and her friends passing by, quickly slunk back inside mumbling about a lost pencil. Giving the girls a good thirty-second lead, I slipped back out with a quick goodbye to Ian and Mrs. Keeper, who was still trying to find my pencil. Eyes constantly scanning for Fiona and her friends, I headed for Simmons Hall to drop off the books I needed for my afternoon classes. The moment I entered the brick building I sensed trouble.

Rounding the corner, I found it.

Taking in the scene before me, I was immediately—unwillingly—pulled back to that day three years ago when everything in my life had changed. I'd had a bad feeling that day too, which had started the moment I woke up and built like a hurricane with every passing hour. Like a wild animal, I often had a way of knowing when something bad was about to happen, a sort of tingling that ran up and down my spine, even when everything appeared normal. Of course, I also felt the same thing when I got excited, and sometimes, to my frustration, I confused the two. Worse, if I was distracted at the time, which happened a lot, I missed the signal altogether. But not this time. I felt danger coming, but ignored it, caught up as I was in my flashback. It had been a horrible day. I'll never forget it.

*T*rouble was brewing—I just knew it. And when I came around the corner to find Tammy "Two-Fist" Cortez, the most popular and powerful girl in the school, taunting a seventh grader, my intuition was confirmed. George Emerson, with his tape-repaired glasses, one lens patched for his lazy eye, overstuffed backpack and too-short, red polyester pants, was her victim. He was also—heartbreakingly so—the misfit of all misfits.

"Watch where you're going, turd-for-brains." Two-Fist shoved a cowering George into the gray lockers. His head smashed into the metal doors and he slumped to the ground, his one eye wide with fright.

"Leave him alone!" I heard myself shouting, the words leaping out of my mouth as though someone else had spoken them for me.

She swung her head around. "Excuse me? Are you talking to me?" Her rough, snide voice made me feel sick to my stomach, but I hid my alarm as best I could. I'd read somewhere that predators could smell fear.

"Maybe you should watch where you're going," I said. "You're the one who takes up most of the hallway." The crowd oohed in surprise and moved in closer, eager to see bloodshed.

"You think you're funny?" Two-Fist demanded.

I took a step away from her. Out of the corner of my eye, I saw George attempting to climb to his feet. "I think the truth hurts, Tammy Two-Ton," I said, hoping to distract her long enough for George to get away.

She came at me like a bull. A sharp pain slashed through my brain, and I fell to the ground with a thud, feeling my eye instantly swell shut. I hadn't even seen the fist coming; and Tammy's fists were big—the size of hams.

"Let's try this again," Two-Fist growled. "Do you think you're funny?"

I shook my head, covering my throbbing eye. "I think you're funny," I said hoarsely. "Funny-looking, that is."

Two-Fist grabbed my baggy shirt and yanked me to my feet. She turned to the crowd. "I think someone here needs to be taught a lesson by the almighty fist." She grinned evilly. The crowd shouted their agreement. "Fight, fight, fight!"

I heard a bell ding twice for round two.

Before Two-Fist could crush me like a mouse, I relaxed my whole body. Not expecting the move, she loosened her grip and I dropped to the ground. And before she could grab me again, I quickly rolled away. Jumping to my feet, an image formed in my head like a movie—Two-Fist's pants dropping to the ground like a magician's sheet. I stared at her, willing those pants to fall down. Just this once. A simple pantsing.

Then the crowd began to laugh and point at Two-Fist. She looked down to see her pants around her ankles. She frantically pulled them back up, her cheeks red with embarrassment.

"Why you dirty . . . !" She lunged at me, and her pants dropped again. She struggled to pull them up, but they immediately slid back down. Now everyone could see that Two-Fist was wearing Little Dolly underwear.

"You could use a belt," I told her. Then I turned and walked away, hoping no one would notice my shaking hands and rapid breathing. Once I rounded the corner, I ran as fast as I could to my next class.

The next day, the story of how I'd made Two-Fist's pants fall down was all over school. The people who'd witnessed it all started talking, wondering how her pants had fallen down without anyone touching them. They'd asked each other with macabre curiosity what, exactly, I had done and how I'd done it. Later that day, one of my teachers had overheard a very garbled version of the story. Someone who hadn't even seen what had happened was telling her friend that Viddie Mors was a witch and that she was preparing to ritually sacrifice Two-Fist in the girl's bathroom. As appealing as that sounded, it wasn't anywhere close to the truth. Anyway, it hadn't taken much to turn a snowball into an avalanche.

Mrs. Cooper had tracked me down and had a talk with me. When I explained what had happened, she seemed to accept my version of the event. What I didn't know at the time was that she'd decided to call my dad to discuss the Incident. That was the phone call the Toad had intercepted. No doubt he'd promised to deal with the problem.

After that, the kids at school kept their distance from me. They were afraid. Even my two best friends. After a couple months of harassment for being associated with the witch they began to avoid me. I let them go.

It was a lonely three years, but I had gotten used to being on my own. At least being alone was safe. Still, there were a lot of times that I had wished my life was back to the way it had been before. I didn't want to be different from everybody else, and I certainly didn't want to scare people away. If only I could go back to that day three years ago, I'd make sure I paid attention to my instincts that had warned me to avoid that hallway, or at least not do what I had done to Two-Fist's pants.

Today the trouble was Fiona, my blonde nemesis. As the memories of the Incident receded from my mind, I took a deep, bracing breath, readying myself to face her. Standing in the middle of the hallway, she and her groupies sur-rounded a heavyset, redheaded girl. The thick lenses of her glasses, which sat at the end of her nose, barely held in place by its round, pinched tip, magnified her blue eyes as she glared at Fiona in defiance. She clutched a large, moss-colored handbag under her arm. She was no George Emerson, but she was in trouble just the same.

Run, I told myself. Just forget you saw anything.

But I couldn't move.

"Give me the bag, Ellie, or I'll tell your dad I saw you smoking in the bathroom."

"I'm not giving you anything, you ditzy, fake-blonde, reality-star-wannabe freak." The metallic braces on her teeth gave the girl a slight lisp.

Fiona scowled. "You'd better give it to me. Headmaster Maguire would not be happy with his little girl getting expelled, would he?"

The heavy girl's lower lip trembled a little. "He won't believe you."

"He believed me last time . . . when I told him you hit me."

"That's because I *did* hit you. And you cried, if I remember correctly. Like a sniveling pukey baby."

Fiona's eyes narrowed. "Well, you'd have cried, too, if a giant pig had hit you." Her groupies tittered. She took a threatening step closer, and they followed her. "Now give me the bag, or I'm going to have to take it the hard way, and then tell your dad you were smoking."

The redhead tightened her grip. She was still determined, but there was no way she could fight all of them herself. She was going to get hurt, maybe badly. "I won't do it!" she shouted.

That was my cue. I couldn't help myself, couldn't stop myself if I'd wanted to. I had to step in. I took a deep breath, put my head down, and ran right at Fiona. The force of my blow knocked her forward into the groupies, and Ellie jumped out of the way. Fiona spun around to face me as I crouched low at her feet. My bag had been jarred loose in the leap, scattering my school supplies all over the place.

"You again!" she growled. "You stupid, clumsy fool. I swear I am surrounded by idiots! What's wrong with you people?"

I let her yell at me as I worked to gather my things at her feet. Finally, I had finished the task of collecting all my stuff back into my bag. I climbed to my feet, searching out the girl named Ellie. She was still there, staring at me like *I* was the idiot. "Sorry about that. I tripped."

The first bell of the day rang—the ten-minute bell.

"You're gonna be sorry," Fiona sneered. "And if I didn't already have two tardies, I'd grind your face into the floor right now." I took three steps back. I didn't want to be anywhere near her when the next thing happened. "Let's go, girls," she ordered, took one step forward, and fell flat on her face. "What the . . . !" she howled as she fought to sit up.

"What's wrong with your shoes, Fiona?" one of the toadies asked.

"The laces got tangled up, rocks-for-brains!" She hastily retied her shoes, stood up, and with a glare at me stalked off.

"Nice work," Ellie congratulated me when they were gone. "Although, how she couldn't tell that you were tying her shoelaces together baffles the mind."

I bit my lip. "Why didn't you run? I was trying to distract her for you."

Her blue eyes narrowed. "I can fight my own battles, thank you very much." She looked as though she could. She stood a good five inches taller than I and weighed at least seventy pounds more.

"But she was going to lie to your dad."

The girl's rounded shoulders dropped. Her ill-fitting uniform protested the movement, settling back into all the wrong places. "She's totally got me on that one. Last time I got in trouble my dad was really disappointed in me. He took away my credit card for a whole month, which was bad, and kept giving me these you've-really-let-me-down looks, which was worse. All because she's a big, fat liar."

The warning bell rang and I turned to go to my first class. Ellie followed after me. "You know you royally screwed up, going after Fiona like that. She's going to turn your life into a living nightmare. Why didn't you just stay out of it?"

I was asking myself the same thing. "I couldn't help it," I told her as we hurried along. "I just had to do something. I didn't want to. I've already run into Fiona once, and I know what she's like."

"So you helped me against your better judgment." Instead of looking mad, she looked amused.

"The last time I . . . did something like this, I lost all my friends." I wasn't sure why I was telling her this.

"You're new here, aren't you?" she asked.

I nodded cautiously.

"Thought so. I haven't seen you before. I take it you got on someone's bad side at your old school, and after that, no one wanted anything to do with you."

"Something like that," I muttered.

"And you didn't learn from that?"

I shrugged. "I never do."

She laughed. "So how old are you? I'm fifteen and a half," she went on before I could answer. "I've got Computer Science now. What do you have?"

I checked my schedule. "Civics." When we compared notes, we discovered that we were signed up for all the same afternoon classes. Funny how I hadn't noticed her on the first day—probably because, after my run-in with Fiona, I'd kept my head down.

"So what's your name?"

"Lavida Mors," I said, but it sounded more like a question.

"Wow. Cool name." Ellie grinned and I relaxed a little. "I'm Ellie Maguire. Wanna do something after school?"

"Do something?" I stared at her. "You mean, like, together?"

"No. I thought you'd do something by yourself and I'd do something by myself, and then we'd talk about it tomorrow."

"It's just that I'm not used to doing things with other people."

"Me either. I think it's because the other girls here are so intimidated by my stunning good looks." She fluffed her hair and pursed her lips like a runway model, then ruined the effect by picking at something stuck in her braces.

"I thought it was because you're so smart."

"That too."

I laughed, feeling suddenly lighthearted. "So what do you want to do?" I asked, interested in her proposal despite myself.

"You could come over to my house."

I frowned. "I don't have any way to get there."

She thought for a moment. "I have a scooter, I'll come to your house. Where do you live?"

"It's a place called Portal Manor."

She gaped at me. "You're joking, right?"

My heart thudded in my chest. "What do you mean?"

"Don't you know? That place is haunted!"

"Why do you say that?" The pounding picked up pace.

"There are all sorts of weird stories around town about Portal Manor."

I thought it might be worth quite a bit to hear what those stories were. "Why don't you meet me outside the gate at four, then."

"Awesome. Can I bring my brother?"

"Sure," I replied as we approached the building where I had Civics.

"Great. See you later." She stopped and turned back. "Say, Lavida?"

"Yes?"

"Thanks for helping me out."

My eyes blurred with emotion as I stared at her in wonder. "Sure, Ellie. No problem."

She grinned and headed down the sidewalk. As she walked away, I realized that she was the first person who had ever thanked me for helping. One simple gesture on her part and I felt stunned and overjoyed and then, inevitably, afraid.

Once Ellie heard the real reason I'd lost my other friends, once she knew what I could really do, she wouldn't want to stay my friend. But until that happened, I would do anything for her.

It was a decision that would come back to haunt me.

CHAPTER TEN
ESCAPE TO KILLIECRANKIE VOOD

Mrs. Keeper was late.

Standing outside Gates Hall, I glanced anxiously behind me to see Fiona and her groupies walking in my direction. I began to sweat as the laughing girls grew closer to where I stood.

Fiona was going to kill me.

Hearing a loud engine, I looked up and spotted Mrs. Keeper's odd, black car barreling toward me. The car pulled up alongside the curb, and I hastily took a few steps back as one of the front tires popped up onto the sidewalk, then thumped back down as the car slowed to a stop. My savior had arrived. The front passenger-side door swung open. I jumped inside and buckled my seatbelt, thrilled to have escaped Fiona's wrath—this time.

Mrs. Keeper stomped on the gas, pulling away from the

curb. Tires screeching in protest, we rounded a curve in the drive far faster than we should have and, without looking, she pulled out onto the main road. I cringed, expecting to be hit any moment, but nothing happened. Once we were on the straightaway, I asked, "Where's Ian?"

"The little devil had to stay after school," she informed me. "Apparently there was some sort of ruckus between him and another boy." She shook her head anxiously. "Things went better for you today, I hope?"

"A little. I met someone. Her name is Ellie. You don't mind if I have her and her brother over after school, do you? I mean, I can tell them they can't come." Although, when I thought about it, I realized I didn't know how to reach them. Ellie and I were only able to chat for a few minutes between classes and we spent that time complaining about our history assignment. No phone numbers were exchanged. Besides, I didn't even know mine.

"Of course, you can have them over. That sounds wonderful. And I'm glad you decided to stick around a little while longer." With a wink, she turned her eyes back to the road and hummed along to a song on the oldies station.

Looking out the window at the passing trees, I remembered that I'd meant to run away this afternoon. What was wrong with me? It was almost as though something was trying to keep me here. I couldn't stay, though. I just couldn't. Too many weird things had already happened to me. And I was beginning to let my guard down.

I would go as soon as the first opportunity presented itself. But first, I had to make sure Ellie was okay with Fiona. I couldn't just abandon her now. Despite her protestations, she needed my help. The trick was to figure out a way to keep Fiona from bothering Ellie after I was gone, without being caught at it. In the meantime, I could figure out why my dad didn't want to return to Portal

Manor. Maybe, if I fixed what was bothering him, he would welcome me back home with open arms. He might even come get me himself!

The more I thought about my plan, the more sense it made to start by exploring the house. Portal Manor was the one connection between many mysteries I wouldn't mind solving—my grandmother's disappearance, my mother's death, and my dad's refusal to return.

The remainder of the ride home, I daydreamed about the joyful reunion between my dad and me after I solved the mystery that had haunted him his entire life. He would be crying—or at least have tears in his eyes—as he told me how amazing I was. I'd just smile and look modestly at the floor.

When we arrived at the manor, Mrs. Keeper let me out by the door to the conservatory before going to park the car. Once inside, I eagerly called to Ms. Penny, dropping my loaded backpack on the ground. But there was no response.

Odd.

Typically, if she didn't come running immediately, she would at least give a whinny to let me know she was still alive. I called again, growing louder and more hysterical with each shout. Ms. Penny hadn't gotten away again, had she? Because if she had . . .

Oh, bugger!

I raced toward the kitchen to ask Mrs. Dooley if she'd seen Ms. Penny anywhere. Rushing through the small door, I froze at the horrifying sight before me . . . Mrs. Dooley was dancing along to the beat of a catchy song, her wide hips swinging back and forth to the rhythm.

"Ooh, baby, baby! Just say yes, don't say maybe!"

But that wasn't the horrifying part. It was seeing Ms. Penny sitting on Mrs. Dooley's shoulder, clinging tightly to her apron as the unsuspecting cook gyrated and bobbed her head to the beat. How she'd managed to get up there without the cook knowing was beyond me. But she was a tricky little beast; I wasn't surprised she'd pulled it off. Spotting the mischievous expression on her face, I knew I had to do something quick, because if Mrs. Dooley realized Ms. Penny was sitting on her shoulder, the raccoon would end up flattened like a mosquito when Mrs. Dooley, fainting from fright, fell on top of her. Though, it would serve the little scamp right for doing something so stupid.

"Oh, Mrs. Dooley," I called, trying to keep my voice light.

"Yes, Miss Laviiiiiiidaaaa," she replied in a singsong voice, swinging around to give me a big smile. Ms. Penny swung with her, and when she saw me, she clung even more tightly to the strings on Mrs. Dooley's latest apron, a red one that read *I could tell you the recipe, but then I'd have to kill you.*

"Things went better today at school?" Mrs. Dooley asked, snapping her fingers to the beat.

"Um, kinda." I couldn't stop staring at Ms. Penny, who was staring back at me and who was going to be in a lot of trouble . . . if she survived. "Um . . . Mrs. Dooley? Uh, my raccoon . . ."

Mrs. Dooley shook her head as she glanced at Ms. Penny, who chattered loudly. "Does this little imp always get her way? She looked so sad and lonely when I checked on her that I took pity on the little mite and brought her in here. Little did I know it'd be like looking after a two-year-old again."

"Oh." I breathed a sigh of relief. "I'm sorry she was so much trouble for you. Just leave her in the conservatory tomorrow. She'll be all right on her own."

Mrs. Dooley raised her eyebrows. "I'll do no such thing, lass. As long as I'm here, she's welcome." She glanced fondly at Ms. Penny. "Now go to your mum, little pet. Tomorrow you can help me make biscuits."

Ms. Penny dashed off Mrs. Dooley's shoulder and scampered over to me. She seemed quite happy to see her mum despite her momentary desertion. She gave me a big head hug then looked around for her treat. I pulled the packet of fruity chews out of my pocket and gave it to her, then strolled over to Mrs. Dooley's side as Ms. Penny nibbled away.

"What're you making?" I peered curiously at a large pie Mrs. Dooley had filled with what resembled some unfortunate creature's innards and wrinkled my nose in disgust.

"Oh, nothing, dear," Mrs. Dooley said brusquely. "Merely trying something new. Not sure it's going to work out, though. There are some fresh-baked cookies in that jar over there. Help yourself."

"Don't mind if I do. Say," I began as I set down Ms. Penny and hustled over to a gingerbread house cookie jar, "we aren't having that for supper, are we?"

Mrs. Dooley threw back her head and laughed heartily. "Not if you stay on my good side. Anyway, it's not for you."

I pulled out a handful of soft peanut butter cookies. "Then who's it for?" If Lady Luck had been smiling on me, Mrs. Dooley would have made that disgusting pie for Ian.

I turned from the jar in time to catch Mrs. Dooley blushing as she deftly covered the pie with a crust. "Take some more of them, why don't you?" she suggested, nodding at the jar. "Take some for your friends, too, while you're at it."

"Okay—" I stopped, my hand halfway into the jar. "How did you know I had friends coming over?"

Mrs. Dooley shrugged. "Had a feeling's all. Let them in the side door so you won't have to open the main gate. Now you'd better run along and change."

"Oh, okay. Thanks for the cookies."

"Help yourself any time."

With one cookie in my mouth and a baggie stuffed full for Ellie and her brother in my hand, I ran up to my room while Ms. Penny stayed behind in the conservatory. It occurred to me as I changed that Mrs. Dooley hadn't answered my question about the pie. Who in this world would want to eat that disgusting stuff? Shoving the remaining cookies and my key into the pocket of my favorite blazer, I hustled down the back steps heading to the conservatory. According to my pocket watch, I had half an hour before they arrived, so I decided to start my exploration of the house, beginning with the Great Hall, where all those doors were located. One of them had to lead somewhere interesting, and better yet, informative.

Leaving Ms. Penny to her cat-pestering, I pulled open the door leading to the Great Hall and stepped inside. Several cats basked on the colorful hearthrug in front of the fire. A fat tabby lifted his head when I walked by, but once he saw me, he yawned and went back to sleep.

When I saw all of the doors scattered throughout the room, it came back to me just how many of them there were. Not sure where to start, I tried something I used to do when I was a little kid. After looking around to be sure no one was watching, I extended my arm, pointed my finger and spun around in a circle until I was almost too dizzy to stand. I opened my eyes to find my finger aimed directly at a large wooden door nestled in the far corner of the room. I'd start there.

My footsteps echoed hollow as drums as I crossed the flagstone floor. When I reached the door, I tried turning the doorknob, but it was locked. Suddenly I remembered the key to my room. Didn't skeleton keys fit pretty much any old lock? Maybe mine would work on this one. I pulled the key out of my pocket and went to stick it in the keyhole, but it didn't fit. Disappointed, I stared hard at the dark iron and, determined to open the door, I tried again. This time, as I shifted and wiggled the key, it warmed to my touch. Not a moment later, the key slid smoothly into the hole. I gave it a turn and heard a distinct click. Trying the knob once more, it turned. I told myself that I didn't have the key in the right way the first time.

But I knew better.

Slowly I pulled open the heavy door and peered into the darkness. In front of me, stone steps, their center worn from the burden of many passing feet, spiraled downward into the blackness. The damp, musty air swept past me, its breath stroking my cheek like a mother's tender caress, but leaving my skin cold. The smells, the darkness, last night's fear all came back to me in a rush. Before I could decide what to do next, I heard the tap-tapping sound of footsteps growing closer and closer, and I froze. Someone very real was coming up the stairs. The deformed shadow of some monstrous creature crept along the wall and I gulped. I nearly slammed the door and ran when a small face appeared, materializing out of the darkness like a phantom.

"Why, Lavida, dear!" Mrs. Keeper exclaimed. "You startled me." My guardian, I realized, looked more disheveled than usual. Cobwebs draped her right ear and wisps of brown hair stuck out from her head like stray threads. A white chalky substance covered her dress, the same one she had worn yesterday.

"What were you doing down there? Cleaning chalkboards?"

Mrs. Keeper smiled as she brushed her hands off on her apron and wiped her face. She pulled off her glasses and started to clean them as well. "Oh, no. Nothing like that. I was trying to cast a spell. I hit one of the walls and the dust from the explosion sprayed all over me."

I raised a skeptical eyebrow. Either Mrs. Keeper was pulling my leg or the wee Brit was one step away from ending up at the funny farm. Since she seemed to be watching me closely for my reaction, I decided that she must be joking. "That's a good one." I chuckled heartily to show that I got it.

Apparently satisfied, she put her glasses back on. "Speaking of good ones . . . how did you manage to open this door?"

I held up my key. "I used this."

She studied the key for a moment. "But that key won't—" She stopped, shaking her head. "Never mind that." She placed her torch in a mount on the wall and closed the door, then turned to look at me. "I want to talk to you, Lavida."

Uh, oh. That sentence never boded well. I avoided meeting her searching eyes, focusing on the ring she wore on the middle finger of her left hand. A thick gold band supported a large, reddish-black stone that seemed to glow with an inner light. The large gem mesmerized me and, for a moment, made me want to follow Mrs. Keeper anywhere. With a mental shake, I pulled my gaze away from the haunting ring. Mrs. Keeper was still peering up at me.

"I think, dear, that maybe you should wait to explore the house until Ian has some free time to show you around. A lot of rooms in this big, old place haven't been kept up. I wouldn't want you getting hurt."

"Mrs. Keeper," I protested with a laugh, sure she was still kidding around, "I'm fifteen years old! I don't need a babysitter."

Mrs. Keeper smiled sweetly. "I know that, dear. I wasn't suggesting that you did. I merely want you to be safe. Why don't you explore the property instead?"

"But I really had my heart set on exploring the house." I

wanted to solve those mysteries, but I also wanted to know what lay beyond the door Mrs. Keeper had shut so firmly behind her.

"Another time," Mrs. Keeper said sternly. This time it was a command, not a suggestion.

"Fine. Since I'm not wanted around here, I'll go outside."

Mrs. Keeper patted my arm. "That sounds like just the thing."

I frowned. She'd totally missed my point. And on purpose, I suspected.

She took hold of my arm and steered me toward the door. "Oh, and Lavida, dear, sometimes wild animals come down out of the hills looking for food. If you see anything strange, quickly find Ian or myself. These animals can be quite dangerous to anyone who doesn't know how to handle them."

"You make it sound like ravenous beasts are just waiting to devour the first person to walk by."

"Well, I wouldn't say ravenous . . ." She smiled. "It's just that some animals find human prey so much more interesting to chase." We were at the door now.

"You're really on a roll, Mrs. Keeper."

The little woman laughed. "Aren't I?" Without so much as a toodle-oo, she scurried off toward yet another mysterious door. I watched her go as the solid heels of her sensible black shoes clacked merrily on the stone.

What was Mrs. Keeper hiding that she didn't want me to see? I didn't believe her story for a moment about the house being unsafe. Yet the way she'd made it sound, going outside wasn't any safer. If I stayed inside, a ceiling might cave in on my head; if I went outside, I could get eaten.

Mrs. Keeper, I saw, had led me to a smaller door right next to the large double doors. I yanked it open in a huff and stepped outside. A brisk wind swept the grounds, knocking tree leaves off their branches and into the vibrant, gray October sky. Flashes of yellow and red and orange danced on currents of wind before swooping in to land like hang gliders on a runway of green grass. I loved days like this.

Taking a deep breath of fresh air, the last of my disappointment faded away. From where I stood facing the drive, the grounds of the estate were extensive, with a lot to explore. Old buildings sat off to my left—a large barn, a four-car garage that might once have been the carriage house, a couple of small sheds painted in a variety of colors, a walled-in area about six feet high and the size of the barn—and then the woods. To my right stretched thirty yards of glistening, green lawn, more woods, and glimpses of the wall that met up with the gate. And the gate itself was about a hundred yards away from the house. I spotted the fountain and thought about getting a closer look at it, but for some reason didn't feel up to it. Perhaps I was afraid of what I might find.

As I looked around, wondering which way to go, the thought occurred to me that my dad must have played here in this yard, amongst these buildings, in these woods. It seemed a strange concept to me that he had walked the same grounds that I was about to and that my constantly working and rigidly uptight dad had actually played.

I decided to head left. I passed the far side of the house and scanned the land behind it. About a hundred feet from the back of the house, the woods began. Hundreds of beech trees dominated the landscape, their silvery bark cool beneath the shade of pear-colored leaves. Very little brush grew under these trees, leaving a carpet of soft, yellow leaves to reign. The woods looked lovely and peaceful, even a bit mysterious. But not dangerous.

Spotting a narrow path dividing the trees, I headed for

Killicrankie Wood. Mrs. Keeper had warned me not to go into the woods, but I could take care of myself. What was I going to do, wander off and get lost? Run into a pack of wolves? Besides, Mrs. Keeper *had* been the one to force me outdoors.

The smell of autumn and decaying leaves filled my nose as I stepped into the cool, dark woods. The smell was fresh, clean and smog-free. Humming to myself, I moved deeper into the woods, gradually climbing upward as the hill rose. As I walked along, I noticed that the woods were abnormally quiet. No little chipmunks chattered or chased each other, no wind blew, no birds called. The silence seemed strange, even to a city girl like myself. I stopped walking and looked around at the trees that stretched up toward the sky.

That's when I saw it, a massive tree the width of the Toad's car, growing in the middle of the woods. I ran toward it, sensing I was about to encounter something miraculous. Breathless, I stepped up onto one of the many thick roots growing like curled fingers above the rocky soil and leaned forward to stroke the brownish-gray bark spotted with bits of pale green lichen. At the same time my hand touched the tree's surface, something tall flashed from one tree to the next off to my left. I turned toward the spot where I'd seen the movement, but saw nothing. My spine tingled.

What was wrong with me? I knew I had an active imagination, but this was getting ridiculous. I was imagining ghosts and goblins behind every tree. Or, maybe someone was trying to scare me—someone by the name of Ian. Determined to ignore his latest prank, I was about to turn my attention back to the tree when another flash caught my eye. Resolving to tell him off, I turned toward the movement and shouted, "Show your face, you coward!" When no response came I walked forward, anger growing with every step. "I know it's you, Ian, you—"

A figure crept out from behind the tree, and when I saw what it was, I forgot all about Ian. Ten yards away from me was a large ball of fur with muscles and teeth. Lots of teeth. I turned on my heel and raced toward the house, knowing instinctively that it was right behind me. A growl erupted only yards away, sounding alarmingly like an evil laugh. I *couldn't* let that thing catch me. If it did, I knew in my gut that I wouldn't survive.

The pounding footsteps grew closer and closer, like a galloping horse riding me down. Knowing I shouldn't, but unable to help myself, I turned my head to look, stumbled over a root, and then regained my footing. I didn't dare look again.

Breaking through the line of trees, I dashed past the high, stone wall of the enclosure and around the first of the sheds, winding in and out of the grouping in hopes of losing my pursuer. For a brief moment, panting hard, I stopped at the edge of one shed to listen, leaning against the rough wood to catch my breath. The rush of pursuit had stopped. My ears strained to catch the merest of sounds, and it came—the padding of paws on dead leaves, like a panther stalking me. My whole body jerked reflexively and I clamped down on my lower lip, drawing blood. My breath, already ragged, came and went from my lungs so quickly that whatever was chasing me must hear its staccato rhythm.

I had to move.

Leaving the maze of sheds, I hightailed it toward the looming barn, my feet slipping on the wet grass. As I neared the building, I searched frantically for an opening, but every door was closed up, locked tight. "Come on!" I cried, tugging on the rusty padlock. There was no way in.

I glanced around, looking for shelter, looking for the creature.

Where is that thing? I thought. Which way should I go? Why hadn't it caught me already? Was it toying with me?

I was stepping away from the barn when a vicious snarl, sounding awfully close to my left ear, burned a path to my senses through the crisp air, the threat of it as deadly as a forest fire. The creature had found me, though I had yet to spot where it was. The house was my only chance, but I'd never make it in time. That thing was too fast, too wily. But I had to try.

My sides ached and my lungs burned as I sprinted, dodging this way and that. The thudding sound of my footsteps on the soft lawn was immediately joined by the thundering of hooves. I wanted to scream, but all the air in my lungs was gone. I could hear the steady pace of the beast's breathing, unhurried, unlabored.

There's no way I should've reached the conservatory door alive, but when I did I yanked it open far enough to slip through and, slamming the door shut, I ducked and screamed as something slammed into the glass pane above my head with enough force to rattle the entire structure.

CHAPTER ELEVEN

THEY'RE BACK...

I rolled myself into a ball and waited to feel razor-sharp teeth piercing my throat. After several seconds, when nothing happened, I slowly opened my eyes. Seeing fur, I cried out. But it was only Ms. Penny squatting in front of me, looking at me as though I'd gone crazy. Her appearance startled me so much that I almost forgot my situation. I leaped to my feet and peered out through the thick, bubbled glass. There was nothing there.

I checked the yard for signs of life, but saw only a small squirrel sitting on his haunches and gnawing on a nut. I'd imagined the whole embarrassing episode, I suddenly realized, just like when I had thought that creature in the tapestry was alive. Mrs. Keeper's story about wild animals in the woods had transformed a harmless rodent into a monster. Feeling like a complete idiot, I could only be thankful that no one had been around to witness my lunatic flight from the rabid critter. Ms. Penny, annoyed by my strange behavior, batted me on the head and scolded me for disturbing her.

I motioned toward the door, hoping to pacify her. "Come on. You can meet my friends. They should be here by now." After scanning the yard once more, I slowly stepped outside, and despite convincing myself that I'd overreacted, I still felt nervous, my eyes searching for signs of danger. With each step, I relaxed a little more, and Ms. Penny ambled along next to me, looking for bugs to play with, and eat, as we walked to the gate.

It took me a while to find the door Mrs. Dooley had mentioned. It wasn't easy to spot, hidden as it was behind a curtain of thick, leafy vines. When I finally uncovered the door and tried the handle, I discovered that it was locked. I wondered if they locked all the doors around here, or only the ones I wanted to go through. Fortunately, I remembered my skeleton key and, taking it from my blazer pocket, tried it in the door. This time it fit perfectly. I turned it and opened the door in time to see Ellie and her brother grind to a stop in front of the gate, each riding a small scooter. The boy slid sideways in the dirt, sending dust up into the air. He caught himself with a tattered red sneaker.

"Over here!" I waved.

"Hey, Lavida!" Ellie called, unstrapping a baby-blue helmet that matched the color of her scooter and made her red hair look even redder. "Like it?" she asked, gazing down at the scooter. "It's a Vespa. We saw them all over Sicily last summer. I liked them, so Daddy bought one for me." Her eyes lighted on the baggie I'd just pulled out of my pocket. "Are those cookies?"

"Yep. Peanut butter. Mrs. Dooley made them. Here, take one." I opened the bag and handed one to Ellie and one to her brother. He studied me frankly as he took the cookie. In looks, he was a smaller version of Ellie. He had her red hair and piercing blue eyes, but his hair was all spiky tufts and he didn't wear glasses or braces. He did have freckles, while Ellie didn't. One of his tennis shoes was untied and his t-shirt spotted with dirt and holes. It looked like Ms. Penny had dressed the unfortunate boy. In the dark.

"This is my brother, Eddie," Ellie said around a mouthful of cookie. "Can you believe we're twins?"

I couldn't.

"Have you had any actual paranormal sightings yet?" he greeted me, tugging on his earlobe self-consciously. I was to learn that he did that a lot.

I glanced over at Ellie. She shrugged. "Better answer him. He's like a rat terrier with a bone."

I thought about my strange experience in the woods, about Loria and Darian. "Um, maybe."

Eddie's freckled face brightened. "Tell me everything!"

Ellie shook her head. "Eddie thinks he's going to be the next Sherlock Holmes."

"Geez, Ellie, will you stop telling people that!" He turned to me. "Don't listen to her. She's just jealous because I want to be more than a couch potato with appendages sprouting from my body."

"Shut up, Eddie—agh!" she screeched. "Something jumped on me!" She turned toward the offending object and came face to face with Ms. Penny. "Eeaagghh! Get it off!" She swung around, trying to shake the raccoon loose. Ms. Penny, clearly enjoying the exciting ride, was reluctant for it to end. She grabbed Ellie's hair and hung on tight.

"Ms. Penny!" I snapped my fingers at the naughty raccoon. Ellie's face had turned a bright red from her exertions, and she looked like she was about to blow a gasket. Giving an exasperated squeak, the little imp jumped off

Ellie's shoulder onto mine just as my new friend was about to bean the raccoon with her blue handbag. She nearly ended up beaning me, but I ducked in time. "Sorry about that, Ellie," I apologized after straightening back up. "That was not how I planned on introducing you to Ms. Penny. Are you all right?"

"Wow!" Eddie stared longingly at my pet. "I can't believe you own a *Procyon lotor.*"

"You know her scientific name?" I was impressed. "For that you get another cookie." I held one out to him, and he took it with a grin. "Most people think she's an overgrown rat."

"Hey, what about me?" Ellie demanded as she attempted to fix her hair. "I never thought she was an overgrown rat." She held out her hand.

I gave her a cookie. "So what did you think she was when you were yelling and dancing around like that?"

"The strangest looking cat I've ever seen," she replied with a straight face.

Ms. Penny tugged at my ear. "What is it, girl?" I cocked my head toward her. "You've never been so insulted in your life?" She screeched loudly. "I'll be sure to pass that along."

"Har de har har," Ellie grumbled. "How was I supposed to know she was a raccoon? Don't they live in the woods?"

"You could make it up to her by giving her some of your cookie."

"You're dreaming."

I laughed. "You wanna hold her? She's really friendly . . . well, most of the time," I added, erring on the side of caution.

Ellie shook her head. "No thanks. I haven't had my rabies shot this year."

"You're such a chicken," Eddie told his sister. "I'll hold her, Lavida." He held out his arms and Ms. Penny jumped into them.

"It's your funeral," Ellie said. "One of these days you're going to find out that you're not immortal."

"We're all going to find that out, one of these days," Eddie said, hitching the raccoon onto his hip like a mother carrying her child.

"Whatever." She pushed up her light blue glasses. "So are we going inside or what?"

"Sure. Come on." The twins followed me through the small door to the other side.

"Holy cannoli!" Ellie exclaimed. The sun was sinking behind the hill, casting a dark shadow over the huge building. "I can see why people think this place is haunted."

"It *is* kinda weird," I agreed as we walked along the dirt driveway. "My dad grew up here, but he hasn't been back since he left the place over twenty years ago."

"That sounds suspicious," Eddie said, kicking at a small rock on the gravel driveway. "Do you know why?"

"I've been trying to figure that out since I got here."

Eddie nodded thoughtfully as he stroked an imaginary beard on his chin. "How very interesting. I enjoy a good enigma."

"Oh, geez, Eddie," Ellie cried in exasperation. "Can't you use the word *mystery* like everyone else?"

He stuck out his pointed chin. "Enigma is a great word!"

"But no one knows what you're talking about half the time."

"That's not my fault." He stubbornly crossed his arms. "Over half the American population is grossly undereducated."

Ellie poked him. "No wonder you don't have any friends."

"And you're Miss Popularity?" He poked her back.

I put up my hands, worried they might want to leave.

"Guys! Guys! Please don't. Why don't we go look at the fountain."

"Okay!" they both agreed, their argument immediately forgotten.

At the fountain, blue-green water spurted into a murky pool, its water blackened by the masses of dead leaves and muck lying on the bottom. I peered at the ornate writing carved into the base of one of the statues. Dried grass obscured half of the saying before I cleared it away. "*The Lost Ones,*" I read aloud.

"I wonder who the Lost Ones are?" Ellie asked, stirring the water with a stick. "Sounds kind of peculiar to me. You don't suppose they're people who got lost somewhere around here, do you?" She looked around the yard and shuddered as a cool breeze passed by.

"Um, guys, those statues aren't human," Eddie pointed out. "Look at them." We looked. Some did resemble humans until you peered closer and saw their long, pointy ears. Others were as small as dolls. "They're supposed to be mythical creatures," Eddie informed us. "Elves and Pixies and the like. Most people don't believe such things exist, mostly because they've never seen any proof that they do. Of course, there's also no proof that they don't."

I continued to stare at the fountain, feeling drawn to it. My eyes moved to settle on the figure I'd seen from the car, the one who seemed to be imploring me to help. I looked deeply into his large, mournful eyes and noticed, with a start, that he looked like Darian. Intrigued and a little nervous, I reached out and touched the statue's cheek, comforted to find that it was cold, solid stone and not warm flesh.

"Let's go explore the house," Eddie suggested. "If we're going to solve this enigma about your dad—oops—for my lexicon-challenged sister, solve this *mystery*, we should start looking for clues. You can fill us in on your paranormal sightings while we explore."

"We better not, Eddie," Ellie said, glancing around. "We didn't tell mom where we were going, so we should probably head back before she notices we're gone."

Eddie sighed. "But we didn't get to hear about Lavida's sightings."

"In my opinion, that's a good thing," she replied, looking uneasy. "And leave the raccoon here."

"Oh, all right," he grumbled. "Goodbye, Ms. Penny." He set her on the ground. "Sorry, girl. I've gotta go." With one last look over her shoulder, Ms. Penny scampered toward the house.

The twins turned to leave, and I followed them to the gate. As they passed through the small door, Ellie said, "Sorry to run, but this place freaks me out. See you at school. Meet me for lunch, okay?"

"Sure," I replied.

I watched them go, the buzz of their engines whining in my ears long after they'd gone. I had the terrible, and yet at the same time, relieved, feeling that they wouldn't be back.

That evening, Mrs. Dooley and I ate alone at the table in the kitchen. When I asked where Mrs. Keeper and Ian were, she told me they were busy with something or other. She was very vague about it and, after that, acted like she didn't hear my questions. I gave up after a while. Questioning the wily cook was like trying to interrogate a rock.

After the meal, she accepted my offer to help her clean

up. When the dishes were done and the food put away, she encouraged me to grab a handful of cookies and head upstairs. In the bathroom, I scrubbed my school shirt as best I could and hung it up to dry. Ms. Penny and I quickly got ready for bed and burrowed under the covers. Tired from her long day of harassing her new friend, she curled up next to my head on the pillow and promptly fell asleep.

While she slept, I immersed myself in *Lord of the Rings*. It was well after midnight when I finished the last page.

Yawning, I brushed cookie crumbs off the down comforter, then snuggled beneath it. Remembering Ian's hoax of the night before, I felt a chill before closing the bed curtains and diving back under the heavy blanket. I left the lamp on next to my bed, just in case.

Last night had been a practical joke, I reminded myself as I lay there shivering. Just a joke.

But when I heard the sound of my trunks scraping against the floor, I knew in the pit of my stomach that my escapade with Loria and Darian hadn't been *just a joke*. Someone was trying to get into my room.

Someone from the secret passage.

CHAPTER TWELVE
VARRIOR'S VALK

When I realized what was happening, I sat upright, my trembling hands yanking the blankets up to my chin. I wanted to yell for help, but I couldn't. I was frozen with fright. I felt like I was in a bad dream where my feet were stuck to the floor and I couldn't run away. I watched in horror as long, slender fingers grabbed the canopy curtain and pulled it open. When I saw who it was, I clutched a pillow to my chest.

Darian had come back for me.

I caught my breath and wound up to scream, but he clapped a strong hand over my mouth, cutting off the sound. I tried to beat him off with my pillow, but he easily pulled it out of my hands.

"Quiet," he hissed in my ear. I felt his warm breath on my skin. "You will wake the others."

I rolled my eyes. "Mmpf oo oo ink I uz rying oo oo?"

He stared at me, confused.

I peeled his hand off my mouth. "What do you think I was trying to do?"

He gazed at me, and the look sent chills up my spine. "If they try to help you, I will have to harm them. Do you want that to happen?"

"I guess not," I replied.

"Move over," Loria said, pushing Darian aside. "Hello again, Human!" she greeted, with more cheer than should be legal under the circumstances. "We have come to bring you to our Mistress. She very much wants to meet you."

"You're taking me to your leader?" They couldn't seriously be thinking I was going to go with them. "What if I don't want to go?"

"You have no choice," Darian informed me.

"Maybe I should take my chances and start screaming."

Darian clamped his hand over my mouth again. "Do not do that," he warned. "We are bringing you to Madrina. She is the leader of our clan. And the Magistrate is the ruler of all Anaedor."

I pulled his hand off my mouth. "Ana-who?"

"An-a-door," Darian said slowly, as though speaking to a dimwitted child.

"Okay, fine. Anaedor. So, let me get this straight"—I looked at the two pale faces staring down at me—"if I refuse to come with you, anyone who tries to help me could 'get hurt.' Right?"

"That is correct, Human," Darian answered. "We have our orders and we must carry them out." He looked deadly serious. Loria, on the other hand, was acting like this was some kind of invitation to a party. She could barely contain her excitement.

"Who's going to make me come?" I asked him. I had

outrun him once. I could do it again. "You or the Fairy Princess?" I nodded my head at Loria.

She beamed at me. "Did you hear that, Darian? She thinks I look like a princess." She twirled around to show off a full-length, green, gauzy dress that floated like clouds around her willowy body.

Darian glared at her.

Loria placed a hand over her mouth to stifle a giggle. "Sorry," she said through smiling lips. "We are being serious. I forgot."

After giving her another irritated look, Darian showed me a miniature crossbow strapped to his right wrist. "I will."

I eyed the nasty weapon. "Can I at least get dressed?" If I was going anywhere tonight, it wouldn't be in a too-short, pink nightgown. "Not in front of you," I added, nodding at Darian.

He gave me a condescending look. He was quite good at them. "Ah, yes. Humans and their modesty."

"Darian, wait in the passageway please," Loria dictated, taking charge.

He regarded her sternly. "Do not let her get away, Loria."

"Oh, Darian, please! I only lost little Souee Piggerel for a few moments. It was not my fault her brother diverted my attention with RedGems while she wiggled through that hole."

"Yell if the Human so much as twitches the wrong way."

She giggled at him. "I will! Now shoo."

Darian turned to go, then spun back. He grasped my chin with his powerful fingers and stared deeply into my eyes. His own were black and deadly serious. I could feel their power in my heart.

"What?" I breathed.

"If you run, I will hunt you down."

Before I could come up with a stinging retort, he was gone.

I slid out of bed and shuffled over to my dresser, where I had unpacked a few of my clothes. I pulled out a black turtleneck, black pants, and my black school shoes. If need be, I could blend in with the shadows in this outfit. I wasn't a ninja fan for nothing.

"You look like a black wraith," Loria breathed admiringly when I'd finished dressing.

"You flatter me," I replied dryly, reconsidering my color choice.

Loria clasped her hands together. "Oh, not at all." She leaned forward confidentially and said, "I love to dress up. But it is even more fun to blend."

I bent over to tie my shoe. "What do you mean, 'blend'?" I asked as I straightened up. It sounded painful.

"Oh, that. We can become whatever, or whoever, we want."

"So, you're not human," I said slowly.

"Oh, no!" she laughed. "We are Blendars. We have to blend as Humans whenever we come to the Upland, you see. For our safety. And Madrina thought it would not be so frightening for you if we looked like your kind."

"Hurry!" Darian called through the crack in the door. "We have very little time," he explained, impatient. "Madrina is expecting us."

"What's with him? He treats you like a child."

"Well, he is my brother . . ."

That explained a lot. They were siblings. Probably twins, they looked so much alike. Though if that was the case, it seemed a strange coincidence that I'd met two sets of twins in less than a week. Pondering this, I quickly checked on Ms. Penny, who remained fast asleep.

"She will not notice you are gone," Loria whispered in my ear as she nudged me to go ahead of her. "I used an old trick while you were dressing to make sure she will sleep a long time."

I shuddered.

Darian held open the secret door. "Follow me, Human."

Loria went down the slide first. When she disappeared around a corner, Darian grabbed hold of me and pulled me onto his lap. His breath tickled my ear as he pushed off and together we flew down the slide.

After landing, which was much softer this time with Darian to take the brunt of it, he scooted out from under me and pulled me to my feet. When he started to drag me along behind him, I had to say something. "You guys might be able to see, but I'm blind as a bat down here."

"Bats are not blind," Darian corrected me. "You Humans so often misunderstand other creatures."

Boy, he must be a real hit at parties. "Can we just get some light?"

"As you wish. I always forget how weak Human senses are." He briefly let go of my hand. A moment later, he grabbed hold again and said, "Awake!"

Light from a small lantern filled the little room. Darian held the lamp in his left hand, which was now very close to my face, and with a shock, I realized that the glowing creatures flitting about inside the glass container were not lightning bugs, as I'd thought before, but tiny, human-like creatures.

"What are those things?" I pulled my hand from Darian's grasp and pointed at the poor creatures trapped in the lamp. Six of them flew aimlessly about the tiny quarters. They had wrinkled, pale-green skin and bulging eyes above a squashed nose. Fuzzy little wings sprouted from their shoulder blades, and their bodies gave off a yellowish-green light. Written in flowing script at the base of the lamp were the words *Lux Aeterna*.

Loria laughed. "Why, silly, they are Starkinders, of course. Do they not give off the nicest glow?"

"Isn't that slave labor? And that lamp, there's hardly enough room in it to move around. They can't possibly—"

"Giving light is what Starkinders do," Darian interrupted me, his dark eyes regarding me coolly. "That is their skill."

"That's a very convenient rationale for everyone but the Starkinders, Darian," I replied indignantly. "You get light, and they get to live in a pickle jar."

"They see serving us as a privilege," Loria explained, looking anxiously back and forth between us. "Starkinders prefer close quarters, anyway, Lavida. They do not like leaving their little homes. The lantern is where they feel most safe."

"Enough of this," Darian growled. "We have more important things to do. Now come with me." He held the lamp aloft and moved toward an opening in the far wall.

I followed him, still seething from our conversation. How did he know what the Starkinders wanted? Had he ever asked them? Of course he hadn't. He simply assumed he knew best . . . just like my dad. He thought he could tell people where to go and they'd hop to it with a "yes, sir" and a smile on their lips. And what was his problem with humans?

Nobody should ever have something forced on them, I decided, then wondered if I included myself in that group. I was always being made to do things I didn't want to do, like now, for example.

Darian entered the dark tunnel, and I followed behind him. He moved stealthily, as though he didn't want to be noticed, so I did the same. I didn't know what was going on, or where we were going, but I decided not to fight it for the moment. My curiosity had been aroused, and it's not like I had any choice anyway, not with that crossbow Darian carried.

The tunnel we were walking through was obviously man-made. After about twenty steps, the surface abruptly changed from smooth stone to coarse rock. I reached out to touch the cool, moist wall. It was bumpy and rough. I could hardly believe it. I never would have guessed that a tunnel ran beneath Portal Manor, leading into an underground cave.

The tunnel soon ended and we stepped into a large cavern resembling an ancient cathedral. The light filled part of the space—enough to make me stop and stare in wonder. Long ribbons of dripstone clung to the walls like grand curtains on a stage and delicate stalactites hung from the ceiling. On the ground, stalagmites thrust upward like rainforest anthills, with only a narrow lane winding through them. The lamp illuminated these natural features like a spotlight as it showed us the way along the trail, a path that appeared to have once been a river of liquid stone, frozen mid-flow. I forgot about being kidnapped and focused instead on watching water drip steadily from the tips of the stalactites, sparkling in the light like falling crystals. An eerie quiet reigned here, with only the sound of our footsteps echoing off the walls to disturb the peace.

Up ahead, a large pile of rocks blocked the path. There seemed to be no way through or around it. Darian showed no concern, leading us to stand in front of a rock the size of a refrigerator and, facing it, spoke strange words. When the stone vanished, my mouth dropped open. That did *not* just happen.

But it had. In front of us, a hole appeared, large enough to walk through with room to spare. I watched Darian step through the opening without hesitation. He motioned me to follow, and reluctantly I did. What if the stone reappeared just as I was walking directly over the spot where it had stood moments ago? When I made it through unharmed, with Loria right behind me, I was actually surprised to still be alive. I looked back to find the stone had returned to close the entry. I *had* to be dreaming this. Disappearing rocks couldn't be real. None of this could be— a hidden world beneath a house, tiny people in lamps, shape-shifting creatures.

After stumbling over a rock, I turned my attention back to navigating the rough path. I was so intent on watching the ground that I ran right into Darian, who had stopped walking to look up at a huge wooden door, knots the size of my fist dotting its dark surface. Light from two Starkinder lamps, one hanging on each side of the door, lit the small room, casting shadows at our feet. In the dim glow, I noticed there were no handles or knobs on the door.

Darian knocked out a complicated pattern of raps and taps and then stepped back away from the door, giving it room to swing open and bang loudly against the wall. I gasped and stepped backward; a big, hairy creature stood in the doorway, almost entirely filling the space. It had a hefty, pumpkin-shaped body topped by a tiny, round head the size of a volleyball. Coarse brown hair sprouted out of its nostrils and ears and from beneath every available opening in its dirt-encrusted clothes. Small, round, yellow eyes peered out of the tiny face and a large, hairy hand pointed a spear at us.

"Run!" I screeched.

Darian caught my arm and dragged me back. I tried to pull free, but he only tightened his grip.

"Let me go!"

"Who goes there?" the creature demanded, sounding like a three-year-old with a lisp.

I stopped struggling.

"Hello, Barg," Loria called as she pushed me forward. "We have brought you something."

The creature called Barg squealed with delight, clapping his hands excitedly. The heavy odor of onions wafted toward me as he stepped forward.

"Oh, lemme see! Lemme see!" He reached out to touch me. "Oooh . . . is she for real?" His hand stopped in mid-air. "Can me touch her? A big hug! Me wants a big hug!"

A fine sheen of sweat coated my forehead as I jerked away from the reaching hand, right into Darian's arms.

"You can hug her, Barg," he said. "But be gentle."

My eyes widened. *Hug* me? "Please don't!" I pleaded to Darian, grabbing his arm and holding tight. "Don't let him touch me!"

Darian pushed me forward. "It is best not to anger a Portal Guard. They tend to break things when they do not get their way." He watched me carefully, challenging me. A muscle in his strong jaw flickered as he waited to see what I was going to do.

"Tell him I'll bite if I'm squeezed too hard and that human bites can kill."

Barg giggled. "Me like her! She feisty. Touch! Touch!"

"It is not so bad," Loria said, putting a reassuring hand on my shoulder. "Barg will be careful, right?" she said, turning to the grinning creature, who nodded eagerly. Once again, it looked like I didn't have much choice in the matter.

I took a huge breath, held it, and stepped forward. I was determined to stay cool in front of Darian—to prove I was tougher than he thought I was. Yet I couldn't help flinching as Barg's large, hairy hands reached out to grab me.

Oh, for the love of Pete, somebody help me!

But it was too late. Barg wrapped his thick arms around

me, picked me up and squeezed tight. His orangish-colored skin was rough against my cheek, and his yellow, broken fingernails bit into my skin. I felt like I was being hugged by a slug with claws.

"Ooooh! She is sooo soft!" he cooed. "Like a Squisher, she is. She is, yes. Me like her. Can me keep her?"

I panicked and tried to pull away. Barg only squeezed tighter. Trapped and unable to hold my breath any longer, I managed to turn my head and whimper, "Help me," through my smushed mouth. Bad move. My nose was right by Barg's armpit now and I nearly fainted from the stench of overripe sweat.

A tiny smile danced at the edges of Darian's mouth. "Let her go, Barg," he told the creature. "Madrina is expecting us. Perhaps later you two can get together and share a meal."

"Get me out of this!" I said through clenched teeth.

"Barg . . ." Darian said sternly.

"Oh, sad is me," Barg whimpered. "See how me weep?"

Barg reluctantly let me go, and I staggered around trying to catch my breath. As I backed away from him, an orange liquid spurted from the corners of his round, yellow eyes. He really was crying.

Loria giggled. "Oh, Barg. You cannot fool us. We know all your tricks." The big creature grinned at her, revealing solid, square teeth beneath flaring nostrils.

After drying his eyes with a dirty, crumpled-up rag pulled from his pocket, he stepped aside. I scooted past him and through the door. I could feel his eyes glued to my back as the others joined me. If it were up to Barg, I'd be his new pet to bring home to mommy. I glanced back.

"Bye, bye!" he called, waving his big hand like a toddler.

"I hope there's another way to get me home," I hissed. "I don't want to go through *that* ever again. He smells awful!"

"We are sorry about Barg, Lavida," Loria apologized. "He loves Humans and he hates baths."

"No kidding." I sniffed my shirt. "Ugh. Now I smell like him."

Darian shook his head. "You say we treat the Starkinders badly, yet you cannot even be civil to Barg, who for some strange reason actually *likes* Humans. All his kind do. I think they sneak to the Upland in hopes of catching a glimpse of one, which, of course, violates the rules." He gave a reproachful sigh. "Barg treated you kindly, and all you can do is talk about how bad he smells. For shame."

"I *was* civil to him, Darian," I argued, knowing I hadn't been civil at all. "I let him hug me," I continued weakly, backing slowly away from his censure. "Besides," I rallied, "he really *did* smell . . . and I have a sensitive no—"

"Darian!" Loria lunged forward, grabbed my arm and yanked me backward. "She cannot see like we do," she scolded.

I looked down to find myself at the edge of a monstrous pit, with no bottom in sight. One more step and I'd have gone plummeting to my death.

"You are right," Darian said in a stilted voice as I shuffled closer to the wall of the cave. "Once again, I have forgotten about your inadequacies."

"I almost died!" I gasped.

"But you did not," he stated coolly. "Now follow me."

I crossed my arms defiantly. "I want to go home."

Darian marched toward me, but just before he reached me, Loria grabbed his arm, pulling him away. "Apologize, Darian."

His lips tightened.

"Do it," she persisted. "This is not the time."

I watched a battle take place within Darian. After a moment, the fire in his eyes died away. Loria, despite her flightiness, seemed to have a certain control over her brother.

"I am sorry, Human," he made a short bow. "I should have been more careful."

"Apology accepted."

Something flashed in his eyes before he nodded brusquely.

"Good!" Loria cheered. "Now you two can be friends." We both gave her a hard look and she snapped her mouth shut.

"We must keep moving," Darian repeated.

His lantern, raised high, showed a narrow stone bridge that spanned the length of the large pit. In the dim light, I could see no other way to get across, and believe me, I was looking.

"I can't cross that," I said in a choked voice. I wasn't afraid of heights, but I was afraid of falling to my death.

"You have no choice," Darian responded scornfully, as though he had expected me to make a fuss. "You cross Warrior's Walk on your own or I carry you on my shoulder."

"You can't make me do this."

He shrugged and reached out to grab me.

"Okay, fine!" I backed away from him, though there was little room to do so on the small ledge between Barg's door and the bridge. "I'll do it myself, but I want it to go on record that I'm doing this under protest."

As I approached the bridge I felt a dizzying sense of vertigo. On either side of the narrow pathway, darkness waited like a gaping mouth. A cool breeze wafted upward, bringing with it a whiff of brine. Portal Manor was a good twenty miles from the ocean, yet somehow the smell of the sea had made it here.

"Put one foot after the other, Lavida," Loria whispered,

sensing my fears. "It is not so bad. Just do not look down."

"Is there anything down there?" I asked, though I'm not sure why, since I didn't really want to know.

"I have never seen it myself, but Anaedorian explorers tell stories of a hideous monster that lives in a deep pool at the bottom of the pit. It has many long arms that could crush you like an Igglebug . . . before it eats you."

Oh, lovely. "Has anyone ever fallen in?"

"Oh, sure," Loria replied cheerfully. She didn't seem the least bit bothered by this fact. "But the ones who fall are the ones who are somewhere they should not be."

Like me, I thought gloomily. "I don't want to end up as somebody's dinner."

Loria laughed. "You will not fall, Lavida."

"Besides," Darian interjected, "you are too small to be much more than a snack." He allowed himself a small smile before turning to step onto the bridge. "Come along now," he commanded, taking the lead. He moved quickly and easily, as though he didn't see the black, cavernous space on either side of his feet.

I followed behind him, with Loria bringing up the rear. But the moment I stepped onto the bridge, I grew dizzy and soon fell behind. The path was so narrow and so long, I felt as though I was walking on a tightrope. I could barely place one foot in front of the other. I slowed down even more. The last thing I wanted was to become some hungry beast's answer to a midnight munchie attack.

Suddenly my foot slid on a patch of gravel. My other foot lost traction too when I tried to catch myself and, as though in slow motion, I began to fall, the darkness rushing up to meet me.

CHAPTER THIRTEEN
WRITTEN IN THE BOOK

A strong hand caught my arm and yanked me back onto the stone walkway. Curled up in an ungraceful heap, I looked up to see Darian standing over me, scowling. He shook his head in disbelief as I pushed myself to my feet and brushed off. I took my time about it.

"You are thinking like a Human," he said harshly when I'd finished. "You must free your mind from your perception. *You* see the darkness of the waiting pit. *I* see a walkway of stone that carries me from one side to the other. For me, there is no darkness."

"Easy for you to say," I muttered. "You live in a cave."

He gave me a pitying look. "You cannot help your weakness, I suppose."

"Not having night vision *isn't* a weakness!"

He simply smiled and shook his head in a patronizing

manner. "Feel free to crawl."

It was too much. I refused to fail in front of this arrogant prig. Taking a deep breath, I focused my attention on the light-colored stone that stretched out before me. I let out my breath slowly, my concentration deepening, and as my sight narrowed and my mind became quiet, the walk appeared to widen beneath my feet. Slowly at first and then more quickly I set one foot in front of the other, determination flowing through me like a river. Soon I was gliding across the stone like a figure skater on ice. If I hadn't felt the stone beneath my feet, I might've believed I was flying. In a blink I was on the other side of the pit, breathless, but exhilarated.

"Lavida!" Loria cried when she caught up to me. "That was amazing. My friends will be so impressed. Most Blendars need many Turns to cross without fear."

"Turns?"

"A long time," she explained.

"A long time?" I looked back at the impossibly narrow bridge just as Darian stepped off it to join us. "But—"

"We must keep moving," he said, pushing past us. He strode purposefully towards an opening in the cave wall. "Come along."

"That dirty rat," I growled under my breath as I reluctantly followed after him, stifling the temptation to step on his heel, but only because I would have ended up tripping myself.

We hiked until my legs grew tired. The light from Darian's lantern, and a few well-placed Starkinder lamps, reflected off bits of sparkling rock embedded in the cave walls. Moving closer, I noticed a series of strange carvings spread out along the glittering surface. Someone had put a lot of effort into etching the curious elongated creatures, the numerous spirals and elaborate designs—circles within circles within circles, squares within squares within squares. I was getting a private tour of a prehistoric cave site.

The sound of moving water caught my attention, the roar growing louder with each step, nearly deafening me by the time I finally spotted the source of the thundering noise. It was a waterfall, plummeting from a cliff high above a dark, round pool. After filling the pool, the water flowed rapidly along about the length of a fallen tree before disappearing beneath a shelf of smooth stone.

"It is called Fenian Falls," Loria shouted in my ear. "It was named after the rebel Blendar, Fenian. He fell from there"—she pointed to a spot at the top of the falls—"a long time ago—just after the Uprising."

I raised a questioning eyebrow.

"The Uprising," she explained, "came about when the Magistrate at the time wanted to take back the Upland for our citizens. Fen and a group of his followers resisted his policy, wanting not war, but a peaceful resolution between Anaedorians and Humans. It is unclear what happened, precisely, but there was a skirmish and Fen fell, or was pushed, as some believed." She gave a romantic sigh. "It is a noble death to die while fighting for something you believe in."

I shuddered and looked away. I agreed with her about giving your life for a cause you believed in. Easy for me to say.

Up ahead, Darian skirted the pool, heading straight for the waterfall. I stayed where I was and watched as he disappeared without hesitation behind the white sheet of water. Taking a deep breath I followed him and, to my surprise, I was able to walk not through the sheet of water, but behind it, into a circular cave. In the damp space, thirteen different-colored doors spaced themselves out along the smooth wall. Delicate white flowers, looking as though they had been concocted from sugared frosting, adorned the faded and beat-up doors. Without thinking, I walked to a red door and tried to open it. It was locked.

"What are you doing?" Darian demanded.

I looked back at him. "Isn't this the way we go?"

"It is, but how did you know that?"

I shrugged, feeling my face grown warm. "Um, because red's my favorite color?"

After giving me a skeptical look, Darian unlocked the red door and held it open for us to pass through. On the other side began yet another passageway. I was beginning to realize how elaborate this underground world was. A number of passageways diverged from the tunnel we entered and, every once in a while, the path would split like a snake's tongue, quickly becoming impossible to remember the way out.

We marched on. I had no idea how long; I just knew my feet had started to hurt. I was used to walking on even sidewalks, not the winding, climbing, dipping, rocky trail we were following. Fortunately, more and more Starkinder lamps lit the way now. I wondered in a dazed sort of way what the tiny creatures would say if I asked them what they did for a living. *Oh, I am light*, they'd reply, and very modestly, too, I'm sure.

Somewhere in the distance, I thought I heard the murmur of voices and I stopped thinking about the Starkinders. Judging from Darian's suddenly increased pace, we were getting close to our destination. The sound of voices grew louder as we approached the end of the tunnel.

At the top of a steep slope, we entered a huge cavern reaching up so high I couldn't see its ceiling. Hundreds of small openings—some dark, some spilling light from within—dotted the walls. Most doorways were reached by stairways carved into the stone, though a few of the highest ones had only knotted ropes to climb.

I looked around me, feeling both scared and curious. Starkinder lamps hung from metal rods protruding from the cave walls, but the cave was still only dimly lit. Shadows leaped up and down the walls like agitated monsters whenever one of the hundreds of strange beings passed by a light. From this distance, they looked like reflections of each other. Most were tall and thin and wore simple, light-colored shifts. Delicate ears poked through their dark, curly hair, and long, narrow noses led the way to rosy red lips. Their skin was white as fresh snow, and big, black eyes nearly twice the size of a human's punctuated their long, oval faces. Despite these oddities, they might've been human.

Many of them carried rough brown sacks slung over their shoulders or lugged colorful clay pots. Some carried small babies in pouches on their backs while others stood behind tables that resembled stone birdbaths, hawking their wares. The tables displayed a variety of items for sale—large mugs and pitchers, woven sacks and fine linens, silverwork, jewels and jewelry, to name a few. Individuals examined the items closely, sometimes dickering over the price. In the open spaces, children played games with sticks and hoops. The bustling scene reminded me of the Saturday market held every summer back home.

A large river flowed through the middle of the cave, most likely the same river that led to the waterfall I'd seen earlier. It served as the major highway for the community, transporting boats resembling Venetian gondolas and long, narrow rafts like English punts, with low sides to protect the passengers or goods traveling on them. Creatures wearing tall, dark hats stood at the back end of each boat, propelling it forward with a long pole.

Not long after we entered the cavern, all the beings stopped bustling about, freezing like wild animals sensing danger. In unison, their heads turned in our direction, but their eyes focused on only one of us—me. My heart rate sped up. I didn't like being stared at, especially with such intensity. It usually meant I was about to get into trouble.

"What are they?" I whispered to Loria as we made our way through the crowd, which divided before us.

"Why, they are Blendars," she replied proudly. "That is what Darian and I look like when we are unblended."

I glanced over at Loria, then at one of the staring Blendars. "The way they're looking at me, you'd think they'd never seen a human before."

"Most of them have not," she replied. "There is little opportunity, since it is unlawful to go to the surface. Also, your presence here worries some of our people," she added in a hushed voice.

"Why?" I whispered back.

Loria looked uncomfortable. "There are things happening . . . I cannot say."

"But you and Darian are blending to look like humans," I persisted. "Why aren't they staring at you?"

She relaxed. "Oh, because they know we are blending. They see who we really are, not the Humans we have become."

"But I saw you as you really are."

"Yes, well . . . that is the other reason why they are staring at you. They have heard you might be the *One*."

"You mentioned that before. What does that mean, anyway?"

"Oh," she replied vaguely, "Madrina will tell you about that."

"But—" I started to protest, then stopped when I saw the creatures were all still looking at me. Wanting to make them stop, I boldly stared back at them. Many of them quickly looked away, intent on studying the ground or the ceiling or a fingernail. I knew, though, that the moment I stopped looking at them, they'd start staring at me again. I hated it when people noticed me—I worried they might see more than I wanted them to see.

We approached a large door at the opposite end of the cavern and I felt a surge of relief. We were finally going to get out of this place. Two Blendars, taller and much more muscular than most of the other creatures I'd seen in the cavern, flanked the door. While the others looked thin and transparent enough to see through, these two had more substance to them. I figured they must be the body builders of the Blendar race.

They acknowledged Darian with a nod, glanced at me— seemingly more out of curiosity than for security reasons— then stepped aside to let the three of us pass. Soon we were standing in another large cave lit by Starkinder lanterns. Most of the lamps gave off a soft, golden light like Darian's lantern. Some lamps, however, glowed blue, green, purple, or red, depending on the color of the glass in the lamp. I was standing inside a rainbow.

The walls and floor of the cave were as smooth and shiny as the inside of a clamshell. Bits of mica fixed within the rock sparkled like stars. Large, soft, brightly colored pillows spilled out from nooks hollowed out of the thick walls of the cave. Carvings similar to the ones I'd seen in the tunnel before the waterfall covered the walls, and I wondered what the symbols meant. Probably something welcoming, like death and destruction to all foreigners. I continued to gaze around the room when something moving close to the floor caught my eye. I looked down and blinked in disbelief. Tiny people, only a foot tall, bustled around the cave. But it wasn't their height that startled me, having seen the

Starkinders, it was their puffy, cotton ball-like hair, which came in fabulously rich shades of greens and reds and purples and blues.

The outfits varied from creature to creature, but each resembled the costumes one might have seen worn to a French ball in the early eighteenth century—very elaborate, with poofy cravats and billowing sleeves. With their round, pale faces and large circles of rouge decorating each cheek they looked like living dolls. Clearly, they were vain creatures, constantly primping and preening, fixing their decadently tall hair-dos or smoothing an invisible wrinkle in their costumes. All wore tiny shoes with heels and the constant sound of clicking echoed in the room as they crossed and re-crossed the stone floor. Full of self-impor-tance, they scurried about, carrying food and drink, tidying the room, talking amongst themselves. One of the dolls strode up to a crack in the wall, flattened itself to the width of a piece of paper and disappeared into the crevice, pulling its hair in after it.

In the middle of the room a regal creature sat in a stone chair, watching me with great interest. Her skin, white as summer clouds, was wrinkled like an elephant's hide. Like the other Blendars, she had large, piercing black eyes, though her curly hair was white. Unlike them, however, she was quite small, literally shrunken with age, so that her head seemed larger than it should. She wore a simple white dress and an indigo-colored cape draped about her shoul-ders. No shoes adorned her long, narrow feet, though a delicate metal bracelet encircled her left ankle like a snake.

Darian left us and went to her side, leaning down to whisper in her ear. I knew he was talking about me, mainly because he kept looking in my direction and scowling. For her part, the tiny woman nodded and smiled in response. Then, with an almost imperceptible raise of her hand,

Darian broke off his explanation and she beckoned to me and Loria.

When I hesitated, Darian took me by the elbow and guided me to the chair. He and Loria bowed down before the little being and I felt impelled to do the same. The tiny woman nodded and signaled for us to rise. She continued to study me for a few moments before saying in a rich, deep voice, "Welcome to Anaedor, Lavida Mors. I am Madrina, Leader of the Blendars. We have been waiting a long time for you to come." She watched me closely, her black eyes sparkling with wisdom and wit.

"But Madrina," Darian protested, "we do not know for sure—"

She held up a wizened hand. "We know nothing for sure, Darian."

"But she is too puny—" He quickly stopped himself, remembering that Madrina herself was quite tiny, but rallied his argument. "She is easily frightened."

"And you are not?" Madrina questioned him, a tolerant smile on her lips.

He straightened to his full height. "I am *not* easily frightened."

"Then why do you avoid the Piggerel Younglings like the purple plague?" Loria teased him.

Darian shrugged. "That is simply being rational. I avoid the little monsters so I do not have to deal with them."

"Is that not what we do with many of our fears?" Madrina asked him with a humorous gleam in her eye. She seemed to enjoy sparring with him.

Darian shook this off with a grimace. "With greatest respect, Madrina, I do not think this Human is—"

"What do you think, Lavida Mors?" Madrina interrupted him. Darian shut his mouth on the remaining words like a turtle snapping up a helpless minnow.

I looked around me, my eyes falling on one particularly flamboyant doll creature surrounded by a bevy of adoring fans. He appeared to be doing an Irish jig. "Think about what?" I hedged.

"You cannot be serious," Darian scoffed. "Madrina," he appealed to her, "please, this . . . Youngling . . . clearly lacks the intellect and commanding presence, not to mention—"

"This is all very strange to her, Darian. Give her time to accept what seems unacceptable to most of her kind." Madrina turned her attention back to me. "Do you think you are the *One*?"

I wasn't sure I liked the direction this interview was going. This whole "one" thing sounded a bit odd to me. Maybe they were trying to get me to admit I was the "one" who stole something of theirs, which, of course, I hadn't. Ms. Penny, on the other hand . . . I replied carefully, opting to sound clueless, playing off Darian's opinion of me. It was a method that often worked. "I really don't know what you're talking about, ma'am. I mean, the one what?"

"The *Prophecies* tell us that the *One* is the only being who has the ability to save Anaedor. This being will possess great powers—the powers of life and death—life for Anaedor, death for the evil that controls it."

Not a thief, then, but a savior, which sounded even worse to me. Every time I tried to "save" someone, I ended up paying for it. "Why do you think *I'm* the *One*?"

"Your name is written in the Book," Darian said.

"What book?" He only stared at me coldly. "Listen, I have no idea what you're talking about." I turned to his leader. "I'm afraid you've got the wrong person, Madrina. I'm really sorry." I shrugged, feeling as though all my insides were sweating.

She looked me in the eye. "Darian has told me about how you were able to see his blend, which should be impossible. About how you crossed Warrior's Walk like you had been doing it forever. He said you knew which door to take in the Room of Doors even though you had never been there. Those are all signs that you are not what you seem. Still, I want you to try something else. Will you?"

I tugged nervously at a strand of hair. "Um, sure."

"What did Darian say to make the gray stone disappear?" She clasped her hands together and awaited my response.

"Madrina!" Darian cried. "That spell is known only to Anaedorians. We cannot tell her—a *Human*!"

Madrina quieted him with a look. "I do not plan to tell her the password. I only wish to see if she recalls it."

I stole a quick look at Darian's face. His expression was blank, but underneath that bland visage, I could tell he was quivering with rage. He didn't like this at all. Loria was no help either. She had drifted away and was gossiping with a group of the tiny beings that milled about her, all vying for her attention. Why not do it? I thought. Having a good memory meant nothing. Lots of people had good memories. Besides, I wanted to wipe that arrogant look of disdain off Darian's face. I took a deep breath and began to speak words that were senseless to me:

Non perium dictor alla sim norasen.
Mey corium betay perius mingum.
En tutum sacre loresan moriseye.
Alaset!

As I spoke, a look of amazement flickered across Darian's face before he stifled it. Madrina, on the other hand, showed no sign of surprise, merely satisfaction. The room was quiet when I finished speaking. I met Madrina's intense eyes.

"What else can you do, Lavida Mors?"

I shrugged, wishing too late that I'd pretended not to

know the password. "Nothing," I mumbled. "I've just got a good memory."

She continued to study me and I started to fidget. She said finally, "I will do one last test, and then I will know for sure." She rooted around in a pocket of her voluminous cape and pulled something out. "Here it is. Now come closer," she beckoned. "I have something for you."

I stepped forward, but not without some hesitation. When someone says I have something for you, it could be a punch in the nose just as easily as a hug.

"The necklace you wear . . . please show it to me."

"How did you—" I clamped my mouth shut and pulled out the necklace. At this point, I wasn't sure I really wanted to know how Madrina had seen a necklace hidden beneath my turtleneck. I reluctantly took it off and held it out.

She leaned forward to examine the pendant attached to the thick, metal chain, but did not take it from me. An unusual design graced the round disc, which I'd never been able to interpret. Madrina's wrinkled forehead puckered even more as she studied it, then she straightened, a triumphant gleam in her eye. "Where did you get this necklace, Lavida?"

"From my Grandma Mors."

Madrina nodded, as though I'd told her what she'd expected to hear. She opened her hand to reveal a round, metal object. It was a pendant similar to the one I wore, complete with an odd design. She placed the one in her hand on top of mine and squeezed tightly. A startling hiss rent the air.

"Now look," she commanded as she lifted her hand.

I looked down and stared in wonder. The two discs had melted together to form one. A new picture decorated the shiny pendant. It was a face.

My face.

"We have our proof!" Madrina exclaimed, lifting my arm in the air like the referee for the winning boxer.

I quickly pulled my arm down, embarrassed and afraid of what this meant. Behind me, the room roared to life, the tiny creatures buzzing with excitement. "I simply cannot believe it!" one said quite loudly.

I spun around only to see a swarm of little people scattering like mice. I turned back around and gingerly took the necklace Madrina was holding out to me. I put it on, sliding the pendant beneath my turtleneck. I couldn't imagine how Madrina had made my image appear on the necklace pendant or why my expression exuded the confidence and strength of a warrior.

Darian looked sick. "If it would please you, Madrina, I would like to have a private word with you."

Madrina studied him prudently, then nodded. "Lavida?"

I took the hint and stepped away from her chair. I looked around to find Loria for company, then realized she had joined Darian and Madrina. So I waited alone, eyeing the little creatures that had gathered about me. They all stared boldly at me and whispered to each other. I made a funny face, and they all stopped whispering and drew back a step. I did it again to the same effect. I was about to try my death grimace on them when something jumped onto my shoulder, startling me. What was Ms. Penny doing here?

But it wasn't Ms. Penny. My visitor was one of the doll creatures, and he was sitting on my shoulder like he had a right to be there.

"What are you doing?"

The creature grinned mischievously, his bright red lips not much larger than one of Ian's pimples. His puffy, dark purple hair, the color of royal robes, rose majestically into the air. His narrow nose tilted upward at the end—a ski jump for ants. His pale green eyes assessed me with the thoroughness of a horse breeder. I recognized him as the clog dancer.

"I am here to serve you, Mademoiselle Mors. Judging by your atrocious hairdo and your inability to dress yourself in anything approaching appealing, you are in *dire* need of fashion help. But never fear, Vesuvius is here! I will show you that there is hope, even for one as fashion-impaired as yourself."

I peered more closely at the little imp perched on my shoulder. Lace and ruffles adorned the green velvet suit he wore and sparkly buckles bedecked the high-heeled shoes that dangled below him.

"Thank you," I replied. "But since I don't plan on joining the circus any time soon, I don't think I'll be needing your services."

The creature snorted. "You do not know what you are saying. But then, you *are* Human, and Humans typically are as dull-witted as the dead." The others tittered at this jab. "But, despite your cruel words, I shall take mercy on you, sparing you from that fate worse than death—a bad wardrobe." The others snickered again, and I started to speak up. "No, no," he held up his hand. "It is too late to protest. If you had wanted me gone, you should have shoved me off your shoulder before so much as a word had passed through these perfect lips of mine."

He leaped to the ground and stared up at me, his tiny hands planted on narrow hips. "Remember, I am called Vesuvius. We shall meet again." Madrina called my name, and he slipped away into the crowd of little creatures all still staring up at me.

"Return to me, Lavida Mors," Madrina called. I rushed back to stand before her, gladly abandoning my new "friends." "Take some refreshment for your journey back."

One of the little creatures presented a darkly polished wooden serving tray upon which sat a shiny silver cup. Warily I took the cup and examined the dark liquid inside. The drink smelled of spices—cinnamon and nutmeg, and a hint of vanilla. The scent made me feel lightheaded. "Drink," Madrina commanded. "It will give you strength."

"But what about—"

"Later," Madrina shushed me. "For now, just drink."

Without any intention of doing so, I found myself taking a sip of the liquid. The strange brew tasted warm and rich and went down smoothly. It vibrated in my mouth, over my tongue, down my throat. I sighed contentedly and drank the remainder of the cup.

I felt sleepy. It had to be late. I wondered how long I'd been gone.

The urgency to get back to my room came upon me like a crashing wave.

Home . . . to Portal Manor.

I had to return . . .

CHAPTER FOURTEEN
REVENGE IS SWEET

The next day, I awoke to Ms. Penny tugging at my ear, and none too gently. This was her subtle way of saying, "Feed me, you lazy biped!"

I groaned and rolled out of bed. Bright light streamed through the window facing the front yard. I crossed the warm floorboards and looked out. The sun was shining today. The light shimmered and reflected off the dewdrops on the green grass below. I stretched luxuriously in the warm light while Ms. Penny did the same, her mouth opening wide as she yawned. I don't think I'd ever slept so well in my life. My body felt relaxed and my mind was free of worries.

Then it hit me, along with a tidal wave of fear—memories of the night before. I pinched the cool cotton of my pink pajamas between shaking fingers. I didn't remember coming back home and changing into them. Maybe I'd finished reading my fantasy book, fell fast asleep, and then dreamed about Anaedor, a fantastical world filled with mythical creatures like in my book. I shook my head, confused and uneasy, then glanced over at where the hidden door was supposed to be. All my trunks were in place. I ran to my dresser. The clothes I thought I'd changed into before going to Anaedor were folded neatly in my drawer, freshly washed and no longer smelling of Barg.

Definitely a dream, I decided, though the most realistic one I'd ever had. I remembered everything so clearly, every detail. The strange sights, the different sounds in the caves, Darian's strong hand gripping my arm. Most dreams don't work like that; they often jump all over the place, typically fading upon awakening.

Not this one.

Swallowing hard, I hurriedly dressed and ran down to eat breakfast. Mrs. Dooley frowned when I didn't stop to talk, but I just couldn't. She saw too much and would probably try to get out of me what had happened. In the car, I kept staring at Ian, willing him to confess his part in this latest incident. Feeling my angry eyes on him, he turned around and gave me a look that obviously questioned my sanity. Mrs. Keeper seemed as chipper and disheveled as ever as she babbled about what a relief it was to have an empty house again. If I hadn't been so distracted by my own chaotic thoughts, I might have asked what the heck she meant by that.

At school, I had a hard time concentrating. I needed to see Ellie. I needed to tell her what had happened. She was so no-nonsense, I knew she would tell me exactly what I needed to hear: that I had a crazy imagination and of course had only been dreaming. When I went to join her for lunch, though, I couldn't find her. Feeling increasingly sick,

I ate my lunch quickly, then hurried to Simmons Hall to pick up my books for my afternoon classes. I'd seen Ellie earlier that morning, from a distance, so I knew she was at school. Maybe she'd gotten sick. *Or maybe she's avoiding you*, an evil little voice said as I slipped down the clearing hallway.

"Fetch me my ballet slippers and my dance clothes," a peremptory voice demanded. It was Fiona. I paused, pulling back around the corner so she couldn't see me.

"What's your combo?"

An annoyed sigh. "Can't you remember anything, Phoebe? I've told it to you enough times! Three stupid numbers! 19-30-23. A two-year-old could memorize that."

"Sorry, Fi. You know how I am with numbers."

"I am surrounded by imbeciles," Fiona bemoaned, rushing past me. She was clutching a moss-green bag. Ellie's bag.

I waited for her to disappear before peeking around the corner. Her friend, Phoebe, was at Fiona's locker, pulling out a bag of clothes. I didn't see Ellie anywhere and she didn't come to any classes that afternoon. I wondered what had happened, how Fiona had managed to get Ellie's purse. I wondered and I worried.

At Portal Manor that night I locked all my doors, left the lamp on, and plotted.

The next morning, Mrs. Keeper dropped me off early at school as I'd asked. Ian wasn't happy about it, but then again, Ian wasn't ever happy about anything. I made a visit to the art room before heading over to

Simmons Hall. Once inside, I put my plan into action.

At lunch, I spotted Ellie sitting alone at a table in the corner of the cafeteria. Keeping a sharp eye out for Fiona and her groupies, I hurried over to sit next to her.

"Hey." She was staring morosely at her lunch tray. "Trade you my green Martian potato salad for a cookie? I know you have cookies."

"I need to show you something," I said. "Quick."

Ellie eyed me warily. "What is it?"

"It's a surprise."

"I'm having a bad day, Lavida. Don't make it worse."

"It's a good surprise. Come on."

She left her tray where it was and followed me. We entered the nearly empty hall and I quietly made my way toward Fiona's locker, with Ellie trailing reluctantly behind me.

"She took my purse," she told me.

"I know. Now be quiet." I found a place to hide where we wouldn't be seen.

Ellie looked at me strangely. "What's this about, Lavida?"

"You'll see."

A moment later, Fiona, as if on cue, entered the hallway with a couple of her friends.

"I could kill her," Ellie growled behind me.

"Just wait." I focused on the group, putting all my attention on them, willing everything I had into making this work.

"Get my dance bag out of my locker," Fiona ordered.

"No," her number one lackey, Phoebe, replied, her hand flying up to her mouth in shock.

"*What?*"

"I, um, well . . . no, I can't."

Fiona's lips curled into a sneer. "Have you lost your

mind, Phoebe Denton?"

"Yes, I have." Phoebe's heavily mascaraed eyes widened, then she clamped her lips tightly together.

"Fine, I'll get it myself. But don't think I won't remember this."

Scowling, she set down her—Ellie's—bag and spun the dial on her locker.

Behind me, Ellie grew restless.

"Wait for it," I told her.

Fiona yanked open the locker and the bucket I'd planted there flew out at her, drenching her and her toadies with thick, oily black paint. They screeched in horror, running around, hands in the air, paint still flying.

"What did you just do?" Ellie hissed, though her expression was delighted.

"I'm going to kill Ellie Maguire!" Fiona roared. "With my bare hands!"

"Ellie didn't do it," Phoebe said, her mouth opening and closing like a wooden puppet. "I did."

"What!" Fiona screeched. "I'm going to kill you!" She launched herself at Phoebe.

Ellie and I smothered giggles as we watched the two wrestle each other, slipping and sliding in the oily mess. Once they went to the floor, fists and teeth full of each other's hair, I grabbed Ellie's arm and pulled her away. Heading out a back door, we burst into roars of laughter.

"How did you do that?" Ellie finally wheezed. "I mean, I assume you set up the paint, but how did you get Phoebe to confess?"

I shrugged. "It's something she's probably wanted to do for a long time. She gets tired of Fiona bossing her around. I just helped her achieve her dream."

Ellie sobered. "How do you know all that about Phoebe?"

I turned away. "I might have overheard her . . ." *thinking*.

"Wasn't it weird how the paint sprayed out like that? Like it was attached to a hose? That was totally freaky."

"Totally." My hands started to tremble. "But nothing a rope and some springs can't manage. Hey, there's still time for lunch. Mrs. Dooley made mine, so I'm sure there's enough to split."

"What did she make?" she demanded, distracted as I'd hoped.

"I don't know. Let's go see."

We found a spot under a tree where I quickly divvied up my ham and cheese sandwich, pickles, banana and three cookies, with lemonade to drink. We sat in companionable silence as we ate.

"Say, listen," Ellie said in between bites. "My parents have to attend a gallery opening this weekend in New York City, and I persuaded them to let me and Eddie stay at home with our housekeeper, Annie. We can come over to your house then."

"Oh, okay." Inside, my heart soared. Ellie must not have guessed my true role in the Fiona paint dousing. "I could ask Mrs. Dooley if she'd make lunch for us."

"I was hoping you'd say that. If the rest of her cooking is anything like this sandwich, I'm moving in with you, haunted house or not." She took another bite and moaned in ecstasy. "This is *so* good!"

"Your mom's okay with you coming over?"

"She doesn't know. If she did, she probably wouldn't let us come . . . because of all the rumors, you know. She's kind of protective."

"So what *are* the rumors?"

"You're probably not going to want to hear this," she said, licking mayo off her fingers, "but better from me than the other girls here."

"Hear what?"

"You have to remember that I've never seen anything myself."

I took a deep breath. Apparently, this wasn't going to be pretty. "Spill it."

She took a bite of her pickle. "Remember that I told you Portal Manor was haunted?" I nodded. "Well, people have said they've heard weird sounds coming from the house, like howling and stuff. A few years ago some kids managed to sneak over one of the walls. They claimed that a wild animal with sharp teeth and hooves, of all things, chased after them." She paused when she saw the color drain from my face. "I think it's a load of hooey, myself. Just a bunch of people with too much time on their hands making up stories."

I shook my head, wondering exactly how much I should tell her. "The other day, the same animal that chased those kids might have chased me too. It certainly didn't look like anything I've ever seen."

Ellie took another bite of pickle. "Are you serious? Go on."

Encouraged, I leaned closer and told her about every-thing that had happened to me since I'd arrived at Portal Manor, leaving out a few details that I thought might hurt more than help. "It seemed so real, Ellie," I ended my story. "It had to be a dream, though, right?" I laughed nervously. "Or someone playing a joke on me?"

She took a sip of lemonade and shrugged. "I'd go with the joke theory. But either way, we should check it out. Eddie will love that, and I'll finally get to meet Ian face to face." She grinned and pushed her dark blue glasses, which matched the color of her tights, back up her nose.

I frowned. "You know Ian?"

Ellie's pink face lit up. "Last year this bully kept picking on Eddie while he was waiting for Daddy and me to come pick him up after school. One day, Ian saw what was going on and told the bully to get lost. They got into a fight and Ian totally made a mess of the other guy, even though the guy easily outweighed Ian by a hundred pounds. Then," she paused dramatically, "he waited with Eddie until we got there. All the guys in town think Ian's really tough. I think he's gorgeous, don't you?"

"No!"

She stared at me reproachfully. "You need glasses, girl."

"Maybe I can't get past his personality long enough to get a good look at him. He's my number one suspect for the joke theory, you know."

Ellie shook her head. "You are *so* wrong about him, Lavida." She sighed dreamily. "He's not a troublemaker, he's a hero."

Really, we had to be talking about two different people here.

Her over-sized glasses slid down her nose. She pushed them back up. "Just make sure you introduce us."

"So Ian is the reason you're coming over?" My stomach roiled. I should've known she'd have an ulterior motive. Maybe she and Eddie were in on the practical joke, too. Maybe they had disguised themselves as Loria and Darian—though perhaps that was stretching it a bit.

"I'm coming for the lunch," Ellie replied easily. "Ian's an added bonus."

I had to laugh. "At least you're honest. Maybe I'll get Ian to serve us."

"Without his shirt?" she asked hopefully.

"No!"

At that moment, the lunch bell rang and we packed up, laughing hysterically.

While riding home with Ian and Mrs. Keeper that afternoon, I realized I was really starting to like Ellie. She was interesting, funny, and she told it like she saw it. She was different from anyone I'd ever met.

The rest of the week flew by quickly. I did my homework, snooped around the house, and talked to Ellie at school. No one tried to get at me through the secret door. In fact, I was starting to doubt its existence. If some kind of opening was there, I couldn't find it. Not even a crack. The only frustrating part was that every time I tried to explore the house, Ian popped up. And every time I ran into him, he got all cranky on me. After the third or fourth time, I couldn't help but think he was purposefully following me around. But why? To make sure I didn't run away, I supposed.

Or maybe he was lonely. If I had his personality, I'd be lonely, too. Maybe I should tell him that stalking people isn't a good way to make friends. Yet, even when I was sure Ian wasn't around, I still had the sense that I was being watched. I didn't feel eyes on me all the time, but every once in a while I'd get that prickly sensation a person gets while being observed. The impression made me nervous enough to put my explorations on hold until Ellie and Eddie came.

Friday night I asked Mrs. Keeper about having them over to visit.

"Of course you may, dear," she replied with an air of distraction before scurrying off on yet another mysterious errand. Something was on my guardian's mind, but I had no clue what it might be.

Later that evening, when I asked Mrs. Dooley about what might be on Mrs. Keeper's mind, the older woman pretended ignorance, then changed the subject to what I would like to have for lunch when my friends came to visit. We spent an hour thinking up decadent ideas and baking. As Mrs. Dooley pulled out a tray of freshly baked chocolate chip cookies, which happen to be my favorite, I asked her who Ian was.

"Ian? Why I believe Mrs. Keeper took him in. Adopted him, actually," she said, sliding another sheet of cookies into the oven.

"Oh. What happened to his parents?"

The cook shrugged as she removed the cookies one by one from the hot tray. After waiting patiently a few seconds for the cookies to cool, I grabbed one and ate the warm treat in three chewy bites.

"I don't know," she answered, scraping the dregs off the pan. "Never asked."

She handed the pan to me and I covered it with fresh balls of cookie dough. I tried again to pump her for more information about Ian and Mrs. Keeper and this place, but she was too good, deflecting my questions like a goalie guarding the net. Her evasion made me wonder what the people living in this house were trying to hide from me.

And, once again, I began to question staying here.

CHAPTER FIFTEEN
THE PLAN

Finally, it was Saturday. My anticipation of Ellie and Eddie's visit had built to a feverish pitch. They'd be arriving any moment and I couldn't stay still. I kept pacing back and forth outside the gate, waiting for them to come. The plan, concocted by Ellie, was to start our day off having lunch. We'd need our energy, she explained, if we wanted to explore the house.

Loud beeps greeted me as the twins pulled up to the gate on their scooters. They removed their helmets, both grinning like crazy. They seemed to be looking forward to the visit as much as I was, which was reassuring. Still, I didn't want to appear too pathetic or needy.

"Bring your scooters inside. Mrs. Dooley is making lunch as we speak."

"Where's Ms. Penny?" Eddie asked as he wheeled his

scooter through the doorway.

"She's with Mrs. Dooley in the kitchen. I think I've been abandoned."

Ellie propped her bike against the wall. "Let's focus on more important things," she said, scanning the yard. "Where's Ian?"

I shrugged as I locked the small door and pocketed the key in my blazer pocket. "I think he went away for the weekend."

Ellie's jaw dropped. "You've got to be kidding me!"

I started laughing. "You should see your face." She gave me the evil eye, which only made me laugh harder. I held up my hands to surrender before Ellie made good on her threat to pull out my hair. "I think he's working on jobs around the house. I'm sure we'll stumble across him when we start our exploring."

"That's better," she said as she twirled awkwardly in front of me. "I'm wearing a brand new outfit." It was a pink velour jogging suit with matching pink glasses. A large pink handbag, smothered by red polka dots, completed the ensemble.

I looked the outfit up and down. "Well, he certainly won't have any trouble spotting you."

Eddie howled with laughter and Ellie crossed her arms. "Like you're a fashion queen." She eyed my faded jeans with the frayed cuffs and my over-sized burgundy blazer.

"What are you saying? Don't you know this is the latest haute couture?" I strutted about, swinging my head and hips back and forth as I headed down the gravel driveway. Ellie burst out laughing so hard that she started snorting. Then Eddie and I started laughing at her, and were still laughing when we passed by the front steps.

"Those lion statues are huge," Eddie exclaimed, wiping a tear off his cheek. "I need a pair of those in front of my bedroom. *Beware all ye who dare enter.*"

Ellie waved at the air in front of her. "Yeah, beware because your room smells like dirty socks and farts."

Eddie beamed as though his sister had given him a compliment. "Maybe I need a statue of someone holding their nose."

"You guys are weird," I told them as we piled through the small door and into the conservatory, but they weren't listening. They were looking around the glass room, clearly in awe.

"That's an African grey parrot," Eddie shouted, pointing up at a dark-gray bird. "And a macaw!" He ran around the large room, pointing and shouting with excitement. "This is better than Biology!"

"I can't believe we're related," Ellie muttered as she wandered over to the pool. She found an open spot between the potted plants, set her pink bag on the concrete and leaned over the wall to stick her hand in the pool. "Not bad. You could swim in this." She nodded her approval. "This place is fabulous."

I fished a large, shiny leaf out of the pool. "When I first arrived at Portal Manor, I didn't want to like it, but it's hard not to."

"You should have a party here," Ellie said. "You'd be the talk of the town."

I shrugged. "I don't know anyone other than you guys to invite. It'd be a pretty lame party."

Ellie sighed. "I don't know anyone I'd want to invite, either. How depressing. Hey, I've got an idea that will cheer me up. Let's go eat." She grabbed her bag and stood up. "I've been a saint all morning and I'm sick of it. If I don't eat soon, I'm going to start chewing on these plants."

"Dinner is served," a voice announced from the kitchen door. Mrs. Dooley waved us in, then disappeared.

"That was Mrs. Dooley," I explained in response to the startled look on Ellie's face. "She has a way of knowing what's on people's minds. Don't you think that's kinda crazy?"

"Definitely, but I doubt that's what she's doing. Anyone who cooks like she does has got to be sane." She looked around and I ducked my head to hide my reddening cheeks. I had been hoping for a different answer. "Eddie! Get down from there. Let's go. I'm hungry."

Eddie jumped down from the tree branch he was balancing on. "You're always hungry," he replied when he joined us. "This place is so cool, Lavida. Someone actually planted belladonna. That's a poisonous plant, you know . . . in case you ever wanted to dispose of someone. Can I live here?"

Ellie pushed him ahead of her. "Like she'd want you around all the time, you big goober."

"You can visit whenever you want," I told him.

He sighed wistfully. "I could learn more from this place than I could in all my science classes, even the advanced ones."

Ellie shook her head. "You are such a nerd, Eddie."

We clattered into the kitchen, where we found a magnificent lunch waiting for us. Mrs. Dooley bustled back and forth from counter to table, adding more treats to the already overburdened table. Monstrous ham and cheese sandwiches, whole dill pickles, bowls of fresh fruit, pretzels and chips, large mugs of chocolate milk, deviled eggs, fried chicken legs, hunks of cheddar cheese, chunky potato salad and a plate of chocolate chip cookies beckoned to us.

The expression on Ellie's face was priceless. "All this is for us?" she asked, her voice filled with the same wonder a child has when seeing Disneyland for the first time. It was very touching.

"Whatever you can eat," Mrs. Dooley told her. "And

you'd better eat up. You're going to be needing your energy for exploring the house later on. The number of rooms in this place boggles the mind, especially when you have to clean all of them." She winked at me. "Don't worry, dear. If anyone asks, I know nothing about what you kids will be up to this afternoon. Now eat. You three are so skinny you're liable to disappear any moment." She clucked and shook her head as she herded us toward the table.

Ellie stopped mid-step to cast a worshipful glance back at Mrs. Dooley. It was obvious the Irish woman had made a friend for life. No one had ever even pretended to imply Ellie Maguire was skinny. She read the quote on Mrs. Dooley's apron aloud—*Don't treat me any differently than you would the Queen*—and grinned. They were two of a kind.

Mrs. Dooley, along with Ms. Penny (who mooched off everyone), joined us to eat. For an hour, she entertained us with stories of the village in Ireland where she'd grown up, many of which related to her job as cook for the most powerful family in the county. The wistful look in her eyes at times told me she missed the Emerald Isle.

"Now don't you be thinking I don't appreciate my job here," she said abruptly. "Working here at Portal Manor is an honor and a privilege. I'd not work anywhere else in the world."

"But still," I pursued, scraping the last of the potato salad off my plate, "to leave your family?" I'd give anything to have a big family who cared what happened to me.

Mrs. Dooley set down her fork. "This job is like none other, Lavida. Someday you'll understand that . . . but not today. Today you have your own job to do and not much time to do it in."

"That was delicious, Mrs. Dooley," Ellie moaned with satisfaction. "I'm glad you're here, even if Lavida isn't." She smirked at me.

"Very funny. I don't want you to go, Mrs. Dooley."

She laughed. "I know, dearie. Now be off with you. I've some work to be doing, myself." She stood and shooed at us with her apron.

Eddie was halfway out the door when Ellie volunteered to help clear the table. He froze in mid-stride and turned back to the kitchen with a guilty look on his face. "We'd love to help," he forced himself to offer.

Mrs. Dooley laughed heartily at the look on his face. "No, no. You run along. I'll do my chores all by my lone-some." She winked at Eddie. "Now scoot."

"Thanks, Mrs. Dooley," Eddie shouted over his shoulder. "You're a culinary genius!"

Mrs. Dooley chuckled, then started singing as she gathered up dishes from the kitchen table.

"Coming, Ms. Penny?" I called. The raccoon violently shook her furry head. She was still eating her lunch. I sighed. Dissed for a melon.

Back in the conservatory, we climbed up onto the pool balcony and made plans about what to do next.

"We're going to have to be rather sneaky," I said. I don't think Mrs. Keeper wants me snooping around the house."

"So what are we doing, exactly?" Ellie asked. She rooted through her handbag and pulled out a tin of cinnamon-flavored hard candy. She held it out to us, and Eddie and I each took a piece.

"Well," I said as I fiddled with my shoestring, "I figured we could look around the house, maybe search for clues as to why my dad has stayed away from here so long."

"Ellie told me what's been happening to you lately," Eddie said. "My theory is that someone is trying to scare you. But I don't think it's Ian," he hastily added after Ellie elbowed him in the ribs.

I looked up at him, surprised. "Then who?"

"Maybe people here don't want you finding out what they're up to, like an illegal smuggling operation." His eyes lit up at the idea. "They could be drugging you. That's why you've been having strange dreams."

I shook my head. "I can't picture Mrs. Keeper drugging me or dealing on the black market." I paused. "But she *is* busy a lot." The more I thought about it, the more I realized I knew nothing about what Mrs. Keeper did all day. Mrs. Dooley knew something, but she wasn't talking. "I don't really think it's likely to be illegal smuggling, but she's up to something," I concluded, "no doubt about that."

Eddie scratched his head, spiking up red tufts of hair. "Whatever she's up to could be related to your dad not coming here."

I drew in a deep breath. Could the two be connected? "This is all so weird," I sighed in frustration.

"What's weird is that I haven't seen Ian yet," Ellie threw in her two cents, popping another candy into her mouth.

I ignored her less-than-subtle hint. "I guess we should get started. I haven't explored the second floor at all. I think there's an attic, too; at least it looks that way from the outside."

"What about the two towers?" Eddie asked.

"Ian lives in one of the towers." After I'd accidentally tried to unlock the wrong door one evening after supper, he told me that this particular door led up to *his* tower room, which was much bigger and better than mine, by the way.

"Ian lives in a tower?" Ellie cried. She twirled a red curl around her finger, her expression distant. "That's *so* romantic."

Eddie made a face. "Is that all you ever think about, Ellie? Romance? Towers were built for defensive purposes, not for romantic ones. At best, they symbolized strength and closeness to God."

Ellie reached over and spiked up his spiky hair some more. "Whatever, Eddie. I still think they're romantic. Haven't you ever read Tennyson's *The Lady of Shalott . . . ?*"—she turned to me and I shook my head—". . . about the lady who lived in a tower and pined away for her beloved Sir Lancelot . . . ?"—still blank on my part—". . . then left the tower and floated down the river to die? Don't you guys *read?*"

"That *does* sound romantic," Eddie replied dryly. "The idea of someone dying makes my heart go all aquiver." Ellie attempted to biff him on the head, but he ducked out of the way. "So who lives in the other tower?" he asked.

I tried to be cool about it, but failed. It wasn't every day a person gets to brag about living in a tower. "You're looking at her."

"No way!" they both gasped at the same time.

"I'll show it to you after we get done exploring, which we should probably start soon. I was hoping to get through both floors of the house, and I don't even know how to reach them. I think I know where to start, though. Follow me."

I guided them to the door that led into the Great Hall, listening to Eddie and Ellie bemoan the fact that their house didn't have a tower. When we entered the large room, they forgot about the tower.

"It's like a castle," Ellie breathed at last, head tilted back to better see the entire room. "And you, Lavida, are the damsel in distress." She could barely contain her enthusiasm, clapping her hands excitedly. Eddie pretended to gag.

"I'm going to have to agree with Eddie on that," I said. "I'm definitely not in distress, thank you very much." Well, that wasn't entirely true. "But if I did happen to be in distress, who would be my Prince Charming riding to my rescue?"

"Ian, of course," Ellie replied confidently. Then she frowned. The idea of Ian as *my* hero instead of hers seemed to rankle.

"No thanks. You can have him." The frown disappeared. "How about you, Eddie? You want to be my knight?" I fluttered my eyelashes at him and his cheeks turned red.

"I think we should just get back to business," he said, tugging at his ear.

I laughed. It was hard not to tease Eddie; he was so serious all the time. "Oh, fine. We'll get back to business." I looked around at all the doors.

"Let's try that one," Ellie said, pointing to a red door in the corner of the room. "It matches my outfit."

Eddie was the first to reach it. He turned the knob, and to my surprise, it didn't resist, opening to reveal a staircase leading upward. Before I could say anything, Eddie had hurried up the stairs. I glanced over at Ellie. She rolled her eyes as she set her bag on a battered leather chair and went after him. I quickly followed.

What we saw when we reached the top of the stairs was

bling the trunk of a tree. Several corridors branched off the
hall, running willy-nilly, with no rhyme or reason to their
layout. I suspected that each passage would have its own
"twigs," quadrupling the number of halls into the hundreds. It would take forever to navigate all the passages,
much less explore each room. This place really *was* bigger
than it looked.

Like Anaedor.

I shuddered and pushed *that* thought out of my mind.

Ellie groaned. "This place is huge! Where do we start?"

"I guess we start at the beginning. Eddie?" I called,
growing worried. "Eddie?"

He didn't answer.

CHAPTER SIXTEEN
THE CALM BEFORE THE STORM

"Edgar Allen Maguire," Ellie bellowed through cupped hands. "Get your butt back here!"

"Shhh, Ellie! We don't want Mrs. Keeper to know we're up here."

"Oops." She clapped a hand over her mouth. "Forgot."

Something crashed to the floor and we ran to investigate. I peeked inside an open room on my left. There was no sign of Eddie in the bright, gaudy room, though I recognized the large dress hanging from the canopy frame.

"I think this is Mrs. Dooley's room. Let's go."

We ran down the hallway and soon found another open door. Peering inside, we discovered what looked to be another bedroom, though this one was more masculine. Glass beakers and jars filled with powders and liquids packed the shelves on one wall, a small chemistry set and an assortment of animal skulls sat on a table close to the door, mayonnaise jars containing dead insects were lined up on the dresser and a thick layer of dust covered everything, telling me that no one had been in the room for quite some time, not even Mrs. Dooley.

"Oh, there you are," Eddie called, emerging from a wardrobe. "Just checking things out."

"Oh, Eddie, I think you've found my dad's old bedroom. I could kiss you!" A horrified expression flashed across Eddie's face as he backed away.

"You're gonna make me break out in hives. We need to be serious." He turned around in a circle, his eyes taking in the décor. "Are you sure this is your dad's room?"

"No, it's the bathroom," Ellie snipped. "Of course, it's his room, dorkwad." She turned to me. "Didn't you tell me your dad is a scientist?"

I nodded. "He's a biochemistry professor."

"Biochemistry?" Eddie echoed. "Wow."

"Well, there you go. And if my deductive skills are working properly," she went on, sounding pleased with herself as she looked around, "I would have to say that this was the room of a budding scientist."

"I can't argue with that," I said.

"Let's get to it, then." Ellie headed for a shelf.

"Well, I guess we could search everything, though I feel weird going through my dad's stuff. I wasn't allowed to touch anything in his office back home." Not that that had stopped me. But here I had witnesses.

"Nonsense," Ellie replied decisively. "If this stuff was so important to him, he wouldn't have left it behind."

"Maybe he didn't have time to bring it with him," Eddie suggested.

"What do you mean?" I asked him, startled.

Eddie shrugged and turned over a dusty jar to look at

the bottom of it. "You said he didn't want to come back. What if someone chased him away?"

"Maybe it's the same someone, or *something*, that's trying to chase *me* away." I sat down on the neatly made bed. "But that doesn't make sense; my dad wouldn't have let me come here if the place was dangerous, would he?"

Eddie shook his head, picking up a large conch shell. "Beats me. He's your dad. Maybe he didn't think *you'd* be in danger." He tilted the seashell sideways and then put it up to his ear.

That wasn't what I wanted to hear. A feeling of melancholy settled over me. Could it be that my dad had knowingly sent his own daughter into danger? Dispatch the troublesome girl to a place where something bad could happen to her and, voilà, problem solved. I had to find out the real reason he'd sent me to Portal Manor. The answer to this question was the true mystery here, one I had a terrible feeling I'd better solve soon.

A huge crack of thunder suddenly shook the house. We ran to the window. The sky grew dark with storm clouds, and the wind thrashed the trees about like tall grass. Lightning flashed and thunder boomed again, rattling the windows.

"Awesome!" Eddie exclaimed, peering out. "A storm's coming. Did you know Lender's Stream floods if it rains more than two inches an hour in a three-hour time span? That's the stream you cross on the main road into Bellemont," he explained. I remembered passing over it on trips to and from school. "The water is so high right now that the next big rain could make the road impassable."

"We should get going, Eddie," Ellie spoke up. "Sorry, Lavida, but I'm not getting stuck here overnight."

I didn't blame her. I turned around to head for the door when I heard someone shouting. I cupped my hand to my ear. "I think that's Ian."

Ellie's eyes brightened. "Ian? We'd better go see who, I mean, *what* he wants."

"I thought you wanted to go home," Eddie said.

"And get all wet?" Ellie glared at him. "No, thank you. Now move it or lose it, you two." Ellie pushed past us like a linebacker and started back down the hallway. We clattered down the steps and into the Great Hall just as Ian was coming out of the conservatory. I managed to close the door behind me before he noticed where we'd been.

"There you are," he said. "I've been looking for you for the last twenty minutes." He ran a hand through his wild hair. "Mrs. K. asked if you guys could help out. The hurricane that everyone thought was heading out to sea has changed its mind. It's coming straight for us."

"I'll help," Ellie and Eddie both volunteered at the same time.

"Cool." Ian looked down at Eddie. "Your name's Eddie, right? We're in the same grade, aren't we?"

Eddie nodded.

Ian snapped his fingers. "Yeah! You're the smart kid. You can help me figure out which windows to tape." Eddie beamed at him, thrilled to be noticed in a positive way for once. "You come with me. Lavida, you and—"

"Ellie," she interrupted, pushing her way forward. "I'm Eddie's older sister."

Eddie shot her a look. "By only ten minutes," he muttered.

She stepped between him and Ian. "What can I do to help?" She fluttered her carrot-colored eyelashes at him and smiled with her mouth closed, probably to hide her braces.

Ian ran his hand through his hair again. I could almost see Ellie's heart beat faster as she watched him. He frowned. "I guess you two can go help Mrs. Dooley. She'll tell you what you need to do. Let's go, Eddie."

Ellie did not look happy as the boys hurried away. Then she smiled broadly, her brace-bedecked teeth gleaming in the firelight. "You know, I think we're going to have to stay the night." She rubbed her hands together and laughed wickedly.

"Here?" I squeaked. My backbone quivered at the idea. What if she saw something weird? What if Darian and Loria came back?

"I'll call Annie and let her know."

Her cell phone didn't get coverage at Portal Manor, which she discovered after several frantic attempts. I reluctantly showed her to the old-fashioned instrument sitting on a table in the corner of the Great Hall. As it turned out, the antique was the only phone in the house—that I could find anyway.

While Ellie made her call, I decided that I would have to phone my dad today. He should be back from his conference by now. But I didn't want Ellie overhearing me ask him why he'd sent me here; it was too embarrassing. Nor did I want her to know I was trying to leave Bellemont. I would have to sneak away later to make the call.

"Annie was more than happy to let us stay," Ellie said smugly as she hung up the phone. "She's probably got her boyfriend there with her. Now let's go find Mrs. Dooley."

We spent the rest of the day listening to the radio for updates on the status of Hurricane Jackson in between filling water jugs, digging out spare candles and lanterns in case the electricity went out, and taping east-facing windows in the conservatory alongside Eddie and Ian. Ellie loved this last activity. She whispered to me that handing Ian the tape was a surefire way of getting to touch his hand.

I rolled my eyes.

Unable to concentrate any longer on what I was doing, I decided to go make the phone call to my dad. I dreaded doing it, but it had to be done. I'd be a basket case until I spoke to him. I told everyone I had to go to the bathroom and scurried out of the room.

In the Great Hall, I dialed my home number with a shaking hand. The phone rang three times before someone picked up.

"Hello?" a gravelly voice answered.

Oh, crud. The Toad. "It's me, Lavida. Let me talk to my dad."

"He only got back last night, Video. He doesn't want to be bothered with your problems."

"Just let me talk to him, or I'll blow the whistle on your little charade," I threatened, sounding as serious as I knew how. "You know, pretending you think he's the greatest thing since the invention of sliced bread so you can get your filthy paws on some of the profits when his next invention hits big—"

"Oh, all right. But make it quick." I heard him bang down the phone and set off to find my father. He wasn't the brightest bull in the barn and, consequently, not a very good student, which was why he had to suck up to other people to get anywhere in life. But, he was wily; I had to give him that.

"Viddie? Is that you?"

"Dad?" He sounded tired, and maybe a little bit disappointed that I was calling. My hopes for figuring out his motives for sending me here plummeted, but I took a deep breath and plunged right into the heart of the matter. "I was wondering if I could come back home now."

There was silence on the other end of the phone, then a sigh. "I thought we'd already discussed all this."

"I know, I know." I looked over my shoulder. "But there

are some strange things going on here, Dad. I don't think I should stay."

"What do you mean by strange things?" he asked sharply.

"I don't know," I hedged. If I told him the truth, he'd have proof that I was crazy, and then I might end up in a worse place than this. "Spooky stuff."

There was a long silence on his end. "It's just that imagination of yours, Viddie," he said finally. "You know you're always seeing things that aren't there."

"How can you say that?" I cried.

"I'm not saying you're lying, Viddie," he soothed. "It's just that . . . well, you *know* you have an active imagination. All your teachers have said that about you."

"Fine. I have an active imagination. But what I don't get is why you sent me here in the first place."

A tired sigh reached my ear. I could almost see him pinching the bridge of his nose, something he always did when he was getting frustrated with me. "Because of your grades, Viddie. How many times do I have to tell you that?"

"My grades have been bad for three years!" I hollered, getting desperate. "Why now?" There was another long silence on the other end of the phone. When it stretched into nearly half a minute, I blundered onward, "If this is about my grades, then why don't you sell Portal Manor and use that money to get me a tutor? Wouldn't that make more sense?"

"I *can't* sell the place," he told me, a hint of anger in his voice. "It was a stipulation of your grandmother's will. I have to maintain that crummy white elephant until I hand it over to you when you turn eighteen."

"Oh," I replied, shocked. "I see." I couldn't believe that Portal Manor was mine. Or would be.

"Listen, Viddie," my dad said, his tone appeasing, "We'll

talk about this later, okay, kiddo? I'm rather busy right now. This invention I've been working on—"

"When am I going to see you?" I asked quickly, before he could hang up.

"Winter break, I suppose. That is, if you want to come home then. You certainly don't have to. I'd understand."

"Do *you* want me to come home?" I asked, tightening my grip on the phone.

There was a click, and another voice came on the line. "I'm sorry to interrupt, Professor Mors, but we really have to finish up this paper. The deadline's tomorrow."

Blast that Toad!

"We'll talk more about this another time, Viddie. I'll call you. Until then, take care, kiddo."

"Dad—"

He said something else before he hung up, but I didn't catch it.

I stood there with the phone in my hand, clinging to it as I listened to the dial tone droning in my ear. Tears welled up in my eyes. I *still* didn't know why my dad had sent me here. Maybe my grades really had been the reason, like he'd said. Or perhaps he was calling my bluff. *I know why your grades have been bad, Viddie. You were trying to get my attention. Well, it worked. You've got my attention, and now you're going to pay the price.* I shuddered. Was it possible that my unconscious attempt to get him to notice me by doing poorly in school had backfired on me?

I sighed and hung up the phone. Staring out at the stormy sky, I suddenly felt very angry. What was his problem, anyway? How could he just dump me like this? I had done nothing wrong, yet I was being punished. Well, I was sick of it. He didn't care about me, so why should I care about him? I made up my mind. After Ellie and Eddie returned home in the morning, I'd walk into Bellemont and buy a bus ticket, even if I had to make Ms. Penny dance for the money. If I didn't leave now, I'd never again find the courage to do so. Every day my resolve to leave Portal Manor was growing weaker, and staying was too dangerous. I would run away, but not back to my dad. He could take a flying leap for all I cared.

I found my friends, taping windows in the kitchen. They were laughing and having a good time and I quietly joined them, feeling sad but determined to carry out my plan.

By suppertime, the winds were blowing hard. The radio told listeners to expect lots of rain, downed branches, flooding, and high winds. At seven o'clock, Mrs. Dooley and the four of us gathered together in the kitchen to eat leftovers. Mrs. Keeper still had business to attend to, or so she said when she popped her head in to say hello, telling us to go ahead without her.

Everyone found a place at the large table. Ellie, Mrs. Dooley and I sat on one side while Eddie and Ian sat on the other. Mrs. Dooley raised a glass. "What a grand group of helpers, you are! Sláinte. Cheers." We all raised our glasses.

After a lively meal, Ian carried a cot up to the little nook at the bottom of the stairs; Eddie refused to sleep in the same room as us girls. I think he was hoping Ian would suggest that he stay with him, but Ian didn't pick up on any hints in that direction. Despite my best efforts, I couldn't get Ms. Penny to join us. She preferred the conservatory, it seemed, and knowing Ellie didn't exactly like my raccoon, I let her stay.

After Ellie fetched her purse from the Great Hall, she

tried to convince Ian we needed someone strong around to keep an eye on us (insulting Eddie in the process), but Ian wasn't getting that hint, either. He left with a promise to check up on us if the storm worsened. At the moment, and much to Ellie's disappointment, it was only raining and a bit gusty.

When Eddie went down to use the bathroom, Ellie sighed and threw herself back on the bed, tossing her purse on the floor. "I really don't get what you see in him. He's so full of himself."

Ellie gawked at me. "Are you crazy, Lavida? He's perfect."

"Give me a break, Ellie. Perfect?"

"If he asked, I'd marry him in a second." She stretched out her legs. "I've already got my whole wedding planned out. We'd look so good together."

The room was getting chilly. Pulling off my blazer, I headed to my dresser and took out a black-and-white-striped shirt, which I donned over my t-shirt, then put my blazer back on. I thought about starting a fire, but felt too lazy. Instead, I pulled off my shoes, jumped onto the bed, and tucked my icy toes under my legs to warm them. "I suppose you've already picked out names for your kids."

Ellie kicked off her shoes too. "Of course. Emma and Anthony."

Ugh. I threw a pillow at her. It had to be done. "You are such a girlie girl!" I laughed and Ellie giggled, right after she chucked the pillow back at me.

When Eddie returned, Ellie and I took turns using the bathroom. Twenty minutes later, the three of us were sitting on my bed, the bed curtains closed tight around us, talking and laughing. The upcoming storm had us too wound up to sleep, and Eddie kept putting off having to go down to the tiny cot at the bottom of the stairs. I had my own motivation for not going to sleep; for as long as I could, I wanted to prolong this time together with my new friends. When I was on my own, I would have a wonderful night to remember. It was a pretty lame substitute for a real friendship, but it would have to do.

We were laughing at Ellie's impersonation of Miss Piggy riding a motorcycle when a chill shimmied up my spine. It's only the storm, I told myself, and the cold of the room. Surely it was nothing to worry about.

I was wrong.

~PART TWO~
ANAEDOR

CHAPTER SEVENTEEN
TAKEN

The room was dark. Only a small lantern lit the cave, making it impossible to get a glimpse of who sat in the shadows. Yet Drefan made no effort to see the face of the Anaedorian who had summoned him. He knew this one did not want to be identified; he had been mind-blocked coming in and would be mind-blocked going out. He would not be able to find this place again. Drefan went along with the game for the moment. Learning his client's identity at a later time, without his or her knowledge, would give Drefan a definite advantage. And he liked having the advantage.

The Creature spoke in a raspy voice, giving away neither gender nor age, clan nor skill. "You understand your task?"

"I do."

"Good. I am . . ." the Creature paused as though searching for the right words, "I am not *pleased* with how events in Anaedor are playing out. We must do everything we can to ensure that Humans are not allowed to enter Anaedor so freely. They are a great threat to us."

Drefan was not sure he agreed, but did not voice his opinion on the matter. His work was easier when he neither held nor shared opinions. He cared only about his clan's survival and was willing to ensure this result at any expense. *Exitus acta probat*—the end justifies the means. His tribe lived, and sometimes died, by this motto.

The creature hidden in the shadows flicked a dismissive hand at Drefan. "Go now. Your Brass is en route to your Clan Leaders as we speak. Do not fail me."

I never fail.

Drefan left the oppressive room. As he strode through the darkness, many thoughts ran through his head. This was not the first time he had done work for this creature, but it was the first time he had been asked to do something so serious. It frustrated him that he, a Black Star mind reader, could not read this one's thoughts or intent. And it bothered him that he desired to do so. Desires could, and often did, lead to a breakdown in discipline. Acknowledging this, he made himself focus on the task at hand. He knew what he had to do, and it would not take long. A simple message began to make its way through a network of minds.

When the creature in the shadows had explained the mission to Drefan, it sounded like a simple process. But Amoral Hunters never took anything for granted. They always believed the worst could happen, even when it rarely did. They made sure they did their jobs well simply by being prepared for whatever might come their way. Even so, to subdue three Humans instead of one presented its own set of potential problems. Not insurmountable to four Hunters, of course, but wanting to leave behind no witnesses, they would bring them all. Drefan would leave it to the creature who had requested his services to decide what to do with them. It made no difference to him.

The wind outside howled like a crazed wolf as the rain pummeled the windowpanes with growing intensity. My door began to rattle and shake as though someone were on the other side of it, desperate to get in. The bed curtains rippled, and a click by the wall caught my attention. I shuddered.

Something was wrong.

Before I could move, a rough blanket enveloped my head and a strong hand pressed against my mouth. A muscular arm wrapped tightly around me and lifted me off the bed as easily as though I were a pillow. I fought to free myself, kicking wildly and reaching behind my head in search of something to grab hold of, but my captor was too quick and strong, and dragged me across the room. Seconds later we dropped to the ground and fell forward down the slide. The ride was fast and the landing smooth, and whoever was carrying me started off at a brisk pace. Yet, despite the speed we were moving, my kidnapper was not breathing hard, scarcely breathing at all, it seemed. Just when I was about to shout at Darian for being too rough with me, the alarming thought occurred to me to stay quiet.

"Heeelp!" a muffled voice shattered the silence that surrounded me. Ellie! "Put me down, you worm, or I'll— Heyyy! Oomph!"

The cave was quiet once more. Whoever was carrying us made no sounds, moving as noiselessly and swiftly as panthers. The blanket over my head suffocated me; I started to hyperventilate.

This isn't right! This isn't right! a voice screamed in my head.

Panic surged through me and I kicked my legs harder and more desperately than before, like a crazed horse. Twisting violently, I found myself on the floor of the cave. Tearing at the blanket covering my head, I kicked out again and yelled as loudly as I could. More shouts joined my own, filling the cave with a chorus of rebounding cries. Strong arms grabbed me, attempting to pick me up, but I squirmed away, leaving the blanket behind. Crouched low to the ground like a wild animal, I looked at each of my four captors, my gaze settling on blazing green, cat-like eyes, and I shivered at the look of cold condescension they directed at me. I bit my lip and returned my kidnapper's stare. In a blink, his scathing glare melted away, swiftly transforming him from dominant to drowning. As we gazed helplessly at one another, I could do little but take in his appearance.

Tall and hauntingly beautiful, his golden hair glowed in the lamplight that highlighted his prominent cheekbones and strong jaw line. He was amazingly handsome—his chiseled features appeared to have been carved from ice and stone. Like the other three strangers, he wore a long, dark green cape underneath which I could see a close-fitting leather vest over a crisp, white shirt and brown leather pants. A scabbard hung from a belt around his hips. But unlike the others, he wore a thick metal ring around his neck—a torque—and held himself as though he were in command. He looked human enough to me and would fit into our society quite easily except, maybe, for the bold black star tattooed on his forehead. Though nowadays, even that wouldn't be too unusual.

Whatever was going on, I soon determined that it wasn't going to be pleasant. Despite the crossbow and threats, I'd never felt truly frightened with Darian and Loria. But this creature was different. He had not come in peace.

With an angry shake of his head, the leader scowled at me, seeming to return from wherever it was he had gone. *You are a fool.* The voice was arrogant and commanding. I looked to see who was talking to me, but couldn't figure out which one of the strangers it was. *Come. You are wasting my time.*

I stared at the stunning creature holding the lantern. His lips had never once moved, but I felt sure now that he was talking to me. And the voice I'd heard had actually come from *inside* my head. The leader's blonde eyebrow lifted in amusement.

I shivered and wrapped my arms around myself. I wasn't just reading his thoughts, he was sending them to me. Could he read *my* thoughts, as well? I wondered.

He smiled a humorless smile. *Know this. I will do whatever I have to do to complete my mission.*

He had answered my question. I glanced helplessly at the two creatures holding squirming, body-like bundles, and a moan slipped out from between my quivering lips. What had I done?

You have made a very powerful enemy and endangered your friends.

The tall, cloaked man clapped his black gloves together. The one who had been carrying me grabbed me once more, though he did not bother putting the blanket over my head.

"I didn't mean for this to happen!" I cried as I watched Ellie and Eddie struggle to get loose.

The bundles stopped moving. "What's going on, Lavida?" Ellie yelped, fear making her voice squeaky under the heavy blanket.

"I don't know, Ellie," I said, wishing that I did, wishing this was one of Ian's practical jokes.

"Ohhh, I hate the dark," Ellie groaned. "Ouch! Stop poking me, you creep!" The three boasting sea-blue stars on their foreheads laughed. They seemed to find her quite amusing. "My dad is going to sue you jerks for everything you're worth!" Her threat only made them laugh harder.

My teeth crunched together in anger. I had no idea where we were, where we were going, or what was going to happen when we got there. I glanced around the tunnel; nothing looked even remotely familiar to me. I had to find a way to get us out of this mess.

The lives of your companions are inconsequential to me. Their screams of agony would bring you back before you had traveled ten paces. Do you understand?

"I understand," I replied, thinking that he didn't need to be so dramatic about it.

He slowly blinked his long-lashed, green eyes at me and smiled coldly. He motioned for me to come forward. When I came within reach he took hold of my arm, his fingers like pythons. I tried to yank free, but his grip was too strong.

After you. He pushed me ahead of him.

I stumbled but he caught me before I fell. *Be careful. I must deliver you in good condition.*

Shaking with fear and frustration, I continued walking. I tried to get a sense of how Ellie and Eddie were doing, but the twins were strangely quiet behind me. I hoped they weren't plotting some way to escape, which sounded exactly like something Ellie would be doing. I could only hope, for all our sakes, that she wasn't.

This guy meant business.

CHAPTER EIGHTEEN
VELCOME TO ANAEDOR

We had been walking for what seemed like hours, although it was probably only a few minutes. Cool, moist air slipped beneath my shirts and blazer like ghosts, and icy water dripped onto my head. I was grateful we hadn't changed into our pajamas, but every time I stubbed a toe on the rough ground, I wished I hadn't taken off my shoes. The occasional bat flitted by, spooking me. I knew their sonar would stop them from flying into my hair. Still, I didn't quite believe in my knowledge, continually picturing one of the leathery creatures getting caught in tangled strands, then sinking tiny, razor-sharp teeth into my neck.

At times the tunnel grew narrow, almost impassable. I kept imagining myself about to be crushed at any moment like a pea between two giant fingers. Oddly enough, during the entire journey we never once passed through any large caves. Our kidnapper was determined to keep us in these awful, cramped tunnels.

We met no other creatures on our trek. Traveling through empty, echoing tunnels without encountering a single soul felt as eerie as spinning through space. Only a few Starkinder lanterns, set far apart, lit the way. Was anyone else alive down here? I shivered, imagining watchful eyes around every corner hiding in every crack and dark nook we passed.

At last, the leader of the group took hold of my arm and pulled me to a stop. "We are going to put your friends down—"

"It's about time!" Ellie bellowed the moment her feet touched the ground.

"I suggest you keep them quiet . . . for their safety and yours," he continued.

Ellie tore off the blanket, threw it to the floor, and stomped on it several times. Breathing heavily she squinted over at me, pretty well blind without her glasses. Her red hair was tousled and she looked mad. "That lousy excuse for a blanket smells like wet skunk."

"I'm sorry, Ellie." I felt awful that she was in trouble because of me, and even more so for being glad she was with me. Eddie emerged from his blanket, blinking rapidly. "I need you guys to promise me that you won't try to run away."

"Well you can tell Mr. High and Mighty here that—" Ellie began.

"This is not a joke, Ellie!" I blurted out, and her jaw went slack in surprise.

The leader regarded her coolly. "I find your courage interesting, but do not doubt my word. You are expendable; I will drop you into a pit if you trouble me. Remember that." His face was amused, but cold.

Ellie bit her lip, then spotted one of kidnappers casually twirling her glasses. "Hey, give me those!" she howled and leaped for them. He lifted the glasses just out of reach, then slowly lowered them. When she grabbed at the pink blob, he yanked them back up.

"Give them to her," the leader ordered after Ellie tried kicking the culprit in the crotch. "We do not need her slowing us down."

The taunter handed the smudged spectacles over without complaint. Ellie gave him a dirty look before putting them on. The ones with the blue stars laughed again, elbowing each other with amusement.

"Quiet!" the leader snapped. "You know what enemies lurk in the dark."

"And in the light," I muttered.

He studied me. "I am not your enemy. But there are many creatures in this world that would be less . . . accommodating than I am. You had better hope you are not here long enough to meet them."

We all gulped at the same time. I could tell by their silence that Ellie and Eddie were taking our kidnapper very seriously. Good. I was going to need all my wits about me to figure a way out of this, and I didn't want them getting any crazy ideas in their heads about being heroes. That, I suddenly realized, was *my* burden.

After several minutes of marching along at a brisk pace, the sound of many voices speaking at once filled the air. Slightly muffled, the voices came from behind large, battered wooden doors that rose up out of the stone floor and disappeared into the shadows above. Two tall stone pillars flanked the entrance. Hundreds of eyes, carved into the surface, stared outward in various forms of appeal, accusation, fear, sadness, and anger. We approached the intimidating double doors, and I realized that the noise sounded exactly like an angry drone of bees defending their hive against attack. A lot of negative energy awaited us behind those doors.

The leader stopped in front of the entry and turned to face our frightened group. "We are about to enter the Great Court. Once inside, we will escort you to the Box of the Accused. Our job is then done, and you will be on your own." He raised an eyebrow at me, as though in challenge, then opened the grand doors by pulling on the massive, black iron rings.

The deafening sound of voices nearly knocked me backward, ricocheting like bullets off the high, rounded ceiling of the enormous cave, and my pupils contracted violently at the unexpected light. Starkinder lamps, hanging from hooks, covered the cavern walls. Hand shading my eyes, I looked up toward the ceiling and spotted thousands of uncaged Starkinders huddling together.

I reluctantly stepped into the huge cavern and followed our captor down a long, narrow aisle. I had expected a small room, like a courtroom, but with its bright lights and hundreds of spectators, the immense cavern looked more like an arena set up for entertainment, not justice. Spread along the walls, standing shoulder-to-shoulder, carved life-like stone statues posed imperiously.

Balconies protruded from the stone walls like pouting lower lips, giving spectators a better view of the proceedings. Brightly colored, uniquely patterned cloths hung from each railing like banners. Stairways carved into the stone led to the different balconies—those closer to the floor ran fifteen feet in length and were packed full; those higher up were smaller, with only a few Anaedorians occupying them. The creatures in these coveted spots drank from ornamented mugs and talked calmly amongst themselves. They appeared to be more civilized than the general riff-raff on the floor, but I imagined their demeanor could—and would—change when they sensed weakness.

At the center of the room a circular platform rose about three feet above the ground, on top of which stood a waist-high, square-shaped wall. This had to be the Box of the Accused our captor had mentioned. Various symbols decorated the front of the box, resembling those I'd seen on my first visit to Anaedor. Twenty or so smaller stone daises, each adorned by a different symbol, formed a large ring around the main platform. Some of the daises had chairs or large cushions while others were free of any kind of furniture.

Despite my tight throat and shaking hands, I couldn't help being mesmerized by all the strange creatures comprising the crowds surrounding us on either side of the pathway. A group of short, hairy men, who resembled members of the mythical Dwarf race, were shouting at each other, faces flushed with fervor. They were so busy arguing that they didn't notice a small object flying low over their heads. It appeared to be a tiny person riding an odd-looking, fat, furry bat with a rat-like tail—a rat-bat. Before I could wonder what the rider was up to, it lifted something the size of a tomato into the air. Just as the little creature passed over the crowd of Dwarves, it hurled the object at one of them, nailing a redheaded Dwarf right in the face. The missile exploded like a water balloon, splattering anyone standing nearby with a thick, brown substance. The brown goo oozed down the Dwarf's heavily bearded face and dripped onto the cave floor.

The victim, not realizing the identity of the real offender, launched himself at a golden-haired Dwarf standing next to him and wrestled him to the ground. The rest of the group formed a circle around the two and cheered them on. The tiny creature flew close to me, stared in surprise, then whizzed away.

Vesuvius?

Before I could call after him, a flash of white caught my eye. A shimmering, long-haired horse with a single horn the color of sapphires spiraling out of her forehead flew toward the center of the cave, her delicately feathered wings rising and falling in great sweeping motions. Landing gracefully, she took her place on one of the smaller stands that encircled the main platform. Next to her dais, a group of Elves, slender of build and of average height, with elegant features and long, pointed ears, bowed to her as she settled to a stop. The winged Unicorn gave a high-pitched whinny, tossed her head, and stamped a silver hoof on the ground in reply.

Somehow our kidnapper managed to lead us all the way to the Box of the Accused without anyone in the arena noticing us. The three followers ushered us into the boxed-in area through a small opening in the wall, one of them giving me a shove when I hesitated. The moment I set foot inside the box, a huge roar erupted throughout the cavern. We had been spotted.

Standing on the other side of the half wall, our kidnapper looked out at the jeering crowd. His eyes narrowed thoughtfully as he watched their reaction to our presence, then he turned to face us. "This should be interesting," he said, his tone pleased. Without another word, he strode purposefully over to a nearby dais where two regal creatures already sat. He nodded to each one, then took his place next to them, his green eyes scanning the room. His three followers flanked the stone platform but made no attempt to step up on it.

"You've got to be kidding me," Ellie exclaimed as we turned to face the booing, otherworldly creatures. "This is crazy! What the heck is going on?"

I stared out at the mocking, hissing spectators, feeling like a heretic during the Spanish Inquisition, and shuddered, recalling what had happened to nonconformists during that nasty period of history. They were tortured and burned.

Ellie scanned the room, disgusted. "Why are they all screaming at us?" She turned her back on the wild crowd to face us. "This has got to be some kind of joke, Lavida."

I studied the crowd behind Ellie, knowing full well that this was no joke. Judging by the looks on the creatures' faces, most of them would happily push the three of us off Warrior's Walk, and pay good money to do it. Filled with rage, this crowd, given half a chance, would gladly take it out on us. I stared at them in shock and fear, wondering why they hated us so much.

Something large, soft and slimy struck me on the head, knocking me sideways. The crowd broke into uproarious laughter as the gunk slowly slithered down the side of my face. I swiped the sticky goop off my cheek and flung it to the floor, hoping against hopes that it wasn't the giant booger that it felt like. As I frantically wiped my hands on my pants, the smell of rot drifted into my nostrils and I nearly threw up.

"Cool!" Eddie moved closer to study the green stuff congealing on the floor of the platform. He bent over to get a closer look and a wad of goo hit him square in the mouth. "Agh!" He ducked down behind the wall, retching and spitting.

Ellie, alert to the danger of getting nailed herself, dove to the floor. "They're throwing things at us!" she cried over the shrieks of laughter. "I can't believe this. Do something, Lavida!"

I bit at a torn nail, then realized with horror that I'd used that hand to wipe away the green goo. "What do you want *me* to do?" I yelled, cowering close to the floor. I could practically feel the waves of hatred billowing toward me, choking me.

"Anything!" Ellie wailed. "Just make them stop!"

But I couldn't do what I needed to do—use magic. I wouldn't. I couldn't let Ellie think I was a freak. I couldn't go through the pain, the humiliation, the loneliness—not again.

I'd rather die.

CHAPTER NINETEEN
GUILTY UNTIL PROVEN INNOCENT

The nasty goo flew fast and hard until suddenly it stopped. The room grew deadly still as all heads turned toward a smaller entrance to the Great Court, opposite to the one we had entered. We slowly rose up on our knees and crawled over to the wall to see what was going on. Peeking over the stone partition, we spotted what had shushed the crowd.

Through a lavishly decorated back entrance, a line of beings entered the courtroom, heralding with raised flags and blowing horns the arrival of two men. The first one was very tall and dressed completely in black. He wore a long cape, which couldn't quite disguise the gut protruding from his middle. His face, dominated by a large, hooked nose, was as pale and bloated as the underbelly of a fish, with only his dark, bulging eyes and thick purple lips for color. His black hair was short and feathered on top, then longer in back, brushing against the top of his sloping shoulders. The second figure to enter the room was an older man. He was of average height and seemed surprised by all the noise greeting him. He wore half glasses, which sat crookedly on his narrow red nose, magnifying his dull gray eyes, which seemed to focus inwardly rather than on the events before him. Long, messy gray hair and a long, straggly gray beard matched the dingy gray robe he wore.

As he walked, he appeared to be muttering something to himself, almost as though he were arguing with an invisible person striding alongside him. Seeing pointy ears through the mess of hair, I thought he might be an Elf, though he didn't look nearly as neat and alert as the other Elves in the arena. With some help, he managed to sit on a stone throne layered with velvety purple cushions, which were definitely more colorful and pleasing to the eye than he was.

The creature in black approached our platform, swooping toward us like a hungry crow. In his left hand, he gripped a glossy black staff, with short, sharp, silver spikes protruding ruthlessly from its top. Alarmed, we all stood up at the same time, ready to run. After climbing the steps, he went to stand behind a stone podium just outside the box. He completely ignored the three of us—didn't even look in our direction, in fact. Behind him a Dwarf used a large mallet to strike a rounded brass gong. Upon hearing the reverberating noise, the crowd waited for the dark one to speak.

"Citizens of Anaedor, you know me as Malvado," he announced, his voice a couple notes higher than the booming one I had expected. "As the communicator for the Magistrate and elected Spokesbeing of Anaedor, I am here to make known the wishes of our great Leader." He glanced back at the Magistrate perched on the large stone chair and acknowledged him with a careless wave of his arm. The

Anaedorian Leader nodded blankly in response. I couldn't believe that this dull, gray man was the leader of anything. He didn't even seem to know where he was. The man in black—Malvado—appeared to be the one in charge. Perhaps the Magistrate was merely a figurehead; in name he was the ruler, but in reality someone else, Malvado in this case, made all the decisions.

At that moment, Malvado turned toward me, fixing me with an intense gaze that made his eyes bulge even more. "You stand accused of a most heinous crime, Human."

"Crime?" I echoed and the crowd booed loudly. He quieted them with a wave of his spiky staff.

"You have crossed the boundaries between the Upland and Anaedor. The Helpers are still allowed to do this, but you are not a Helper, are you?"

I shook my head no.

The crowd booed again, and this time they wouldn't quiet down so quickly. They were like sharks smelling blood, and I was the bag of chum.

"That is not all," he continued, his voice shrill. "While you were here, you poisoned our water source, killing many of our citizens."

My mouth dropped open. "I don't know what you're talking about—"

"Silence!" Malvado roared. "You are the accused. Until this matter is resolved to my . . . our satisfaction, you have no rights."

Eddie boldly met Malvado's eyes. "You can't do that. The law states that we're innocent until proven guilty."

Malvado gave Eddie a cold look. "That is a Human law, and Human law holds no power here." He peered into Eddie's eyes, his own glowing madly. "Tell me exactly what happened when your friend was here in Anaedor, and I might let you live."

Eddie stared back at him, his eyes becoming distant and glassy. I felt a shiver of fear tremble through me.

"Lavida poisoned the water. She has belladonna. She used it to make the poison."

"Eddie!" I cried. "What are you doing?"

"Leave us alone!" Ellie yelled, glaring at Malvado.

He turned toward Ellie, focusing his intense gaze on her. Her blue eyes glazed over. "My brother tells the truth," she intoned. "Lavida poisoned the water."

The crowd gasped, then howled with anger.

"Ellie!" Panic bloomed in my chest like a fungus. How could she! I looked helplessly at Malvado. He gave a victorious smile and returned my stare, his eyes deep pools of malice. I clenched my fists tightly as my stomach churned.

"Tell me what I want to hear," he demanded, "and this will all go away."

I heard myself begin to speak. "I . . . I did . . ."

"Say it! Say it!"

The crowd grew quiet.

"I did *not* do this!" I shouted, sagging as my knees buckled. I caught myself on the half wall, holding on tightly to keep from falling over.

Malvado's whole body convulsed with rage. He stared at me again, willing me to speak against myself. I tried to look away from him, but I couldn't. My mind whirled like a sandstorm and I began to shake from the strain. Maybe I should give in, I told myself. Plead for mercy. But admit that I poisoned someone? I couldn't do that. They'd kill me for sure. Nevertheless I was weakening. My temples throbbed and I trembled from the effort, a quaking leaf on the verge of falling. I sucked in air like a drowning victim, held my breath, and centered all my energy on Malvado, willing him to back off, willing him to look away. At last, just as I was about to give in, his eyes shifted from mine out to the crowd.

All pandemonium broke loose, the noise in the room reaching a deafening pitch.

"Silence!" Malvado shouted, his jowls quivering. "Silence, I say!" The room slowly quieted. "You all witnessed what happened here. She is obviously guilty, but she will not admit it. The only way to make her tell me what I need to know is to torture her."

My knees folded beneath me again. Had he really said *torture*?

There was a movement behind Malvado. A noble being had risen from his seat on one of the smaller platforms and now strode purposefully toward the Box. It was one of the Elves. He stood higher than the other Elves, but shorter than Malvado by a good foot. Yet the way he held himself made him look taller than he was. The rich, dark brown cape that cloaked his straight, dignified back added to the effect. He wore his golden-brown hair, which matched the color of his eyes, relatively short for an Anaedorian. The cut exposed much of his long, pointy ears, one of which had an ornate silver ring piercing its tip. With great dignity, he climbed the steps to the podium and said something to Malvado that I couldn't make out.

Malvado shook his head defiantly.

The Elf spoke again. This time, although Malvado narrowed his eyes, he bowed.

"Council Elder, Agranden the Elf, wishes to say something," he announced, and took a step back.

Agranden glanced back at Malvado, then turned toward the crowd. He cleared his throat and the room quickly became quiet. "Citizens of Anaedor," his strong voice filled the cavern, "by now all of you should know quite well my position on allowing Humans in our beloved world." He smiled charmingly and the crowd laughed, cluing me in to what that position was. "However, while I feel it is time we broke free of their influence, I do not want to *entirely* alienate them. Until we can better understand what has happened here and what we want to do next, the Humans should be placed under the Crushers' care."

The crowd shouted their disapproval, but stopped when Agranden held up his hand. As slender as it was, it emanated power. "If you will, cast your minds back to a time when we reacted rashly to an unclear situation. You remember the Uprising, when so many of us died and Anaedor was nearly destroyed. Let us do this right. We will be patient. We will gather the facts, using torture only if necessary." The crowd grumbled, but generally kept their thoughts to themselves this time.

The Elf scanned the room, then gave a satisfied nod. "I am sure the Magistrate will agree that it is best if you all return to your homes peacefully and let the Council determine how to proceed. I promise you we will resolve this with all possible haste."

The large crowd quickly dissipated, talking excitedly. Many of them stared boldly at me as they passed by the Box, but I was too tired and miserable and frightened to care. My friends had betrayed me and I was about to be tortured. My life couldn't get any worse. Only the creatures on the platforms that ringed the Box, along with Malvado and the Magistrate, remained. I heard voices behind me and turned to see a group of Blendars, their dark, curly hair flowing behind them as they approached an empty dais.

Two of the Blendars carried a simple, dark blue litter that resembled a hospital stretcher. On it sat Madrina, dignified as a Queen. The two Blendars placed the litter on the small stone platform. Hope surged up inside me: She knew the truth. She would get us out of this mess.

"It is good to see you could finally join us, Madrina of

the Blendars."

Madrina returned his gaze, unflinching. "We were detained, Malvado. I would explain, but I am sure you already know the reason why."

He sneered at her, then turned his back on her to address the group. "Council Leaders, we are now confronted with a grave crisis. We must decide what to do with this murderous Human and her followers. It is my opinion that torture be used to make her admit the truth, even though Agranden is afraid of doing so. He does not seem to realize how important it is that we find out what this loathsome Human was doing, sneaking around in our world, and whether we should prepare for any more vicious attempts on Anaedorian lives."

"I completely agree," a cool, silvery voice interjected. I jerked my head toward the icy voice and then stood up to get a better look. Scanning the cavern, my eyes came to rest on three of the strangest people I'd ever seen; they resembled ice sculptures more than humans, their skin as transparent as a newly frozen river. Icicles, ranging from thick and fat to needle thin, sprouted from one of their heads, hundreds of ice bubbles covered another's scalp, and the third—the leader, judging by the elevated position of her chair—wore curly ice snakes, a frozen Medusa. Their eyes, cold and pale as afternoon snow, regarded the room unperturbedly. White flakes drifted around them, coming to rest on the luxurious, black fur coats each of them wore. Either it was actually snowing over them, or they had a serious dandruff problem.

Malvado nodded toward the leader, then gave her a slight bow, his puffy features smug. "I am glad you support me, Moire."

She held up a translucent hand. The dark fur coat slid up her pale arm, revealing rivers of blue veins. "Let us be clear,

Malvado. I do not support you." Malvado pursed his fat, purplish lips. "I simply do not want Humans in my world. They are stupid, destructive creatures, and so unclean." She shuddered delicately. "It would be more efficient to simply eliminate the Humans and be done with it."

"It is of my most exalted opinion," I heard a piping voice say, "that we should not forego the torture. Such fun it would be to see the Humans suffer . . . in return for all they have done to us." I turned to see a group of tiny silver-winged creatures dancing about on one of the platforms. They looked like Fairies. Not the good kind, though.

The winged Unicorn blew air from her nostrils and shook her narrow head from side to side. Her silvery white mane floated in the air as she crossly stamped a silver hoof.

"Oh, you are so boring, Unkeros!" the Fairy leader squeaked. She crossed her arms. "What is wrong with a little torture?"

"Torture is not the answer, Peerie," Madrina spoke up, her deep voice filling the cavern. "We cannot violate our treaty with the Helpers. As some of you may remember, they spared our world during the Uprising, and have peacefully assisted us for Centions since. If we go back on our word, we will only harm ourselves in the end."

"I agree wi' the dragonfly," a Dwarf said gruffly as he nodded toward Peerie.

"I am not a dragonfly, you . . . you Mucklemouth!" Peerie replied indignantly, hands on her hips.

The Dwarf snorted, obviously of a different opinion. "We have tae act noo. Oor clan must return tae oor work in the mines—RedGems dinna dig themselves up. We canna spend all oor time being polite and getting noowhere. This must be finished noo!" He raised a short-handled sledge-hammer into the air. Based on his urgency to return to work, I could only surmise that 'noo' meant now.

His fellow Dwarves lifted their hammers into the air and chanted "Finished noo!" several times before Agranden silenced them. "I understand your desire to move quickly, Gruamach," Agranden sympathized, "but Madrina is right; we cannot violate our treaty. For now, we will leave the prisoners under the Crushers' care at Miseria until we can decide what to do. You are free to return to your clans now. You will be called to meet when all the facts have been gathered, and we will vote on the matter."

Gruamach grumbled, but nodded his acceptance, giving due respect to Agranden's decision, even if he didn't agree with it. Peerie rolled her tiny eyes before flitting away, the other Fairies following close behind her. The rest of the Council began to leave as well. In the sudden crowd, I looked around, frantically trying to find Madrina. At last I spotted her; she was speaking urgently to Agranden, but he didn't seem persuaded by her argument. It was obvious Madrina couldn't help me, or she would've done so already.

A moment later my eyes found Darian in the throng—he was looking directly at me. I shivered at his intensity, unable to look away from his dark eyes. He was in Blendar form, I noticed, but he didn't seem all that different from his human form. His nose was a little longer, his eyes larger, and his ears a little pointier. Maybe all that blending as a human made him look more like us every time he did it. Dropping his eyes, he turned to go. I wanted to beg him to help me, but I couldn't make myself speak those two simple words. In the past, asking for help had never done me much good. People were more inclined to either ignore my pleas or do the exact opposite.

As the room emptied, I could only stand there with a leaden feeling in my gut, imagining Malvado heading off to sharpen the blades and ready the rack. Beside me, Ellie and Eddie shook their heads dizzily.

"What happened?" Ellie asked as she looked around.

I bit my lip to keep from crying. "You both told Malvado that I was the one who poisoned several Anaedorians and now they're going to torture me."

"We did *not!*" Ellie shouted indignantly. "We were defending you and . . . and . . . oh, I don't remember. It's all a blur."

I stared at her, not believing what I was hearing. "You said, and I quote, 'Lavida poisoned the water.' Eddie even told them I had belladonna. I thought you guys were my friends!"

They said nothing in their defense, only blinked at me in confusion, as though I were speaking Greek. Before I could say more, four stocky, well-muscled men, each holding a small bow armed with a deadly arrow, approached us. One stepped forward.

"You are to come with us. If you try to escape, know that my life's greatest pleasure would be to kill you, Human scum."

We did as we were told.

CRUSHER

CHAPTER TWENTY
TURBLES IN PARADISE

The one who had spoken directed us like a general, commanding us to follow him in a single line. He led the quiet procession, followed by two others like him—one with a long face, the other flat—and a short one bringing up the rear. I could see where the name "Crusher" had come from. Built like boulders, with muscles sticking out from places I didn't realize muscles existed, they looked like they could crush anything with their hands alone. If their hands were not enough to do the job, the short sword each one possessed would do the trick.

Around each of their necks, except for the leader, hung a thin, gray rope looped through a heavy, donut-shaped stone. Their close-cropped hair, thick skin and tightly fitted uniforms matched the gray stone around us, allowing them to blend in and disappear if they wanted to. I imagined hundreds of them lining the walls, watching me with their dull eyes. Moving rapidly, we left the cave of the Great Court through yet another opening and were now traveling through a wide tunnel.

After a stretch of heavy trekking, we entered a large cave. Starkinder lamps lit the open space, their light reflecting off the black surface of a wide, rapidly flowing river. Half a dozen objects, shaped like giant flat-topped bike helmets, bobbed in the water.

"Fig, take the lead," the head Crusher ordered the flat-faced one. "I will take Mo and these two Humans; you take that one." He pointed to me, his expression thoroughly disgusted as his gaze met mine. "Loo," he told the long-faced Crusher, "you will follow us to protect the rear."

Satisfied that there'd be no trouble from us, he headed toward the floating objects waiting in the water. He approached the one closest to him and did something strange: he reached up and knocked three times on the raft's surface, then, when he pulled his hand away, the object started to back out of the water and up onto land. The "raft" had legs and a head! He knocked on the backs of two more of the amphibious creatures, then snapped his fingers at Loo and Fig to join him.

"It is a Turble," the Crusher called Mo told us as we stood before the strange beasts. Mo was the shortest of the four Crushers, and not nearly as well built as the others. He actually had a little rounded belly and a double chin.

Eddie leaned forward to examine the giant reptile's shell. At one time, the structure had been rounded at the top like a regular turtle shell. Someone had notched small steps into the thick, ridged material and leveled the top to create a four-by-four platform.

"I get the 'Tur' part for turtle, but what's the 'ble' for?" Eddie asked over his shoulder. He tapped on the shell, watching the animal closely for any reaction. The Turble ignored him.

"That is for the bubble part," Mo explained, glancing nervously over at the other Crushers. When he saw they were still talking he went on happily, "Turbles create giant bubbles over their backs from air pouches located beneath their shells. They use the bubble to protect their young until their shells harden and they are big enough to defend themselves. If you are standing on the Turble's back before the bubble forms, you will be kept safe when you go underwater."

Eddie stroked the dark shell. "I wish I could try that some time."

"You are in luck, my friend," Mo told him excitedly, his broad, innocent face beaming. "To get to Miseria we will travel underwater on the Turbles' backs."

"We get to *ride* on the Turbles?" Eddie echoed in disbelief. "Yes!"

"No way am I going underwater on one of those things," Ellie announced, shooting Eddie a dirty look. "I happen to be allergic to drowning . . . and to genetic mutations."

The leader, hearing Ellie's steadily rising voice, marched over to her. "You have no choice," he said, towering over her. "Now climb on that Turble right now or you will swim the whole way."

Ellie narrowed her blue eyes. "I don't like your attitude."

"And I do not like your kind," he retorted, glowering at her. It was his turn to raise his voice.

"Ellie," I hissed at her, "let's just do what they say. We don't want to make things worse than they already are."

She crossed her arms and scowled. "This is so unfair, Lavida." She placed her foot on the first step, tested its sturdiness and then, satisfied it wouldn't cave in, carefully stepped onto the flattened back of the Turble. As she moved to the center, her nose wrinkled in distaste. "This thing smells like rotten fish."

"This is amazing," Eddie said as he hopped on behind her. "I'll have to study this creature more thoroughly. I could do a whole thesis on Turbles. Perhaps get published . . ."

The other two Crushers joined the twins on the Turble, flanking them to ensure they could not get away. Ellie threw me a pleading look while Eddie, on the other hand, didn't seem to care—or get—that we were all going to die.

Mo gently grabbed my arm and guided me onto the back of the next Turble. The flat, carved-out surface was rough under my socks. Ellie was right about the smell. I tried holding my breath. It worked, but only lasted as long as I didn't need to breathe. I gave up and tried not to think about the stench creeping up my nasal passages and bur- rowing into my brain like larvae.

Mo tapped his foot twice and a glistening bubble began to rise up from around the edges of the Turble's shell. In seconds, the bubble had formed a protective shield over us. I gazed at the shimmering material in wonder, then poked it with a finger. It wiggled like Jell-O, but held firm.

"The bubble's actually pretty hard."

"It will not pop." Mo paused and frowned. "Well . . . that is, unless we are attacked by Pirudons. And then, only if they get their teeth in good."

"Pirudons . . . ?" I asked.

The Crusher squinted and wrinkled his forehead as he thought about this question. "They are kind of like a fish and kind of like a leech. They are very big and their jaws are strong enough to break rocks."

I tried to see into the water. "Are there any Pirudons in this river?"

He patted my arm. "Do not worry. Pirudons tend to

avoid Turbles. Turbles are tougher than they look. Though, come to think of it, this *is* the Pirudons' feeding season. They get so hungry after hibernating that they go after pretty much anything that moves. Let us hope for the best." He smiled broadly at me. "Well, here we go." He tapped his foot on the shell three more times and the large creature waded into the river.

I studied the black water, searching for monsters, shivering as I thought about starving Pirudons and what else might lurk beneath the mirror-like surface. "I can't believe this is happening," I murmured, half to myself.

"I hope you do not try to escape while you are with me," Mo said, the worry evident in his kind eyes. "My brother, Hedl, assigned you to me so he can blame me if you get away. He does not want to look bad before the Council Elders." He looked around as though afraid he might be overheard. "I will tell you something else . . ." he whispered, "the other reason he wants me to take you is he does not like Humans. He thinks they are unintelligent, interfering, freakish eejits. But *I* like Humans. They are . . ." he paused and his eyes sparkled merrily, "*cool!*"

"Where did you learn that word?" I asked, surprised to hear it coming from an Anaedorian. "We use it a lot in our world."

"I know," he replied excitedly. "My best friend, whose brother is in the Upland Reconnaissance Crew, told it to me. He has gone on many missions; he knows all about Human culture."

"The Upland Reconnaissance Crew?" I repeated. "Is that like the CIA or something?"

"CIA," he echoed, savoring each letter. "I do not know about that. The URC was created some time ago to study everything Human, everything of the Upland—where you live, that is." He looked down at his wide, sturdy boots, suddenly shy. "Is your name *really* Lavida Mors?"

"That's what it says on my birth certificate." I wondered what the big deal was about my name. I wanted to ask him, but I had other things I needed to know first. "How come you're being so nice to me? According to Malvado, I tried to poison your people."

He waved his hand in the air as though swatting away my words. "When Hedl told our family the story, I did not believe it for one moment. Besides, I heard the truth from Loria." He smiled dreamily as he said her name. Then he frowned. "She was speaking to Hedl about it and I happened to overhear. She likes him, you know, but she should not waste her time. Now that he is in line for a promotion in the URC, simply being in the same room with him is dreadful."

"He does seem a bit arrogant," I remarked.

Mo nodded vigorously. "He spends a lot of time looking at his muscles in mirror pools—quite sickening, really." He flexed his arm, squeezing the bicep. "*I think my muscle grew another thumb width, Mo!*" He rolled his eyes in disgust.

"So what did Loria say to your brother about me?"

"She said you were with her and Darian the whole time you were in Anaedor. She also told me that she was positive you have not been here any time since then."

I was about to ask how she would know this when I realized the Turble was going underwater. I grabbed his arm. "I hope this bubble thing works for humans." I could see it now—my head, unable to handle the change in pressure, slowly imploding like a rotting jack-o'-lantern.

Mo laughed, then frowned uncertainly. "You know, I do not think we have ever tried the bubble with a Human passenger." He slapped me jovially on the shoulder. "I believe you and your friends will be the first to try it. Good luck!"

I grimaced and tightened my grip. Up ahead, Ellie and Eddie's Turble was nearly submerged when I heard Ellie scream. I would not have been surprised had all of Anaedor heard her. She was still alive, which was heartening, though poor Eddie probably had a burst eardrum or two. As my own Turble sank deeper and deeper into the water, I felt the urge to scream myself, but a blue-green glow coming from a large school of tiny, luminous fish swimming alongside the giant turtle distracted me. Mesmerized by the pretty light, I stared at the odd creatures in delight. They seemed entirely unaware they had an audience.

The tugging of the Turble's legs was rhythmic and soothing. Once I realized I was still able to breathe and that my head had maintained its original shape, I relaxed a little. I could actually see myself getting used to this peaceful, underwater world. Perhaps I could stay down here forever—they couldn't torture me if I was in a bubble, could they?

"Do you know what they're going to do to me?" I asked Mo.

He rubbed his broad forehead. "No one outside the Council has ever resisted Malvado's powers . . . until you came along, that is. That, and being Human, are two counts against you, I am afraid."

"Resisted Malvado's powers?" I repeated. "What do you mean?"

"Malvado is a great mind worker. He can read your mind and make you do what he wants you to do. After the Uprising, each clan chose one skill to practice and make their own."

"Like magic?" I breathed, stunned. Could I really have something in common with these creatures, these Anaedorians? I had "skills" same as theirs, though I had never been forced to choose only one. Of course, I'd also never worked to perfect any of them, either.

"You could say that," Mo agreed. "Amorals chose to be mind workers. Some are better than others at their clan's skill, and Malvado is very, very good at his."

"Is he good enough to make my friends say what they did about me?"

Mo shook his head. "He can only make them tell the truth. That is the law of the court."

Unless I was sleepwalking and had done what Malvado had actually accused me of doing, he had made my friends lie. They hadn't betrayed me, after all. Thinking my friends had betrayed me was almost more painful than the thought of being tortured, but now a wave of relief passed over me.

"So who was the guy that brought us to the Great Court?"

Mo shrugged. "I do not know. I was not there at the time." He looked disappointed. "Mother does not like me attending those events. She says they are barbaric. I tried to go, but she sent me on an errand on the other side of Anaedor."

"He was blonde," I told him, "and had a black star on his forehead. He seemed like the leader of the group that kidnapped us."

Mo's eyes widened. "You mean Drefan."

"I guess."

Mo nodded. "That sounds exactly like him. He is Hunter Leader of the Amorals. A mindworker, like Malvado. Some say he is even more skilled than Malvado. My mates and I, we stay away from him. Well, we stay away from all Amorals. They are ruthless. And Brass means more to them than life."

"They sound lovely," I murmured.

He gave me an odd look. "Does that mean bad? Because

if it does, then yes, they are very lovely."

"Ah."

Up ahead, a wavery orange light reached out to us, and Mo turned his attention to it. The Turbles swam toward the light and surfaced with a great whooshing sound. The beasts parked near the bank of the river, lit by Starkinder lamps, where they waited patiently for us to disembark. I was wondering how we were going to get out when our shield popped like a soap bubble, freeing us. Mo jumped to the ground, then reached up to help me down.

Once on solid ground I looked around and saw that we were now standing in a cave similar to the one we'd left behind, except tiny flecks of light sparkled on the surface of the rock, creating the sensation that I was looking up at a starry sky. Flat-faced Fig was guarding Ellie and Eddie while Hedl and Loo stood waiting at a large wooden door. A skull's head had been burned onto its dark surface. Hedl knocked, then beckoned Fig to join them.

I eyed the door nervously. "What's going to happen to us in there?"

"Well . . ." Mo began.

"Well, what?" Ellie demanded, hurrying over to us with surreptitious glances over her shoulder at the talking Crushers. Eddie, after one last longing look at the Turbles, joined us.

"Mo, this is Ellie and Eddie. Guys, this is Mo." Eddie and Mo exchanged a wave; Ellie crossed her arms and gave him a suspicious look.

"I was about to tell Lavida that most prisoners who enter Miseria have never left. After a while, they just disappear." He glanced toward the door where his brother stood, then said in a low voice, "Some say the prisoners in Miseria are fed to the Onyx."

Ellie's face turned an unpleasant shade of white. "Fed

to who?"

"The Onyx," Mo repeated. "Nobody knows exactly what it is, but it lives underwater and has lots of tentacles and a giant mouth like a beak, with razor-sharp teeth, and eyes the size of your head." He saw the horrified expression on our faces and hastily backpedaled. "I mean . . . it is, well . . . it is just a rumor. I do not believe the Onyx exists at all." He nodded confidently. "I am absolutely sure there is no such thing."

"The Onyx *does* exist," Eddie announced. We all turned toward him with wide eyes. "I believe what Mo is referring to is the giant squid, or *Architeuthis*. These creatures are so elusive they were once called the 'aliens of inner space.' Evidence has been scarce, but scientists are still pretty sure giant squids exist, mainly because of all the eyewitness accounts and from stories like those about the Kraken. Think *20,000 Leagues Under the Sea*," he suggested. "Not too long ago, pictures surfaced of a giant squid washed up on shore, and more recently of a live one going after a baited fishing line. They can grow up to sixty feet long, maybe longer—possibly 175 feet, by one unconfirmed report. These marine creatures are extremely intelligent and very fast. They're considered voracious predators, worse than sharks, and some of the larger ones actually attack sperm whales." Eddie rubbed his hands together. "Here's the best part. These squids are so big their eyes are the size of a dinner plate and their tentacles—they have eight in all, two longer than the others—covered with tooth-lined suction cups, which they use to capture prey and draw it to their bird-like beaks."

No one said anything; we were all shocked into silence.

Ellie was the first to recover. "Well, I don't know about you guys, but I eat squid, not the other way around." She looked up at Mo and fluttered her carrot-colored eyelashes at him. She said they were her best feature and liked to use them accordingly. "I don't suppose you could help us out, you handsome devil."

Mo shook his head, blushing. "Oh, no! I could not do that to my family. Your escape under our watch would bring great shame to us. But I can keep you company while you are in Miseria." He flashed her a beaming smile. "You can tell me all about your world. My mates will be so jealous. The Upland has the *coolest* stuff. I have heard rumors that you can speak to someone who lives the length of a river away from you."

"Even farther than that," Eddie told him. "We use something called telephones. I'll tell you more about them when you come visit us in prison. You could tell us all about your world, too."

"I *have* heard of telephones," Mo said, his gray eyes glowing with excitement.

"But we'd like to learn *all* about your world, too," Eddie whispered conspiratorially. "I'm sure you know lots of cool stuff to tell us about Anaedor. Maybe you could even find out what's going to happen to us."

Mo grinned. "My mother does say I am very inquisitive."

"Mo!" Hedl hissed. He had pushed past Loo and Fig and stared at his brother, "Are you talking to the prisoners?"

Mo looked innocent. "They were talking—"

Hedl narrowed his eyes. "You better not be consorting with the enemy." His hand clasped the handle of his short sword.

When he turned back to the door, Mo stuck out his tongue. "He is such a . . ."—he looked around, searching for the perfect insult—"such a *nerd!*"

"Good one," Eddie nodded approvingly. "When you come visit us in our cell, we'll give you some more names to call your brother."

Mo grinned.

Finally, the door opened. Hedl stalked over to our group, rounded us up like a herd of cattle, and marched us toward the forbidding entry. A heavily muscled guard, who looked like Arnold Schwarzenegger back in his body building days, stood watch. Acknowledging Hedl, he touched his forehead with his fist in a kind of salute, but our captor pretended not to see him, marching past him down a long, dark corridor that stretched endlessly before us. All along its length, other corridors branched off like tree roots. Several Crushers bustled through the main passage, crossing back and forth between the offshoots, looking very important and busy as they scurried about. When they saw us, they saluted Hedl, fists to foreheads, then stepped aside to watch us pass with suspicious eyes.

Another hundred yards farther on, Hedl stopped to look back at us, then disappeared around a corner. When we reached the spot where he'd vanished, I saw a steep stairway leading downward, straight into Hell. At the bottom—I counted fifty worn steps—was another stout wooden door where a Crusher guard waited. He unlocked the door and waved us through.

Hedl strode through the entrance into yet another long, bleak corridor, with only a few Starkinder lanterns to light the way. The three of us, after some prodding by Loo and Fig, fell in behind him. The hall smelled of mold and rot, and was cold and damp and dark as a crypt, despite the Starkinders' efforts.

Passing several doors, we stopped at one with a small, barred window set at eye level—for normal-sized people, that is, not me. The same guard who had unlocked the door lifted a heavy wooden beam that barred the doorway. He pushed open the door, and it thumped dully against the stone wall inside the cell.

"All of you in." Hedl shoved each of us into the small, dark cell. My heart beat wildly as I fell to the floor. Unable to see a thing, I didn't want to move from where I'd landed, so I just sat there, frozen. The thick door banged shut behind us, the bar clunked into place, and we were left alone, with only the sound of dripping water and the smell of death to keep us company.

"You can't shut us in here!" Ellie yelled as she beat on the door with her fists. "I know my rights! I want my one phone call."

No one replied.

"This is crazy," she moaned. "We're never going to get out of here." She continued to pound on the door, shouting "Free the Human Three!" over and over.

"Ellie, stop that." I crawled over to her, pushed myself to my feet, and pulled her away from the door. "You're going to hurt yourself," I scolded as I clumsily draped my arm around her shoulders. She leaned against me as we sank to the floor. "We've got to stay calm."

"We're going to die in here, Lavida. I don't know why I need to be calm about it."

She had a valid point. In reality, I wanted to join her in her panic, but somehow I believed that if I kept my cool, things would work out.

"There better not be any rats down here," Ellie said. "I hate rats."

"No need to worry about the rats, girl," a raspy voice wheezed out at us from a far corner of the room. "The Terradors scare them off."

Ellie screamed.

CHAPTER TWENTY-ONE
MISERIA LOVES COMPANY

We could see nothing in the darkness of the cell.

"Eddie, do something!" Ellie demanded, clutching me tightly.

Eddie, being the male and therefore nominated to confront danger first, bravely called out, "Who's there?" in a shaky voice.

"Your worst nightmare," the voice growled like a wild animal.

"Stay back!" Eddie shouted. "I know karate."

"Oh, keep your knickers on," the creature snorted. "I can't even see you. And speak up, you're no louder than a bug in my ear. My hearing ain't what it used to be since a Terrador roared in my ear."

"Aren't you delightful," Ellie replied acerbically, quite

recovered from her fright.

"Who are you?" I asked.

"I was here first," the creature snapped. "Who are you? No one too bright by the sound of you."

Before Ellie could say something else sarcastic that got us nowhere, I intervened. "This is Ellie and Eddie. And I'm Lavida."

There was a moment of silence. "Lavida, did you say? Odd name. Mine's Piper, which isn't much better. I think it is, anyway. Ha. I've been here so long, I can't even remember my own name."

Ellie groaned. "You've been here *that* long? So what did *you* do wrong?"

"Well, that's the corker," Piper cackled. "I don't exactly remember."

"Oh, Mother of Mary!" Ellie exclaimed. She leaned toward me. "She's a loony, Lavida. We're stuck in here with a loony."

"Just because she can't remember things, doesn't make her a loony, Ellie," I whispered. "She might know a way out of here."

"Oh, nice," Ellie replied a bit too loudly. "I'm sure she has lots of great ideas, seeing how successful she's been at escaping herself."

"Now see here, girl," Piper responded crossly, "I'm not entirely deaf."

"Sorry," I quickly apologized for Ellie. I could tell by her mumbling that she wasn't about to do it herself. "Do you know what's going to happen to us?"

"How should I know? Probably the same thing that happened to the poor sap who was in here before me."

"Poor sap?"

"The Terradors got him." Piper hooted. "All they left behind were his dry old bones."

"Brilliant!" Eddie exclaimed. "What are Terradors?"

"White Dragons," Piper informed us, a hint of macabre glee in her voice. "The Crushers let them come up to Miseria once in a while to clean out the cells, if you know what I mean." We all sat in silence for a minute, digesting this bit of news.

"Listen, Diaper, or whoever you are," Ellie spoke up, "we don't want any trouble. I'm tired, and I just want to go home. Can you help us or not?"

"I think not," Piper said and yawned. "I'm going to sleep now, so keep your traps shut." Before I could say another word the sound of snoring filled the air.

"Don't tell me she just went to sleep . . ." Ellie exclaimed. "I told you guys she was a loony."

"Shhh, Ellie," I cautioned. "She might hear you."

"She said she was deaf."

"She seemed to hear us just fine," I reminded her.

"Man, I hate this place. We're surrounded by freaks!"

"They aren't freaks," I said quietly.

"Show me one person we've met here who isn't an aberration," she demanded.

"Ummm . . ." I struggled. I couldn't think of anyone.

"When the guards return we'll ask for a light," Eddie said, interrupting my efforts. "That should help a little. Maybe we should try to get some sleep."

"You've got to be kidding me," Ellie said with a shudder. "I'm not sleeping in here. Didn't you hear what Piper told us about the Terradors coming up to feed?"

"The likelihood of today being that day is pretty low, Ellie," Eddie reassured her.

"The likelihood of being kidnapped is also pretty low and look what happened," she muttered.

"If we're sleep deprived, we won't be able to think straight. We obviously aren't acclimated to the circadian rhythm for cave dwelling—thirty-four hours awake, fourteen asleep. We simply can't go that many hours without rest."

"I agree with Eddie. We need sleep." I felt tired, more than I should. Going up against Malvado had taken a lot out of me.

"All right, I'll sleep," Ellie reluctantly agreed. "But only if I get to sit between you two."

Eddie and I were okay with that, so the three of us slowly made our way toward one of the walls opposite where Piper sat. We were almost there when I tripped over something round that clattered hollowly across the stone floor. I shuddered and hugged myself tightly. *I don't even want to know.* We sat down and leaned against the cool, moist wall. Strange sounds filled the air, startling everyone from time to time. We fought sleep, afraid we might not wake up again, but at last each one of us slipped into an uneasy slumber.

"Wake up, Humans! It is me, Mo!" A bright light shone through the metal bars in the door's window.

Ellie yawned and stretched, banging Eddie and me on the head with her elbows. "I don't think I can handle any mo', Mo," she muttered sleepily.

"Humans?" Mo's eager eyes peered through the metal slats, darting around trying to see us. "I have brought food for you. You too, Piper. But you have to promise you will not try and escape like last time."

"I think she's sleeping," Eddie told him.

"Perhaps. She is a tricky one," Mo replied. "Tougher than she looks. And quicker." He rubbed his forehead gingerly, remembering their last encounter.

"So why is she here?" I asked him.

Mo shook his head. "I do not know; my brother never tells me anything. But some say she is a rebel and a spy. Anyway, I have brought something for you to eat. My mother is a master food preparer."

"What did she make?" Ellie asked, sounding grumpy. "Barbequed bat wings?"

Mo smiled in the light of his lamp. "How did you guess?" Ellie's eyes widened. "Though I do not know what barbequed means, so not that part. I have also brought you seaweed-stuffed mushrooms, crayfish, and guano juice."

"Guano juice?" she repeated, sounding a bit sick. "Doesn't that mean bat droppings?"

"Um, yes," Mo replied. "I never thought of it like that. In Anaedor we consider guano a great delicacy."

Ellie crossed her arms. "I'm not drinking bat poop or eating seaweed. I'll puke."

"Why don't you bring it in?" Eddie suggested, ignoring Ellie.

"I am not allowed to enter the cell—not after the last . . ." Mo left off, then recovered. "But I can push it through the slot on the door." His face disappeared from the window and reappeared by a small narrow opening at the bottom of the door. He peeked inside, his eyes gleaming.

Eddie pulled through several clay plates and set them down in front of Ellie and myself. We stared morosely at the food. Even Eddie looked uncertain.

Mo popped back up to peer through the small window. "I have something to tell you," he said excitedly.

I delicately pushed the rancid smelling plates in front of me far away—I think it was the bat wings—and leaned forward to listen.

"Malvado has convinced most of the Council Elders that Lavida is behind the poisoning. He has always wanted to prohibit Humans from entering Anaedor, looking for a good reason to make the ban a law—"

"And Lavida just happens to be that good reason," Eddie concluded.

I chewed on my thumbnail. "They're going to torture me, aren't they?"

Mo looked uncomfortable. "Well, you see, that is why I came . . . to tell you it might be easier if you confessed to the poisonings."

"She didn't do anything wrong!" Ellie cried indignantly. "They can't convict her just because we ratted her out."

"Actually, I don't think that you did, Ellie," I confessed, wishing I'd said something earlier.

"Then, what happened?"

"I think, from what Mo has said, that Malvado brainwashed you and made you say those things." I cringed, waiting for the anger.

"Brainwashed, hm? Well, that's a relief," she confessed, surprising me. "I didn't think I'd do anything like that on purpose. Well, not to a friend. I'd rat out that freak of nature Fiona in a heartbeat."

I laughed feebly.

"Sorry I brought up the belladonna, Lavida," Eddie put in. "Who knew he could get that out of me?"

"I'm just sorry I didn't believe in you." I really was. I finally got friends and the first thing I did was accuse them of something they didn't do.

Mo frowned. "Are you saying that Malvado made your friends lie?" He paused, looking puzzled. I don't think he knew what to do with that information. He said nothing for a moment, the wheels churning in his head.

"You were saying something about the Council . . ." I prompted him.

"Oh, yes. Malvado has nearly collected enough votes from the Council of Elders to use torture. My brother's favorite device is the rack—"

"Your brother!"

"Oh, yes. He is very good at it. He will stretch your arms and legs until all your bones break."

I swallowed hard. "If I admit I did something, they'll never let me out of here. But if I maintain my innocence, they'll break my bones. That's like drowning a witch to prove she's innocent. I can't win either way."

"Can't you just let us go?" Ellie pleaded with Mo.

"I am sorry, Ellie," Mo told her, his broad, innocent face pained.

"It's not your fault, Mo," I soothed, though a tiny part of me wished that it had been. I wanted someone to blame for this mess—someone other than myself for once.

Sensing he was off the hook, the Crusher grinned, promptly changing the subject to a more pleasant topic. "So what new names do you have for me to call my brother?"

"Ellie has quite the arsenal," Eddie muttered. "Ask her."

"Do I ever!" she responded heartily. "I personally like the classics—doofus, hoser, dorkwad, lowlife. Reeky, beetle-brained, maggot pie for those jerks who really annoy me. Then there's stoner, rocks-for-brains . . ."

I was about to stop Ellie's "helpful" hints when Mo said, "Thank you for those wonderful names, Ellie, but I have to go now. Malvado is coming."

"What! He's coming now?"

Mo's head disappeared and we heard his footsteps hurrying away. The cell was dark again, and quiet. It wasn't long before the foreboding sound of another heavier set of footsteps approached. Malvado's maggot-pale face filled the opening. He scanned the room before fastening his dark, hypnotic eyes on me.

"Are you ready to confess?" he asked, his voice slippery and thin.

"She didn't do anything," Ellie answered for me. "You made us lie!"

"I did no such thing," he growled at her. "That would be breaking the rules of our august court." He smirked, knowing there was no way we could prove anything. "You have one more tock to change your mind, Human, before I change it for you." As quickly as he had appeared, he was gone.

"And in that time," Eddie calculated, "he'll get the remaining votes he needs to go ahead with the torture. That's the only reason he's delaying, anyway."

"This really stinks," Ellie grumbled.

I seriously considered trying to do something myself to get us out. It was dark, Ellie and Eddie wouldn't be able to see a thing. I would have to be tricky about making the attempt; it would be risky, but I owed it to them, especially after believing they'd betrayed me.

"Never fear!" a high-pitched voice announced grandly, startling me, "Vesuvius is here." Ellie shrieked as the little man appeared before us in a halo of soft pink light. The light came from a Starkinder sitting on Vesuvius's shoulder, nestled against his fluffy hair. It cowered there nervously, as though afraid of the big world around it. "I come bearing greetings, and chocolate."

"Vesuvius!" I cried, feeling hope for the first time in hours as I grabbed the Hershey bar he was balancing on his big hair. "Where did you get this?" I tore off the wrapper and divided it into three parts, which we stuffed into our mouths. Even Ellie, who was studying the visitor with undisguised distaste.

"Why, I found it in your room, of course," he replied as though there really could be no other answer.

"What were you doing in my room?" I asked suspiciously, using my sleeve to wipe off any chocolate that might have found my cheek or chin or nose, instead of my mouth.

"Looking for things, darling." He glanced over at Ellie and Eddie, his light green eyes speculative. "Mercy me!" he burst out, staring at Ellie, who was staring back at him. "What are you wearing on your face, dear girl?"

Ellie's revolted stare turned surly. "They're glasses."

"Of course, they are! I have never seen this kind of accoutrement in such a daring color. They look absolutely divine on you. I must try them on some time. Do *not* break my poor little heart and say no."

Ellie looked at him, then she glanced over at me. "What is this thing, Lavida?"

"That *thing* is Vesuvius. He attached himself to me in Madrina's cave—she's the Blendar leader I told you about. He thinks I have no fashion taste."

She snorted. "He's right." Fingering her pink glasses, she looked at Vesuvius. "So you like them?"

"That's not a compliment, Ellie," I told her. "Look at what he's wearing."

"What's wrong with what he's wearing?" She reached out and stroked the tiny fur cape. "I love it."

Vesuvius gave a little bow. "Of course, you do. You obviously have good taste . . . unlike some other creatures in this room." He threw me an exasperated look. Ellie bit back a giggle.

"Forgive me," Eddie interrupted. "But what exactly are you?"

Vesuvius hopped up onto Eddie's knee and patted his face. "I am your savior, dear, naïve child." He jumped down and straightened his cape.

"I mean, *what* are you?"

"Oh, yes, of course. I . . . am a Zephoo."

"Zephoo?" repeated Eddie.

"Bless you." Ellie sniggered.

"Yes, yes. Have no doubt, I have come to get you out." He preened for a moment, then said, "There is only one teensy, weensy problem." He examined his nails critically.

"What's that?"

He looked me up and down. "Your gargantuan *size* is the problem." He clasped his hands together and sighed. "I *did* so want to be a hero. I was going to lift the bar, but they locked it down, so I nixed that idea. Instead I had to slide in through that slot by the door, which, as you can imagine, I did *not* like doing; it wreaks havoc on the do." He fluffed his hair. "I suppose none of you can shrink . . . ?"

My hopes plummeted through the floor.

"If only Ian were here!" Ellie wailed. "He'd get us out of this."

"I can get you out," a rasping voice rent the air. We all swung toward the back of the cave. It was Piper. I'd forgotten about her.

"Mercy me!" Vesuvius jumped back, his hand pressed against his heart. "What is this Uggums, may I ask?"

"Watch it, Tinkerbell," Piper said gruffly, swinging her head toward Vesuvius. "You'd make a nice snack." He scooted away from her, looking quite appalled that she would suggest he might be food.

We leaned closer to get a good look at Uggums—er, Piper—but she was hard to see in the Starkinder's muted pink light. All I could make out was what looked like a pile of old rags sitting against the wall, topped by a mop of long, greasy hair.

"I told you all before that I had a way out of here,"

she grumbled.

"No, you didn't," Ellie said.

"Shut up, Ellie!" Eddie hissed at her.

"Come see." Piper motioned us over. "I'm busting through the wall."

Eddie bravely volunteered to check out the hole while the rest of us hoped this wasn't some kind of trap. He bent over, picked up a rock and banged it on the wall. Something heavy hit the floor.

"The wall is weak here," he called back. "I think we can break through."

I was all for trying. "Eddie and I will work on the wall. Ellie, you watch the hallway. Vesuvius . . . well, you just stay out of our way, okay?"

"Done and done," Vesuvius assented and hopped aside.

Eddie and I took turns pounding on the wall with a large stone and pushing the rubble away. The wall was surprisingly brittle in areas and crumbled easily. Piper ordered us around and Vesuvius babbled on and on about his new shoes and their shiny buckles.

I was banging as hard as I could against the collapsing wall when Ellie screeched. "Hurry up, you guys! I think I hear them coming!"

Eddie joined me, and we both hammered and pounded on the wall, scraping our knuckles and bruising our hands, though I didn't feel the pain—only my heart beating and my head throbbing with adrenaline.

"Come on, come on!"

One stubborn layer of rock remained impervious to our efforts. "Stand back, Eddie," I said. I didn't want him to see what I was about to do. To cover my actions, I put my hands on the wall and pretended to push. At the same time, I concentrated my energy on the stone, directing all my force into it. Blood pulsed through my veins and a splintering sound, like ice cracking, came from beneath my hands.

"I think I found the weak spot," I yelled. I grabbed a stone, and after one big whack, my hand broke through the fractured rock. "Get over here, Ellie. Help us knock out the rest of this wall."

She dashed over to us and threw her weight into it—literally. The size of the hole was soon large enough for a small dog.

Just a little farther . . .

Voices came from outside the door.

"Stand back, you two," Ellie told us. She ducked her shoulder like a defensive lineman and slammed into the wall, bringing huge chunks to the ground. We had our hole.

The sound of the wooden bar banging against stone startled us. I glanced toward the door and made out the outline of someone's hair in the small window. Malvado. I pushed Ellie and Eddie through the opening. "Go!" I turned to the old woman. Her hair had parted, revealing sunken eyes and a strong nose. "Come on, Piper. Let's go!"

"Get out of here," she wheezed. "Your incessant babble is giving me a headache."

I shook my head. "We're not leaving you behind. You saved our lives."

"Scat!" Piper shouted. "I can handle myself."

I tried to see into her eyes, torn over what to do, but she made the decision for me, all but throwing me through the opening. Vesuvius jumped onto my shoulder and clung to my neck as I wiggled the rest of the way through. Once on the other side, the Starkinder squeaked in terror and flew away, leaving us in darkness.

"Never trust a freed Starkinder," Vesuvius muttered in my ear.

The prison door scraped against the rocky floor and

banged loudly against the wall. I shot to my feet and ran two blind steps before tumbling over Ellie and Eddie huddled together.

"Why aren't you moving?"

"Shush."

"What's that sound?" A rushing, babbling noise surrounded us.

"It's a river," Eddie informed me, his voice unusually anxious. "Annual flooding must have weakened the wall. That's why we were able to break through."

I bit my lip uncertainly. We were out of Miseria, but now faced a roaring river. Behind us, footsteps filled the prison room. "Have you made up your mind, Human?" a voice demanded. The sound of a scuffle broke out. "Answer me!"

"Did you come to ask me on a date, young sir?" Piper cackled crazily. "I might be going blind, but it doesn't take eyes to see how much you like me!"

"Where are they, you old bat?" Malvado roared.

"Where are who, darling? It's only you and me. Just the way you planned it, I'm sure. Give me a kiss. Oh, you brute!" Piper crowed. "I thought you loved me!" She laughed even louder, then a grunt cut through the air and was followed by an ominous silence.

"Guards!" Malvado bellowed. "The Humans have escaped. Go after them!"

"We have to jump, you guys," I told them around the lump in my throat.

"But I just had my hair done," Ellie fretted.

"Me, too," Vesuvius echoed.

"Oh, for Pete's sake, you two, will you shut up about the hair! We jump or we die. Now, on the count of three. One, two—"

"This way!" a voice came from behind, echoing through the cavern. Light shone into the river cave, and the roaring river came into focus. It looked cold and dark and very deep.

I stepped back. There had to be another way . . .

"Stay where you are!" a guard shouted, only feet away.

A hand brushed against my arm, then tightened. My blood froze. With a wrenching twist, I yanked free.

"Three!" I shouted and leaped as the hand struggled to regain its hold. I had expected my feet to reach water right away, but the fall was long enough to scream my lungs out of air. There was no time to draw another breath before I hit the river.

I plunged deep into the icy water, then kicked my way to the surface, gasping for air and searching for any sign of Ellie and Eddie.

They had disappeared.

"The Pirudons will get them now," I heard someone laugh as the river carried me swiftly away. "And if not, the Falls of Death will do the job."

CHAPTER TWENTY-TWO
VERGE OF DEATH

The water was frigid and running fast. I couldn't see anything in its murky depths. The tunnel was nearly black, illuminated by occasional glimmers of light that only briefly alleviated the darkness. Starkinders. When their lights flashed on, I looked around as I struggled to stay afloat, hoping to spot Ellie and Eddie. Where were they?

The rough walls of the cave rose steeply up from the water. If I could manage to swim over to the side, which seemed virtually impossible in this torrent, I might be able to climb up on a ledge and spot them.

"Ellie! Eddie!" I shouted, gulping down water.

No answer.

I tried swimming against the flow, but the current was too strong. I reluctantly turned to face downstream and at last spotted Ellie's and Eddie's heads far ahead of me. They were alive! I was paddling toward them when something the size of a cat jumped on my shoulder and seized hold of my ear. I gasped in horror, remembering the Pirudons. Coughing and spluttering water, I swiped at it as best I could before swallowing another mouthful of water.

"Do you mind?" Vesuvius panted. "I am trying to save myself."

"Vesu—" I began to say before I slurped up more water. "Let go!" I tried to loosen his grip, but had to give up when I started sinking again.

He grabbed a fistful of my hair. "I shall save you."

"*You* . . . save *me*?"

"Lavida!" Ellie shouted. "Is that you . . . you . . . you?" Her voice echoed in the tunnel. "Did those guards say something about a waterfall?" The frigid water was making her voice shake; or maybe that was fear. It should be fear. I sensed trouble ahead, and this time, there was no mistaking it.

"Maybe," I hedged. There was no sense getting her riled up. She was bad enough when she was *un*riled up.

"There's no maybe about it," Eddie yelled. "I'm detecting a change in water speed. At the rate we're traveling, we'll reach the falls any minute."

So much for protecting Ellie.

Vesuvius whistled loudly in my ear. "Well, Mademoiselle Mors, it has been fun, but now I must run." In the dim light, I watched in dismay as a round fuzzy creature whizzed straight for my head. It was the rat-bat. As it passed over us, Vesuvius stood up on my shoulder and grabbed onto its tail, using the makeshift rope to swing his entire body up and onto the fat creature's back.

"Vesuvius!" I shouted after him. I would've raised my fist and shaken it at him if I didn't need both hands to keep from drowning. "Get back here, you coward!"

"Ta, ta," he sang and disappeared into the darkness.

"Lavida," Ellie cried out. "Something just banged into me!"

I felt my blood go cold. At the same time, something big and heavy slammed against me. The force of the blow knocked me under the dark, turbulent water. My heartbeat pounding in my ears, I kicked my way to the surface and came up spluttering. "Swim, Ellie! Swim, Eddie!" I shouted wildly. "Toward the edge of the river. We're under attack!" I swam as hard as I could. But each time I got close to the walls of the cave, the beast lurking beneath the water knocked me back toward the middle of the river as though herding me.

I was tiring. I wouldn't be able to swim much longer. The roar of water filled my ears, loud as a tornado, and grew louder with each passing second.

"We're almost at the falls," I called out. "Swim!"

"I can't swim anymore," Ellie cried. "My arms are numb."

"Look!" Eddie shouted. "There's a light up ahead."

I spotted the bright glow just as a massive head broke through the black water in front of me. Two more heads appeared on my left and right, surrounding me. The first arrival opened its giant mouth, revealing a gaping hole filled with row upon row of sharp, glittering teeth. There was little doubt in my mind that these were the dreaded Pirudons. They were so close to me now I could've counted each individual, terrifying tooth. I gulped air and the smell of rotten fish infiltrated my nostrils. Bile rose up from my stomach.

"Get away from me!" I blurted out.

Resisting Malvado and breaking through the rock had sapped the last of my strength. I could only slap the palm of my hand on the water. The nasty creature roared and ducked beneath the surface. The remaining two beasts followed the first, bellowing at me before diving beneath the foam. The appalling thought occurred to me that they had gone underwater so they could get at me from below. I jerked my knees to my chest and searched anxiously for the twins; they floated several feet ahead of me, the current whipping them down the river. We were fast running out of room.

"Grab the rope!" a voice shouted from the bank.

Up ahead, three figures stood on a ledge overlooking the river. One held a Starkinder lantern aloft and the other two, Loria and Darian, gripped a rope. Boy, was I glad to see them. Working together, the siblings tossed one end of the long, thick rope out into the swift river current. Ellie and Eddie arrived at the line first: Eddie snagged it before it sank and hung on tight; Ellie reached for the rope, but her hand slipped and she whizzed right past it. She tried to swim back toward the rope, but she couldn't make any progress against the current. Clutching the rope with one hand, Eddie reached out for his sister.

"Stretch, Ellie!" he yelled, reaching as far as he could. Ellie flailed desperately in the water, trying to grab hold of Eddie's hand. Their fingertips touched, then she slipped away. "Ellie!" Eddie screamed for what he thought would be the last time, when she suddenly stopped in the current, her body flipping around to face upstream, rushing water parting on her face as though she were being dragged behind a speed boat. She had caught onto the rope trailing Eddie.

I moved quickly downstream toward the line, too quickly I realized. I had only one chance to grab hold.

Eddie reached for me as I swept past him. I lunged for his hand with my right and missed, but I caught Ellie's hood with the other. Fighting hard to hang on, I brought my right hand around and grasped the line.

"Pull us in!" Eddie shouted.

We were safe, I thought, relieved, then I remembered the Pirudons lurking below the surface. The Blendars yanked hard on the long rope and I felt myself moving toward the riverbank. Eddie was at the front, followed by Ellie and myself, dangling at the tail end of the rope like a baited worm.

Behind me a terrifying roar battered my eardrums. I don't know what made me turn around—I thought I'd learned never to turn around when something horrible was trying to get me—but turn, I did. One of the Pirudons raced toward me as swiftly as a shark, its horrendous mouth bearing down on me. Terrified, I whipped my head back toward the shore.

"Hurry!" I cried.

Darian and Loria swiftly pulled the rope hand over hand, their pale faces taut with the effort. The other Blendar set down the lantern and hurried to the ledge to pull Eddie, then Ellie, onto dry land. I was the last one. Darian dropped the rope and reached down to help me up. As he grabbed my wrist, my footing slipped and I slid back down the bank, screaming. But before I disappeared back into the water, he seized the collar of my blazer and hauled me up. I flew into his arms, where he grabbed hold of me. After a few moments, I realized I was hugging Darian so tightly he couldn't have gotten away if he had tried. I let go of him and quickly stepped away, unimaginably embarrassed.

Drawing myself up into a dignified stance, I was about to thank him when he grabbed my arm and jerked me roughly away from the edge—just as a large mouth snapped shut where I'd been standing.

I found myself in his arms for the second time within the

space of a minute. I felt surprised, and a little worried, to realize I wasn't in any hurry for him to let go. For his part, Darian didn't seem too eager either.

"Whew!" Eddie wheezed. "That was a close one."

Darian stepped away from me, an odd look on his face as he reached down to pick up the lamp. "You have no idea."

The three of us, shaking and dripping water, peered into the darkness. Eddie and I shuffled forward and looked over the edge. Water dropped away into a black pit of nothingness. Three more seconds in the river and we'd have gone over the falls.

"Just in the nick of time," Eddie declared unsteadily as we backed away from the precipice. He bumped into Loria, who was standing behind him, peering over his shoulder to see the falls. "Excuse me," he apologized, then looked up at Loria. "Wow!"

She looked spectacular. Like Darian, she was in her Blendar form and, also like him, she didn't look all that different from her human disguise. Or maybe I was seeing what I wanted to see, what I was comfortable seeing. She wore an all-black outfit, and a tall hat topped her dark, curly hair. Her apparel was curiously similar to what I'd worn my first night in Anaedor, with the addition of the hat. It appeared that I was, for the very first time in my life, a trendsetter. I couldn't wait to tell Vesuvius the good news, if I ever saw the twerp again.

"I've never seen anyone so beautiful," Eddie said sincerely, wrapping his arms around his shivering frame.

"Oooh!" Loria cooed, pinching Eddie's cheek. "You are so little, and so cute."

"I am but nothing in the light of your beauty," he proclaimed, drawing himself up with as much dignity as someone who looked like a drowned rat could.

Ellie appraised Loria, then turned to Eddie. "Well, well,

well," she purred, "I never thought you had it in you, Eddie Maguire—making goo-goo eyes and spouting poetry." She laughed and leaned forward to nudge him.

"Stop it, Ellie," he hissed at her over his shoulder.

"I'm merely pointing out," she went on, indifferent to his reddening cheeks, "that earlier today you were saying I was too romantic. And now you come up with this?" She smiled sweetly at Loria. "My brother says he doesn't believe in romance."

"I never said that," he replied through clenched teeth. "I merely implied that you overdid it . . . like you do with everything."

"I do not, you—"

I glared at the two of them. "You guys! Loria and Darian just saved our lives."

"Excuse me," a high-pitched voice exclaimed. "*I* saved your lives." Vesuvius swooped down on his little creature and jumped off to land agilely on my shoulder, grabbing a strand of my wet hair to keep himself from falling off. The rat-bat flew off with a chirp.

"It was I who told them where to find you, missy," he grandly informed me, "just in time to throw you the rope. They were heading in the wrong direction, you see." He glared at me, his tiny hands planted on his hips. It wasn't easy looking at someone who was an inch away from my head and whose hair had puffed out to the size of a basketball. I kept hitting my nose on his tight curls. "I would like an apology for being called a coward, Mademoiselle Mors. I might be vertically challenged, but I am *not* a coward."

I sighed. "I'm so sorry, Vesuvius. You're my knight in shining velvet. You saved the day." I bit my lip. "Oh, and nice hair, by the way." He made a horrible face at me, which I could see out of the corner of my eye, but chose to

He crossed his arms. "I expected a better apology, but that will have to do, I suppose. Humans are not known for their way with words." After another dirty look at me, he turned to face Ellie, who was attempting to dry her glasses on her wet shirt.

"You did not lose your glasses!" he said, drawing Ellie's startled attention up to him. "Loria, look at them." He deserted me, hopping down to the ground, using his coat to slow his descent, and ran over to Ellie, his heels tapping on the floor. "They are simply fabulous."

Loria skipped over to look at the glasses, which now sat on Ellie's nose. "They are so beautiful," she announced after delivering a chorus of oohs and ahhs.

"Thanks," Ellie said, her eyes wary as though she expected them to attack her at any moment. "I bought them in Paris." She relaxed her guard a little as the two begged her to tell them about her shopping experiences in the great city of fashion, which she did with increasing enthusiasm. Close by, Eddie took turns staring at Loria and emptying the water out of his tennis shoes.

I looked over at Darian to see how he was taking all this, only to discover that he was staring at me as he gathered up the rope. He bowed. "We meet again."

"Yes, we do," I replied with a shiver. "But this time I'm glad to see you."

Darian frowned, before a little smile played around the corners of his mouth. "Likewise."

Tying his shoe, Eddie piped up, "Don't you think we should be putting some distance between us and Malvado?"

"He probably thinks we went over the falls," I said.

I hoped.

Darian shook his head. "Malvado would not leave that to chance. No, he is right. We must keep moving. I will introduce you to Gille first, though." He waved toward the other Blendar hovering in the background, the one who had helped pull Ellie and Eddie from the river.

Gille didn't look like a typical Blendar, being shorter and more rotund. His hair was a thick, reddish-brown and grew not only on his head, but on his arms and chest, sticking out from the neckline of a tan shirt. His nose was round and piggish, rather than long and pointy. He actually looked more like a Dwarf than a Blendar, except for his abnormally large eyes. Besides the Blendars, I'd seen no other creature in Anaedor with those eyes.

"Even though he is new to Anaedor," Darian said, which explained why Gille looked so different from the other Blendars, "when he learned that Loria and I were attempting to find a way to get you out of Miseria, he volunteered to help us." He proudly clapped Gille on the back.

Gille sniffed loudly and rubbed his pug, reddened nose before bowing stiffly. "Thank you, Darian," he said nasally as he straightened up, "but I think any noble citizen of this great world would do the same. I feel honored simply being here."

"Well, thanks. All of you," I said. "I thought we were goners, that no one would help us." Darian looked at me sharply when I said this.

"Just keep in mind that it was I who rescued you," Vesuvius exclaimed, beating his tiny chest dramatically. "*I* am the hero of this story!"

Loria picked him up. "Yes, you are, Vesuvius," she soothed. "I shall tell everyone about your heroics when we get back to the compound."

Appeased, Vesuvius tugged at his tunic. "That is more like it."

"What's that sound?" Eddie asked, and we all turned to look at him. He stood up and cocked his head to the side.

We stopped to listen and heard shouting. Angry shouting. "They're coming!" His eyes brightened.

"This way," Darian urged. He motioned us toward a dark opening in the cave wall.

Vesuvius mounted his hovering rat-bat and we all left the roar of the river behind, following Darian into a small nook. Our footsteps echoed and multiplied as though there were twice as many people in the cave. I glanced around nervously, spotting three animals waiting patiently for their riders to return. They looked like llamas but were shorter with wider, flatter backs and bigger heads. Their pale golden fur was thick and soft. Luxurious manes—full as a lion's—encircled their broad faces and flowed down their long necks onto their backs. When I saw their large, sleepy eyes, which were white as snow, I realized with a sense of dismay that they were blind.

"Quickly now." Darian attached his Starkinder lamp to the collar on one of the animals. Loria and Gille did the same. "I will carry Lavida with me on my Huffer. Gille, you take the other Human female."

"I *do* have a name," Ellie said dryly. "It's Ellie. This is my twin brother, Eddie."

Darian straightened. "You are twins, as well?" He seemed taken aback by this information. I looked at him. Something was going on inside that brain of his. "I am Darian," he introduced himself, regaining his composure, "and this is my sister, Loria." He motioned toward her.

"These are the ones who took me into Anaedor that first time, when I thought I was dreaming," I explained.

"Well, that solves that mystery," Eddie said. "Can I assume you two are the *other* set of twins?"

Darian nodded absently. "The *Prophecies* say there will be two of a kind, and two of a kind, and then three," he murmured. "Could it be we are—"

Long, blood-curdling howls reverberated through the tunnel behind us.

"Darian," Loria cried, "they are crossing the river!"

He nodded. I couldn't believe how relaxed he seemed. My heart was beating wildly, and if I hadn't been so cold and wet, I'd have been a little pool of sweat on the floor by now. He swiftly mounted his Huffer and held out his hand to me. I took it and he pulled me onto the patient animal with little effort. "Little Eddie will go with Loria."

"It's not *little* Eddie," Eddie grumbled as he struggled to climb onto the wide back of the Huffer.

"You will have to hold onto me," Loria told him as she grabbed the leather reins. "Huffers are a lot faster than they look." She laughed at the look of alarm on Eddie's face. "Do not be shy. As you Humans like to say, I do not bite." With a sharp command, she snapped the reins and the beast took off like an arrow. Eddie managed to grab onto her waist to keep from flying off. They disappeared into the darkness of the tunnel leading from the nook.

"Loria," Darian called after her, "wait for us." He frowned, turning back to Gille. "That sister of mine . . . we must go now or we will never catch her."

Gille nodded, then turned to Ellie. "If it pleases you, I advise you to hang on tight." After a moment's hesitation, she wrapped her arms around him and squeezed him like an orange in a juicer—his face actually turned a bit purple—as he spurred his furry steed.

"Sekar, ride!" Darian commanded. I grabbed him around his narrow waist and we leaped forward. Vesuvius tore off ahead of us on his fat rat-bat, singing a ridiculous song about the wonders of being a Zephoo.

Despite the obvious danger of our situation, I couldn't help but feel exhilarated as the cave walls rushed past. Although the Huffers were blind, they seemed to know exactly where they were going. And they were fast. Faster than anything I'd ever been on. I heard myself laughing out loud and clapped a hand over my mouth. I was as bad as Eddie.

"You find something amusing?" Darian asked over his shoulder.

"As a matter of fact, I do. I *really* like these Huffers."

"Yes," he agreed. "They are good, gentle creatures."

"And they're *really* fast."

"Indeed. Shall we overtake Loria?"

I laughed again. I never would've thought Darian had it in him. "Yes!"

Darian nodded. "Sekar, go!"

Sekar shook her big, furry head, then accelerated like a race car. We passed Gille and Ellie, and it wasn't long before we narrowed the gap behind Loria. She glanced back to see us closing in on her. She grinned and urged her Huffer on. The light of our lanterns threw shadows onto the wall as we galloped by and lit Eddie's pale face and wide eyes. He hung on tightly.

"Eddie looks like he's going to throw up," I said to Darian.

"That is an unfortunate side effect of riding Huffers," he explained. "You are not sick?"

"Not even close. Go faster!"

Darian cracked the reins. It didn't seem possible that Sekar could run any faster, but she did. We'd almost caught up to Loria when out of the corner of my eye I saw something whiz past my head. Vesuvius? No, he'd already passed us.

"What was that?" I glanced back over my shoulder. I could see Gille and Ellie galloping toward us. Behind them, large shadows loomed just around the corner. Hooves clattered on the stone floor. Someone, or some*thing*, was coming. Fast.

"Get your head down, Lavida," Darian yelled. I clung to him, feeling his stomach muscles tighten under my hands. "They are shooting at us." He slouched down and called out to the other two, "Loria! Gille! Our enemies are upon us!"

As quick as that, our little jaunt became serious. Darian twisted around, a muscle ticking in the hollow beneath his cheekbone. I shuddered. Strapped to his wrist was his crossbow. He took aim and let loose a bolt from his bow. His eyes were completely black and deadly serious now; no longer was he as human looking as I'd thought. I shivered again, truly understanding how real all of this was. At exactly that moment, a sharp burning pain ignited in my left arm. I looked down to see an arrow piercing it and blood dripping off my elbow. I blinked several times before finally realizing what this meant. My stomach seized up as a wave of dizziness gripped my brain.

"Darian," I gasped as a terrible weakness made my body heavy.

He reached back and took hold of me before I fell off the Huffer. Wrapping a strong arm around my waist, he somehow managed to pull me in front of him. The Huffer slowed and Gille, oblivious to what had happened, skirted around us, moving on ahead.

"Hold onto Sekar's mane," he said in my ear. He sounded far away. I wove my numb fingers through the thick fur and tried to keep them closed. It was hard.

He found the shaft of the arrow in my arm with one hand while the other snapped the reins, urging the Huffer to move faster. "You have been hit by a poisoned arrow." He sounded distressed.

My head dropped forward of its own accord. I couldn't raise it.

He shook me. "You will die soon. Are you listening? If

you are truly the *One*, then you must heal yourself. You have the power, use it now!"

I felt my blood grow cold. "I can't," I groaned, wanting desperately to throw up. My stomach spun like a whirlpool and I felt so weak. "I've nothing left."

Darkness rushed into my mind.

PIRUDON

CHAPTER TWENTY-THREE

MUNGULAS AND CRUSHERS AND TROLLS, OH MY!

Darian shook my injured arm, reviving me. "You must try!" he urged. "Like when you crossed Warrior's Walk—you have to believe you can do it. You *have* to believe, Lavida!"

"They might see me!" I gasped. "I can't let them know—"

"What are you talking about?"

"They'll think I'm a freak." I wanted to give up and go to sleep, but the excruciating pain in my arm kept me awake. It felt like someone was jabbing a hot poker into my muscle.

"And that is terrible because . . ." I couldn't answer, so Darian did it for me. "Because to you Humans, anyone different is a freak," he sneered, his abrupt change shocking me. "And you feel the same way. About Barg, about me and

Loria, about all of us. You are as bad as the rest of your kind!"

Despite my drowsiness I felt myself growing angry, the emotion energizing me a bit. "You don't . . . you don't get it. Agh! I can't . . . talk!" My tongue was coated in cement.

"Then stop talking. Focus on what you need to do. You must destroy the poison, or you will die."

You will die.

Ellie and Eddie were far enough ahead; they wouldn't know what I was doing. I felt so drained, so tired and empty, as though my soul had deserted me. But I had to try. My veins pulsed and my head throbbed to the beat of my heart as I tried to concentrate all my energy on destroying the poison. A part of me fought against my efforts; I was so used to focusing on helping others. Yet when it came to saving myself, I wasn't sure how to go about it. I almost felt as though I didn't deserve to be saved.

If you die, you won't be able to get your friends out. You'll have failed them.

The words, bitter and true, cleared my mind and I was able to focus once more. In mere seconds, my body grew feverishly warm as I brought my mind to bear on the poison in my veins fighting its way up to my heart, my lungs, my brain. Breathing was hard. Everything was hard. My whole body shaking, I forced the effects of the poison back down to the bone-white shaft lodged in my arm, commanding the malevolence to go away. It struggled against my will like a wild stallion and I dearly wanted to give up.

And then, slowly, slowly, my mind began to clear and I felt myself returning to reality. My eyes opened. Except for a small area in my left arm, the pain had almost entirely faded.

"You are back," Darian whispered in my ear. He

sounded both surprised and relieved. "I feared you were lost. Now hold on. We are in for a ride." He sat up straight and snapped his reins. When we caught up to the others, Darian cried, "Now, Loria! Now, Gille!" Their Huffers swerved to the left and darted into a dark, narrow tunnel. Without prompting, Sekar followed after them, arrows whizzing past her big, shaggy head. Quick as spilled ink, the passage became darker than a black hole. The Starkinders had doused their lights. Closing my tired eyes once more, I wrapped my arms around Sekar's long, thick neck. Seconds later, I realized I could no longer feel her rhythmic stride beneath me. I opened an eye, wondering what was going on.

The frightening sounds of howling and growling burst out behind me. Twisting around, I spotted Crushers mounted on large, long-legged, wolf-like beasts. From a ledge over-looking a deep abyss the gray men were shooting arrows at us like machine guns. Their mounts, with matted brown fur dripping water, snarled and snapped ferociously at us. They looked hungry.

Wait a minute . . . if the Crushers were standing on the edge of a bottomless pit, where were we?

It didn't take long to figure out that something was wrong with this picture—we were falling into the pit!

Before I could panic, Sekar shifted her body and took a sharp right. My eyes adjusted a bit to the dark and I looked down to see Sekar's front and back legs stretched straight out from her sides, a flap of skin connecting them. She looked like an oversized flying squirrel. The webbing caught the air and held us aloft, soaring along like a hang glider. I was relieved to find we weren't plunging to our deaths. Unfortunately, we were now heading into a deep, black pit. I had a sinking feeling this was the kind of place where trespassers didn't live long enough to warn others what lurked in the shadows.

The lower we sailed, the darker it grew—so dark that I couldn't see my hand in front of my face. On the plus side, the Crushers had stopped shooting arrows at us. Either they'd given up because they couldn't see us, or they knew something we didn't about what awaited us below.

"I can't see a thing, and I'm cold," Ellie complained, her teeth chattering.

"I am cold, as well," Gille remarked stuffily. "Much to my chagrin, the cave environment does not seem to be very good for my health. I have a rather delicate constitution, I think."

"Please!" Darian entreated. "We must be quiet now. We do not want to disturb the savages that hide here. They would tear out your throat just for the pleasure of watching you die."

In the darkness, I could swear I heard Ellie's jaws snap shut. They stayed closed for about three seconds before popping open again. "Now wait a dang minute, Darian. Just because you're incredibly attractive doesn't mean you can tell me what to do. I want to get out of this messed-up world of yours, ASAP. You can drop us off. Anywhere around here would be good. And if you'd point us in the right direction, we'll find our own way back home."

"If that is what you want," Darian replied. His voice was calm, but I could tell by the tenseness in his arms that he was struggling to keep his tone even. "I would not want to force you to stay in a place you find loathsome. But I must warn you, Ellie, the moment you are left alone, you will be captured. And I guarantee that whatever creature finds you will not be as kind to you as we have been."

There was a moment's silence. "Okay, fine. I'll stay with you," she grumbled. "But I'm not happy about this."

"Me either," Vesuvius seconded. "My hair is in ruins, I

have not changed my clothes in four tocks, and I think I have Igglebugs in my shorts. I simply cannot *take* it anymore."

"Oh, Vesuvius," Loria giggled. "You are so dramatic."

"I take offense to that, dear Loria," Vesuvius drawled. "I am not *dramatic*, I am *entertaining*."

"You are certainly entertaining, Vesuvius," Darian shot back dryly. "And you are welcome to go ahead and change."

Vesuvius said nothing, so I guessed that he'd decided to stick with the group. Which made me wonder what lived in this place that scared Vesuvius enough to chance the apparent horror of wearing the same clothes for longer than four tocks, whatever those were. Hours, maybe? Hopefully not minutes. That would be a bit extreme, even for Vesuvius.

"Where *is* our destination?" Eddie asked the same question I'd been pondering. "You're taking us back home, right?"

"We cannot do that yet," Darian told him. "The Healers must attend to Lavida first. She is hurt."

"Hurt?" everyone echoed in disbelief. They all started talking at once, forgetting Darian's warning to stay quiet.

"Did he say *hurt*, Lavida?" Ellie cried out. "What happened? Talk to me, girl!"

"I'm fine!" I shouted, feeling panicky. They were going to find out what I'd done. "Darian's exaggerating things."

"I am *not*," Darian answered as he tightened his grip around my waist. "You have a Crusher arrow in your arm. Only a Healer can remove it."

"No one survives the wound from a Crusher arrow," Gille said. "She should be dead already."

"You're going to die?" Ellie lamented. "You can't die on me, Lavida! You're my only friend! Breathe, girl! Breathe!" She breathed loudly, in . . . out, as though reminding me how it should be done.

"I'm okay, Ellie," I assured her, thrilled to hear that I was her only friend. "I hardly feel it anymore."

"How can that be?" Loria asked.

"That is what I would like to know," Darian replied. "The poison comes from a Mungula and has never failed to kill its intended victim . . . until now, that is."

"Maybe it isn't a Crusher arrow," Eddie suggested.

"Eddie's probably right," I said hurriedly, willing Darian to stop talking.

He shook his head. "The arrow is definitely Crusher. They use fresh Zephoo leg bones to construct the shafts." He paused when a loud moan rent the air. "Sorry, Vesuvius. I did not mean to remind you."

"Oh, the sheer brutality of it all!" Vesuvius lamented. I imagined him placing the back of his hand to his forehead. "How could they do that to my kinfolk?"

"That's so sick," Ellie sympathized. "I can't believe they use your bones to make arrows."

"It is probably my poor grandpappi's leg bones," Vesuvius sighed, likely wringing his tiny hands together. "And maybe Uncle Thadius's, as well—"

"Vesuvius!" Loria scolded. "Remember that we are talking about Lavida right now."

"Who? Oh, her." His barely veiled attempt at "forgetting" my name did not go unnoticed. "Mademoiselle Mors will be fine. According to her, she does not need help from others to save her from drowning. She is the One, after all. Hard as that is to believe when she dresses like an Eenie Meenie."

"What the heck are you talking about?" Ellie demanded.

"According to the Prophecies, darling," Vesuvius took it upon himself to explain, and I wanted nothing more than to slap a muzzle on him, "the One has great powers and uses them to battle evil."

"Powers? What kind of powers?" Ellie asked warily.

"It's nothing, Ellie," I said quickly. "Just a story. I'll tell you about it when we get home." It was a lie. I had no intention of doing so. I could not tell her the truth, not after hearing that appalled tone in her voice.

The Huffers leveled out and were now drifting toward a dull light shining from an arched opening in the pit's wall. Below us, the pit continued to drop, for who knew how far. Darian grew tense behind me, and my body automatically mimicked his response. Something was about to happen.

"Be ready," Darian whispered. His warm breath tickled my ear and I shivered. "We have visitors."

"Visitors?"

"Trolls."

My blood curdled. I'd read about Trolls, of course. Every kid knows a little something about them. Yet I had a sneaking suspicion that these were not the little, fuzzy-haired Troll dolls most of us have come to know and love. No, I was pretty sure this was the other kind of Troll—the stupid and mean kind, the kind that can move faster than a cheetah, the kind that is always hungry, constantly on the prowl for food, eating whatever crosses its path.

And we were in its path.

As we glided toward the light, I scanned the ground inside the opening for any sign of the predators, but could see nothing. Then, out of the corner of my eye, something moved—a black shadow, a grotesque, spider-like creature the size of a large dog scurried down the wall's rough surface. I blinked twice. When I focused on the cave wall again, I almost couldn't bring myself to believe what I was seeing.

The whole wall was moving. Not only that, the Trolls—hundreds of them—surrounded the cave opening. And more were coming.

"Oh, crud." I grabbed Darian's hand on Sekar's reins.

"What's going on now, Lavida?" Ellie called out.

"Say nothing," Darian whispered, slipping his free hand over mine. My heart skipped a beat. "Trolls can hear your heartbeat as it accelerates with fear, and fear increases their appetite."

I took a deep, shuddering breath. "I bumped my arm, Ellie. No big deal."

"You've got to be careful, Lavida," Eddie warned. "You don't want to push the arrow all the way through your arm. I read once about this guy who tried to pull the arrow out and it got stuck and the doctors had to amputate."

"Eddie! Don't tell her that!" Ellie shrieked. Something odd happened at that moment—the creeping black figures not only stopped crawling, but ceased to move at all, as though stunned. As soon as Ellie's mouth closed, they started to move again, creeping slowly toward the cave entrance.

Darian squeezed my hand. "Keep her talking," he whispered. "This entry is the only way out of the pit for us."

I nodded nervously and said as enthusiastically as I could with my heart in my throat, "I'm fine, Ellie. Don't worry about me. Um . . ." I began, then floundered. What could I say to keep her talking? We were nearing the opening, and I could smell the Trolls now; they stank of rotten meat and rancid blood. I was starting to feel alarmed when an idea popped into my head. I had to make Ellie laugh. But how? The last thing I felt like doing was making jokes.

At last the words came to me: "I really wish Fiona were here right now."

"What!" Ellie squawked and the Trolls froze. "Why would you want that bimbo here?"

"Um . . . we could use her for bait."

She laughed loudly. "She'd be terrible bait! There's hardly any meat on her bones, and what there is would taste like old goat!" She slapped her thigh, guffawing at full volume. The whole time she was laughing the Trolls remained where they were, cowering against the cave walls and covering their large, hairy ears. A knot of the black creatures surrounded the tunnel opening, unable to do anything but cringe in agonizing pain.

Ellie sighed despondently, her laughter suddenly gone. "I hate this sorry excuse for a world. I can't wait to get out of here." She sighed again, then settled into silence. Released from their suffering, the Trolls began to move again. More of the skinny creatures gathered about the arched entry, readying themselves to pounce on us. We would be passing by them at any moment.

"Sing, Ellie!" Eddie shouted. "You *have* to sing!" He had not only seen the Trolls, he had somehow figured out what I was trying to do to stop them.

"What are you talking about, Eddie?" Ellie demanded. "You know I need at least half an hour to warm up my voice."

"Then warm it up with a simple song," he said. "We need something to cheer us up."

"Have you gone crazy, Eddie Maguire? I don't feel like singing—"

"Oh, please do, Ellie," Loria begged innocently. "I would *so* like to hear a Human song."

"I would be happy to—" Vesuvius offered.

"I'll do it," Ellie quickly relented. "If you insist. But I still don't see—"

"Sing!" Eddie and I shouted at the same time, and so, with a shrug, she began.

"I am woman, hear me roar," she bellowed, snapping her fingers to the beat. "I am too big to ignore!"

She sounded absolutely terrible and the Trolls seemed to agree, scrabbling over one another in their hurry to get away from the horrible racket. Squeals of pain echoed throughout the cavern as claws dug into skin and bone. I watched in fascinated horror as the surging mass of hairy limbs and emaciated bodies fled from the cave opening.

"What the heck is that noise?" Ellie shouted. An ominous silence filled the cavern as she waited for an answer. The Trolls, freed from torture, crawled back toward the opening.

"They're Trolls," I said, my voice trembling. "And your singing is scaring them off."

She snorted. "Very funny, Lavida."

My lungs contracted in panic. The Trolls were now close enough to jump onto the Huffers. One, just above the cave opening, lifted itself into a pouncing position. "I'm not kidding, Ellie. Your voice is so, um, powerful. I don't think they can handle it."

"That's the dumbest thing I've ever—"

"Ellie!" Darian and I were nearly at the cave opening.

She gave an exasperated sigh, but started singing again. All the way into the tunnel she sang her heart out, sending the Trolls fleeing, screeching, clambering for safety.

Once past danger, the Huffers landed and began running in close formation down the passageway.

"You did it, Ellie!" Eddie cheered.

"And what did I do exactly?" Light from Starkinder lamps lit the way once more, showing a disgruntled Ellie. I think she was starting to put two and two together.

"No offense, darling," Vesuvius said as he hovered on his rat-bat by her head, "but you are possibly the worst singer I have ever heard."

Ellie's lower lip stuck out as she crossed her arms. "I don't think I'm *that* bad." She glared at him. "I've had a lot of voice training, you know."

"You did not let me finish." Vesuvius straightened his cravat. "I was giving you a compliment. Your atrocious voice saved our lives, Ellie darling."

Darian groaned softly behind me. "You really know how to make a girl feel good about herself, Vesuvius."

"You are overreacting," he replied, sounding peevish.

Ellie looked around at the group. "Are you saying I sang *so* badly that I scared away *Trolls*?" She ducked her head and covered her face with her hands. Her shoulders started shaking.

"Oh, Ellie!" Loria exclaimed. "Do not cry. You saved our lives!"

Ellie took her hands from her face. She was grinning. "I'm not crying, Loria." She started giggling wildly. "No wonder my dad makes me practice in a sound-proof room."

We all burst out laughing, as much from our relief at escaping Malvado and the Trolls as about Ellie's poor dad. Eventually our chuckles died down and the Huffers drifted into single file, moving quickly down the tunnel. We weren't completely out of danger yet.

"Will you take us home after we see the Healers?" I quietly asked Darian.

"I need to speak to Madrina," he replied, leaning forward. His breath stirred strands of my hair. "She will decide what to do next."

"Can't you just take us home?" I pleaded. "I'm sure we'll be safe there. I can see a doctor to remove the arrow." Though what I'd tell her about how it ended up in my arm, I couldn't imagine.

"I am not so sure you will be safe in the Upland. Malvado is persistent. He has already had you brought back, even though such an action violates all protocol, and judging by that sham of a trial, he has proven how little he cares for our laws. He will think nothing of violating them again. Besides, I promised Madrina I would watch over you. I failed her once, I will not make that mistake again."

"Are you doing this for me or for your own conscience?" Silence answered me. "I want to go home, Darian. I don't want my friends to know . . ." *that I'm a freak,* I continued in my head, remembering what he'd accused me of thinking.

A part of me wondered if he was right . . . that I did think that way.

"I cannot take you there. I *will* not."

My arm throbbed and my head ached and I couldn't argue with him anymore, much as I wanted to scream and shout and fight against staying. But I was too tired. All I could do was close my eyes and hope to forget. If I were lucky, I would sleep, waking up to discover that all this truly was a dream.

I drifted off.

And dreamed.

TROLL

CHAPTER TWENTY-FOUR
A MATTER OF LIFE AND DEATH

Galloping hooves pounded across a crisp carpet of golden
leaves; the mare's muscles rippled beneath my thighs as
strong arms encircled my waist, rooting me to the black
horse's broad back. I hoped that the hunters had given up
their pursuit. I didn't have the will to run anymore. I
turned my head to see who had rescued me. When I saw
the pale oval face framed by dark hair and large gray eyes
peering into my own, I felt like I was looking into a mirror.

The face gazing down at me was my own.

And yet it was not.

I was looking into the face of a woman, not that of a
fifteen-year-old girl. Shallow crevices crossed her forehead
like cracks in the dry desert sand. Strands of gray brightened her black hair and one of her front teeth was chipped.
It was her eyes that struck me most. Despite the thin lines

spreading like tiny riverbeds from each corner, they sparkled with life.

She studied me, her expression speculative. "You are
safe for now, my child," she told me. "But yours is a peace
that will not last." Her eyes grew troubled. "There are those
who wish to see you harmed. You *must* be careful who you
trust, Lavida."

"What do you mean?"

"Someone you know will betray you."

"Tell me who," I begged. "An Anaedorian? Or one of my
friends?"

"I wish that I knew," the woman sighed. "I only know
that you must beware the servant. That is all I can tell you."
She spurred the glistening black horse onward. "You need
to understand, Lavida, that the path you must take will be
difficult. But take it you must."

"Why?" I croaked, my voice barely above a whisper.
"What do you want from me?"

"I want only to guide you as I have always done."

"I don't understand."

"Your dreams, child. I have sent you dreams. So many
dreams."

"*You* gave me those dreams? Those nightmares? How
could you? They've haunted me all my life!"

She looked shocked, as though I had struck her across
the face. "I sent those dreams to prepare you, Lavida!"

"For what?" I gasped.

"For what is coming."

My head pounded. "What is coming?"

Her expression was grave, distant. "I cannot tell you; I
cannot see."

"Who are you?" I asked, wondering whether I could trust
someone who had frightened me for as long as I could
remember.

The woman's eyes softened. "Why . . . I am you, Lavida."

I shook my head groggily. "You're me in the future?"

The woman smiled. "Not quite. I am only one small part of who you are. A drop of water in your ocean."

"What does *that* mean?"

She laughed. "It will all one day make sense, Lavida. For now, you must believe what I have told you. So many have sacrificed to make you who you are—to make you the *One*."

I shook my head again, trying to sort it out, but it was hard to think straight. I was so tired. The senseless words she spoke echoed in my mind, quickly blurring together. I closed my bleary eyes.

I am you . . .

A drop of water . . .

So many have sacrificed . . .

To make you the One *. . .*

Beware, Lavida. Beware...

The servant . . . the servant . . . the servant . . .

The confusion of words swirled and danced in my mind, flying around and around like fall leaves caught in a wind devil, faster and faster, dizzying me, slipping and sliding in and out of my grasp.

Stop it!

I started violently and the words disappeared. I opened my eyes and saw that I was lying in a bed beneath cool white sheets and soft blankets. A clean white bandage covered my left arm where the Crusher arrow had been. I flexed my elbow. The pain was gone.

"I have been waiting for you to come back," said a voice off to my right. Madrina. "Blanca, you may go."

I looked to my left. A small figure draped in a dove gray habit stood and shyly faced me. I could not see her features through the thick, white veil covering her face, but sensed they might resemble those of a mouse.

"It has been an honor," Blanca squeaked and bowed to me as though I were the queen of England before scurrying out of the room. I realized then that she had been sitting in the wooden chair by my bed, keeping a vigil.

"Where am I?" My fuzzy voice sounded exactly how my mind felt.

"You are safe here in our Blendar home," Madrina reassured me. Her dark eyes were kind. "The poison in the Crusher arrow nearly killed you before you rendered it harmless. Using your powers exhausted you. Darian brought you here, and Blanca the Healer removed the arrow."

I struggled to sit up. "I don't think that arrow was poisoned, Madrina."

The tiny woman leaned over. "Lie back," she commanded and I meekly did as I was told, too weak to argue. She pulled the covers up around me and took my cold hand in her own. "It is time you knew the history of Anaedor and your place in it."

"*My* place?"

Madrina nodded. "I know all this seems strange to you, but I ask you to listen and keep your mind open to what I am about to tell you." She paused and gave my hand a reassuring squeeze.

"Long ago, Anaedorians walked the Upland as freely as you Humans now do. And, yes, we actually lived amongst your kind. However, it was not an easy way of living. Humans were afraid of our kind. They were afraid of our powers and our beliefs. They did not understand us, so they sought to destroy us. Over time, anyone believed to have magical powers was forced to flee. If we wanted to save our lives, our cultures, our species, we had to hide ourselves from Humans and their ignorance. And so we did, believing, hoping, that at some future time, when

Humans evolved in their understanding, we would be able to return to our homelands and live in harmony with them.

"But that was not to be. The places where my ancestors hid whilst living in the land across the waters were sought out and plundered. A few with powers stayed behind— some succeeded at staying hidden, some blended in with the humans. Most clans, however, were almost completely destroyed, though some individuals escaped, crossing the long waters in tiny boats. The journey was perilous, and many perished. Our ancestors eventually landed on the shores of a new land, with enough survivors to start a new life. Humans lived in this place, but not nearly so many of them as do now. And having learned not to trust your kind, we prolonged our hiding, hoping that with time we could show Humans that we were not a threat to them.

"But we allowed too much time to go by, and we grew afraid of even trying to venture out amongst Humans. As ages passed, Anaedorians came to accept the reality that they could never return to the lives they once led." Madrina sighed as she stared off into space, her wrinkled features growing wistful.

"Once, when I was a Youngling, my parents sneaked me to the Upland. They thought the heat of what you call the Sun might cure my crippled legs. It did not, as you can see, but I shall always remember the great, comforting warmth I felt in the short time I spent basking in its light. I miss it so . . ." She shook her head, her white hair moving in the slight breeze, and released my hand. "But that is neither here nor there. There is more to the story.

"We had to create our own world, separate from Humans. By fate, our ancestors found this place hidden deep below ground. Within these caverns and tunnels we built the world of Anaedor, though our kind was not the first to occupy these realms. There had been others before us, called Seers; beings who could see the future," she explained. "What they saw, they carved into the walls, along with accounts of the lives they led, how they came to be.

"Long after they were gone, a Blendar woman named Jamen found the cave of carvings. She translated the words and wrote them down, filling four books. She called these writings *The Chronicles of Anaedor* because much of what was written spoke of Anaedorians, whom the Seers never knew—our lives before we arrived, our journey to this place, and what has happened to us since then. Jamen was amazed at how accurate the writings about these events were." Madrina shook her head sadly. "Unfortunately, the books have been lost to us for hundreds of Passings now, and no one has been able to find the cave containing the original writings."

I sat up and propped my chin on my hand. "Then how do you know what the *Chronicles* say if you've never seen them?"

Madrina smiled. "Jamen knew the writings and, not long before she passed from this world, she related to her daughter the prophecies in tales, all of which made the disturbing prediction that our world would one day be in grave danger. She called these lost writings the *Prophecies*.

"Over time, these words were repeated again and again to members of our clan, and to other Anaedorian clans as well, until the *Prophecies* became as much a part of Anaedor's history as real events. Much has been lost in transmission, but we do know this part for sure." She checked to make sure I was listening. I was. "In the beginning, there would be a period of peaceful co-existence in Anaedor in which all the different creatures that sought refuge within these walls would work together as one clan to build the world you see now. And this was fulfilled; we all had the same goal . . . to make a world safe from those who wished to destroy us.

"The *Prophecies* then foretold the coming of a change. It was written that an upheaval of great proportions would come about, during which time chaos and mistrust would seize hold of Anaedor and threaten to destroy our way of life."

Madrina clenched her long-fingered hands together, gazing earnestly at me. "I already see this coming true, Lavida. We no longer know ourselves as Anaedorians. We are Blendars, Healers, Elves, Zephoos, but not Anaedorians. We have cut ourselves off from each other. Even in our own clans, we are at odds. We no longer know who we are or what we believe in. The wise ones teach us that to know where one is going, one must know where she has been. Yet many Anaedorians no longer remember what our ancestors suffered—where we have been. We have forgotten our history, and so we do not know which way to go, neither in our present nor in our future." She stopped talking and looked at me expectantly.

I sat up straighter. Madrina's story was fascinating, but surreal. On some level, the idea of Anaedor made sense to me. I mean, where did our knowledge of Elves and Dwarves and Unicorns come from if they'd never existed? Most legends have some foundation in truth.

"So what does all this have to do with me?" I asked.

"There is more to our story," Madrina warned. "The most important part. The *Prophecies* told us that you were coming."

"Me?"

"Yes, you, and by name. Listen . . ." She began to speak in a quiet, yet powerful voice. "*In the 1000th Passing, great chaos and confusion will commence. A Creature, more powerful than anything Anaedor has ever seen, will* embark on a campaign of both insidious and blatant destruction. Out of the turmoil, a confluence of great power will arise and destroy this most hateful and spiteful Creature. And Anaedor shall know their savior as *Life and Death*.

"The 1000th Passing is *now*, Lavida, and these are very troubled times in Anaedor, as you have seen."

"I still don't see how this means I'm the *One*."

"You are Life and Death."

I blinked at her.

"Your name," she began again, more slowly, "Lavida Mors, means *Life* and *Death*."

"W—well," I stuttered, my heartbeat speeding up, "that's not—my name doesn't mean—"

"Lavida—" Madrina began in a soothing voice.

"No! Please stop talking! I don't want to know any more about you or this place or my name. Don't make me do this. Please! I can't get involved—not again. I don't want to be the *One*. I just want to go home." When I had finished my rant, I fell back into the pillows, buried my face in my hands and cried real tears for the first time in a long time.

Madrina smiled sadly. "Jamen was my ancestor. She carved your name into the wall of her cave home, which is now mine, so that we should always know it. I have gazed at your name myself—too many times to count. This is your destiny, Lavida. No one else can fulfill it."

I lowered my hands, my chest heaving from suppressed sobs. "What do you want from me, Madrina?"

She leaned back in her chair. "It is simple, really. You have to show us the way back."

I stared at her. "You mean, across the ocean? I don't think I can do that. I don't have a passport and—"

Her large eyes sparkled, amused. "You are thinking too literally, Lavida."

"Oh. You mean, you want me to help you symbolically, as in finding the way back to your roots."

"In a way."

"But why do you need me for that?" I nervously rolled the top part of the sheet into a ball and dried my face with a trembling hand. "Can't you guys figure out the way for yourselves?"

She looked troubled. "I wish that we could, but sometimes, when souls are lost, they need guidance."

I pulled myself up tall. "I'm not the person for the job, Madrina. The people here hate me. They'd never listen to me, even if I knew what to tell them."

She smiled at me, her wrinkled skin buckling into deep furrows. "You are the *One*. You will figure something out."

I shook my head. "That's circular logic, Madrina. Like asking, why are we here? And answering, because we are."

Madrina shrugged. "What is wrong with that?"

I pressed my lips tightly together, feeling more and more trapped. I had to get out of this. Once I was pulled in, I'd never be able to walk away. In the past, I had tried to resist getting involved, but I never could. It was time to make a change.

"Okay, let's look at this another way. Why would the *Prophecies* name a human as your savior? We're the enemy, right?"

"We did not foresee that you would be a Human," Madrina acknowledged. "But that is the way of life, is it not? Full of surprises. Besides, it is possible that the *Prophecies* mentioned that the *One* is Human, but since we do not have them in any but the most cursory form, we cannot know for sure."

I blinked my eyes rapidly, fighting back fresh tears.

Madrina looked at me kindly. "I know this is hard to accept, Lavida, but you must."

"That's easy for you to say! I'm only fifteen years old!" I cried, conveniently forgetting that only yesterday I'd have said fifteen was old enough to do as I chose. "Please don't ask this of me . . ." *I'll lose everything*, I silently finished.

Madrina paused, weighing her next words. "I have some advice for you, Lavida."

"And that would be . . ."

Taking in my combative expression, Madrina chuckled. "Do not worry. It is relatively simple to follow. When you accept who you are, you will know what to do."

"And if I never do . . . ?"

Madrina laughed and snapped her fingers. Two muscular Blendars entered the room, carrying her litter. "I know you do not want to do this, Lavida, that you do not want to accept this role. And I know you have your reasons why. Think about what I have said." She smiled at me as the two Blendars lifted her onto the portable bed. She settled herself into place, pulling a blue lap robe over her legs. Her attendants grabbed hold of the long poles and lifted her up.

"So what happens if I accept it?" I hurriedly asked her. I needed to know more; I needed more advice.

Her expression darkened. "That is when the real battle begins, Lavida." She looked away from my stunned expression. "You have a visitor to see you now," she said as she was borne away.

"How are you feeling?" Darian asked as he strode into the room. He looked tired.

"I'll live, I guess."

"Blanca, the Healer, confirmed that the arrow was poisonous," he said, watching my face closely.

I wriggled uncomfortably beneath the soft blankets. "There's got to be a logical explanation for what happened," I replied, my breath jerking in and out of my lungs.

He gave me a long look, his features unreadable. "I cannot deny what I witnessed, Lavida." I felt a chill run through me. What was he doing? He was the one person I could count on to argue that I was a weak, helpless Human who couldn't do anything. "You ran across Warrior's Walk like you had wings. You repeated word for word a secret spell after hearing it only once. You resisted Malvado's powers in the Great Court. You survived a poisoned arrow. And your name is in the *Prophecies*."

With each word he spoke, I felt a growing sense of doom. I didn't want this. I didn't want to be different. I didn't want anyone depending on me. I only wanted to be like everyone else. I rubbed my aching temples. I hadn't fought for myself at my old school and look what happened. They had made me an outcast. I couldn't let that happen again.

"Okay, so let's say the arrow *was* poisoned," I conceded. "Maybe the poison didn't get into my system. Maybe it was bad poison and didn't work like it was supposed to." I looked at his disbelieving face. "That could happen!"

"You are fighting the wrong battle, Lavida," he replied. "I have to say that at this point in time, your evidence for disproving that you are the *One* is not enough to convince me."

"Then try this," I argued desperately, feeling a growing hysteria. "I got myself across that bridge through sheer luck. Malvado probably isn't nearly as powerful as everyone believes. And people are always making up new names for babies!" I was shouting now, but couldn't seem to stop myself. "Even if I were the *One*, which I'm not, I don't want to be. That's all there is to it. So drop the subject. *Please*!"

There was silence. I peeked up at Darian through my bangs. He was studying me, something he seemed to like doing. I waited for him to add something more, but he simply said, "I imagine you are hungry."

I nodded, wondering what the catch was.

"I will see what I can do—"

Just then Ellie and Eddie burst into the room, followed by Loria and Gille. Eddie waved a deadly looking arrow around in the air like a conductor's baton. Shorter now after having been cut to remove it from my arm, the arrow still looked wicked enough not to need poison to kill someone.

"This was in your arm!" he cried in awe as he jumped onto the bed. He bounced excitedly a few times. "Loria said the poison in this arrow could take down an Eenie Meenie—which I have to assume is either quite large or very tenacious—in less than a minute. And *you* survived!"

I glanced over at Ellie to see how she was taking this.

She avoided my eyes. "I'm starving!" she said heartily, turning her back on me.

My heart sank. What did she know? What had they told her? I glanced at her.

"In fact, I'm so hungry, I might even take some of that bat poop you guys have."

Loria giggled. "None of you will have to partake of guano. I will personally make sure of that."

"Gille," Darian directed, "let the food preparers know the Humans are ready for sustenance."

Gille bowed to Darian. "Of course," he sniffed, rubbing his red nose miserably. "That is what I am here for . . . to help others. It is an honor."

"Do you need anything else for the moment?" Darian asked.

"A ride home?" Ellie suggested.

Darian shook his head. "I am sorry, but it would not be safe for you right now." He motioned to Loria. "We will return momentarily."

Silence took their place as they left. Eddie explored the

room and examined the Starkinders in their lamps. Ellie twirled a ringlet around her finger, her expression stony, almost angry.

"Well?" she said, breaking the stifling stillness.

My heart thudded in my ears. "Well what?"

"What's going on here, Lavida? How the heck did you survive a poisoned arrow? Gille and Loria wouldn't tell me anything, just kept whispering to each other about you being the *One*. What the heck is that? Are you one of these . . . things? And don't lie to me this time. I hate liars."

The look of disgust on her face made me feel sick inside. My mouth dried up, my tongue froze. "Uhhh . . ." She knew. She knew, and she was going to hate me. She hated freaks. She'd said so in Miseria. My last chance at having a friend was gone. Blown away. I opened my mouth to speak, to reassure her that it wasn't what she thought, but at that moment, Darian, Loria and Gille entered the room, carrying three delicately forged wrought-iron trays.

"For our guests of honor." Loria set her tray down in front of Eddie and rubbed his head playfully. He quickly scooted over and she sat down.

"We are serving—" Darian began as he deftly placed a tray in front of me.

"No, no, no!" Ellie interrupted when Gille set down her tray. "Don't tell me; I don't want to know."

With a sniff and a bow, Gille excused himself and left the cave. Darian leaned against the wall with a thoughtful expression on his face while Loria watched us proudly. I only picked at my food, unable to look Ellie in the face.

When Gille returned to the cave a few minutes later, Ellie pushed her cleaned plate away and yawned.

"I have prepared a room for the other two Humans," he announced. "Shall I show them the way?"

"Please do, Gille," Darian replied.

Loria stood with a reluctant sigh. "I am going, too," she said, running her hand over Eddie's wild hair. She seemed fascinated by the spiky cut. "I am sure Madrina has errands for me to run—lately she always has errands for me to run!"

Eddie and Ellie said goodnight to everyone, though Ellie didn't look at me once as she shuffled after a beckoning Gille. I waited for Darian to follow them, but he hesitated, lingering to be sure they were gone, then came to stand by my bed. I looked up at him, feeling suddenly nervous. I wondered what he was going to say.

Clearing his throat, he kneeled down. "I must apologize for my earlier behavior. I have strong," he paused, his dark eyes roving the room, "I have strong personal reasons why I do not want a Human to be the *One*. I have seen what they do, not only to each other, but to other beings."

Having seen and experienced first-hand what humans do, I could empathize with his reasons.

"Wouldn't I know it if I were the *One*?" I asked him and my eyes teared up. I quickly looked away from him, down at my cold, shaking hands. "Wouldn't I feel it?"

He took my hand in a surprisingly warm gesture, then he reached out with the other and turned my face toward him. "Look at me, Lavida." Slowly, hesitantly, I looked up into his dark, serious eyes. "Remember what Madrina said to me about our fears? How we avoid them? I think that is what you have been doing for a very long time."

We gazed into each other's eyes for a breathless moment, then he abruptly dropped my hand and stood.

"Sleep now, Lavida. We will talk more when you wake." He bowed to me and swiftly left the room.

I lay back and closed my eyes, more confused and upset than ever. When at last sleep pulled at my consciousness, clouding my senses and easing my mind, I was grateful. I didn't want to hear any more about being the *One*; I didn't want to think about how many people were counting on me. And I certainly didn't want to think about my fears.

Because right now, my worst fear was coming true.

CHAPTER TWENTY-FIVE
EENIE, MEENIE, MINEY, BARG

The sound of shouting filled my ears. I blinked sleepily and looked around the room, disoriented. Where was I? My eyes caught sight of the Starkinder lantern hanging on a peg by the doorway, and it all came back to me. I was in Anaedor, and I was being hunted.

Someone was coming.

"Lavida!" Gille cried hysterically as he dashed into the room, a handkerchief pressed tightly to his nose. "Malvado and his guards are coming! We must flee!"

"But what about Ellie and Eddie?" I spluttered.

"There is no time. We must leave now!"

I rolled out of bed and fell onto the floor. Gille's eyes widened. "Get up! Get up!"

"Turn around!" I directed as I untangled myself from the sheet that had tripped me. "I've got to get dressed."

"Hurry!" he yelped as he looked away. He shakily blew his nose and peered anxiously out the doorway. "They are coming! I can hear them!"

I tore off the white gown and clumsily pulled on my own clothes, which someone had cleaned and mended. "We've got to get the others," I insisted again as I pulled on my last sock.

He shook his head. "We cannot do that. There are too many of them. They will catch us all if we delay. No. Darian told me what I must do and that is what we will do."

"But my friends! He'll hurt them!"

"They will be all right," he tried to assure me, but he didn't sound too convinced. He wiped his nose one last time then stuck the handkerchief in the pocket of his tan pants. "Malvado does not want them. He only wants you."

I took a deep breath. He was right. Malvado was after me. And if I left now, he might never find Ellie and Eddie. "Let's go, then."

"Follow me." He ran out of the cave, easily mounting a waiting Huffer in one jump.

I, on the other hand, had a little more trouble. "Help me, Gille!" I yelled after I'd landed on my butt for the third time.

He looked back at me in surprise. "But Loria told me you are the *One*! Use your powers!"

"I'm a little tired," I told him. "Please, just give me a hand!"

Gille shook his head but helped me onto the Huffer. He gave the proper command and the furry animal leaped forward. Soon we were flying down a dark tunnel, part of an elaborate network of passages running behind the walls surrounding the main Blendar cavern.

"Where are we going?" I asked, as we galloped along.

"To safety," Gille replied. It wasn't a very specific

answer, but anywhere that Malvado was not was good enough for me.

We traveled on and I wondered how Eddie and Ellie were doing. Had Malvado found them? I fervently hoped not. Had I done the right thing in running? Would they think I'd abandoned them to save my own hide? My heart ached at the thought. As we rode, I fretted about my decision, only noticing after some time that the tunnel floor now sloped downward. We seemed to be heading deeper and deeper into the realm of Anaedor. Up ahead, a faint light emerged from the darkness and I could hear voices. A chill went through my body.

"Oops," a high-pitched voice sang wildly (and a little flat), "I think I did it again!"

That was Mrs. Dooley's favorite song! But who would be singing it down here? Maybe there were other humans down here, maybe even Mrs. Dooley herself. Maybe Drefan and his Amorals had kidnapped her, too. Mo had said that Malvado hated all humans.

"Who is that?" I whispered to Gille.

The Blendar shrugged, sniffing a little. "I do not know, but I think it best we steer clear of them. A tunnel branches off to the right up ahead. We will take that one."

"No, wait!" I said suddenly. If it was Mrs. Dooley, I had to help her. "I have to see who's singing that song. A quick peek and then we'll go."

Gille shook his head doubtfully. "I do not think that would be a good idea. Malvado could be right behind us."

"Please, Gille!" I pleaded. "I haven't heard anyone behind us for ages."

"If you insist," he sighed and rubbed his red pug nose. He slowed the Huffer to a trot, and we cautiously approached the cave. When we neared the entrance, he stopped the animal and we both slid to the ground. I sneaked up to the edge of the wall and peeked around the corner into a large cavern. What I saw in there sent a violent shudder through me.

"It's a roomful of Bargs!" I croaked in stunned disbelief. How could there be more of those big-bodied, little-headed, hairy creatures?

"Eenie Meenies," Gille corrected me, looking over my shoulder.

"So *that's* what an Eenie Meenie is. Hey! Those are what Vesuvius said I dressed like!" I tightened my hand into a fist. I'd get that little, big-haired snob if it was the last thing I did.

At that moment, one of the Eenie Meenies approached the entrance. Gille and I flattened ourselves against the wall, pulling the Huffer close to us. Seconds later, I sneaked another quick look as the Eenie Meenie passed by the entryway, staying inside the cave. Then, peering further into the cave, I watched the Eenie Meenies as they poked at each other with sticks and bellowed loudly in response each time one of them got it in the eye. Not particularly surprising behavior, I surmised, judging from my past encounter with Barg. Many were doing what might be called singing—if you were tone deaf, that is— along to songs blaring from a battered radio. Others drank messily from large mugs of frothy brew and chattered like squirrels to whoever would listen.

A small group of Eenie Meenies self-importantly sorted through large piles of what looked suspiciously like garbage. Every thirty seconds or so, one of them climbed onto a stone platform and lifted something high up in the air. Everyone would stop what they were doing to examine the item with a gravity that belied their childish antics. As if on cue, they collectively passed judgment on the object, either by cheering or booing boisterously. Then the Eenie Meenie

would reverently set the item onto a designated pile or toss
it over his back, depending on the judgment. This time the
object of interest was a hairdryer. One of the Eenie Meenies
looked down the drying end as though gazing through a
telescope. Then he pointed it at the others. They all raised
their hands and screeched loudly before bursting into
raucous laughter. From the looks of it, they were having a
trash party.

Carried away by curiosity, I leaned farther in to see what
they'd pull out this time. I wasn't expecting what happened
next: big, hairy arms plucked me off my feet and slung me
over a wide shoulder like a sack of potatoes.

"Aha!" a high-pitched voice squealed excitedly. "Me
thought me smell Human." The creature lumbered through
the cave opening, taking me with him.

"Let me go, you big lug!" The big lug ignored me. I
pounded on his broad chest, but stopped when my hand hit
something sticky.

I frantically wiped it off on his hairy back. "Ew! What
was that?"

"Is where Barg sneezed."

"Ohh," I groaned, but not only because of the snot;
either all Eenie Meenies were named Barg, or I'd just been
reunited with my smelly friend. "For the love of Pete, Barg,
put me down!"

The massive Eenie Meenie ignored my pleas as he
shouted to the others, "Look! Look! Me got Human! Come
see!" A massive roar erupted from the crowd. The mob of
Eenie Meenies surged toward me, their tiny heads bobbing
excitedly above their bouncing, pumpkin-shaped bodies.

Unaware of the danger, Gille shook his finger at Barg's
broad back. "Now see here just one tick. This is unacceptable."

"Go away." Barg turned and pushed two thick fingers

against Gille's forehead, knocking him right over.

"I would if I could!" he cried indignantly as he hopped back up, checking himself for injury. "But I must see to it that she is taken to a safe place."

"Me find her, me keep her. That be the rule."

The other Eenie Meenies began to surround us. "Gille!" I cried. "Help me!"

The handkerchief was back in his hand and he pressed it to his nose. "I knew we should not have stopped here. This is all your fault. He is going to be so mad at me!"

"No, he will not! Darian would want you to help me!"

Like killer bees, the Eenie Meenies swarmed us. They began petting me and pulling my hair. They stroked my clothing and stuck sausage-like fingers in my ears. One tried to stick a finger up my nose but, thank goodness, it— the finger—was too big, and he only succeeded in smushing my face. I never thought I'd be thankful for small nostrils, but there it was.

"Stop it!" I finally yelled when I figured it was safe to open my mouth without getting a finger shoved into it. My voice echoed in the cave. The Eenie Meenies took a few steps back, staring at me in awe, their yellow eyes wide.

"Eenie Meenies like you, feisty one," Barg piped up. "Us keep you, yes?"

He held me up over his head and waded through the crowd. I scrunched my eyes tightly closed. I felt rather than saw that he had climbed up onto the stone platform. I wondered if I was going to be judged and thrown into a sorting pile—only which pile would they choose?

"Catch!" he squealed, lifting me into the air.

Catch?

All right, that was the last straw! I was not going to be the Eenie Meenie's newest toy. Gille was useless. In fact, at that very moment, he was standing over by the entryway ready to make a run for it. I had to get out of this by myself.

I scanned the room. To my left I spotted a large stalactite hanging from the ceiling about ten feet away. I don't
know what came over me, but I had the idea that I might be
able to grab onto it if I jumped. I'd never done anything like
this, of course; I wasn't Spiderman, for Pete's sake! I'd
probably end up landing on a stalagmite and skewering
myself like a shish kabob. But when I looked down into the
crowd of Eenie Meenies leering up at me—some were even
drooling in their excitement—I changed my mind. I'd
rather get myself killed trying to escape than end up as an
Eenie Meenie trophy.

Surprising Barg, I swung my legs up and around his
neck. Giving myself no time to think, I straightened up so
that I stood precariously on his broad shoulders. Using his
little head for support, I crouched, took a deep breath, and
leaped.

EENIE MEENIE

CHAPTER TWENTY-SIX
NOWHERE TO BE FOUND

Ellie sat up, clutching a soft blanket to her chest. Gille had shown them to a tiny cave outfitted with colored lamps on the walls and large, brightly patterned pillows and thick blankets covering the entire floor. She and Eddie had slithered under a blanket and fallen immediately into a deep sleep. She'd been right in the middle of a great dream involving both Eric Hermoso, a famous pop star, and Ian asking her out on a date. She was telling them she couldn't see why she couldn't date both of them when something awakened her.

"Eddie, wake up!" she hissed, shoving him. "I heard something." She pushed back the thick, downy comforter and rose slowly to her feet.

Eddie moaned, "Eddie's sleeping," and rolled over. Ellie grabbed her pillow and threw it at him. "Hey!" He sat up, rubbing his eyes. "What do you want?"

"Something woke me up. I don't know what it was, but I have a bad feeling about it. We better go check on Lavida." She found her glasses and slipped them on.

Eddie was immediately awake. "You think something's wrong?"

"Maybe."

Eddie jumped up and the twins ran down the corridor toward Lavida's room. "Lavida!" they called in hushed voices.

"Where is she?" Ellie demanded, looking around the empty room.

"Maybe she's using the bathroom," Eddie suggested, hoping he was right. He had the same feeling as Ellie that something strange was going on. Of course, something strange was always going on in Anaedor—that's why he liked the place so much.

"Do they actually have bathrooms here?" Ellie asked. "Which reminds me . . ." she trailed off as a look of panic crossed her face. "Ooohhh!" She crossed her legs and hopped up and down. "Now I've gotta go!"

Loria entered the room with a tray. "Oh, hello! You are awake already."

"I've got to use the bathroom," Ellie said, getting right to the point.

Loria's eyes widened. "Oh, dear! Oh, yes. I learned about this unusual Human necessity in one of my classes. Um, come with me. I am sure we can find something."

"Find something?" Ellie said uncertainly as they left the room. "Are we talking a bucket here?" They passed Darian as he entered the cave.

"Where is Lavida?" he asked, scanning the room.

"We think she might have gone to find a bathroom," Eddie replied.

"What do you mean?" Darian demanded.

Eddie bit his lip. Ellie was not going to be happy.

"We cannot lose her," Darian continued. "Where is Gille? He was supposed to check on her and report back to me."

"Maybe they're both using the bathroom and will be back soon." Eddie shook his head angrily. "Sorry, Darian! I'm really not using my head. Judging by Loria's reaction, I must assume your people's digestive systems don't function like ours. Fascinating . . ." Eddie's eyebrows drew together as he pondered this interesting new fact. What did Blendars do instead? he wondered, nearly forgetting about Lavida and Gille.

Darian picked up Lavida's discarded gown and clutched it tightly, his knuckles white, his expression grim. "Something is wrong. She has changed into her clothes."

Loria and Ellie returned to the room at that moment. "The bathroom really does consist of a bucket," Ellie informed them, "and Lavida wasn't anywhere near it."

"Gille's missing, too," Eddie told her. "Something's definitely wrong."

"Wrong?" Loria repeated, turning toward her brother. "We must do something, Darian. Gille is so new to Anaedor. He does not know his way and is not very . . . well, he is no warrior."

Darian grimaced. "Before we do anything, I will have to speak with Madrina."

"By the time you find Madrina and figure out what she wants to do about all this, Lavida could be Troll food," Ellie argued.

Darian turned on Ellie, his eyes cool. "You do not understand our ways. We must go through the proper protocol. I will speak to Madrina first; then we will take action."

"Well, Eddie and I don't have to follow your rules," she

replied. "You two can go talk to Madrina; my brother and I are going to look for Lavida, and then we're heading home."

"Do not be foolish. You do not even know where to start."

"I know we need to get out of this place before Malvado finds us!"

"She is right, Darian," Loria spoke up. "They will be safer in the Upland."

"I know!" he said through his teeth. "I know. But there are rules."

"Rules are made to be broken," Ellie argued, her hands planted defiantly on her hips.

Darian stared at her. Finally, he threw up his hands in surrender. "All right. You win. We will go with you. I shall have to deal with the consequences of my actions later." He did not look happy about it. "Loria, take the Humans to the Huffer stable. I will meet you there."

She grabbed his arm. "Where are you going, Darian?"

"To ensure that we will be ready for whatever we encounter." He strode out of the room.

Inside the Huffer stables, the smell of seaweed, wet fur, and manure filled the air. Loria quickly went about preparing the animals for their pursuit. She expertly slid a silver bit into each of the Huffer's mouths, draping the reins on their flat, fuzzy backs. She then attached lanterns to each of their collars.

"Awake," she told the Starkinders sleeping in their lanterns, and they obliged.

Darian hurried into the room carrying a leather sack. He reached inside the bag and withdrew two objects. He handed one to Ellie and the other to Eddie. "For your protection," he explained as they studied the small crossbow in their hands. "Attach it to your wrist."

"I'm not wearing this thing," Ellie protested. "I'll end up

putting an arrow through my foot." She saw Eddie eagerly strapping on the contraption. "And neither are you, mister." She tried to snatch the bow away from him, but Eddie dodged her, jumping behind Darian.

The Blendar looked flustered. "The weapon is for your protection. Might I remind you that there are creatures in Anaedor who would swipe off your head with one claw?"

"One claw?" Ellie's mouth hung open as she looked to Loria for confirmation. She nodded seriously. Ellie looked down at the crossbow. "So this strap," she said brusquely as she fitted it to her wrist, "goes where?"

"I will show you," Loria volunteered. "And just so you know, Ellie," she said as she tightened the strap, "these arrows will not harm the creature they hit. They only take them to a place far away."

"Oh," Ellie laughed. "Well, I guess I can't send myself away from myself."

Loria looked uncomfortable as she strapped on her own crossbow. "Well, actually—"

Darian quickly interrupted. "Just do not shoot yourself. Then there is no worry."

"Could you actually send that part of yourself to another place?" Eddie asked with wonder.

"Yes," Darian sighed.

"Cool!"

"Edgar Allen Maguire!" Ellie roared. "Don't you dare do it as one of your so-called experiments. Mom will kill you if you come back without all your parts. Besides, you'd be an even bigger freak than you already are."

"Aw, Ellie, you're no fun."

"*I'm* no fun? See how fun it'll be returning to our world with only half a body. You'd only be able to shop at half-off sales and all your arguments would be one-sided. You'd never be more than half the man you've always wanted to be."

Eddie's lips twitched. "But I could be a halfback in football." They started to giggle, a little hysterically.

"I think we had better get going, Darian," Loria said. "I am afraid they are getting a bit . . ." She tapped her head meaningfully.

Darian nodded. Humans were so very strange. He really did not understand them at all. Of course, maybe they had been underground too long and it was addling their minds. He had read of such things.

"Eddie will ride with Loria," he dictated. "Ellie, come with me." He climbed up first, then, with little effort, pulled Ellie up onto the furry beast, settling her behind him.

"Just as long as you understand that I get motion sickness," she told him after a few shuddering hiccups. "So don't go too fast or take the corners too tightly. That Gille, he was a terrible driiiiiiaaaggghhh!" Darian had flicked his wrist and they bolted like lightning down a tight corridor.

Darian led the way in their search, traveling through tunnels and caves at such a rapid pace that Ellie, with her eyes shut tightly, missed everything. Eddie tried to take in all he could but couldn't help feeling sick whenever he opened his eyes for more than a few seconds.

As time wore on they began to lose hope of finding Lavida.

"Where is she?" Ellie wailed. "I just want to find her and get out of this place. I have the worst luck—"

"Quiet, Ellie," Darian admonished. "There is no need to alert every creature in Anaedor to our exact position."

Ellie clamped her mouth shut.

And for once, it stayed that way.

CHAPTER TWENTY-SEVEN
KEEP YOUR ENEMIES CLOSER

What had I done? Flying through the air with arms flung wide, I slammed into the massive stalactite. My arms wrapped around the smooth surface, attempting to grab hold. Struggling to maintain my grip, I slipped again and again until I curled my legs around the slick cone like a sloth and hung on tight.

I had survived, but now what? My imagination conjured up all the different things the Eenie Meenies might do to get their hands on me: throw rocks at my head, poke me with sharp objects, play smash the human piñata. I couldn't stay here.

Before the stunned crowd could react, I slid down the rest of the stalactite like a firefighter on a pole and dropped to the floor. Landing on my feet, I ran directly at the crowd of staring Eenie Meenies, feinted left and shot to the right, hoping to confuse them. It worked. The bumbling creatures stumbled and piled up on each other, grunting and shouting accusations.

At last I dashed through the opening with the Eenie Meenies in hot pursuit. Gille sat on the Huffer, head ducked low, mumbling to himself. When he saw me, his eyes brightened and he wrung his hands. "How did you get away?"

I didn't bother answering as I jumped onto the Huffer, this time without any trouble. Amazing what a little adrenaline can do for you. "Go, Gille!" I wrapped my arms around his thick waist, then turned around to see how close the Eenie Meenies were. I was surprised to find Barg standing in the cave entrance, looking like a little kid whose pet dog had run away.

Without thinking, I reached in my pants pocket and pulled out my watch. After giving it one last look, I tossed it to Barg. He caught the shiny disc and stared at it with awe. Then he looked up at me with a big-toothed grin and a wave. Oddly enough, he no longer looked so creepy to me.

As we galloped along, I heard drums and horns echo in the distance like the thunder of an approaching storm. My stomach gurgled. My pursuers no longer sounded so far away. A moment of déjà vu washed over me like a mighty wave: I was the hunted beast in the tapestry and Malvado and his Crushers were the hunters. But this time I didn't think a woman on a horse would be riding to my rescue. There was only Gille on a Huffer. Not exactly confidence inspiring.

The sound of a whisper startled me out of my bleak thoughts. I looked around and saw nothing except the empty tunnel stretching out before us. Gille was hunched down low, urging the Huffer on with snaps of the leather reins. I cocked my head to one side, hoping to catch the sound again. I knew I'd heard something, had the stomach-dropping sense it was danger, but I couldn't see anything anywhere. I opened my mouth to warn Gille that something was up when I felt a large object brush against my leg. I looked to my left and was startled to see another Huffer, a sleek black one, running right beside us. The rider was cloaked, but I knew immediately who it was.

Drefan.

Greetings, Human.

"We've got company!" I shouted to Gille. I knew only one reason why Drefan would be hunting us . . . Malvado had paid him good money to do it.

Gille looked over and his eyes widened with fear. He spurred the Huffer to go faster.

"Leave me alone!" I shouted.

That I cannot do. You know why.

I did. "You'd do anything for money, wouldn't you?"

I could feel him grin in the dark.

"I don't believe it," I cried, wanting to buy my own words. "There are some things even you wouldn't do!"

His laughter rang out, echoing down the tunnel. Gille stiffened and I realized that the Blendar was trembling. *You do not know me at all.*

"Maybe not. But I do know one thing for sure; I'm not going with you."

You have no choice. I have yet to fail a mission and do not plan to start now.

"There's a first time for everything. Step on it, Gille!"

But before the Huffer could pull away, Drefan plucked me off its back and swung me into the air as though I were a paper doll. Before I could react, I found myself sitting on Drefan's short-haired Huffer, his muscular arm wrapped tightly around my waist. Drefan tossed Gille an arrogant wave, then turned on a dime and slipped into a side tunnel. Gille gaped speechlessly at me as he and his Huffer fell far behind.

"Let me go, Drefan!" I struggled to get away.

Stop squirming.

"You have no right to do this!"

I am not your enemy.

"You've said that before."

I have a job to do, and I am doing it. My task is neither wrong nor right, merely a task.

"If it's only a task, then take me back to the Blendars. They would pay you for your troubles." I wasn't entirely sure that they would, but I had nothing else to bargain with.

There is someone who wants to meet you.

I felt a chill. "Why?"

He wants to test you.

"Test me?" The chill intensified. "You know, this is not a good time. I have to find my friends, and I was poisoned recently and—"

Excuses are for the weak.

"But I can't do this—"

Silence!

Considering the circumstances, I thought it would be in my best interest to do what I was told for a change.

As we rode toward our unknown destiny, Drefan slackened his grip, but only a little. His arm, still wrapped tightly around my waist, made it clear I wasn't going to escape any time soon. With each stride the Huffer made, my stomach tied itself further into knots. I was worried . . . about my friends, about upsetting Drefan, about being tested. I hated tests. I desperately wanted to nibble on a fingernail but there wasn't much nail left. How was I going to get out of this?

After a half hour's journey, full of agonizing about what to do, Drefan pulled on the reins, slowing the Huffer to a walk. He quietly approached the narrow entrance to a cave. An orange glow spilled from the edges of the opening like candlelight from a jack-o'-lantern. About twenty yards from the entry, Drefan dismounted, and with his help, I slid off the beast, his hand remaining firmly attached to my arm.

A rhythmic chant vibrated the air around us and a shiver ran up my spine.

Watch me closely. Do not speak, and keep your mind-work hidden. You are about to encounter strange and powerful beings.

He crouched down to peer inside and I peeked around him. Leaning sideways, the inside of the cave slowly came into view. What I saw nearly made me cry out. Drefan's hand flew to my mouth and covered it just in time. Inside the cave a huge, roaring bonfire flickered and danced. Figures wearing monk's robes and hoods formed a half circle around a man standing close to the fire. The apparent leader held a tiny, squawking Eenie Meenie by its foot, dangling the little creature upside down like a chicken. The poor thing was obviously frightened half to death.

When the baby Eenie Meenie mewled pitifully, it hit me like a ton of bricks what was happening—they were going to sacrifice it! I felt sick to my stomach.

"We give thanks to the gods for granting us power," the monk intoned. He raised the ugly, little wretch higher into the air. "We offer you this soul for your continued protection of our clan."

The others chanted softly at first: *"Take our sacrifice, return our power."* With each repetition of their incantation, their voices grew louder and the words came faster.

I pried Drefan's hand off my mouth and hissed, "You've got to stop them. They're going to kill that Eenie Meenie!"

Leave them be, he told me forcefully. *They are sorcerers. You do not want their attention focused on you, unless you would you like to trade places with that annoying little brat.*

I stared at him in horror. "You can't let them do this! They're going to kill an innocent baby if you don't do something. It doesn't deserve to die."

He shrugged and his green eyes glinted in the firelight. *I have more important things to worry about than an Eenie Meenie. As do you. Look away if you must.*

Glancing back at the fire, I saw the monk raise a long, sharp dagger into the air. "No!" I shouted, yanking my arm from Drefan's tight grip. Before I knew what I was doing, I was running into the cave, sprinting straight for the tall figure clutching the kicking Eenie Meenie. I launched myself into the air, crunched my eyes closed, and waited to slam into his body. I slammed into *something*, all right.

Right into the dusty, stone floor.

CHAPTER TWENTY-EIGHT
NOT WHAT YOU THINK

They were about to give up the search for Lavida and Gille when Loria spotted something up ahead. "There, Darian, against that wall!"

It was Gille. They dismounted and ran to him. He was drenched in sweat and bleeding from a cut on his forehead. His eyes widened in fear when he heard their approach, but his shoulders slumped in relief when he realized who it was. "I knew you would come," he exhaled. "Someone ambushed me. I did not see him very well. He took Lavida!"

"Where did they go?" Darian demanded.

"I do not know!" Gille sniffed.

Loria laid a hand on Gille's shoulder. "Calm yourself, Gille. Let me see that cut; it is bleeding."

"Bleeding?" Gille cried and his knees gave out. Darian caught him and propped him up against the cave wall. "I must have hit my head when I fell off my Huffer." The exhausted animal was standing a few feet away, panting.

"What were you doing on the Huffer in the first place?" Eddie asked suspiciously.

"A Blendar caught me in the corridor while I was going to check on Lavida. He told me that Malvado and his guards were coming, so I had to get her away before he caught her, just as you told me to, Darian."

"Who was the Blendar that told you that?" Ellie commanded. "Malvado wasn't there. No one was there."

Gille looked up at her in surprise. "I do not understand. A Blendar told me that Malvado was coming."

"But who was the Blendar?" Darian asked harshly. "We need to know, Gille!"

"I do not know," Gille cringed before Darian's anger. "I have never seen him before. He wore a green cloak. I could not see his face."

Eddie snapped his fingers. "That sounds like the guy who kidnapped us. I'll bet *he* was the one who told you Malvado was coming." He rubbed his chin. "He followed you, waited for the right moment, then grabbed Lavida."

"Are you referring to Drefan, Amoral Hunter Leader?" Darian looked worried. "He has a black star on his forehead."

"That's the guy," Ellie answered. "He's the one who brought us to the trial. I didn't like him."

"Few do." Darian shook his head, looking around the cave, his finger working the trigger of the crossbow. "If Drefan took her, then she is in trouble, indeed."

"What should we do?" Loria asked, eyeing her brother.

"What we should have done in the first place—consult Madrina."

A flying object whizzed by, startling Ellie. She started

swinging at it before realizing it was only Vesuvius on his flying rat. "I thought you were a Crusher arrow," she wheezed.

"I will forgive you for thinking that, dear, fashionable Ellie," he said. "Human perception is *so* . . . inadequate." He picked invisible lint off his shoulder as he hovered near her head. "I heard the news that Mademoiselle Mors has gone missing. Just my luck to miss all the excitement; I was getting my hair done." He fluffed his puffy do without actually touching it.

"How did you hear so fast?" Eddie asked, skeptical as always. "We just found out ourselves."

"We have our ways, little Human," Vesuvius told him. "We Zephoos are known for our amazing communications network."

"That only means they love to gossip," Loria clarified.

"So what are we going to do now? I am here to help," he offered grandly.

"Drefan kidnapped Lavida and is taking her to Malvado," Loria told him morosely.

"Drefan, hm? Well, you know I am no good when it comes to dealing with the Amorals. Such dull dressers! What would we talk about?" He patted his rat-bat's head, and she squeaked happily. "Perhaps we should work behind the scenes while the rest of you go after him."

"Does Madrina know where we have gone?" Darian asked.

"She might. I saw her from a distance as I was leaving. She looked quite angry."

"Angry about what?"

"I have no idea."

Darian's eyes narrowed. "Are you sure?"

"I could make some guesses."

"Please do."

Vesuvius rubbed his chin. "Hmm, yes. What was it she said . . . ?"

"Vesuvius!" Darian roared. Everyone jumped.

"Calm yourself, Blendar," Vesuvius replied blandly, fanning himself with a white-gloved hand. "I am getting to it. Genius must not be rushed."

"If you are a genius, Vesuvius," Darian growled, "then I am Malvado."

Vesuvius eyed him up and down. "The way you are curling that upper lip of yours, I can scarcely distinguish you from that hideous beast." Darian clenched his fists. "I am of a mind not to say a word with you looking at me like that."

"You are pushing your luck, Vesuvius," Loria warned him. "You know Darian does not get angry often, but when he does—"

"All right. All right. Touchy, touchy. Madrina was shouting your name, Darian."

"Shouting my name?" He looked stunned.

"Nothing to worry about, I am sure. She was probably only looking for you."

Darian looked doubtful.

"So what are you going to do about Drefan?" Ellie prodded. "Go after him?"

"Malvado is likely to have her by now," Darian said. "There is no time to notify the Security Squad. We must go now . . . alone, despite the consequences."

Gille was petrified. "Amorals"—he sniffed—"are awful!"

"Do not worry, Gille," Loria soothed.

Darian nodded. "Yes, Gille. Vesuvius has given me a good idea."

"Of course, I did. That is what I do. Now, I have a lunch date and must not be late. Ta ta." He whizzed away, his dark purple hair bobbing up and down in the wind.

"What's your plan?" Ellie asked Darian when Vesuvius was gone.

Darian was about to explain when a loud bellow, coming from the direction they were heading, filled the passage-way.

"The horn of the hunter!" Gille called out, his eyes widening in fear.

"Run!" Darian commanded and everyone raced to mount their Huffers. The terrified group spun around and fled the spot.

As they sped away, Ellie eyed the crossbow on her arm. Would she use the weapon if she had to? What if she accidentally shot herself in the stomach? She peered at the gently rounded mound and lifted an eyebrow. Maybe that wouldn't be such a bad thing, after all.

The horn sounded louder, and she tightened her grip on Darian. "Are we going to have to fight?" she shouted.

"Fighting is always a possibility," he replied. "Are you ready?"

She was about to reply no when an arrow flew past them. Without thinking, she spun around, aimed her crossbow, and fired. "Ah! I hit one. Oh my gosh, I shot somebody."

"Keep firing," Darian yelled to her.

"I—I . . . okay." She turned and fired five more times. The horn stopped. "I think I hit that blasted horn," she told him, feeling pleased.

He laughed. "I believe you did. That should delay them long enough for us to initiate my plan. Loria! Gille!" The two riders turned around to face him. "Pull into this tunnel, quickly!"

The group swiftly ducked into a narrow passage and pulled their Huffers to a halt. Darian dismounted, followed by Ellie. Eddie and Loria joined them on the ground. "Gille,

I want you to take the Huffers back home. Once you are there, tell Madrina that Malvado is hunting us. She must send reinforcements as soon as possible."

"But I do not know my way back!"

"The Huffers know," Darian told him. "Just let them lead you home. It is important that you go quickly. We are going to need Madrina's help."

"I do not like this," Gille moaned. "If she is angry with you—"

The sound of a horn blared in the distance. "Looks like they found their horn," Ellie remarked. "I was hoping I'd sent it to New Jersey."

"We have to make haste," Darian said. "Go, Gille. The Huffers will take care of you." Without waiting for a reply, he slapped Gille's beast on the rump and she galloped away. "Follow," he told Sekar. She gave him a questioning snuffle, then she and Loria's Huffer took off after Gille. Huddled in a small nook off the main tunnel, they waited for Malvado's militia to arrive.

Moments later, loud, echoing footsteps filled the corridor. Ellie shivered. "They're coming," she whispered to Loria and Darian. When they didn't answer, she turned around and saw two tall blonds wearing dark cloaks. Each wore a green star on his forehead.

They were Amorals.

CHAPTER TWENTY-NINE
BEWARE

I looked around the cave, stunned. How in the name of Pete had I totally missed an entire person? I struggled to sit up, readying myself to run. To my surprise, the fire had completely disappeared, along with the baby Eenie Meenie. The other monks had moved to form a complete circle around me. Biting my lip, I counted them and came up with thirteen—definitely not a good sign.

The lone sorcerer pulled off his large, enveloping hood to reveal short, dark hair and a trim beard ending in a pointy goatee. His nose was thin and it protruded from his narrow face like the sail of a sailboat. He looked surprisingly young to me. Maybe it was the dark blue graduation cap, complete with yellow tassel that he had produced from the folds of his blue velvet cape and placed on his head.

"Paying your exorbitant price appears to have been worth it, Drefan," the leader said to the approaching Amoral. "She definitely has the potential to be the *One*. Did you see how she leaped at me like a Mungula?" He rubbed his hands together gleefully. "We will need to test her further!"

I quickly closed my eyes and lay back on the ground. Maybe I could pretend to be dead.

On your feet. Everyone here knows you are awake.

I sighed and opened my eyes. Drefan's outstretched hand reached to me. I grabbed it and a vision flashed through my mind like lightning. In it, a man riding a white horse raced across an endless field of green grass. *Freedom!* a deep voice shouted joyously. Then the image disappeared and I was on my feet, feeling wobbly and out of sorts. I was shaking my head to clear it of the strange vision when I noticed Drefan staring at me, looking shocked. Oh, crud. Now I'd done it. He glared at me as though he wanted to kill me, then his handsome face went as blank as the gray walls around us. He turned away from me and stepped toward the group.

I studied the peculiar company surrounding me. The room was darker now without the fire, lit only by torches held high by two of the monks.

"This is Lavida Mors," Drefan announced. "I am sure you will find some use for her."

The leader bowed to me. "Welcome to Anaedor, Mistress Mors. I am Sabero."

I stared at him. "What happened to the fire and the little Eenie Meenie?"

His brown eyes sparkled with amusement. "What you saw never existed, Mistress Mors. Magic is not allowed in Anaedor for anything but self-defense." He put a finger to his lips, mischievously winking at me as though we were in cahoots.

So they had frightened me on purpose. "Who are you?"

"Who are we?" Sabero raised a dark eyebrow. The gesture made him look impish, definitely up to no good. "An interesting question, and most difficult to answer. We come from a race that once lived beyond the Great Sea, where we were known as Druids." His expression darkened. "But history—and mankind—distorted who we were and what we did."

"I've heard of Druids," I said slowly, scanning my memory. "They're priests, and they're supposed to be wise and powerful. They also made sacrifices to pagan gods—human sacrifices," I whispered, suddenly remembering the human part.

"We certainly do not make sacrifices." He looked around at the rest of the group, all of whom had removed their hoods. The others, young like Sabero, nodded in agreement. "None of us feels the need for that here. We have other ways of ensuring that we get what we want."

I swallowed hard, deciding I didn't really need to know what those other ways were. "So what *do* you do?" I asked, figuring this was a safer question to ask.

"Long ago, after the Uprising, the Council of Elders voted to outlaw the use of magic in Anaedor, as I mentioned. The Council reduced our role to that of record keepers for Anaedorian affairs, stripping us of any practical skill or power." He snorted. "We became mere scribes, existing only to serve others. When our ancestors protested, many of them disappeared. The remaining members of our clan decided to hide our true identities, doing nothing to draw attention to ourselves. For a very long time, we could not risk practicing our magic for fear of discovery. But now, I, and the Druids you see in this circle, have decided to return to the old ways, to regain the power and influence we once enjoyed."

"So why did you send for me?"

"If you are the *One*, Mistress Mors, then you can free us to be who we really are. Therefore, we must determine if you are truly what the rumors say."

"How are you going to do that?"

"As I said before, we have our ways."

My eyes widened anxiously. I glanced around the dark cave, looking for an escape route. I was stuck here alone, surrounded by a bunch of grown men running around in robes. Who knew what they might do?

"Do your *ways* involve torture?" I whispered.

He laughed and chucked me under the chin. "Do not worry, Mistress Mors. We have already begun our tests, and you have passed the first. But there are others. There is so much that I need to know about you."

My stomach roiled. "I can tell you everything you need to know right now. I'm not the *One*." I looked at Drefan, whose eyes slid upward to focus on my forehead. "Will you take me back to the Blendar caves, Drefan?"

He smiled. The rat was enjoying this. *I am afraid I was not hired to do that. However, if you have the Brass to pay me . . .* I stared at him in dismay and the smile grew wicked. *To perform services that have not been paid for would not be good business.* He looked me over. *Are you sure you have nothing with which to pay me?*

I thought of my empty pockets. The necklace I'd gotten from my grandma was the only thing of value I had on me. My hand rose to stroke the metal pendant, reassuring myself that it was still there. The metal disc felt different under my fingers. I glanced at Drefan and saw him staring at my hand, a speculative look on his face. I dropped the necklace, releasing it to fall back beneath my shirt. I wouldn't part with my necklace ever, despite the fact that it was different now, or maybe because it was.

Drefan continued to stare at me thoughtfully. *That is unfortunate. Perhaps we shall meet again.* Before I could chase after him, grab his dark green cloak, and beg him to take me with him, he was gone, melted into the shadows of the cave. I was left alone with the Druids. Turning back around, I found that only Sabero remained. The others had gone.

"What's going on?" I demanded, trembling.

"I will be happy to escort you back to the Blendar dwellings, Mistress Mors," Sabero said. "And I hope you will agree to answer a few questions on the way . . ."

I looked at him warily, wondering if I really had any choice in the matter. "All right. I'll answer your questions. Just bring me back to my friends."

He bowed. "This way," he motioned and turned to walk away.

We left the cave, Sabero moving swiftly as a jackrabbit on a sugar high. I had to run to keep up with him. We kept up this pace for at least ten minutes longer than my limit normally allowed. Inevitably, I tripped on a rock and sprawled onto the hard, rocky ground. I didn't even bother trying to get back up, wondering why I hadn't thought of collapsing earlier.

"I . . . need . . . to rest," I gasped as Sabero crouched over me.

"Perfect!" He sat down on a stone. "You rest, and I will ask questions." He leaned forward, his bearded chin propped on his hand, the yellow tassel swinging back and forth, mesmerizing me. "Now, I must know . . . Why did you throw yourself at me in the cave when you were so clearly outnumbered?"

I shrugged as I sat up and lifted my sleeve to examine a skinned elbow. "I guess I wanted to stop you from hurting that Eenie Meenie."

"But why did you want to protect the creature? I have it on excellent authority that you have every reason to despise Eenie Meenies." He grinned when I looked at him in surprise, wondering how he knew that.

"He was only a little baby. He was helpless."

"How did you think you were going to fight me and my fellow Druids? You *are* only one little girl."

I pulled my sleeve back down and picked at a rust-colored scab on my hand, avoiding his eyes. "I didn't think that far ahead." And even if I had, the result would have been the same.

"Apparently."

"But you didn't harm me, so I guess I made the right decision."

He snorted. "You have a strange way of thinking. I am not through with you yet, you know."

My throat tightened.

"What do you think of Drefan, then? He is no more than a servant to those who pay him. Would you save him?"

"*You* seemed to trust him. That should make him save-able."

"Are you absolutely sure about that?"

I stared at him. "I'm not sure of anything, much less absolutely." I rubbed my temples.

"Can you trust me?" he asked.

I shrugged. "I don't know. Maybe. I've got to trust somebody, right?" Funny I should say that when I trusted no one, not even my friends. Not even myself.

He examined me, his expression calculating. "Perhaps. But trusting the wrong person could destroy you."

"How do I know who to trust and who not to trust?" I implored. What was the formula?

"You know by their actions," he replied simply.

I gave a bitter laugh. "Going by that, I should trust Malvado just as much as, or maybe more than, I trust other people."

The Druid looked dubious. "Why is that?"

"Because I know upfront that he doesn't like me. Everybody knows that. He's not going to suddenly want to be friends with me. The people who are pretending to be your friend, but aren't, are the ones you've got to watch out for."

Like you.

He stroked his beard as he pondered his next question. "All right. Let us say you have determined at last who your enemy is, how would you go about defeating him? And I hope you have a better method in mind than leaping at him."

I shrugged. "They don't exactly teach enemy-overpowering techniques in human school."

"What if I showed you some ways? Would you be willing to try them?"

"Maybe," I cautiously agreed, wondering what his intention was. Another test? A plausible excuse to kill me?

"Good!"

"But first I have my own question."

His head tilted sideway. "Yes?"

"You called Drefan a servant, right?"

"I did. Why?"

"Oh, nothing. Just something someone said to me once." *Beware the servant.* Had my dream woman been trying to warn me against Drefan?

I shivered suddenly, remembering something else Sabero had said. *We became mere scribes, existing only to serve others.*

Two servants, two men whose motives I couldn't understand . . .

Beware, Lavida. Beware . . .

CHAPTER THIRTY

DUTY

The cavalcade of hunters marched past the narrow tunnel. The small group hiding inside held their breath and waited, hoping against hope that Malvado's guards wouldn't discover them. It was only a small Crusher Crew. Malvado and his militia were not with this troop. Darian, in his guise as an Amoral Hunter, watched them pass and breathed a sigh of relief. Had there been Mungulas they would have found them for sure; their sense of smell was incredible.

"Let us go," he whispered to the group. "We are going to follow them. Be silent." He looked directly at Ellie.

She frowned. "Why are you looking at me? I can keep my mouth shut."

"Then, do," he counseled sternly. "Are we ready?"

Everyone nodded. Stepping out into the corridor, Darian scanned the tunnel. When he sensed that no one was bringing up the rear, he motioned to the others to join him and led them down the passageway. It wasn't long before they caught up with the slow-moving party.

"Why are we leaving the hunt?" one of the Crushers asked.

"Because Malvado commanded it," another one snapped. "He thinks someone may be helping the Humans and wants to release the wild Mungulas to go after them."

Darian felt sick at this possibility. Wild Mungulas were frighteningly unpredictable.

"Why do we always have to do what he wants?" the first one snorted. "He acts like *he* is the Magistrate. We should only take our orders from the Magistrate himself, not this charlatan who thinks he rules us."

"Better not let him hear that, Loo. He would throw you into Miseria himself."

"He is not here to listen, Hedl."

Hearing Hedl's name, Darian winced. He did not like the Crusher, though Loria did. From all appearances, she felt a spark for him. He looked over at his sister to see if she had realized who they were following. The dreamy look on her face told him she most definitely had.

"The walls have ears," Hedl warned.

"Yes. And you have a mouth," Loo retorted. "I imagine you would tell Malvado what I have said in order to advance your rank."

"I would never do that," Hedl protested weakly.

"Likewise, I would never tell what I know about you and a certain incident in the Upland. That is unless—"

"You would never . . ." Hedl growled.

Loo laughed. "Like I said—"

"Shhh!" the Crusher Leader hissed. "I hear something."

The band halted. Darian stopped his group with a hand signal. Everyone froze.

"What is it?"

The Crusher cocked his square-shaped head toward the direction of Darian and the others. Suddenly he unsheathed his bow. An arrow was in the track and aimed at them before Darian could take another breath.

"Come out now or I will fire," Hedl commanded.

Ellie and Eddie's eyes widened, both looking to Darian for instructions. "Go on," he whispered. "Look like prisoners." The two raised their hands above their heads. "What are you doing?" he hissed.

"This is how we do it in our world," Eddie explained. "It shows we can't grab our weapons."

"Good idea," the Blendar acknowledged. He was also pleased to note that both of them had tossed away their crossbows. It appeared as though at least some Humans used their brains on occasion.

Ellie and Eddie stumbled forward into the light of the Crusher party's lamps. Hedl chuckled. "Grab them," he motioned to his men. "Good work, Amorals. You have captured two of the Humans."

"Our good work will cost you fifty RedGems," Darian stated coolly. "Each."

Hedl studied Darian for a moment, then slowly nodded. "Agreed. They will serve as bait for the other one." He cupped Ellie's chin with his right hand and gave her a hard smile. Her lips twisted, her eyes flashed defiantly.

"Where is the other Human?" Hedl asked.

"We are still searching for her," Darian told him.

"Well, keep it up. She is the one we want." Hedl motioned toward a Crusher to his left. "Pay him, Loo." The Crusher handed a bag to Darian. As Darian counted the Brass, Hedl asked, "What is your name, Amoral? I have not seen you before."

"We have just completed our Passage," Darian replied, pointing to the green star on his forehead. He did not want to give a name—names were all too easily checked. And the Amorals would not be pleased to find out that Blendars were masquerading as one of them.

"Ah, new Hunters. Well, congratulations on your first bounty. Your Elders will be pleased."

Darian nodded, sneaking a glance at Loria. She was staring intensely at Hedl. "Thank you," she replied before Darian could speak. The deep voice—all Hunters were of the masculine gender—sounded strange coming from her mouth. "Where are you taking the Humans?"

Hedl raised an eyebrow. "Once the trade is made, Amoral, you do not ask questions. You should know this."

"Forgive my partner," Darian quickly interrupted, pushing Loria back behind him. "He has always been too curious for his own good."

Hedl stared at Loria suspiciously. "Teach him to hold his tongue. Others are not as forgiving as I am."

Darian bowed. "That I shall." He did not make the mistake of apologizing. Amorals never apologized. "We must go now." He pivoted on his heel, hoping Loria would follow him without further words.

"We are meeting at the Arena," Hedl called after them, "in case you find the other Human. There is a large bounty on her head, but I am sure you already know that, Hunter."

Darian nodded. Now they would be able to follow the group without notice. Lavida would never forgive him if he let anything happen to her friends. Why her opinion mattered to him so much now, when he had once despised her, he was not sure. But it did. He intended to do whatever he could to protect Ellie and Eddie.

"**N**o, no, no!" cried Sabero, throwing his hands into the air. "You are not focusing!" He was angry, nearly distraught.

"I'm trying," I said, even though I wasn't. If I gave Sabero proof that I could do magic, that would be like pounding the final nail into my own coffin. I would become one of them, and in doing so would share their fate—Exile.

"To be a powerful sorcerer, Mistress Mors, you must start with the trivial."

"A powerful sorcerer?" I felt a chill run up my spine.

"Real magic is nothing more than learning to control your mind and teaching it to do things it has never done before."

"If I was really the *One*, I should just be able to do magic, right? But I can't."

"I know what you are doing; you are hiding your powers from me."

I opened my mouth to protest, then closed it.

"I know you have them. But can you control them? Or do they control you?"

I didn't answer.

He stood abruptly. "Come along."

I stared at him. "You're not going to kill me?"

His eyes narrowed. "Why would I do that?"

"Because I failed you."

"You failed yourself," he said. "I will take you to the Blendar compound now. You are no use to us."

I gazed at his stony profile. What did he mean by that? I was protecting myself. That wasn't failure.

That was survival.

Neither noticed the figure stalking them in the dark shadows of the cavern. Drefan followed the two with a tiny smile on his lips. He had successfully completed the job he had been hired to do. Easy, really. Almost boring. Except for the Human—she was more interesting than he had thought anyone could be.

And then there were her powers . . . At first they had disturbed him, but now he would give anything to be touched by them again, if only for an instant. The strange images she had stirred in his head, they had kindled something inside him. She was like Scrumpy, the seemingly harmless drink they served at the Cavern Tavern. The brew was delicious and intoxicating, and very dangerous for a man in his position, which is why he never drank it. He knew he should stay away from *her* as well, but he would not do it.

He *could* not.

One thing about her made him wary: she had refused to do magic for the Druid, even thinking that she might die for her refusal. She might refuse to perform for him as well. A strange feeling filled his chest—a tight, scratchy, burning sensation. He did not like it; it made him feel helpless and small, made him want to bellow and roar. He must break her.

A thought appeared suddenly in his mind, distracting him. Drefan placed his hand on the hilt of his sword as he listened to the message playing in his head: *We have disguised ourselves as Amorals.* Some impudent Pizzer was attempting to pose as one of his own. His Hunters had a flawless reputation. He refused to let some young buck ruin it. He reluctantly turned his Huffer about to go search out the Hunter imposters. He wanted to stay and see what happened next to the Human. Though what he wanted more was to look into those endless gray eyes of hers and be transported to that strange, enticing world he had glimpsed.

But there was his duty to attend to first.

Duty.

For the first time in his life, work felt like a burden to him. If he had possessed any skill at labeling his feelings, which he did not, he would have said he was starting to hate this burden with a very un-Amoral-like passion.

And when an Amoral begins to feel anything with the least bit of conviction, woe be to those in his path.

CHAPTER THIRTY-ONE
BETRAYAL

As the twins headed toward the Arena, Loria finally broke her uncharacteristic silence. "Do you think Hedl would ever care for someone like me?"

Darian had a feeling this question was coming and had prepared his answer. "He would be an eejit not to like you, Loria."

"Hmm. I did not give us away, did I? With my question?"

"I think not," he replied, patting her shoulder awkwardly. He wanted to comfort her, but did not know how, especially when she looked and sounded like an Amoral. "Besides, the result did us good; we now know where they are taking the Humans. We can follow them without getting caught."

Loria was quiet for a moment. "The Crushers appear to

support Malvado."

Darian nodded. "I think most of them do. They do not have much choice, though. They are under his command."

"Hedl, too?" She unconsciously pulled at the short, blonde strands of hair tickling her ear.

Darian sighed. He did not want to hurt her, but he could not lie to his twin. "Hedl is ambitious, Loria. If he wants to obtain a powerful position in Anaedor, his best chance is to go through Malvado."

"But there are other ways to advance," Loria surmised.

"There are other ways, yes," Darian agreed. "But none as swift."

She simply nodded and they were quiet for a while. They were passing the seventh cairn, the sacred tower of stones signaling their proximity to the Arena, when Loria spoke again. "They will be okay, will they not?" She turned to face him as they walked, searching for reassurance.

"Of course," Darian replied, looking away from her on the pretext that he needed to scan the area ahead of them. The real reason he could not look her in the eye, though, was that he was not so sure they would be. "I will not let anything happen to them."

"Darian," she asked, hesitating before continuing in a whisper, "do you . . . do you think Lavida is the *One*?"

He paused for a moment before answering. Finally, he shook his head. "I do not know, Loria. She is not anything like I had imagined the *One* to be."

"She is certainly brave!" Loria exclaimed, her bright eyes sparkling like no Amoral's would. "Look at what she has done since she came to Anaedor. I only wish I could be as courageous as she."

Darian nodded in agreement. The Human had done things he would only have attempted after a Turn or two of training. "She *is* brave . . ." *or very dense*, he thought. "But being brave, Loria," he emphasized her name, wanting her to hear this, because she was so bull-headed and romantic about such things, "is *not* enough to defeat Malvado and his forces. He is too strong and does not care who he hurts to get what he wants."

He rubbed the green star on his forehead; the brand was starting to irritate him. "Everyone believes the Magistrate is our Leader, but it is clear that Malvado has him under his control. One of these Cycles, he will eliminate our Leader altogether and take over the Council of Elders. The *One* is supposed to lead us in our fight against the evil in our world. Can you imagine Lavida doing that?"

Loria shook her head. "It is hard to imagine in some ways, but in others . . . I do not know . . . she *shines*."

"Yes," he replied distantly, "she certainly shines. I will grant you that, sister."

A light appeared up ahead and they stopped. They both crouched down.

"The Arena is so bright," Loria observed, shielding her eyes from the glare. "They must have lit every lantern and torch in there."

"As though preparing it for a battle," he murmured, half to himself.

"Do you think?" Loria breathed. "With whom?"

"Let us move closer for a better look." Darian quietly made his way toward the tunnel entrance. "Wait here."

When he did not hear Loria answer, Darian spun around. What he saw made his blood go cold. He raised his crossbow.

"That would be unwise," a hauntingly familiar voice said, and Darian froze. A hooded figure held a gleaming dagger to Loria's throat, his other hand lazily tracing the green star on her brow. "Did you think I would let this go? Impersonating a Hunter is a serious offense, Darian of the Blendars.

You know that quite well, I am sure, being a member of the URC."

"It is for a good cause," Darian tried to explain. "We—"

"I know why you are doing it, Blendar. That is not a good enough reason."

"We must find the Human, Drefan. If she is the *One*—"

"I am not so sure she is, and neither are you."

"*I* am sure!" Loria cried. Darian winced, willing her to stay still so long as the deadly blade pressed up against her throat. "Someone has to believe in her," she went on, ignoring the knife. "I do."

"How nice for you," Drefan replied blandly. "Your sister, Darian?" He looked the Blendar directly in the eyes, challenging him. "She is not as distrusting as you are, is she? She has the faith of a Youngling."

"Leave her alone. She is only helping me. I am the one you should punish, not her."

Drefan chuckled. "I will punish you both. You are equally guilty."

Darian shrugged, forcing himself to remain calm. "Then do it. We are running out of time." He glanced at Loria, trying to assess how she was doing. She made a strange face at him, which triggered a memory of a game they used to play when they were younger.

"Now!" she shouted, slumping in Drefan's arms. Darian launched himself at the Amoral, but before he could reach him, he was gone, leaving Loria in a pile on the hard stone floor.

"Are you all right?" Darian searched her for signs of harm.

"I will be," she answered shakily.

"I cannot believe I scared off a Hunter."

"You did not." She pointed. "They did."

Darian looked up. Crushers surrounded them. "Look

what we have here," Hedl smirked. "It seems our friends wanted to give us an escort."

Darian thought quickly. "We wanted to make sure the other Human was not already here. Otherwise, why waste our time looking for her?"

Hedl swept his arm toward the Arena. "Why not come see for yourselves? Follow me."

Loria gave Darian an uncertain look. He shrugged his shoulders. "Follow my lead," he mouthed to her as they stood up. She nodded bravely, but he knew she was scared.

Moments later they entered a large, empty cavern brightly lit by Starkinder lanterns. The ground had been cleared of stalagmites and rocks. Scuffs marred the gritty layer of gray dust coating the ground and scorch marks peppered the walls. The Arena was where the Anaedorians met for various forms of entertainment—games, performances, festivities, mock battles, formal duels . . . and executions. Some ancient "games" required the use of wild Mungulas and, at the moment, some twenty or thirty of the nasty, ornery beasts were locked within the rusty bars of sturdy cages, barking and howling at the newcomers.

Something else occupied one of the barred enclosures: Eddie and Ellie lay sprawled on the ground, motionless. His stomach turned at the sight. Loria gasped when she saw them and tugged on his arm.

"Hide your feelings, Loria," he whispered. "Remember who you are."

She frowned, but kept her mouth shut tight.

Strutting arrogantly, Hedl led Loria and Darian to a band standing on one side of the Arena. "I found these two Hunters lurking outside the cavern," he declared as he approached the group. "This one said they wanted to know if the Human has been captured yet. What should I tell him?"

The one to whom he spoke, wearing a black cloak, his back turned to them, suddenly spun around.

Malvado.

This was not good. Not at all. Loria hated Malvado, and when she got emotional, she had a hard time maintaining her morph. Darian felt her shaking beside him. She was trying to control herself, but she was losing the battle. Her hood slipped backward, her features began to pop in and out, the green star faded. Within half a tick, it was obvious to everyone in the Arena that she was not an Amoral. She had returned to her Blendar self—her dark hair curly and wild, her eyes large and black and angry as a thwarted Fairy. Darian sighed and morphed back to his own Blendar self. He was going to have a hard time talking them out of this one.

"Let our friends out of that cage!" Loria cried.

Darian shook his head. Their predicament had just gotten a lot worse.

"What is this?" Malvado demanded, annoyed at being interrupted.

"It appears to be two Blendars," Hedl told him.

"I can see that!" Malvado growled, his nostrils flaring.

"Of course you can see that, sir," Hedl agreed obsequiously. He rubbed his square hands together nervously. "These two are the ones who 'sold' us their find. I thought they might be plotting to get in here and sabotage our plans, which is why I kept a lookout for them."

"Anyone could have seen that, you cretin," Malvado snapped. "It seems we would be doing the Amorals a favor by holding these two while we search for the other Human. The more we can use as bait to lure her here, the better."

"Good idea, sir," Hedl said.

"You cannot put us in jail, Hedl!" Loria reached out to touch him. He jerked away from her outstretched hand and she pulled it back as though he had tried to bite her. "I—I thought you were my friend."

"You know this creature?" Malvado gave Hedl an equally speculative and appalled look. "She is a *Blendar!*" He sneered at her as he would a lowly Igglebug.

Hedl's gray face turned red, as though he had been standing too close to a lava pit. "She is my *brother's* friend," he hurriedly explained. "You know Mo"—he laughed nervously—"he is always picking up strays."

Malvado curled his fat upper lip. "Well, this time it appears he has picked up garbage."

Hedl laughed loudly at the moronic joke and Loria's face fell, her large eyes melting with pain and humiliation. Darian's blood heated up.

"Now look here, Hedl," he challenged, clenching his fists. "You *are* Loria's friend."

"*Friend?*" Hedl snorted. "You are mad. Blendars are no friends of mine." He was about to turn his back on them, when inspiration struck. "Human-lovers," he spat at them, the spittle hitting the ground by Darian's left boot.

"Enough!" Malvado roared, angrily swinging his spiked staff back and forth. "Put them in the cage with the others. We have an outlaw to hunt down."

"As you wish, sir," Hedl replied, bending stiffly at the waist. "Loo, cage them."

Darian looked around quickly. Crusher guards surrounded them, the expression on their chiseled gray faces bland, but watchful. They might not be the most intelligent clan in Anaedor, but they were very good at what they did. The situation looked hopeless. Still, Darian refused to give up without a fight. He owed it to the Humans and to his sister.

When a Crusher guard reached out to seize him, Darian spun away and grabbed his attacker's hard smooth arm, twisting it behind his back and driving him to his knees, screaming in pain. Another Crusher rushed Darian and he let go of his victim, leaping into the air in a flying kick. He nailed his assailant in the chest, sending him flying back a good ten yards. He was about to take out another guard when Loria cried out. Hedl had a tight grip on a fistful of her wild mane of hair and was twisting it ruthlessly.

Darian stopped fighting, panting hard, willing himself to stay calm. "Let her go."

Hedl smiled evilly. "Stop fighting."

Darian held up his hands. "Just let her go."

Two more Crushers secured him roughly.

"No!" Loria cried. "Fight, Darian!"

He shook his head. "I cannot," he replied and winced inwardly when her shoulders slumped pitifully. He had no choice, though; there was no winning this battle.

He watched in silence as Hedl dragged his sister to the cage and shoved her inside. She stumbled and fell to her knees on the hard, dusty floor. The other Crushers flung Darian next to Loria and slammed the door shut, locking it with a large iron key.

Loria struggled to her feet and staggered to where the Humans lay. "Darian, look at them." Her lips trembled.

Darian rose and moved with her, brushing dust from his hands, then knelt down and checked both of the Humans. The smaller one, Eddie, had dried blood streaking down the side of his head . . . and looked very pale. Ellie lay very still, too still. "They are alive, but barely so," he told his sister. "I do not think they will last much longer. They seem to be under some kind of malignant spell."

"And you shall join them," Malvado hissed, peering through the bars of their cage. When they turned to face him, he pointed the tip of his staff at them, a triumphant sneer on his evil, bloated face.

A zapping noise sizzled through the large cave, and the two Blendars fell, unconscious before they hit the floor.

CHAPTER THIRTY-TWO
DISCOVERING THE HORRID TRUTH

At last, the route looked familiar to me. Sabero and I stood at the bottom of the slope that led up to the entrance of the Blendar compound.

"This is as far as I go," Sabero told me. "We shall meet again, Mistress Mors. And when we do . . ."

"Go on." I had to know. "Finish your threat."

His eyes narrowed. "You will stop playing games and perform your magic for me."

With a low bow, he spun about and left me to wonder who he was, what he really wanted from me. Was he the servant my dream lady had warned me about? I shivered. My whole body felt cold, my mind numb. I was facing an unknown enemy who could attack me at any time, and I was alone. That enemy could even be the Blendars, I realized, as I approached the entrance. Still, I feared I had little choice but to go to them. I had to find my friends and I didn't know my way home. I was trapped here.

Lifting my shoulders in a pseudo show of bravery, I slipped into the large cavern. All the Blendars stopped in their tracks to watch me as I made my way toward Madrina's cave. For most of the way, I kept my eyes on the floor. When I had nearly reached the other side, a young Blendar giggled and I glanced up. I didn't see the little one, but I became aware of something else as I looked around. The Blendars standing closest to me gazed at me with such an expression of reverence on their long, narrow faces that my heart stuttered slightly. They bowed to me as I passed by them, their eyes glowing with wonderment, creating a pathway for me as I hurried to reach the entrance to Madrina's cave. The experience was kind of eerie, even humbling, but also a welcome change from what I'd been experiencing.

"I want to see Madrina," I told the two burly guards blocking my way into her cave. They looked down at me.

"She is not seeing any visitors," the one on the left told me.

"But this is an emergency. I *have* to see her."

"We are sorry," the right guard droned, scanning the room over my head, a bored look on his face.

"You don't understand. I'm Lavida. The *One!*" No! I did not just say that! "She knows me," I said, attempting to cover my slip.

The first one laughed. "Did you hear that, Tirus?"—he elbowed his partner in the ribs—"She thinks *she* is the *One.*"

Tirus snorted. He tapped his head knowingly with a finger, raising his eyebrows. They both laughed.

"Why don't you think I could be the *One?*" I asked, intrigued. With a sweep of my arm, I indicated the rest of the cave where the Blendars remained, watching. "Everyone else here seems to think I might be."

"They are misinformed," Tirus said arrogantly. "Croner and I have heard the rumors about you, undoubtedly started by Zephoos—they do it all the time—but we are not naïve like our kinfolk."

"Besides," Croner remarked as he reached down and mussed my hair, "you are too small to be the *One*. The *One* will be big like us." He flexed his arm and a muscle bulged, like an orange trapped under his skin, and they laughed a deep belly laugh.

"Okay, you've had your fun," I grumbled. "Now will you let me in? This really is an emergency. My friends are here and I need to make sure they're okay."

The two Blendars quickly sobered. "The other Humans are gone. Now go. You are distracting us from our duties."

"But—"

"Tut, tut, tut," Croner scolded. "Duties. Now run along." He shooed me with his hand. "Go on."

Stunned, I turned to go. The Blendars in the cave stared at me as I passed through their parted sea, but I was too upset to notice. My friends had gone. But where? With Malvado? No, please not that. I felt dizzy, sick—

"There you are!" a voice shouted triumphantly in my ear.

Startled, I nearly fell into the river. I turned to see Vesuvius hovering by my head on his rat-bat. "Vesuvius!"

"I knew I could do it if I put my mind to it!" he exclaimed, his little face beaming as his ride fluttered around me. "Brilliant. I told you there was more to me than stunning good looks and fabulous clothes. I cannot wait to tell Ametrius all about my amazing deductive skills."

"You found my friends?" I asked excitedly.

He looked down his ski-slope nose at me. "No. I found you. Your friends are out looking for you."

"They are? You mean Malvado didn't get them?"

"He was nowhere near the compound."

"Do you know where they are now?"

His little eyebrows rose. "Of course, I do. Brilliant, remember?"

"Oh, Vesuvius!" I cried, happy for the first time in hours.

"But you must let us ride on your shoulder," he informed me. "Woo-woo is getting tired."

The leathery creature settled onto my shoulder and wrapped its legs around my neck. "All right," I agreed, shuddering.

Together, our little group left the Blendar cavern in search of my friends. Vesuvius directed me to grab a Starkinder lantern on the way out, which I did even though doing so went against my principles, and then instructed me to take the narrow tunnel off to the right.

"They are not far from here," he told me in a stage whisper. "I left them to attend a lunch date, but I found you instead. Ametrius will simply have to wait." His little smile was pettily satisfied.

We had been walking for quite some time, maybe half an hour, when I finally lost my patience. I was ready to pull my hair out, or better yet, Vesuvius's hair. He was a horrible backseat driver.

"Are you blind!" he yelled more than once. "No, not that way. This way. Watch where you are going, will you, I am getting wet."

"I thought you said they weren't far," I managed to grind out after he pulled my hair, again, in an attempt to steer me.

Vesuvius shrugged. "Now that I think about it, Darian did mention a plan—something about going after Malvado."

My stomach dropped. "What do you mean? I thought

you knew where they were! What are you up to?"

Hearing my shouts, the rat-bat began to stir. She let go of my neck, stretched and lifted off my shoulder. "She gets hungry after sleeping," Vesuvius said, grabbing the tiny reins attached to the halter muzzling her blunt nose and mouth. "See you around!" With a squeak, the tiny creature tore off.

"Wait. Where are you going?" I called after him as he flew away. "Where am I? Vesuvius!"

But he was gone. A large, flat rock beckoned and I dropped down onto it, frustrated and lost. It seemed that Vesuvius had set me up, leading me on a wild goose chase. Or maybe not so wild, I thought with a chill. Perhaps he was leading me to the enemy. Either way, Vesuvius had managed to lure me away from Blendar territory and then had abandoned me, leaving me on my own in a strange world filled with creatures who hated me. He might even be going for reinforcements now, Woo-woo's hunger only a ruse to put me off guard.

Dazed and frightened, I stood and hurried in the opposite direction we'd been heading. The black ink closed in around me, leaving only the small circle of light cast by the Starkinder lamp. A growing sense of doom flowed through me like mud in my veins. I imagined a cavalcade of Amorals and Crushers and Druids racing after me.

I began to run.

A thundering sound echoed in the distance and the feeling that I'd been this way before came over me. When I saw a familiar red wooden door spotted with white gypsum flowers up ahead I knew I was right. I was close to the waterfall, which meant I was on the path toward home. I raced toward the door. When I reached it, I discovered that it was locked. Crud. I was so close to freedom!

Shivering from fear and cold, I slid my hands into my

blazer pockets to warm them, wondering what to do next. As I did so, my left hand hit something metallic. Slipping my fingers around the metal, I pulled it out and examined it. My house key. I stared at it for a moment, feeling a growing sense of hope, then slid the black key into the lock. The metal glowed for three or four seconds, and once the light faded, I wrenched the key to the right. The latch clicked. Pulling the skeleton key out of the keyhole, I pocketed it, then cautiously opened the door, uncertain who might be on the other side. I didn't want to get careless now.

The small cave was empty when I entered it. The red door shut behind me and I spun about, spotting the other doors in the room. Excitement coursed through me like electricity. Maybe Ellie and Eddie had headed this way. Maybe Darian and Loria were taking them home.

With renewed vigor, I quickly passed through the cave and around the waterfall. With each step I took, the briny smell of ocean grew stronger. Close to the end of the tunnel, where the unusual cave carvings decorated the walls, I thought I heard someone yelling. A light shone up ahead and I ran toward it. It had to be Ellie and Eddie.

But why were they shouting?

"Somebody help me!" a frantic voice cried out.

I sprinted toward the sound, oblivious to everything but reaching my friends. Exiting the tunnel, I almost pitched headlong into a huge pit, which I'd forgotten about in my hurry. Waving my arms like a whirlybird, I focused hard, imagining I had wings, and only just stopped myself from plunging downward. I steadied myself and slowly took a step back from the edge of the gaping chasm. When I was on stable ground, I scanned the dark cave. A cold shiver of dread ran down my spine when I spotted a figure lying on Warrior's Walk—the same bridge I'd crossed my first time in Anaedor. Next to the body, a lantern struggled to ward off the darkness.

"Help me, Lavida!" a voice begged. "I have hurt my leg. Please hurry!" The victim reached out a shaking hand. "Hurry!"

I set down my Starkinder lantern and ran out onto the bridge. "Don't move. I'll help you. And whatever you do, don't look down."

The figure groaned and coughed. I gasped as he began to stand up. "Gille!" I shouted, suddenly realizing who it was. "You're going to fall!" But he only continued to stand up.

And then he grinned.

CHAPTER THIRTY-THREE
THE SERVANT

My whole body began to tingle. Something was terribly wrong.

Gille straightened to his full height and studied me, a sneer marring his face. "I find it hard to believe anyone could even contemplate that you are the *One*. Your powers are not even strong enough to get you on a stupid Huffer. Still, you are a threat to my Master's plans and, as my Master's servant, I must do as I am told."

I didn't hear his last words—another voice was echoing in my mind. *Servant, servant . . . Beware the servant.*

"But you're a Blendar!" I protested.

"One of those spineless imbeciles? I think not." He curled his lip in contempt. "My Master used magic to transform me into one."

Something clicked in my head. "Of course! You don't

shimmer like a Blendar. Why didn't I catch that?"

"You did not catch it because you are breathtakingly stupid. I poisoned those Anaedorians at the Cavern Tavern and no one suspected me, not even you, just like my Master predicted."

I stared at him. "*You* poisoned the Anaedorians?" It was so obvious now. Gille's master could only be Malvado. He was the one Anaedorian who hated humans enough to concoct such a scheme. He wanted everyone to think a human had been responsible for the poisonings so that he would have an excuse to ban them from Anaedor forever. But why go to all that trouble? No one even knew this place existed, and wouldn't want to come here if they did. "So you weren't taking me away when we ran from the Blendar compound?"

"Not quite," he agreed, almost giggling at my naiveté. "I was taking you *to* my Master."

"How could you? I trusted you, Gille!" The words were out before I realized what I was saying.

Gille's pudgy face turned deadly serious. "That was your first mistake, *Human*." He rubbed at his red, runny nose. "I have grown tired of this game. If that interfering Drefan had not taken you, this would be over by now." He flexed his fingers and his knuckles cracked. "It is time we end this. I am as anxious to be myself again as the Onyx is to meet you."

The Onyx? Why did that name sound familiar? Then I remembered what Mo and Eddie had told us about the Onyx—a giant squid with eight tentacles and a claw-like beak and giant eyes. A distant bellow rose like a bad memory from deep down in the black hole.

Gille chuckled evilly. "The Onyx has risen to the surface, something he rarely does. He must be very hungry."

I bit my lip. I didn't want to die here.

"You're just like everybody else!" I accused him, stalling, hoping to come up with a plan. "Bossing me around, making me do things I don't want to do!" I clenched my fists, breathing heavily, my scheme for coming up with another plan forgotten. When did I ever get a choice? When did I ever get to decide what I did and did not want to do?

Never.

And I was sick of it. "Just because I'm a freak doesn't mean I don't have a brain. I make the decisions for my life. Me!" I jabbed at my chest. "So you can just take your arrogant attitude and shove it!"

Gille yawned. "Are you through ranting now?" He bent down to pick something up, then leaped at me with lightning speed.

The impact knocked the wind out of me. Struggling to breathe, I realized with a feeling of horror that he was trying to push me off the stone bridge. I tried to grab onto something—anything. My hand found his hair. I seized hold and yanked hard. He screeched. I yanked again, pulling myself to my feet, and he squealed like a pig. I pushed away from him and ran down the narrow bridge, the fact that I should have been petrified with fright far from my mind.

Until his wicked laugh caught up with me.

In that instant, I saw in my mind's eye a scene, a possibility. I stopped on the spot, turned to face him and, seeing him rushing toward me, I squeezed my eyes shut and jumped straight up. When I opened them, I was high over Gille's head as he passed below me, unable to stop on the slippery gravel on the Walk.

I landed on the ground and turned to face his back. He spun around.

"It seems you are more of an adversary than I thought," he snarled. His eyes turned yellow. "But you are still no match for me!" he cried, his voice rising from a low growl to an eerie, wolf-like howl. He lunged, swiping at me with hands that had transformed, sharp, deadly claws protruding from the end of each finger.

I shrieked and jumped back, nearly going over the edge. I thought my heart couldn't pound any harder, or faster.

Gille laughed a high-pitched cackle and settled his weight back on his haunches. He lunged again, but missed as I spun away from the edge like a ballerina and skittered to a stop several feet away.

He had doubled in size now, his arms and legs lengthening like chewing gum. Thick, spiky hair covered his entire body and large, sharp teeth sprouted in his snarling mouth. His hind feet had transformed into hooves and he balanced on them like a rearing horse. A memory surfaced. The woods. Teeth. Running. Hoof beats. Gille had come after me before.

He leaped at me again. I dove beneath him as he flew over me, but not in time to avoid his long claws. The sharp weapons tore through my favorite blazer and shirts to scrape the thin layer of skin just above my ribcage. Pain surged through my entire body and I gave a startled gasp. Gille's laughter echoed in my ears as I peered down at the tear in my clothes. I was surprised to see so little blood, because the cut hurt like mad. He'd only scratched me, but I felt like I had a cleaver in my side. I began to feel dizzy, like when the Crusher arrow had pierced my arm. A nauseating wave of pain coursed through my gut and I crunched my eyes tightly closed.

But this time I didn't have the leisure of willing the poison away. When I opened my eyes, Gille's gaping mouth was only inches from my face, his breath as fetid as fly-infested road kill. He grinned like a deranged hyena; his yellow teeth glistened in the lamplight.

I scuttled away from him as best I could on the narrow ledge. My eyelids quivered, wanting desperately to close. The poison had depleted nearly all of my energy. I couldn't fight anymore. I curled myself into a ball and waited for the end.

The sound of his hooves echoed in the cave like a countdown as the beast stalked toward me. "Prepare to meet the Onyx," he growled. He was almost upon me when he sucked in a spasmodic breath, as though surprised, and then another, and another . . . then he sneezed, a startling explosion in the vast space. His balance upset, he shifted too near the edge and one hind leg went over . . . then the other, almost in slow motion. He fought to dig his front claws into the stone path, screeching shrilly as the weight of his body drew them steadily along. His hind legs scrambled for a hold, breaking away chunks of clay and stone. His eyes bulged in fear and disbelief. "Help!" he cried, suddenly changing back into the old Gille, stubby fingers reaching out. "Do not let me fall, Lavida!"

I automatically put out my hand to grab his. I couldn't just let him fall. His eyes narrowed with delight as he reached out to grasp it. But before he could latch onto my outstretched fingers, a terrifying bellow rent the air. Startled, his foot lost the hold it had found and his thrashing, rotund body went over the edge, supported only by his fingertips. His eyes met mine for an instant. A short scream burst from his gaping mouth as he lost his final grip, and he sank out of view.

When I didn't hear anything more, I crawled toward the edge and peered over the side. I saw nothing but shadows and darkness. Suddenly a taut-veined hand shot up from nowhere and gripped my arm. I screamed and tried to shake him off, but I was too weak from the poison. He clung to me like a giant leech, pulling me over the edge.

"Aaaagh! Somebody!"

The Onyx thundered again, and in a moment of clarity, I saw what would happen if I fell into that pit. I would die a gruesome and painful death.

"Somebody help me!"

You are the One, *Lavida*, a voice whispered in my ear. *You are the* One.

The sound of those words, even though I didn't want to believe in them, warmed me like a fire in my belly. The heat radiated throughout my body, and my skin glowed as brightly as a million Starkinders. The pain in my side faded away. Fear left me. Strength filled my will and my limbs. Gille stared up at me in horror. He jerked his hand away from my arm as though it burned him and he fell into the abyss. As he plummeted into the pit, he changed back into the hairy creature he'd been while fighting me. The Gille I had known was gone.

Seconds later, colorful, flashing lights lit up the darkness down below. The Onyx, or whatever it was, trumpeted once more, then an ominous silence filled the air.

The glow pulsing from my skin dissipated like fog before the sun. I stood up, shaky, and felt relief that I'd survived. At the same time this thought entered my mind, an evil, mocking voice echoed through the cave.

"Abandoning your friends?"

Oh, crud. It was Malvado. I turned to run.

"You shall not escape," he called after my retreating figure.

"Yes, I *shall!*" I shouted back.

"And leave your friends?"

I jogged to a halt and turned to face him.

"Your friends and those traitorous Blendars are, shall we say, *waiting* for you."

He had to be bluffing. "Why should I believe you?" I

challenged, hoping against hope that he was lying.

"Oh, I have them, all right." He held up something pink—Ellie's glasses. "If you come with me,"—he smiled coldly—"I will let your friends go. I only want you."

The Toad had taught me all about deceit. He was one of the many reasons that I didn't trust people. I understood quite well that Malvado wouldn't let my friends go. Still, I had no choice but to go with him. I couldn't abandon Ellie and Eddie.

"All right. I'll go." I crossed the rest of the walk.

As soon as I reached the other side, two Crushers grabbed my arms, pinning them behind me.

"Take her to the Arena," Malvado commanded, then turned and stalked away.

I didn't make it easy on my guards during the march, letting my entire weight drop so they had to drag me, and stomping on their feet (which was about as effective as kicking a rock) whenever I could. It wasn't much, my little rebellion, but it made me feel better.

After passing a large, cone-shaped pile of rocks, we encountered a giant archway spilling light like a beacon. As revenge for my lack of cooperation, one of the guards twisted my arm before shoving me through the opening. I stumbled into a large cavern and fell unceremoniously on my face, skinning my left knee. I pushed myself backward to check out the damage, falling on my butt in the process. From this humble position, I looked around the Arena in awe, forgetting my knee. Spotting an assortment of deadly weapons hanging on the wall, I wondered what kind of vicious games they played here. My hands began to shake.

One of the guards jerked me to my feet and dragged me to a row of metal cages. When we reached them, the Crusher pushed me to the ground again and I bruised my other knee. I wished now that I hadn't rebelled. Two of the cages were empty, two barely contained several snapping, snarling wolf-like beasts that looked just like Gille, and one seemed empty—the one in front of me. But it was not. I pushed myself up from the ground and studied the four still figures curled up on the floor. They looked dead. My stomach churned.

I turned to face Malvado, my voice quiet, quivering. "What have you done to them?"

He laughed coldly. "Oh, just a little something to keep them quiet. If you do not cooperate, however, they will stay that way, permanently."

I stared at their motionless forms. It didn't look like they were even breathing. I had done this. I had abandoned them, and now they were either dead or dying. "What do you want from me, Malvado? Whatever it is, I'll do it; just make my friends better."

"I want nothing from you, Human," he replied scornfully. "I simply want you to disappear. If you are the *One* as rumor says, then I want you to be gone from Anaedor . . . forever."

"Done! It's a deal. We're out of here."

"You misunderstand me, miscreant. I want you *dead*."

I gulped.

"Oh, yes. I will convince the Council Elders that you are a danger to us, and you shall die."

A drop of sweat rolled down my forehead and onto my cheek. "But I haven't done anything to you. Why would you want me dead?"

"You have not done anything?" He shook his black staff at me in accusation. "You have poisoned my citizens and ignited a rebellion amongst us. You are despicable!"

"I didn't do any of that! You're the one who told Gille to poison the Anaedorians! He bragged about it before he fell into the pit."

Hedl, who was hovering by the cage, peering into it, whipped around. "Who is Gille?"

"I do not know anyone named Gille," Malvado hissed. I stared at him. I had the strange feeling he was telling the truth. "She is trying to fool you, and she made an easy job of it." He snapped his fingers at the guards. "Put her in the shackles. But be careful—we do not know what she can do. If she tries anything . . ." He stopped talking and strutted over toward the wall where the weapons waited to be used.

The guards grabbed my arms and dragged me toward the wall where iron clasps hung like giant lobster claws. Out of habit, I reached up and clutched my necklace. I squeezed the pendant tightly in my sweaty palm.

Lavidaaa, a voice called, coming from all around me.

"Who's there?" I whispered.

You are so lost . . . you do not know what to do.

"I know I don't!" I cried, startling the guards. They moved faster, wanting to get me safely into the shackles. "After the Incident I tried not to use my powers, especially around other people. And I was doing all right until I came to Portal Manor. But now my friend thinks I'm a freak and she's going to leave me. They're all going to leave me!"

You were simply following your calling, Lavida. That does not make you bad.

"Then how come every time I use my powers, I scare away the people I love?" My father, who had distanced himself from me long ago; my friends at school, who had stopped talking to me; Ellie, who was already suspicious and refusing to speak to me; Ian and Eddie would be next, followed by Mrs. Dooley and Mrs. Keeper.

"Lavida?" a shaky voice called. I looked back. Ellie stood on wobbly legs, staring out through the bars of the cage. She looked deathly pale, her blue eyes wide and frightened. "What happened? Where are we?"

"Malvado has us. He's . . . he's going to . . ." I couldn't finish the sentence, but Ellie knew what I'd been about to say.

She sank to her knees. "Oh, no!"

I stared at her, watching her cry in fear, and my heart twisted with pain. One of the Crushers spun me around, slammed my back against the wall and slid the first cold shackle over my wrist. Just as he was about to clamp it shut, I tore my hand from his grasp, gave him a violent shove and broke free.

"Catch her!" Hedl shouted.

I ran, my legs like cement, my heart threatening to burst.

"Stop her!" Malvado shrieked, waving his spiked black staff maniacally. His dark cape flapped about him like a raven gone mad as he stalked toward the cages. "What are you waiting for? Release the Mungulas!"

The Crushers rushed to open the cages and the hairy creatures poured out like overgrown rats from the sewer. Catching sight of me, they raced after me, howling and baying. Their hooves clattered hard against the stone floor, the sound echoing loudly in the giant cavern. I glanced back over my shoulder as I darted in and out amongst the cages. One of them, faster than the others, started to gain on me, closing the distance quickly. I knew I couldn't outrun him. I had to fight. My lips trembling, my breath coming fast and short, I turned to face the Mungula, my foot knocking against a large rock. Toes throbbing, I picked it up and heaved it as hard as I could. The heavy stone hit the creature squarely on the forehead and knocked him down. Immediately, he bounced up again to land on his two hind hooves. The look he aimed at me seared into my eyes.

"Do I have to do everything myself?" Malvado screamed

at the Crushers and Mungulas.

He flung out his hands in my direction, as though throwing a broad net at me. An invisible object slammed into me and I flew backward against the wall, the impact knocking the wind out of me. As I struggled to get my breath back, I realized I was pinned to the wall like a butterfly in an insect collection.

I was trapped by magic!

MUNGULA

CHAPTER THIRTY-FOUR
THE CASUALTIES OF WAR

Malvado howled triumphantly.

I thrashed about in a futile attempt to break free while Malvado calmly polished the smooth end of his staff on his black robe. "Consulting the Council is no longer necessary. I have plenty of witnesses here who will attest that you have used magic in Anaedor. The Council will believe me when I tell them what a danger you were to our world."

Were?

"I didn't use magic!"

He smiled evilly. "What does that matter?"

"But it's a lie!"

He shrugged as he raised his hands again. "Guilty. Now prepare to die." He pointed his staff at my heart and mumbled a spell under his breath.

"Lavida!" Ellie screeched. "Help!" One of the wild Mungulas was smashing against the cage, trying to get at her.

I chopped frantically at the invisible strands bounding me. When that didn't work, I thrashed my body from left to right, trying to free myself. But nothing budged. I was imprisoned as firmly as my friends. We were all going to die in this underground world, and all for nothing.

"Cease and desist!" a voice cried out. My head whipped toward the source of the echoing command, my heart pounding. There in the entrance of the cave stood Mrs. Keeper and a messy-haired Ian. What were *they* doing here?

Malvado scowled and raised his hands. With a poof, two balls of white light appeared in each one. "*Cremare!*" he screamed and hurled the fiery orbs at Mrs. Keeper. The glowing balls flew at her like malevolent comets streaking through the sky. She squinted in the blinding light. Ian pushed her to the ground and placed himself in front of her.

"Get down, Ian!" I yelled.

"Ian!" Ellie cried from the middle of the cage. "Help him, Lavida!"

I stared helplessly at her. The only way to help him was to use magic.

And she would see me do it.

Ian and Mrs. Keeper, too.

The graffiti at my old school flashed in my mind. *Lavida Mors is a witch!*

The note Phoebe gave me in class . . . *Freak! Freak! Freak!*

And that painful question Ellie had asked me . . . *Are you one of these . . . things?*

"Now you will know that I *am* one of them, Ellie," I

whispered, "because I can't let my friends die."

The orbs were only inches away from Ian and Mrs. Keeper. I threw out my hands and the balls of light shuddered to a stop like someone had hit the brakes. Just as quickly, they took off again—back toward me. The fiery globes picked up speed. My hands automatically rose to protect my face.

This would be my last sacrifice, giving my life to protect others. And this time, it was my choice to do it. At last, I would be free.

I closed my eyes and waited for impact.

When nothing happened, I slowly opened one eye. The orbs sat, one in each hand, as though waiting for their next command. I looked at each hand in surprise, then raised my arms high into the air, slowly, deliberately. I searched for Malvado and saw his dark eyes widen in horror. With all my strength, I flung the white balls of light at him. Like diving hawks, they sped toward the black-cloaked figure.

But they did not hit Malvado or the staff he held out in defense. Instead the balls swirled around him like tiny tornadoes, igniting strands of his hair. He screamed in anger and pain. The balls spun faster and faster until a loud pop shattered the still, expectant air. Smoke filled the Arena, and when it cleared, Malvado was gone. My knees gave out and I slid to the ground. My eyes landed on Mrs. Keeper and Ian. Both stared at me, then at the cloud of smoke that had once been Malvado. Hedl, sensing defeat, pushed the other Crushers aside and dashed from the Arena. The rest of the Crushers and Mungulas followed in a swarm of chaos.

When the cave had cleared, Mrs. Keeper and Ian ran to me.

"Are you all right, dear?" Mrs. Keeper asked, kneeling by

my side. She gently brushed my hair off my forehead.

Ian kneeled, too. He looked me over, then, satisfied that I was okay, he punched me on the shoulder. "What were you thinking, Lavida? You could've been killed!"

"What are you talking about?" I asked, clutching my arm. I squinted up at him. My head hurt as though someone had used it to break rocks.

"I'm talking about the mess you've made of things," he growled.

"You can congratulate Lavida some other time, Ian," Mrs. Keeper said dryly. "Right now you'd be of more help if you could lend a hand sitting her up."

He shook his head, as though he wanted to refuse. Still, he propped me up so my back was against the wall. "You should've told us what was going on."

I couldn't believe what I was hearing. "What was I supposed to say, Ian? 'Hey there's a secret world full of magical creatures living beneath the mansion'?"

"Sure, why not?" he said smugly. "We know all about Anaedor, and that monster Malvado."

I gaped at him. "Then why didn't you warn me about him?"

Ian blushed and shrugged, looking away. I realized with a growing sense of horror that I could have avoided all this, and Ellie would never have known that I could do magic. I could have saved things between us! My lungs constricted. Air seemed so elusive. "I lost my friend!" I choked. "My last hope!"

"We're still here," Mrs. Keeper soothed as she patted my hand, trying to calm me. "We won't leave you, dear."

I stared at her helplessly. She didn't understand. And why wasn't she freaked out? I'd caught fireballs in my hands and thrown them at another person. I'd done magic!

What was wrong with these people?

"Somebody get me out of here!" Ellie shouted, cutting off my rising hysteria. I looked to see her gripping the bars of the cage, her eyes focused solely on Ian.

"I'm coming!" he called and hurried over to the cage. Mumbling under his breath, he fiddled with the lock and soon had it undone. He swung the door open and helped Loria and Darian as they woozily staggered out of the cage. Darian grabbed Loria before she fell and lowered her to the ground. He sat down next to her, anxiously looking her over to make sure she was okay. Mrs. Keeper helped a bleeding Eddie out of the cage. A white handkerchief appeared as though from nowhere, and she swiftly applied the cloth to the wound on his forehead.

Ellie was the last to come out, leaning heavily on Ian. "Thank goodness you've come, Ian. You're so strong." Grinning, he helped her sit down next to Eddie, who was now holding the makeshift bandage himself. His color had returned and he looked a bit better.

Ellie hadn't yet looked at me, not once.

"What happened out there?" Darian asked, turning to me.

I chose to misinterpret his question, putting the focus on Gille instead. "Gille kidnapped me. He was actually a Mungula in disguise. And his master sent him to do his dirty work. Then Malvado found me and tried to finish the job."

Ian was watching me closely, waiting, it seemed, to find out if I would say anything more about what had happened in the Arena. I didn't.

"Gille was a Mungula?" Loria exclaimed. "I cannot believe it."

"I saw him turn into one when we were fighting on Warrior's Walk. He said his master used magic to turn him into a Blendar."

"I should have expected something like this from Malvado," Darian said ominously, shaking his head. "Things are changing in Anaedor."

"Yes, they are, and not for the better." Mrs. Keeper broke off. "We must get Lavida and her friends back home immediately."

"Amen to that!" Ellie seconded. "I'm tired, I'm hungry, and I can't see a thing." She turned toward Ian and squeezed his arm. "You'll help me, won't you, Ian?"

"It'll be my pleasure," he said in a manly voice.

"We will escort you to the outer boundaries, Keeper," Darian offered as he stood and dusted off his brown leather pants.

Mrs. Keeper nodded. "We would be honored, Darian. Thank you."

"Let's get out of here." Ellie leaped to her feet and blindly started marching toward the back of the cave. Ian grabbed her arm and suavely turned her around, aiming her toward the exit.

Darian held out his hand to me and I allowed him to pull me to my feet. "I want to apologize for failing you, Lavida," he said quietly. "I should have known about Gille. I should have—"

I squeezed his arm. "You didn't fail me, Darian. I was the one who shouldn't have run away."

"I did fail you, and I will make it up to you." His voice was determined.

"This can't be fixed, Darian. What I feared most has happened."

"You saved your friends' lives, Lavida. How can that be bad?"

"I know, and I'm so glad that I did. I'd do it all over again in a heartbeat. I just hate that in doing so, I had to lose them."

"You have not lost me, Lavida."

I glanced up at him, startled, and he smiled. It was a very nice smile.

Even for a Blendar.

CHAPTER THIRTY-FIVE
UNDERSTANDING . . . A LITTLE

I woke suddenly and sat up in my bed. Next to me, Ellie slept soundly, snoring like a chainsaw. During the trek back, she had spent her time chattering to Ian, asking him how he'd found us. He was evasive in his answers, but said enough to keep her happy. Not once did she mention what I had done to Malvado.

After checking on Ms. Penny, who had found her way back to the room sometime in the night, I quietly slid out of bed, pulled on my faded red hoodie and hobbled down the front steps to check on Eddie. He, too, was sleeping quietly, his arm wrapped tightly around his pillow. Continuing down the steps, I made my way to the Great Hall, where I found Mrs. Keeper enveloped in a blue plaid robe sitting on the large couch facing the fireplace. A battered and worn leather book, the same one she'd held when I first met her on the steps of Portal Manor, lay on a wooden coffee table in front of the couch.

"I'm here." The heat of the roaring fire reached out to me and I shivered at the sudden warmth.

Mrs. Keeper turned around, not in the least surprised to see me. "Sit down, Lavida." She rose and took my hands. I walked around to the front of the couch and sat down on the soft cushions. Mrs. Keeper settled by me, still holding my hands. Her skin was soft and warm. Her large, brown eyes were shiny as she looked up at me. "I'm so sorry, Lavida." Her voice was small and full of pain.

I stared at her. "Why are *you* sorry, Mrs. Keeper? Malvado's the one who should be sorry."

She squeezed my hands, giving me a grateful smile. "I should've told you from the beginning about Anaedor. If I'd said something right away, none of this would have happened."

"But you couldn't have told me about Anaedor my first night here. You barely knew me."

"I wasn't sure how much of your father's daughter you were," she admitted. "Whether you'd believe me or not."

"I probably wouldn't have. I can hardly believe it now."

"Still, the knowledge might have protected you. I went to see Madrina after you told me your true name. When she heard what it was, she felt positive that you were the *One*. She warned me that it wouldn't take long for the other Anaedorians to hear about you, and when they did, you would be in great danger." Mrs. Keeper gave a guilty shrug. "She was right, it didn't take long. A Zephoo overheard our conversation and soon made it known that a human named Lavida had come to Portal Manor. The little scamps are insatiable gossips and this was a good tidbit, so I suppose I can't blame them for spreading the story. It would have been found out anyway, especially after Loria and Darian had discovered you."

"So you knew I'd met them, trying to rescue Ms. Penny? And that they took me to see Madrina?"

She shook her head. "I had no idea. But Madrina is wiser than I. She knew you had to be warned, and I imagine she took matters into her own hands by sending for you. For my part, I thought that if you weren't *the* Lavida Mors of the *Prophecies*, why should I worry you over nothing? I had my doubts that you were the *One*; you seemed so young. So I waited." She chucked me under the chin. "You poor dear. How strange it all must have seemed to you!"

"Like a bad dream," I admitted. "When Drefan and his Hunters kidnapped us, that's when I started to believe."

"Drefan? Oh, dear. That is exactly what Madrina had feared might happen. Once word got around who you might be, Malvado was bound to take action."

"Well, it's nice to know *you* don't think I'm the *One*."

Mrs. Keeper studied me pensively. "I *thought* it was impossible, that your gran's giving you that name was only wishful thinking on her part. But now I believe you might be that person. How else could you have fended off Malvado's magic?"

"Maybe those fireballs were only an illusion." It was a weak argument, but all I had.

Mrs. Keeper stared at me for a long moment, her small, dark eyes behind her glasses sharp and speculative. At last she asked, "How did you know to come down? And here, to the Great Hall?"

I shrugged. "I just did."

"Don't give me that! You knew because you read my thoughts, Lavida. You heard me call to you in your mind."

Mrs. Keeper's insistent voice in my head had awakened me from a deep sleep. "But maybe *you're* the psychic," I argued, purposely avoiding saying what she wanted me to say.

She pulled her hands away from mine and sat up straight. "You know I'm not talking about myself, Lavida," she scolded. "My psychic abilities are decent, but very rudimentary. All I did was send you a message and hope it was received. Obviously it was, for here you are. And while I have some powers, *you* are the telepathist. And I'll wager you can do much more than that with your mind."

I stared up at the dark ceiling. A part of me wanted to own up to Mrs. Keeper, to admit that I had done some pretty strange things. After all, she had said she had psychic abilities. But I couldn't say the words, at least not out loud, and certainly not to anyone else. It would be like digging my own grave . . . with a bulldozer.

Mrs. Keeper patted my knee. "I know this is hard for you to accept—it would be hard for anyone. It was for me." I looked at her, surprised. "You see, Lavida, Portal Manor is not just an ordinary house; it is a sanctuary. The person who runs this house, the Keeper, has a very important job to do. Our job is to make sure the Lost Ones find their way safely into Anaedor. We are the only sanctioned way for them to get in."

"The Lost Ones . . ." I murmured, wrinkling my brow as I tried to remember where I'd heard that before. Then it came to me. "That's written on the fountain."

She nodded. "The Lost Ones sense that we are here. This home is like the magnet to their metal, pulling them to us. That fountain and this ring"—she held out her hand so that I could see it—"let the Lost Ones know this place is safe, that I am safe."

"Is that why you've been so busy this week? You've been helping Lost Ones?"

"I'm so sorry about that, Lavida. You were a lost one yourself, but I didn't see that. I was so busy helping others that I forgot about how much you, too, might need me."

"I'm used to doing things on my own."

"Even so," she persisted, twisting the ring on her finger, "I could have helped you."

I shrugged. "I survived, didn't I?"

"You almost didn't," she said seriously. "And to think . . ."

"What?"

She shuddered. "To think that Gille was in this very house that first day you arrived."

"He was here?" I wrapped my arms around me.

"He left a short time after you arrived."

I nodded, putting two and two together. "I saw him when I first arrived. He also chased me that day when you sent me out of the house."

Mrs. Keeper wrung her hands. "Oh, dear! I was transferring a group of Lost Ones over to Loria and Darian, and I didn't want you to find us. I didn't want to frighten you." She smiled grimly. "So I sent you out, right into danger. If only I'd known Malvado had sent Gille to spy on me." She stared at the fire, then muttered to herself, "He's probably been doing that for a while. He's so paranoid about this house and the Keepers. Of course, he'd want to keep an eye on what I was doing." She looked over at me. "I was a right dolt not to have been more careful."

"You were doing your job, Mrs. Keeper. You *did* tell me not to go into the woods, but I went there anyway. That's my own dumb fault. And I could have said something to you and I didn't . . ." *because I didn't trust you.*

"Still, Lavida,"—my guardian shook her head miserably—"I'll never forgive myself for what happened to you. You were my responsibility. I should have done better by you. I just never thought to question whether any of the Lost Ones might be other than what they appeared. I, of all people, should know better."

"Please stop beating yourself up about it, Mrs. Keeper. It doesn't do any good."

She took a deep, shuddering breath. "I won't let you down again," she promised and I shivered. She sounded like Darian, and that worried me. Her idea of making things up to me might not coincide with my idea of a pleasant time.

Before she could elaborate on her ideas, I asked her a question that was bothering me. "How did you start doing something like this? It's not exactly the kind of job you're going to find advertised in the Help Wanted ads."

She chuckled and sat back against the plump cushions. "A year after my parents died, my great-aunt Lucia, who'd moved to America with her husband years earlier, tracked me down and asked me to come live with her here in Bellemont. One day, while taking a walk, I met your grand-mother. Despite our age difference, we became good friends. So good, in fact, that she trusted me with the knowledge of Anaedor."

I stared at my guardian in disbelief. "Grandma Mors knew about Anaedor?"

"More than that . . . she was once the Keeper here. A long line of Keepers flows through your blood, Lavida. It also flows through my own, something I discovered after meeting your gran. Through her I learned as a Helper how to do what I do now as a Keeper."

"Like opening doors without touching them," I con-cluded, feeling strange and tingly. Mrs. Keeper could do magic, too. The pieces were falling into place.

Mrs. Keeper smiled mischievously. "Among other things, yes."

"So if my grandma was a Keeper, how come you're the Keeper now?" I was growing interested despite myself. I was finally learning something about my family, about why I was the way I was.

"One night, your gran went into Anaedor and, for reasons unknown, never came back. I wasn't sure I wanted the job of being a Keeper, and though I knew something of Anaedor, I was ill-prepared to take over. Nevertheless, we had few options. Your gran had hoped your mother would be the next Keeper, but that wasn't to be."

"My mother? How could *she* be a Keeper? She didn't live here at Portal Manor, did she?"

"No, no! She was a Bellemont, remember, and her family's connection to the Mors—well, your gran never did get a chance to explain all that to me. Anyway, your mother had the same kind of power your gran and I did, only stronger. She would have been the strongest Keeper Portal Manor had had for centuries. But she chose to go with your father when he left Portal Manor for good." She shrugged as though she couldn't understand why anyone would want to leave this place.

The news stunned me. My mother had powers—just like I did. For the first time ever, I felt a connection to her. The thought warmed me and made me feel stronger inside. "So what happened to her?" I was almost afraid to ask the question. Had she, like myself, been driven to help others, despite the danger? Had she made the ultimate sacrifice to protect someone else?

"She returned to Portal Manor only once," Mrs. Keeper answered quietly. "Then she died."

I leaned closer, my chest tight. "How?"

Mrs. Keeper looked at the fire, her expression grim. "She died in Anaedor. Many claim that hers was not a noble death."

"What?" My heart beat faster. I remembered now what Mrs. Keeper had said about my mother when we'd met that first day. *I believe you are the spitting image of your dear mother, may she rest in peace. Though I don't know that she does, poor lass, after* . . . After what? What had happened to my mother? What had she done?

"This all happened shortly after your birth, Lavida. Malvado summoned your mother to him. She went down to meet him and was killed. Your gran had followed her to find out what was going on, but never returned. I believe Malvado killed both of them. Your gran's body was never found, but I know she's dead." So there had been no trip to Alaska. "She would've returned. I know it. She loved this home, and she loved being a Keeper. She would've come back." She wrung her hands, her face etched with loss.

"But what happened to my mother?"

Mrs. Keeper picked up the book lying on the table and distractedly flipped a few pages. She took a deep breath. "A Blendar named Deemor found her body and carried it to Portal Manor. Malvado told everyone she'd threatened to kill the Magistrate. The Anaedorians were outraged that a human had made such a threat against their leader, turning their suspicion of everything human into something worse. Many began to hate us." She sighed. "It didn't help that several upstanding Blendar citizens were killed in the fight between Malvado and your mother. Many blamed your mother for their deaths, of course."

"I can't believe my mom would kill anyone." I'd never known her, but the smiling woman in the picture sitting on my bedside table would never have hurt anyone. I felt sure of this now. She was kind and good and incapable of harming another being, human or otherwise.

"I never believed it myself," Mrs. Keeper said, turning to look at me. The tears in her eyes threatened to spill over. "But I couldn't do anything about it. I had to take over the role of Keeper, and there was so much to do. Luckily,

Winifred agreed to come help with the cooking and cleaning, among other things. She's been a wonder."

"Does she know about Anaedor and your job?" I asked, pretty sure I already knew the answer.

"She's definitely one of us, Lavida. Winifred has always felt a bit of an outsider herself with her gift for mind reading."

"She feels like an outsider, too?" She seemed so confident, so at peace with who she was.

"Oh, yes. Anyone who is different goes through that."

I nodded slowly, still thinking about my mother. "If Malvado killed my mom and I look like her, maybe that's why he had it in for me."

"You're being coy again, dear," Mrs. Keeper said quietly. "You know very well by now that there are those who believe you are the *One*."

"I'm not sure I believe any of that."

"There's not much to believe; your name is in those books."

"I know Madrina's ancestor found the *Chronicles*, but maybe all the prophecy meant was that I was going to be the next Keeper."

My guardian studied me, taking in my hopeful expression. "Time will tell," she said eventually. "I saw what you did with Malvado. You have the potential to be even more powerful than Willa Mors. She built this house hundreds of years ago and what she was, and did, still affects Anaedor and its people."

I felt my heartbeat speed up as I repeated the name softly. "Willa Mors. She's the one in my dreams, isn't she?"

"The one in your dreams, dear?"

"A lady comes to me when I'm dreaming and she tells me things. Well, she used to. Now she comes when I'm awake."

Mrs. Keeper frowned in thought. "It is quite possible that you dream of her, perhaps feel her presence through all these centuries. Anything is possible with your kind of power."

She sat up straight and held out the ancient book to me. "Take this. It contains the Keeper's Decree—a chronicle of the history of Anaedor—as well as loads of beneficial bits of wisdom." I took the heavy book, nearly dropping it, and wrapped my arms around it. I was tempted to open the book right away and see what answers lay within its fragile, yellowed pages.

Then a thought occurred to me: "How come my dad's not the next Keeper?"

Mrs. Keeper shook her head sadly. "Your gran never told him about Anaedor. She thought he was too much like his father, too scientific, too rational. She didn't want to harm him with knowledge he couldn't accept." She started petting the fuzzy black fur ball of a cat that had jumped onto her lap. "Anyway, he hated it here," she went on. "Your gran was never around, always busy with her role as Keeper. When your dad was ten, his father passed away, leaving him on his own in this big old house full of odd happenings and weird noises. I think he blamed your gran for abandoning him and vowed never to return.

"He didn't even come here when your mother was ordered to bed rest for the final months of her pregnancy. He had gone on a trip to South America to do field work before the decision was made, so he had a legitimate excuse. Your grandmother fetched your mother and she came here to stay, against your father's wishes, but he was obligated by contract to finish the job and could do nothing about it.

"A few weeks before your mother's due date, she went into labor and you were born. I had no way of letting your father know—he made his phone calls from a nearby village—there was no way to reach him. A few days after you came into this world, he called Portal Manor to let your mom know that he was back. He wanted her to return to the city with him.

"He was shattered, of course, when he found out your mother was dead. By then, your gran was missing, too. I didn't know what to tell him about her, so I said she'd left for Alaska not long after he went on his trip—she sometimes traveled to help Lost Ones who lived far away. There had been a blizzard during that time so it didn't take much to imply that she might have been caught in it. Thinking she'd abandoned your mother, he blamed your gran for your mother's death. He was so upset he didn't pursue your gran's disappearance—not until he had to prove she was dead to get his inheritance—and by then, I'd pulled a few strings to back up my story. He was also angry with me for allowing your mother's burial to go ahead without him. But with her injuries, I couldn't permit a regular funeral. There'd be questions from others, from him. Questions I couldn't—wouldn't—answer.

"I met him in Bellemont. He still refused to come to Portal Manor, which was for the best, anyway; I didn't want him looking at things too closely. He took you away with him, along with a letter from your grandmother she'd left with you."

I fingered my necklace. This must have been with the letter, too.

"I imagine that's how you got your name," Mrs. Keeper went on. "Your gran saw something special in you. She must have insisted he name you Lavida. Perhaps told him it was the name your mother wanted. He shortened your name to Viddie, maybe so he wouldn't be reminded of your mother every time he said it." She sighed wistfully. "I heard from him occasionally—he kept me on as a housekeeper, part of your gran's will, I expect—but I never saw him again. Then he called a month ago and asked me to take you in so you could attend Bellemont Academy. I said yes, of course. I've often wondered what had become of you. When I'd see you again, if ever."

"I wished he'd left me here with you," I said angrily. "He might have taken me away with him when I was a baby, but he didn't want me, not like this."

"Your father didn't know what to do with you, I think. Perhaps a part of him blamed you for what happened to your mother. He thought she had died giving birth to you." I stared at her. "I'm sorry, Lavida. I didn't know what else to tell him. And then . . . well, you do look an awful lot like her. Seeing you every day would have reminded him of what he'd lost. On top of that, there were your, um, special abilities. I imagine that when you were little, you didn't know enough to keep them hidden from others."

She was right about that. But I'd learned pretty young to hide what I could do by not doing it at all—if I could help it. The Toad was like a radio—I couldn't help but hear him, and others like him. Otherwise, I kept the switch turned off and rarely attempted to turn it back on. I never liked what I heard, anyway. At some point along the way, I'd kind of convinced myself that I wasn't any different from anyone else, that what I could do was my imagination playing tricks on me; that it wasn't me doing anything, just coincidence. I hadn't really fooled myself, though. Still, it didn't seem fair to be punished for doing something that helped others.

"I don't want to be different, Mrs. Keeper. Every time I help someone with my . . . well, I lose my friends."

She smiled sadly at me. "I understand, lass. I truly do." She pulled me to her and stroked my hair. Relaxing in her warm, soft arms, I stared blankly into the fire, mulling over everything I'd heard, over what I should do now.

"So how does Ian fit into all this?" I asked, pulling away. "I mean, how does he know about Anaedor? Can he . . . do stuff?"

"He learned about Anaedor from me. Just as your gran needed backup, so do I. He is my Helper. And yes, he has powers."

That explained how he always won his fights at school. "But who is he? Where did he come from?"

"I guess you could call him a human Lost One," Mrs. Keeper said, gazing into the fire. "I found him one day when he was just a babe. Someone had left him at the gate. I heard the crying and went to see what all the hullabaloo was about."

I laughed, startling the dozing cat. "That sounds like Ian. Always complaining." I sobered suddenly, realizing what this meant. "So he doesn't have any parents?"

"Not that he knows of," Mrs. Keeper answered, then yawned loudly. "But he has me. And now you." I grimaced and Mrs. Keeper laughed. "You'll learn to love him. He's just a bit tetchy at times. Now, it's time you were off to bed. I'm tuckered out."

I stretched, suddenly realizing that I was tired, too. "What day is it, anyway?"

"Only a few hours have passed since we found you missing, though I guess that it felt much longer to you. Time in Anaedor runs a bit strange that way. It's being underground that does it, I think."

"Only a few hours . . ." I said in wonder. "What about Hurricane Amy?"

Mrs. Keeper patted my hand. "She passed quickly by us with only a few branches knocked down and a little flooding before heading back out to sea. Now run along and get your sleep. You'll need to start training soon, before Malvado regains his power. You have much to learn."

I stiffened. "You mean he's not—"

"Oh no, dear. He's very much alive."

"He's not going to come after me here . . ."

"He could. In any case, you must be ready if he does."

I clutched the book tightly to my chest. "I can't do this, Mrs. Keeper."

"You can, and you will," the little woman said simply. "If you don't, Anaedor will be destroyed, taking you along with it." My eyes widened.

"Now close those worried eyes. Tonight you will sleep well."

"Good night," I murmured drowsily, already half asleep. "Mrs. Keeper?"

"Yes, dear?"

"How did you know we were gone?"

Mrs. Keeper laughed. "Your Ms. Penny alerted us. She went looking for you and found Ian instead. When he went to take the little mite to your room, he saw that you were gone. He noticed the secret door was open and knew right away what had happened. We immediately went after you."

"I'm glad you did," I said sleepily.

"As am I," Mrs. Keeper answered, gazing at me fondly. "Seeing Malvado get back some of his own was quite a thrill. I think he'll be feeling this one for quite some time."

"Serves him right," I murmured, the words barely making it out of my mouth. I was so tired I wasn't aware of Mrs. Keeper guiding me up the stairs to my room, then tucking me into bed, where I drifted into dreamland.

CHAPTER THIRTY-SIX
IT'S NOT OVER

The sun shone brightly through the high windows, illuminating the room with light and hope. I sat up and stretched luxuriously. It was going to be a beautiful day. Ellie snored loudly beside me and Eddie was nowhere to be seen, probably still sleeping in his cot at the bottom of the stairs.

In the quiet of the room, I thought about all I'd experienced during the last several days. I'd never imagined that my dream, the one that had frightened me for so long, would turn out this way. I had sensed that coming to Portal Manor would mean the end of my life as I knew it, and I'd been right. My old life was gone, a distant memory, replaced by a link to a strange, new world filled with creatures who needed my help.

In a way, I felt connected to the Anaedorians. I knew what it was like to feel lost, to not fit in. I knew what it was like to be ostracized, sent away, simply because of who you were. Even so, to think about how much the Anaedorians depended on me to help them find their way again was scary. I was still so lost myself. Most of me dreaded the thought of taking on this monumental responsibility, but a small, crazy part of me actually liked the idea of being able to help so many. If I couldn't have friends in my world, at least I would have them in another one. I knew one thing for certain. Despite what had happened in Anaedor, despite losing my only friend, I was going to stay at Portal Manor. I liked it here—the accommodations were much nicer than back home and the food was to die for. More importantly, Mrs. Dooley and Mrs. Keeper, being different themselves, accepted me for who I was. I couldn't say that for my dad.

Heaving a sigh, I rubbed my eyes and stretched again. Then I waited for Ellie to wake up so I could stop mulling over all the painful scenarios of how she might end things, from declaring she never wanted to see me again to telling the whole school I was a freak.

I was about ready to wake her myself when the bed started to shake. I clutched the covers, fear surging through me.

"Hey, who's rocking the bed?" Ellie exclaimed as she sat up.

"It isn't me, Ellie!"

We looked at each other, understanding dawning. Our eyes widened in mirrored fear. "Malvado!"

"Eeeh, eeeh!" We looked up to see an irate Ms. Penny shaking the bedpost.

"Ms. Penny, get down here," I commanded. She landed on the bed between us. Ignoring our stern looks, she ran back and forth between us, taking turns swatting us on the head.

"I think she's getting revenge on us for leaving her behind," Ellie said dryly, leaning down to grab her bag. She reached in and pulled out a pair of glasses. "I can't believe I lost my favorite pair." She slipped on some bright red ones.

"I can't believe you're complaining about losing your glasses, Ellie. You almost lost your life!"

"So it wasn't a dream?" Eddie spoke through a yawn as he walked through the door. "It all really happened?"

I nodded slowly. "Um, yes, it did." I told them everything Mrs. Keeper had said to me, leaving nothing out, then I waited for them to make their goodbyes and hightail it out of here.

"So we have to protect Anaedor," Eddie summarized the situation. I blinked in shock. "We can't say a word about what happened to anyone."

"What would we say?" Ellie snorted. "Hey, everybody! We discovered an underground world filled with frea— fascinating beings. Come on! We'll show it to you." She shook her head. "Yeah, right. You might as well hand me the straightjacket now 'cause we're off to the loony bin." She laughed.

"But I'm one of them, Ellie," I said. "Don't you remember?"

She shook her head. "All I remember is my friend saving my life." She was staring at me intently.

"Really?" I breathed. "You're sure?"

She nodded. "As long as it wasn't against your better judgment." She grinned at me.

"No. This time I chose to do it."

"And next time you'll let me know when you're going to do something freaky? You won't keep things from me? I don't like being lied to. That's what made me so mad, you know."

"I'll try my best," I replied, hoping I could follow

through. I'd spent so many years hiding my true self, so many years hiding the truth.

"Don't try, just do it."

I nodded and my heart grew instantly lighter, my mouth curved into a grin. "Mrs. Keeper wants me to do some training. Do you guys want to do it with me?"

Ellie gave me a disbelieving look, her thick glasses magnifying the disgust in her eyes. My heart sank. "Me doing exercise?" she said. "No way." She crossed her arms.

"Did I mention that Ian would be training with us?"

"You didn't let me finish," Ellie said quickly. "No way . . . could you stop me. That's what I was going to say." She giggled. Eddie and I started laughing, too.

Ian walked in on us as we were laughing hysterically. "What's so funny?" he asked, checking his pants zipper. We laughed even harder. "All right. Knock it off," he muttered, blushing. "We've got a lot of work to do, Lavida. That hurricane made a mess of things."

"I'll help," Eddie volunteered, jumping down from the bed.

"We'll all help," Ellie added. "We won't let you do it alone, Lavida."

Something in her tone made me look over at her, then at Eddie. The matching expressions of determination and loyalty on their faces made me feel a glow inside. They were going to stand by me even after what they'd gone through in Anaedor, after I'd accused them of betraying me, after I'd abandoned them, and best of all, after what they'd seen me do.

A feeling of happiness surged through me as I slid off the bed. "There's work to be done!"

"Breakfast first!" Ellie hollered.

"Of course," I laughed. "Breakfast first."

The four of us headed for the kitchen, laughing the whole way.

D refan smiled to himself as he crept away. What he had heard about the Human defeating Malvado was true. She had done something no other Anaedorian would dare to do. More importantly, she had done it on her own. He now understood why Malvado had paid all that Brass to have the Human kidnapped and accused of poisoning Anaedorians; she was a great threat to the Spokesbeing's position in Anaedor. She could see what he was about, could destroy everything he had worked to achieve.

Of course, Malvado was not the only one who would be happy to see the Human die. Others in Anaedor knew the Human as a threat, others who had plans and schemes, others who had plenty of Brass at their disposal. If Malvado were not Drefan's secret client, there were plenty to fill his place. Having witnessed the Human's powers, they would want to ensure that she be eliminated.

Drefan, however, was not sure that he could accept every job likely offered to him, even though his decision would anger his clan Elders. He could not be a part of any plan that would bring harm to the Human whose name was Life and Death. In this, he was not being kind or sentimental. No, the Human had something Drefan wanted, something he needed. He must protect her from them all.

No matter what.

ALSO AVAILABLE FROM
VARIANCE PUBLISHING

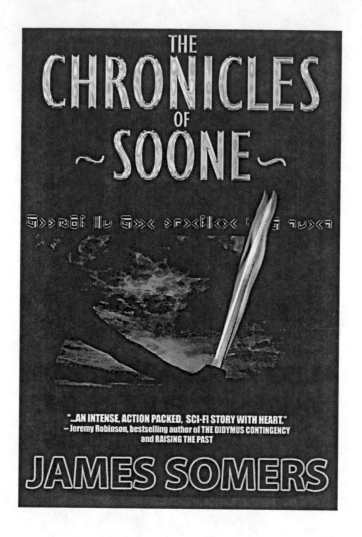

"... A fun action novel that makes an underlying theme of God not feel out of place."
-- Fantasybookspot.com

"James Somers has written an exciting debut that promises to be as epic as Star Wars."
-- Wren Reviews

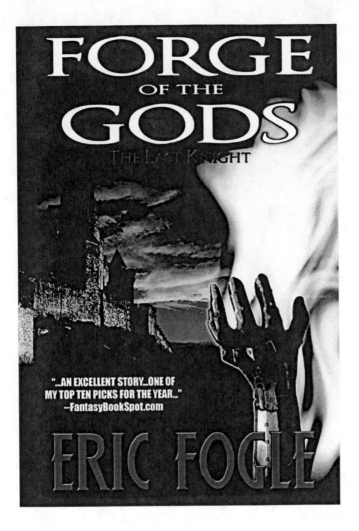

"... Engaging ... this has real potential to become a small-press fave."
-- Bookgasm

"This will definitely be one of my top ten reads of the year and I would recommend that this book makes everyone's "To Read" list."
-- Fantasybookspot.com

ABOUT THE AUTHOR

Kristina Schram has a Ph.D. in Counseling Psychology and enjoys incorporating the mysteries of the mind into her books. She tries to fit her writing in between raising her three boys, spending time with her hubby, and cleaning up after a troublesome dog and three cats. She has been writing "books" since she was a mere youngin' (the first was about what she wanted to get for her birthday—a castle was mentioned, I believe). She also enjoys photography and trying to green up her life for a better world tomorrow. She and her family currently reside in the state of New Hampshire, where you can "live free or die." It's up to you!

Visit her website: **www.KristinaSchram.com** for more information, book updates, blogging fun and some good old Mischief, Mystery and Magic!

LaVergne, TN USA
03 April 2011

222646LV00003B/3/P